# SPLINTERS OF HEAVEN
## BOOK I OF PAX TERMINUS
Theo Tsirigotis

Cover Design by Ryan Mulford

Cover Art by Kyle Enochs

First paperback edition February 2026

ISBNs: 979-8-9940400-0-3 (e-book), 979-8-9940400-1-0 (paperback)

www.theotsirigotis.com

*For my parents,*
*who filled our house with books*

# PART I

*Upon the wheel, there shall be a sundering and a breaking,*
*When brother murders brother, and mother smothers child,*
*When the great serpent will burst forth, around the worlds snaking,*
*The children of the heavens must still those of the wild,*
*Or be cast down into the abyssal void, formless, forsaking,*
*Another generation consumed and to the Rift exiled.*

—Fragment attributed to Andwen II (unconfirmed),
Library of Ministry of Fate, Section: Prophecy, Guiding Axioms

# OUTSKIRTS AND ENDINGS

The priests said that the earth, the worlds, and every life upon them spun upon prescribed paths, and Syl couldn't help but despise whichever god had set his own little wheel rolling. Of every gods-forsaken piece of land in every corner of the empire, it was beyond belief that he was back in Getacia.

It was a consolation to him that at least they would be done here after tonight. Their hunt for the last of the escapees had led them here, to these scrubby croplands. They arrived as dusk fell, and the cold was setting in with a vengeance. Along with the five other members of the team, he stopped where the road met an old, dying oak, well shy of the firelight that spilled warm and inviting from the small windows of the nearest farmhouse. The other scattered houses were close enough for their own flickering lights to be visible. They would be too far away to hear anything if their quarry put up a fight.

After a huddled minute of half-whispers, the team split up, four quickly fading into the twilight, shapes blurring against the high grasses and scattered trees as they joined the rest of the cordon. Syl made a few adjustments to the timepiece in his hand, an intricate series of concentric metal circles. The rings started to move. He placed it in a pocket of his cloak and nodded to Kass. They started toward the farmhouse.

Kass strode ahead, sparing an impatient look back when he slowed to examine the squat little barn beside the house. Her long brown hair was pulled back into an ornate knot and framed an angular face, made sharper with irritation. Her silent glare was a judgment on Syl, this hovel, those inside, and likely on the entire assignment that had seen them spend the last two weeks hunting through the muddy farmlands of this province, so far from the empire proper.

There was the impression of momentum halted from inside his cloak, and there came a high tone, like a tiny bell struck, traveling no further than his own ears and barely there. The others should be in position. The other rings kept ticking forward. Closing the final distance, he knocked on the door—three polite but insistent blows. The weight of the aegis gauntlet lent the knocks a certain sense of command.

"Open up."

There was a shuffling behind the door, and the sound of surprised whispers. From her position by one of the windows, Kass held up three fingers. Their informant had spoken of a widower and a daughter. So, that left only the one to worry about inside, and this far from the Riftgate at the imperial capital. It would be almost too easy. Likely not the only one hiding here, but the team would take care of any others.

He knocked again, a little harder.

"Open the door, by order of the Exarch."

This time there was an answer, heavy with the local accent.

"It's late. Who's there?"

As if they didn't know. "Open the door. Don't make me ask again."

Syl closed his eyes, savoring the sense of knowing exactly how the next few seconds would pass. An interaction acted out so many times in so many places that it had taken on a sense of ritual. A pause. A consideration. And a final acceptance that there had only ever been the one option. They could see where the choices led, but they always chose the one that delayed the inevitable for as long as possible. Syl didn't begrudge them that.

And...there it was. A shuffle and the sound of a bolt being drawn. Then another. Maybe a third. And then something heavy dragged from in front of the door, set to the side. So many useless obstacles against the inevitable.

The door cracked open to show a short, wiry man silhouetted by a low fire inside. A thin, leathery neck and windburned face poked out from clothes that hung limp, heavy with dirt from the day's work.

Syl threw the door wide and pushed in, brushing the man aside.

Kass flowed in behind him. "Why, thank you, goodman. Kind of you to invite us in."

The farmer frowned slightly at that, but a mixture of fear and perhaps even some residual sense of propriety stopped him from saying more. Besides, there was no un-opening that door.

"If you say so."

Syl scanned the room. Low beams and a thatched roof. A space made cozy by the large oven in the corner and slightly repellent by years' worth of close-pressed, unwashed humanity. The rest of the room was filled, ceiling to floor. The odds and ends of life hung from hooks, crowded shelves along the walls, and covered most of the large table that dominated the center. Behind it stood two women who looked nervously between him and the farmer. The one with long brown braids fidgeted with her hands, while the other, with short black wisps curling above green eyes, stared with unabated suspicion at their new guests. Impossible to tell daughter from fugitive. A thrill ran through him. They would know soon enough.

The farmer grew visibly more agitated and concealed it poorly. He would say something now. They always did.

"What brings you here, sirs?"

The farmer had the deep, raspy voice of someone who had spent too much time outdoors during those long weeks where the blighted, ruined cities of the Breaking vented their ashen misery on the rest of the world, or at least where the wind blew it, like these unfortunate northern provinces.

"We are here on behalf of the Exarch. Is that not enough?"

The question hung heavy in the air, long enough for anger to flash briefly across the man's face as he squirmed for the right answer. Good. A man used to honesty. That always made this easier. And it was too late for the right answer. Syl waited patiently.

"Meant no disrespect. Late though. Weren't as if we were expecting visitors." The man's attention shifted toward where Kass circled the room. Her movements were languid, lazy. A lie against her capabilities. He cleared his throat and turned his attention back to Syl. "What can me or my daughters do for you?"

Syl stared at the farmer in mild disbelief and even a little amusement. How could he pretend that this night could end any other way than the obvious? Still, they had time to kill before the team closed the noose. He could play along.

"You're right. We've been rude. My name is Scyllus, and this is my partner, Kassara. We're here to ask you a few questions. Would that be alright?" Syl paused, as if honestly waiting for an answer. The man gave a stiff nod. "And your name is Andrec, is that right?"

"Aye, that's what they call me. And of course, sir, ask away. We've nothing to hide."

Kass coughed back a laugh, missing a beat from where she hummed behind the two women. The corner of Syl's mouth twitched up.

Andrec cleared his throat and gestured toward the table. "Please, have a seat."

Syl swept his cloak off, placing it carefully on the bench seat and revealing the high-collared uniform underneath. Badge and gauntlet made the evidence of their fears incontrovertible, washing away any illusions the farmer might have clung to. Andrec's face lost a few shades of the little color it had, but he composed himself admirably. The women behind him less so. They had taken on the panicked look of deer, eyes flitting between him and Kass, who continued to poke around the edges of the room. Syl still couldn't decide which was their quarry. From her continued circling, Syl could tell that Kass couldn't either. They would probably be bringing them all in anyway, but he knew he should want to try to separate the dangerous from the merely guilty. He would give Andrec a chance to save his family. More than Syl had gotten, and certainly more than Andrec deserved.

Lowering himself onto the bench, Syl gestured for Andrec to sit. With the resigned air of the sentenced, he did. To clear any lingering doubts, Syl placed his hands on the table. One thudded down, iron on wood. The gauntlet that encased his left was built of overlapping bands of metal and ossanite. The thin black cloth hiding the delicate patterns underneath did nothing to soften its impact. The other was placed gently, but the oathknight's tattoos peeking out from the hem of his cuff were another promise.

"I see you recognize the uniforms?" Syl ventured.

"Aye, I do."

"Then perhaps you can guess why my friend and I have come all the way out here to your farm?"

"No, can't say I can, sir."

Syl raised an eyebrow. "Really? You couldn't possibly guess why two of the Vigil's Hunters might be at your door? Do you at least know what we do, then?"

"I'm not one for repeating rumors."

"Say you had to."

"Had to, eh?"

"Yes."

"They say you hunt and kill any as would touch the Rift. Men, women, children. They say it's all the same to you. Devils in black." Andrec shifted uncomfortably. "To hear them tell it."

Syl couldn't keep the disdain off his face. Didn't want to try. Perhaps it wasn't so bad to be back in Getacia. He had forgotten how much he hated these people. You tried to help them, to bring them into the empire and give them a chance to survive the next cataclysm, and they rejected it. The out that Syl was trying to give Andrec tonight, thrown away just the same.

*He doesn't deserve a chance.*

*He doesn't know how much he has to lose.*

"Wrong. We hunt those too weak to resist the stain of those souls reaching out from the Riftgate. Stained, threnics, mages... The names don't matter. The price of peace. A peace that depends on people not doing what you're fucking doing, Andrec. Even so, I think it's fair to give you this one chance." Syl gestured magnanimously across the table. He watched the women out of the corner of his eye, waiting for a reaction. Still nothing, even now. "Andrec, tell me why we're here. Give me the answers you know I need. It's that simple. There's no need for this night to end in violence." It was true, and part of him even wished he meant it.

Andrec glared at Syl for a long, sweating moment. He broke eye contact. "Can't say I can help you."

"Of course you can't," Syl sighed. He gathered himself, feeling the momentum building. "Andrec, I want you to remember that the people you're hiding understand what's about to happen to you. And they are willing to watch it happen, because they might have a chance of saving themselves for a few minutes longer. I want you to understand that you can choose what's about to happen." He watched for a reaction from one of the women. What was she waiting for?

There was another chime from the timepiece, just loud enough for him to hear. The team would be hitting the barn. Andrec's time was up. "So, for the last gods-damned time...tell me where they are. Now."

This was part of the ritual too. Chance or no, there had been no doubt in Syl's mind where this conversation would end. He readied himself for the next part, pulling from the six sanctioned conduits bound to him. He could feel their borrowed strength rush in along the lines drawn into his skin, as reassuring as always. Power drawn through the Riftgate, through their bodies, to his own with binding runes. He watched Andrec gather himself too, preparing for the most important decision of his life.

All that remained to be seen was whether Andrec or the Stained broke first.

Syl hoped it was Andrec. Here in an outskirt province, the Stained's connection would be weak. They would deal with her, but it was Andrec's inability to see how deeply he had failed his family that was most infuriating. The man's resignation hardened into resolve. Syl could practically watch the wheels of his mind turning as they came to what no doubt felt like a decision. The only one he had ever really had.

Pushing backwards from the table, Andrec screamed a single word toward the window. "Run!"

The dam broke. Syl vaulted the table, scattering the crockery and slamming into Andrec. He was clawing for a knife at his belt when Syl broke his neck. Whirling, he saw the woman with the braids pull a long knife from the folds of her dress. Syl turned to the other. There was the real threat. Kass threw the one with the knife into a wall with enough force to leave her a crumpled pile of braids, limbs, and skirts.

As Syl lunged toward the last woman, gauntlet held before him, it suddenly felt as if he were pushing his way forward through water, his limbs fighting resistance in the air. They struggled toward her, desperate now. This wasn't possible. And yet, it was happening. They had vastly underestimated her. The arcane aegis of the gauntlet around Syl's forearm blazed with light, stuttered, fell dark. Too much energy, too little time to dissipate.

The Stained slowly walked over to where he struggled, a fly in amber. She moved unhindered by the impossible thickness of the air, but sweat beaded across her brow. The hand she reached toward the table to select one of the simple knives was shaking with the effort of holding them both there. He was pulling everything he dared from his conduits, and it still wasn't enough. To hold two oathknights at once was insanity. The strain was tearing her apart. Not quickly enough.

Syl let out a strangled sound as his own channeled strength was slowly overcome by the waves of power coming off the woman. Muscles strained and tore and healed in unnoticed agony. He could see the panic in Kass's eyes as she watched, trapped like him, knowing she was next. The collars they had on their belts that would have cut her connection to the Rift were less than useless. Nothing but weights dragging them down to their deaths.

She came close and considered him, nose curled. "The price of peace?" she sneered. "Hunting me and my family, and you have the nerve to talk about *peace*?" Holding them in place was taking its toll, and sweat started to drip off her pale face, which had taken on a sallow, sunken quality. Veins of light worked their way up her arms and along the edges of her scalp. The green in her eyes was fading, a lighter shade taking over. "You killed them? For what? You could have done anything, could have just collared all of us." She paused, considering. Then she laughed, high and tinged with the madness of the soul that infested her. "It's the missing patrol that led you here, wasn't it? Should have known there wouldn't be any hiding that one. But don't you worry, I'll bring you to them."

There was a third and final chime. Or perhaps Syl simply wanted to hear it badly enough to imagine it.

The Stained stopped too though. The sneering smile that had been growing on her face disappeared, and she cocked her ear toward the window. "No, no, no... Oh, you cowards. You wouldn't come alone, would you? How many are there?"

Syl said nothing. He didn't think he could.

She looked unsure of herself now, fear back, but not for herself this time. "Shit." She turned to the door, then considered the Hunters before her again, trying to find a way out where there was none, frantic. A few more beads of sweat pattered onto the wood. "Shit, shit, shit!"

She made up her mind. Another step closer, staying just out of reach of Syl's grasping hand. His face was red with effort and mouth locked in a silent scream as he reached toward her, still straining with everything he had. Knowing she would be killed right after him didn't count for much.

"Out of time, aren't we?" She gave a sad laugh, all the madness gone and just her left. Syl thought those last few drops of sweat might have been tears. "I'd ask you to spare my children, but I know what your kind thinks of prayers like that. See you in hell, Hunter."

Raising the knife, she plunged it toward his neck.

... And lurched sideways, as if one of the many gods had decided to intervene. A god that had sent two crossbow bolts thudding into the room in quick succession. A very practical, if inaccurate god.

The Stained cursed as she struggled back upright, one bolt having barely cut along the front of her delicate neck, a thin red line that was in that unreal transition between skin opening and insides bleeding. Another fingerbreadth would have torn her throat out. The shock of it broke her concentration for the barest moment.

It was enough.

Syl's limbs regained their hard-won speed, and he exploded forward. He closed the distance in a silent instant. He pulled her toward him with one hand and sent the other, gauntleted and heavy and unforgiving as judgment, through her face.

Syl shuddered with involuntary relief. He let her fall. Her face was a ruin. One green eye stared back at him, wide and surprised, the original color returning. He tried not to think about her last few words, but he couldn't shake that last look of utter helplessness, of despair. It was usually all over before that. The cut on her throat from the crossbow bolt had started to bleed.

From the thin window, a ghoulishly cheerful face peered in at them. Leon. Gods damn it, of course it was. He would have to keep his thoughts about gods and saviors, practical or otherwise, to himself. It would already be at least a month before he heard the end of this one.

"Everything alright in here?" He took in the scene and raised an eyebrow at Syl.

Another near miss to add to the list. Syl composed himself, smiling back as nonchalantly as he could manage. "We had it under control."

"Damn you, Leon. You insufferable little bastard." Kass was kneading her hands, trying to hide the trembling as her body worked through the adrenaline. "Maybe you could try for a better shot next time? Or better yet, not wait so damn long?"

Leon laughed. "Apologies. I'll stay out of your way next time."

With an effort, Kass pulled back on her usual cold demeanor. "Tell me you found the others."

"Course we did. Also had a bit of trouble, if I'm being honest. But I think you missed one." Leon pointed behind them.

Syl and Kass spun around, still a little on edge, to where an old woman lay in a small loft above them, unnoticed before now. Andrec's mother, most likely. Tears glinted among all the wrinkles.

"Drag her out," Leon said. "Domarik has another outside."

Kass went to go roust the last resident, and Syl tried to take some satis-faction in their victory. Another Stained dead. Another one of those who had taken the life he should have had, dead and no longer a threat. But the woman here had been unusually powerful. Impossibly so. This should have been an easy collar.

Syl told himself that was what was bothering him—that Rift-users resurgent in a restive province were what was making his head pound and putting the lump in his throat. And yet, it was when he looked back along the long, dark arc of his life that he found the truth, the definite thing about this night that he already understood perfectly, because he had lived it. It had been her final prayer, that helpless fear. He tried not to look at the Stained as he stepped out into the dark to find Leon.

# BROKEN RITUAL

Waiting outside next to Leon was Domarik, their team's Primary. He towered over Syl, his Secondary, and dwarfed the wiry Leon. In late middle age, a few layers of fat now covered his dark frame, but there was no mistaking the heavy slabs of muscle underneath.

"Report?"

"One inside, taken care of." Syl ignored Leon's mock indignation at not being mentioned. He'd thank him later. "Outside?"

"Four. Two legionnaires dead though. Assuming you ran into the same issue we did."

It hadn't been a question, but Syl wanted to ask his own anyway. "Why?"

Domarik nodded, understanding. "Unclear. But before we left, I received a report. Gregoris's team is missing. This might explain it."

Syl and Leon exchanged a worried glance. Casualties were fairly common on Hunter teams. Collaring a Stained around the capital was especially deadly work. But for all Domarik's characteristic understatement, an entire team going missing was something else entirely.

"Wait." Syl fell into step beside him. "We are so far beyond the range where this should be possible... I mean, one, with an exceptionally strong connection to the Riftgate...maybe. But five?"

Domarik wiped his long blade clean with a rag as he walked. "It's always something. Three prisoner convoys attacked in a month, patrols missing, spotty reports from the North. Everything from pre-Breaking ruin discoveries to blind prophets wandering around proclaiming the end. Team missing, and word of a new pretender to the Northern throne..."

"There's always one of those," Leon said, even as Syl waved for him to shut up.

"Governor's nervous. Exarch has some theories. They tell the judiciars some, me a little less." Domarik shrugged his huge shoulders and sheathed the blade, half again as thick as any carried by the other Hunters. "I know what you're thinking. But every time there's a revolt, or a few too many emergences, the priests love to scream about the end. It's pointless. We wait, we watch, and in the meantime, we do our job."

Syl knew Domarik was right. And he knew better than anyone that managing bloody revolts and crushing uprisings was half the business of an empire. Perhaps they were simply due for one here. The legionnaires from the cordon were everywhere now, little arclamps bobbing about, blue light reflecting on black armor.

"Is it separatists who are organizing this, then? Doesn't explain the Stained either way," he said, not wanting to let it go. Domarik might be right about doomsayers—probably was. But the trouble with anyone prophesying the next cataclysm was that they were always eventually right.

Domarik ignored him to watch the soldiers, who were grunting and cursing as they hauled what was left of the patrol from a cellar next to the barn. The limbs, relatively well preserved in the cold underground space, were at least easy to carry. As if that would make it easier for the families that would see their children or parents returned in pieces. They were making a pile of their rings, coins, and medallions that the flamewardens had imbued with trace energy from the Rift a week ago, something for bloodhounds to latch onto in the case of this very eventuality.

"A full patrol," Leon muttered. "Twelve fully armored and kitted soldiers. Fucking embarrassing. They don't make 'em the same anymore."

Syl tried not to let Leon's words get under his skin. They deserved more respect than that, but there was a measure of truth to his words. These sorts of incidents only occurred occasionally, and only around the capital. Getacia was about as far as it was possible to be from that locus and still be in the empire. Another point for the doomsayers.

A soldier walked by, more grim-faced than the others, but not struggling at all under the load over his shoulders. Small, bony, pale limbs. Syl turned away to follow Domarik as he kept walking. He tried to put the final words of the woman out of his head. She had been right, in the end. It had been a useless prayer. Syl wondered if that boy was one of the four that Domarik was counting. Almost certainly. You had to count the little snakes too, and Syl had written enough reports to know you had to stay consistent in how you counted. Practically the basis for a civilized society.

On the far side of the barn, the rest of the team waited with two prisoners. The old woman lay in a collapsed pile, ignored by all. Kass was holding another, a girl with a collar around her neck. The other two members of the team, Liora and Lucky, were waiting with her. Kass yawned, delicately covering her mouth and looking back in the direction of the provincial capital, Rasovus, clearly eager to be on the way to the Exarch's estate, where a bath and sleep waited.

Liora, the newest member of their team, squatted on her haunches and looked at the two prisoners, hands playing a nervous beat on the sheathed longsword held across her legs. Syl remembered being the new member of the team as well. It wasn't only being new; it was knowing that you were the replacement for someone whose boots you could never truly fill. Hunters rarely retired. Lucky, their bloodhound, was one of the sanctioned bondmages capable of sensing the signature of the arcane energy of the Rift. Gangly and barely into adulthood, he stood apart with a look of distracted distaste, as always. The cordon platoon's lieutenant stood back respectfully, waiting for instructions. The men and women under his command flowed out of the barn, search complete. Torches flared. Thatch fired and crackled. They started to load the bodies onto a cart and prepared to leave.

Black-cloaked, uniformed, and with the tanned skin only found south of here where the sun still shone often enough, the team was barely visible against the pale grasses around them. The girl was by contrast a wayward spirit, pale face covered with stringy black hair. The null collar Kass held her by stood out like a warning sign around that frail neck. The plain peasant's smock she wore was stained and filthy. It was also not so dark that Syl couldn't see the resemblance to the Stained from inside the farmhouse. To those little limbs carried out of the barn. Another little snake. Part of him wished she had made it past the cordon. This was never easy, even if it had to be done.

Domarik grunted, clearly reaching a decision regarding the two. Syl had been staring at the girl, lost in thought. The noise stirred him. He wanted to say something, but knew it would be pointless. He almost did anyway. He saw a world where he would have, heard the words he could have used, but then a higher, clear voice cut the night.

"Domarik..."

Domarik quit his examination to turn to Liora. Syl was horrified and exultant at the same time, throat catching. Domarik waited expectantly, as did the rest, curious why she would speak up. Even Lucky turned to watch, engaged for once.

Liora couldn't meet Domarik's gaze, but she forged ahead, voice gaining momentum. "We could leave them. It's only a girl and an old woman."

"Do you think that's a good idea?" Domarik asked, head cocked. He sounded genuinely, terrifyingly curious.

*New, and she's done it now. Not a smart move.*

Syl could only watch as Liora wilted under that glare. He had liked her. She had potential. But you didn't un-swear the sort of oaths they'd sworn, and those oaths left so little room for interpretation. The girl had to die. So, it was all the more surprising to hear someone use his lips, move his tongue, to repeat the same nonsensical plea.

"Domarik..."

Their Primary's glare didn't hold the same power for Syl. You didn't work together, run the risks they had together, and not trade in some of the respect and fear you probably should have kept for a measure of familiarity.

He told himself it was too late to do anything except forge ahead. The memory of the woman's face was burning a hole in him. It wasn't her fear, or the hate, but the helplessness. That, and being back here... The old griefs spilled out and swept him along in a rare moment of passion. The painfully grateful look on Liora's face was clear, and there was a warmth to it that wasn't entirely washed out by all the others around him.

"We can send her to the judiciars. To one of the camps." It wasn't a good fate, he knew that, but it was a sight better than death. He didn't bother mentioning the old woman. "The girl hasn't done anything. Collar her and send her north."

Syl hated that Domarik knew why he had spoken up. After all, Domarik had been the one who had found him at the end, so long ago. He didn't bother addressing Liora anymore. Syl was his Secondary and had been on the team long enough to be allowed an opinion, even if he apparently was set on using that privilege in the most self-defeating way possible.

Domarik shook his head, unapologetic. "It's not what she has done, Syl. You know that. It's about what she *will* do. Look." He strode forward suddenly and grabbed the girl's jaw, squeezing and twisting her sobbing face upward to the firelight of the house, which now roared behind them with a comforting warmth. The girl's greasy locks fell back, and Syl recoiled from what he saw there. Terror and grief, yes. Hate, certainly. And one eye that was almost completely black, as if the hate had been more than her little form could bear and was making its way out the only way it could. "Look at that. Even I've never seen something like that. Who knows what's burrowed its way in there from the Rift?"

"Domarik, she..." Liora tried.

"You do not speak," Domarik said, not bothering to look her way. "I had my doubts about you. Do not press now."

Syl was more unsure than ever now, but he tried again. He saw the eye, the hate, but he saw another there as well, bright green and full of fear. "Domarik, she's barely more than a child. She likely had no part in any of this, and she won't be doing anything from one of the camps," Syl insisted. His voice was steady, but he was pleading now, and pleading for a lost cause. With the chaos in this province, this was hardly the time to be making exceptions. Both he and Domarik knew it, but Syl couldn't bring himself to back down.

He could feel the pressure of the stares from the others. He looked around, seeing no sympathy from any beyond Liora and maybe a thoughtful look from Lucky, a deviation from his usual sour expression. Kass appeared wickedly delighted at the little drama, a distraction from the dirt and the cold. The poor lieutenant was holding as still as possible, as if that would help the rest of them forget he was even there.

"This is not a discussion, Syl. This is the way it has to be." Domarik studied him, curious. "You of all people should know that."

Syl had one more card to play. "Then let the Exarch decide. The judiciars will have questions, and maybe she can answer some of them. Given everything happening, you can't say we couldn't use any information she might have. And I guarantee they will want to study whatever is in her. Bring her with us." He looked hopefully at Domarik, who still absently gripped the girl's face. She was squirming silently in pain, tears glinting on her face and teeth bared. Domarik was still as he considered. Then a brief nod. Syl let out a breath he hadn't realized he'd been holding.

"Fine. But the old woman dies here. Charge of helping to harbor fugitives from the Vigil. You do it. Actually, no—Liora does it. You make sure of it. We're done here."

With that, Domarik released his hold and started away from the farmhouse. The others followed, Kass dragging the mute girl along. Liora gave Syl another grateful look, but he couldn't meet her eye. He had told her himself how mercy was at best unprofessional, and at worst a betrayal of their charge as oathknights in the Vigil. There was nothing wrong with sending collared Stained to a life of service and exile at the borders of the Empire, far from the temptation or possibility of communion with the Rift, but their duty was caution first, second, and always. Better a thousand innocents die than Stained like these be allowed to destroy the world again. He knew that better than anyone. And with patrols and teams of Hunters missing, they could ill afford sentimentality. This final little distasteful task was Domarik's way of telling him there would be more to come from this. All in all, a stupidly sentimental end to an otherwise successful raid.

He hated that it still felt good.

Liora smiled. "Thank you."

Syl grunted. They would probably examine the girl's affliction, ask their questions, and she'd be dead within the week anyway. "It's nothing. Probably a mistake."

"I don't think so. She's so young. They don't listen to me, but you…"

"Let's get this done." The walls were up again, and the throbbing in his head worse than ever.

*She just had to say something.*

*So did you, didn't you? Can't forget, can we?*

Liora was studying him now with those hazel eyes that seemed incapable of hiding what she was thinking. *She'll have to lose that,* Syl thought, and something about that thought made him unreasonably angry. He straightened, glaring back. That infuriatingly sympathetic expression pasted across a heart-shaped face framed by a short, practical cut, the back end standing up absurdly from where her hood had found a new direction for her hair. *Ridiculous.*

"You cannot, *cannot,* give your opinion like that. Or even *have* an opinion like that. Leaving them here? That was never an option. Do you understand what will happen to you if Domarik reports you as unfit for the team?"

"I do."

"Do you? Really?"

"Yes, Syl. I do. I'm not a gods-damned child. I know what happens."

Syl shook his head again in disbelief. At her, at himself, he wasn't entirely sure. "Good. Good! Now let's get this done. And if you so much as suggest leaving her here, I swear I'll report you myself."

The sympathy was gone from her face, and something far less clear made its home there as she drew in on herself. Syl told himself he couldn't care less. They needed to speed things up if they were going to catch up with the others. He turned to the old woman, who had been an unwilling third party to their exchange. The crone's face glistened with tears. Syl thought he could see some measure of gratefulness too though. An old woman's life for that of a child. What could be more natural? They were only here to help hasten nature along a bit. Wasn't that what civilization was all about?

"Be quick about it, devil," she spat.

Perhaps more hate than gratitude then. Syl could understand that. After all, what did she see when she looked at him? A tall, dark, scarred Southerner who had murdered her family. If only they could look beyond their own little miseries and provincial resentments, they might see the absurdity of harboring the sort of people that had brought a dozen cataclysms since the Breaking. The ones that the Fallen who still prowled the world would use to bring another and slowly drown their world in ash and ice. Maybe then they could see that they left the Vigil no options. Left *him* with no options, forcing him to do what he did and making Liora do the same.

"Domarik was right though. You need to do this."

He circled around behind the old woman, drawing a long knife from behind his back, holding it out to Liora. She balked.

"Why?"

"Because you still don't seem to get it. The ones in there?" He pointed angrily back to the burning farmhouse with the knife. "That's the easy part. That makes sense, feels fair. But this is how we actually save lives. You think she didn't know? Wasn't happy to be a part of it? People that are incapable of looking beyond their own self-interest like that don't deserve forgiveness. Mercy now is how you get another patrol killed."

"This *isn't* fair," she protested, shaking her head. "You can't pretend she's a threat."

Syl's arm was still, the offered blade a demand, not an invitation. Liora needed this, not more explanations. She hesitated, foot raised as if to step away. But she took the step forward. And another, until the knife was in her hands. Syl tried not to notice that slight tremble. She was brave, there was no doubting that. He'd seen her records. This was something different though, and he was relieved she had come forward. Wasn't sure he could have done what he would have needed to do otherwise.

"I promise you, it gets easier," he offered. "But you have to do this, there's no two ways about it."

She was beyond answering now, but her hands were where they were supposed to be. Syl still remembered his moment here. Everyone in the Vigil had one. Some came with reluctance, others with distaste, like Kass, and a questionably fortunate few with a worrisome eagerness, like Leon. Liora would have to face it in her own way.

She faced it.

The crackle of the fire split the cold quiet of the night. They began the long walk back to where the team had staged. Syl thought he should feel pride, or at least a little vindication, but all he felt was sick. It had been the girl, he realized. She had brought Syl back to the past, and that was never a good place for him to go. Run through your memories often enough, and they became dreamlike. But even if they lost their edges with time, those dream-memories inevitably returned, heavier with guilt and more expansive with the knowledge of every path not taken, ready to crush him. Tonight was proof of what happened when you let the past bleed into the present. Better to forget it. Who he was now was what mattered.

It was a lesson Liora would have to learn sooner or later.

# A LITTLE GLORY

The riders below weaved their way through the trees, apparently unwilling to dismount from their short, stocky horses. Guttural curses and sharp laughter echoed from the loosely organized column. The men and women were covered in a mix of bright cloth, furs, and assorted scraps of armor, riding with the easy confidence born from a life in the saddle.

Above, behind a small ridge, Vali lay with his cheek pressed into the dirt, peering through the smallest of slits in the fallen log ahead of him, listening as the conversations below mixed with the calls of birds, who warned one another of the invaders in their territory. They had done the same when Vali and the rest of the soldiers of the auxiliary rangers had set up in the gray morning, but had eventually returned. Proof that time makes a place home and newcomers neighbors. It was a bright day, flashes of weak sunlight filtering through the clouds and the thin layer of leaves that remained on the trees above. A foul wind from the blightlands to the south, an expanse of dead marshes and ancient battlefields, made the air heavy and conjured images of decay and dark places. For today's work, they could hardly have asked for a better breeze to mask their presence.

Slowly, so as not to disturb the leaves beneath him, Vali turned his head to the side to look down the line of soldiers who waited, still as fallen statues. With their cloaks and furs threaded with leaves and twigs, they nearly disappeared, even at this distance. Nothing but a line of human-length lumps. The arrows that were stuck into the ground close behind tree trunks, hidden from the riders' line of sight, were the only man-made silhouettes that disrupted the natural patterns.

His mates, Lucan and Marika, were piles of leaves and fur to his right. Lucan caught his gaze and gave him a nervous grin. Friends from childhood made into family over the long years. Their families had advised his father for decades. No need to break with tradition. To those two, he was Vali, while to the half dozen scattered beyond them, he was still Valerek dal Costranis, the younger son of their lord who sent them out here to fight on the eastern borders of Getacia.

At this point along that border, there was only a narrow strip between the blightlands and the mountains, and it was anything but hospitable. Walls and forts lay ahead on the riders' path, and they were here today to ensure that these invaders never got even that far. This was the largest scouting party from the Tribes they had seen on this side of the empire, and Vali knew it would be in everyone's interest if it were the last. These sorts of people were incompatible with the unquestioning unity the empire needed to weather any future cataclysm.

The "Thousand Tribes," as they called themselves, rarely came this way though, and Vali absently wondered what would have driven the ones below to try. They would have already had to pass through a good portion of noxious, deadly swamps to reach this point, and their horses would be near useless in the lands here. These horsefuckers would ram themselves through any opening they could find though. The two broad, high mountain passes to the far east, the Gates, were where they usually tried, with the predictability of the seasons. Auxiliary ranger units like his were the force before the dams of other fortresses at smaller gaps, like the one behind them.

Farther down the line, their unit's commander, Captain Askaris, was yet another lump, distinguished only by the fact that his head was up, hidden behind another log. He was using a small mirror to respond to a signal from their far left. A few flashes later, and he was focused again on the loud group down below, trying to judge the perfect timing. It would be soon, Vali knew. They couldn't let the invaders' lead element get past their far positions.

They had been lying here since the early morning, and Vali had thought he might freeze to death in those hours before the sun reached the horizon. The marshes might stay warm with the sickly, never-dissipating heat of all the blightlands, but here on healthy ground, the chill cut deep. Now he was sweating though, his wolf cloak, heavy tunic, and leather armor all more stifling with every minute. Vali was burning with the need to move, to release this energy. He had to fight like a god today. He wasn't worried about proving himself to his fellow Getacians. He needed to outdo the captain and to outdo those two other killers he brought with him everywhere, the other legion oathknights. It was those three he needed to impress if he ever wanted a chance to become one of them. Vali channeled all his impatience into his grip on his bow, trying to crush the wood in his hands and willing his impatience away. He was ready. That was enough.

He felt as much as heard the signal, the bird cry that wasn't quite a bird cry. All around him, shapes shed their extra coats of leaves and emerged from the forest floor, statues coming to life.

Then the killing began.

Vali sprang up. There were so many milling down below. *"Pick your target, and see nothing else,"* his father always said. Same principle when you stumbled on a group of deer. Don't let the others distract you. This was no different.

He set his sights on one, wheeling around on his mount, round fur hat coming to a sharp point and framing a flat, broad face. He focused on the spot right where the head met the shoulders. Practiced movements found the fletching on his cheek.

Vali released and reached for another arrow without waiting to see if it connected. That would be a problem for later. All around him, the hiss of arrows was drowned out by the cries of pain and confusion below. A few of the horsemen were trying to rally together, small shields up and looking up into the woods for an angle of attack. Let them search. Vali knew they would find nothing. Death ahead and the swamps behind. If he had to choose, he wasn't sure which way he would have gone either.

Reaching for his last arrow, Vali saw one of the figures drawing more and more of the riders together. A big, pale, bearded bastard, roaring and directing the others. They were sending arrows back into the trees now, but it was an impossible shot. Vali and the others were too well concealed, and they held the high ground. He could see the man below coming to the same conclusion. As Vali sighted down the point of the arrow, he saw the man gesturing in the opposite direction. They wanted to try the swamps. They might not know it, but the arrow would be better by far. This shaft, however, missed their leader and only barely clipped a large woman behind him before disappearing, spending its fury in the dirt or a tree beyond. No matter. He heard the captain's shrill whistle. Time to finish things.

Captain Askaris was already over his log and sprinting down the steep slope, heavy longsword drawn. The rest followed a heartbeat behind. They had all been silent until now, a row of wolves picking the enemy apart.

Now it was time to break them. They gathered their courage and hate for these savage outsiders. No banners of the Imperial Phoenix here, or horns blowing. Howls and roars and furious war cries sounded across the ridge as their skirmishing party rushed down the slope in a tide.

The three Helians were far faster than the rest. Anointed oathknights of the legions with the black patterns on their skin tying them to their conduits back at Heliopolis, they sped toward the enemy with the strength of the Rift flowing through their veins. Beyond that, they were warriors who had proven themselves countless times before on the bloodiest battle-fields. Vali watched as they closed the distance and made impossible leaps, slamming into the riders like loosed ballistae and immediately wreaking bloody havoc with those long, heavy blades.

A bitter twist in his guts drove him forward. Vali picked his man. He was quiet now, saving his strength. The long-handled axe pumped beside him as he charged forward, wolf cloak streaming behind him. He locked eyes with the tribesman ahead of him, whose face was twisted in a rictus of fear and rage.

For a moment, he saw himself as the man saw him. A tall, bearded figure beneath the maw of a skinned wolf. Another savage at the borders of the empire. Vali hated him all the more for that and snarled as he sidestepped a weak cut to smash the man into the ground with a brutal blow. Vision blurring and blood pumping in his ears, he whirled, hungry for the next.

The ambush had turned into a confused melee, riders slashing about the thicket of spears and axes that reached for them like hungry branches. Vali exchanged a series of furious blows with one of the invaders. He hooked the bottom curve of his axe blade into the man's side and felt his blood flood with elation.

Another rider came at him, unhorsed but howling in his barbaric, nearly unintelligible version of Common as he ran at Vali. The man was missing an eye, but that did nothing to dull his speed. The short, curved blade sent shocks up his arms as he deflected and blocked the furious cuts and stabs. The man was strong as well as quick. Vali grinned as he took the measure of his enemy. Not strong enough. Not quick enough.

Vali had trained since before he could walk. With his father, and with the best masters-at-arms and tutors that could be lured to their faraway province with all his father's wealth. The man in front of him didn't know it yet, but he was dead already. Still, Vali felt the weight on him, knew there was so little time. There were so few opportunities to be noticed, to be selected. In a few sets, he could find an opening and finish the man. It would be over in seconds. But he didn't have seconds.

He trusted reflex, strength, and youth to save him. Pushing the rider's next swing wide, he threw his axe at the man, who twisted out of its way. However, he didn't have long to enjoy his success, with Vali close behind the axe, tackling him to the ground, overwhelming him with his huge frame. Barely nineteen, but tall and muscled like an ox. Vali straddled the smaller man, pinning his sword arm and drawing his own dagger. The long knife punched forward, and Vali's knuckles smashed into the man's bristly chin. At first, he thought he had missed. No, it was just too sharp. He thrust it forward twice more. It was like he was punching the man in the neck and jaw, blade disappearing each time and the warmth making his grip slick.

"Behind you!" someone called.

Vali threw himself down and felt the passage of something heavy and fast where his head had been. Hooves thundered past, inches from his face. As he rolled to the side, his hand found a spear half buried among the leaves. The man it belonged to was dead, lying nearby. Another mound in the forest again.

"To me! Getacians! To me!"

Captain Askaris's command rang out above the tumult. For Vali, it was a clarion call, the smooth Helian accent unmistakable. He sprang up. The fight around him had devolved into the tail end of a slaughter, but where that voice rang out, the enemy had organized enough to surround a group of soldiers. On their quick, undersized horses, they circled furiously, curved blades flashing, their short bows given up for this close work. In that circle of horseflesh and metal were the Helian oathknights and another few Getacians. Concern and excitement warred for primacy in Vali. They needed him. This was his chance.

Outracing those around him who had also turned to the calls for aid, he hurtled toward the horsemen, axe somewhere on the ground behind him and spear held tightly in one hand. There wasn't time to think. Instinct would guide him. He sprinted as fast as the wind, faster, flying across the last few strides and leaping forward, using the barrel chest of a fallen horse to propel himself upward. For a beautiful moment, he could feel himself suspended in the air, spear poised and impossibly high above the ground. A wolf leaping for the kill.

No. A phoenix.

He had the briefest flash of grim satisfaction as the spear sank home into the leg of one of the riders, pinning him to his horse. This would break their line, he knew it.

From within the circle, Captain Askaris stared up at him, eyes wide. And then time caught up with Vali.

He fell with the horse and rider, and realized, too late, that he hadn't quite broken their momentum. The rider and the horse he had downed would do that—along with him.

The rest of the circling riders plunged into them. There were stuttering images of hooves, screams human and equine, and pain beyond description. Something smashed into his right leg. Vali cried out, grateful and terrified that no one could hear him. There was a blow to his head. It cut off his scream and shocked him out of his body. He knew, in a distracted sort of way, that the pain was immense. He thought he might still be screaming. Finally, blessedly, he felt another jolt, and the black of the void opened before him. Vali raced for it, plunging into darkness.

# A NEW WAY

They were trying to be quiet, they really were. But the sucking sounds of marshland mud and splash of the thigh-deep water were constant as they struggled away from the killing fields. Darya looked to the front of their small group to where her brother, Mikael, led the way, peering into the gangrenous fog from his mount. Mikael was everything to her, older brother and mentor and protector all in one. Along with competent, and brave, and all of the good things that Darya wished she could see in herself. Even now, worried as she was, Mikael was at the front, leading the survivors, scanning from above a beard that was a little heavier every year. She remembered teasing him for the wispy thing it had been. That had been a long time ago.

Stuck in the sickeningly warm marshes as they were, it seemed to Darya in that moment that if being a leader meant anything, it was taking the front when everything had gone to shit. And there was no denying that things had gone well and truly to shit today. Even the wan sunlight of an hour ago was retreating now. Darya thought she couldn't get any more frightened after the slaughter of the ambush, but after wandering for hours, the thought of being lost and blind in these endless swamps made her breath catch. Less than twenty of them remained now, out of a force that had numbered over two hundred, and half of them without horses. It seemed a bad omen that none of their ambushers had bothered following them here.

Every step stirred the vile, fetid water and assaulted the senses, making her eyes water. The brackish liquid—water was too generous a word—gave off an acrid vapor, and the horses grew uneasy as ripples spread and splashes echoed beyond their sight. These lands were poisoned. Rotted remnants of a battle past myth and memory poked out of the water and made jagged islands of rusting metal that they were careful to skirt far around. Outlined by the sunset behind them, the bones of some massive, long-dead machine of war cut the horizon, most of it sunken back into the earth. The little debris and the behemoth behind them were all rusted and falling apart, original functions impossible to tell, but they should have been dust—the Breaking of the world was thousands of years ago. These blighted lands were decay themselves, but without end. And she knew not everything in these places was dead.

They had to get back to their camp, to the warband. The Arkhan had it in his head to find a new way past the empire's forts and the black-clad crows, the legionnaires who guarded every pass south, and her brother had been charged with scouting a way through here. Scouting a way through and finding allies, the sorts from the stories, who were touched by the souls of the dead. Darya knew, in theory, that they were real, but they were so far removed from the reality of the Thousand Tribes that the whole venture seemed a bit absurd to her. They also told stories about fiery saviors and deliverance to promised lands of warmth and sun, but Darya had always thought those who took the idea of the gods sending anyone to save them a bit too hopeful and more than a little childish. This might have felt the same, but she also knew that the Arkhan and his warlord, Janbek, were deadly serious. Serious or not, it still struck Darya as a terrible reason to die, hunting for these semi-mythical allies. She also knew, thanks to her brother, exactly who had planted that idea. Not that there was ever much doubt. The mysterious outsider who was never far from the Arkhan's ear—Vels. The useless, thrice-damned, hooded and bandaged old bastard who had led them here along a narrow strip of land, and then had fled once the killing started. It wasn't his failure that Janbek or the Arkhan would see, unfortunately.

She could already see the hard glances at her and the others without wounds, the muttering behind her brother's back. To her side rode one of the other women in the scouting party, Alina, a friend from childhood. A bloody rag was tied around the muscular woman's head, where an arrow had taken a strip of scalp, matting the usually annoyingly lustrous hair on that side a crusty red-brown. She had an arrow nocked and was scanning the water. Darya wished she had some measure of her friend's strength, or maybe just her seeming ability to take everything in stride. Alina was built for fights like that ambush. As another splash left her flinching,

Darya couldn't escape the conclusion that she, with her too-thin arms and entirely overactive imagination, was not. Alina noticed her examination.

"Does your brother know where he is going?"

Alina's voice fell flat in the heavy air. Some of the men were up to their waists now. And all of them had heard Alina's comment. Including Bohdan. From his half-submerged position, he did his best to studiously ignore it, and Darya was grateful for that. He came from their tribe as well. Practically a stranger a few years ago, the fact that the tall, lanky man was one of the only four left from their home put him squarely in the category of friend, given the strange peoples of the Thousand.

Darya gave Alina a sharp look. She sidled her horse closer. "Of course he does," she said. Her voice sounded unconvincing, even to her. "Please don't start. Can't you hear them already?"

Alina considered her skeptically. For all her friend's usual cold cynicism, Darya could see the panic just below the surface. There was no taking today in stride; she was scared too. Whether of the swamps, her close association with Mikael, or both, she couldn't tell. Alina lowered her voice too. "Fine. But we need to get out of this swamp, Darya. And fast. That old bastard warned us about this area."

"There wasn't any choice," Darya protested. She didn't like their situation any more than Alina, but she trusted Mikael.

"Always feels like that, doesn't it?" Alina muttered.

A loud splash sounded to their right. The entire column halted, all searching by the twilight's eerie light to see what had made the sound. Ears strained and silence reigned around them as they held a collective breath.

A wet cough broke the quiet. One at first, and then an uncontrollable fit of thick, racking coughs from a man behind her. It looked like he had been shot in the chest. It was a wonder he had made it this far. He kept coughing, blood and spittle dripping from his lips.

"Shut him up!" A shouted whisper from the front.

Darya felt bad for the man, but they were right. The loud coughs were an invitation that they did not need right now. She didn't think he could stop though.

With a casual movement, one of the man's fellows slid forward, pulled his head back, and slit his throat. The coughing turned to a gurgle, and the body fell into the water with a splash. Seeing the look of horror on her face, the man gave Darya a wide, gap-toothed grin. The column began moving again in the relative silence of the regular squelch and ripples of their forward progress. There were only a few muted whispers and a couple hisses of disapproval to mark that anything had happened at all.

Beside her, Alina nodded in approval. She caught Darya's troubled look. "What? What would you have done?"

Darya opened her mouth to reply, then closed it, reflective. "I don't know. Not that. We could have waited, maybe?"

Alina snorted. "Wait with him if you like."

<hr />

It was completely dark now, and a few of the men had lit torches. The mud was firmer beneath their feet, but the water was deeper. Darya wasn't sure if that was better or worse. They moved faster without having to drag their feet out of a trap every step, and the water smelled a bit less sour, but the splashes around them were louder and more frequent now. All things considered, Darya decided she liked this considerably less. They were stopped now, another noise to their left leaving them peering into the dark, blinded by their own torches.

"What do you think it is?" Alina whispered. Her horse fidgeted beneath her.

"I don't know, maybe a—"

Darya's guess was cut off. There was a scream from behind them as one of the Easterners was dragged under. Followed by utter stillness as they all looked in shock to where he had stood. The only signs he had been there at all were a few bubbles and ripples spreading from the spot.

Then another scream from the rear. This one was not over quickly. It was the one who had slit the wounded man's throat earlier. He was thrashing and screaming for help, a knife out and stabbing wildly at the thing that held him. In the dim firelight, Darya had an impression of gray scales and a long mouth filled with pale needles. Some sort of remnant. A creature left from before the Breaking. Panic overtook the group.

"This way! Follow me!"

She couldn't see him, but she heard Mikael's voice and pushed her mount toward him, heels digging into its flanks with desperate urgency. Her horse and Alina's surged forward, seeking to close the gap between them and the lead riders. Anything to put distance between them and the screams behind them. The water had become a churning mess as man and horse sprinted for the closest thing to safety. She didn't want to think that safety right now might just mean not dying alone.

Darya chanced another glance backwards and immediately regretted it. Another man went down, piercing cry turning into a gurgle and his torch hissing as it hit the water. Not before she saw a dozen more shapes, pinpricks of light glinting above the water and long bodies undulating toward them.

A little half-scream, half-whimper escaped her throat, terror over-whelming most rational thoughts. Except for one. *Why?* Why had she insisted on coming along with her brother? She had refused to stay in the camps, where most of the other women remained. Wanted to see the world, explore. Wanted to make a name for herself. Be like her brother. A brave and beautiful warrior woman. A leader like their mother.

"Stupid, stupid, stupid," she hissed to herself, a mantra.

She made a solid promise to the Sun, the stars, every god, and to herself to give up this idiocy, if only she could survive the night. And then, out of the darkness, there was light. A beacon of hope in the distance. She could see a single pinprick of fire ahead, the distance impossible to judge. A torch from one of theirs who had escaped the ambush? A local? They had all seen it and redirected with unspoken agreement. No one cared where it came from all that much; any light was better than the dark around them. Those few who were on foot were falling farther behind, but Bohdan remained close, somehow having kept pace with her and Alina.

"Let me on!" he gasped, reaching for Alina's reins. His chest was heaving, face dripping.

"No, he can't take the weight!"

Darya wanted to help, but she could feel her own horse straining through the high water. He was infected by the group's panic, snorting and eyes rolling back in his head. There was no chance for a second rider. They started to inch ahead of Bohdan, whose steps became slower and slower. She turned away from him, feeling the betrayal. But there was nothing she could do. The light ahead grew closer and closer. Darya allowed herself to hope. They would make it.

With a sick lurch, Darya's horse twisted sideways, screaming in an inhuman pitch as something tore at him from below. She was falling, foot caught in the stirrups, incapable of doing anything.

"Wait!" she screamed to Alina, right before she plunged into the murky waters.

The waters were a shock, sweating and panicked as she was. Immediately, the filth began working its way into her nose, and her body spasmed, trying to expel the liquid she had gasped in when she had fallen. She could feel her horse struggling madly, wrenching her along, but she was able to reach down and feel for the stirrup. She could feel something else down there, brushing against her arm, hard scales and furious movement. Darya tried to block it out of her mind and focused on the one chance she had: pull her boot out of the stirrup. Escape. But try as she might, she couldn't remove it, the odd angle and her horse's panicked thrashing drowning her. The fear became all-consuming. It was all Darya could do to remember the stirrup. She could feel the water, along with something more viscous, seeping ever further into her nose from her position and had a vague sensation of being upside down. Another spasm wracked her, and she snorted in more water. Every conscious thought fled. Darya started to claw and struggle as mindlessly as the horse.

Suddenly, she could feel another presence, feeling along the stirrup. Another hand, beside her own. Together, they pulled her boot from the stirrup. She was starting to see spots at the edge of her vision, and there was a burning sensation as the water in her nostrils burned its way down. She righted herself, seeking the bottom with her feet. Darya exploded out of the water, coughing and sputtering and blind.

The light. She and Alina needed to find their way back toward the light. "Move!"

Rough hands pulled her along through the water, not waiting for her to come to her senses. Strong, large hands. Looking to her side, she saw Bohdan, soaked in water, sweat, and something darker, dragging her along. Alina was nowhere to be seen, but she could see shapes silhouetted against the lonely flame that was once again before them.

The water was shallower, but still they thrashed through it, expending all their energy to move at a jogging pace. It was like sprinting in a nightmare. Their heavy coats and furs that were such a comfort against the cold were killing them now, heavy and constricting. She could hear hissing behind them and the rippling splashes of the creatures as they closed in.

They were both beyond screaming now. There would be no warning when one of them went down. One less breath heaving in the dark. Darya could see the shapes beneath the light now. They were so close. But they would never make it. She glanced at Bohdan as she struggled forward. He caught her gaze before taking a quick glance backward. She could see the fear. He knew it too.

Darya's foot slipped under her as she pushed against the mud beneath. She wanted to scream. Floundering, she thrashed her way back upright and couldn't resist looking back. They were close enough for her to see the oily sheen of the scales, the sinuous and segmented bodies. And their speed. Whimpering, she clawed her way forward, the light so close that she could practically feel the warmth. Too far still, and now Bohdan was a step ahead of her. Something animal was screaming inside of her. It screamed that she could live, that she *had* to live, to take the only chance left. It made sense, it made sense, she needed it to make sense. Did he know too? What if he came to a decision before her? She knew he would do it. Darya knew she didn't have a choice.

She sank her knife into Bohdan's side.

His eyes bugged with pain and surprise. Was that a sense of betrayal she saw in them too? No, he just couldn't believe she had beat him to the only decision they had left. She lunged away, pulling her bloody knife with her, but she was too slow. With a speed she didn't think he had anymore, one of those hands reached out and grabbed her, pulling her back.

Sense fled, and hysteria took over again. Breathless, she started slashing frantically with the knife, past aiming, but doing anything she could to get him to let go. Darya felt a searing pain across her forearm. She had cut herself. But the grip was gone too. A last flood of adrenaline pushed her on. She didn't look back, but she could hear when the teeth started to tear him apart. And she had been wrong after all; he still had enough breath to scream. Tears blurring her vision, she kept moving, trying to catch up. Those cries pushed her on. The water was only at her calves now.

She ran into a shape before the torch. Crying out, she instinctively lashed out with the knife, but it was knocked out of her hand and disappeared with a splash. Strong arms pulled her close in an embrace. She tried to collapse, but they held her up. It was Mikael. He had come back for her.

"Bohdan?"

Darya shook her head, tears streaming down her cheeks. She sobbed with the release of the tension and the shock of what she had done. Red warmth soaked her sleeve.

Mikael pulled her closer, like he had when they were children. "It's alright. It's over. I'm here now." He pulled her along, to where the water was barely deep enough to wet the boots.

"Who was there?" She was gaining some of her breath back and needed to think of anything else but what was behind her. "From the camp?"

Mikael didn't have a chance to answer. Vague shapes loomed out of the darkness as the few remaining survivors joined them at this shallow point. Alina was among them and was avoiding looking at Darya. Between them all walked a solitary figure bearing a torch, slim beneath black robes and with nearly every other bit of skin covered with wrappings. The rest split apart, making more room than necessary. Some looked away or spat over their shoulders. Intelligent green eyes sparkled over a smile filled with perfect teeth.

Vels.

# A QUESTION OF SCOPE

S treams, forests, seas, and vast fields of ice stretched as far as Syl could see. Further than he could reach, at least. Lovingly carved and painted, the central piece of the Exarch's outer office was a work of art. A great inland sea stretched across the length of the table, dividing the landmass nearly in two, and split in turn by the crumbling gray lines of the old sea walls. Massive deserts started at Syl's end, gradually transitioning to the green and fertile lands of the Helian Empire.

The table and the land went on, picturesque islands and croplands turning into dark forests and uncharted, snowy mountains. That part was accurate as well, Syl thought ruefully, looking out the window of the Exarch's estate and past the spread of the barracks, past the stone and timber lines of Rasovus, north to the toothy white horizon. The west end of the map petered out in a vague depiction of the blackened and burned blightlands, separated from everything else by a great scar gouged into the wood. Further yet along the table, great plains of scrubby grasslands spread endlessly to the east and were in turn swallowed by the advancing maw of snow and sheets of ice that marched their way south from where the Exarch and his chief judiciar stood, listening to Domarik's brief.

The plain black robes the Exarch, Demarhis, wore were augmented with richly decorated vestments, threads of crimson and gold forming fantastical patterns. The Exarch's brown eyes were those of a kindly father, but Syl knew a word or gesture from the small, rotund man would see any one of them on the rack or with a noose around their neck before the day was done if he deemed it in the interests of the empire. Judiciars and Hunters might enact the will of the Vigil, but even governors knew better than to cross the exarchs of their territories. Prayer beads hung at his belt, five strings of five, for the aspects of the *Vox Caelorum*. A brilliant, flashing sun hung from his neck and rested, half concealed, under folded hands that balanced on a well-fed belly. It was a twin to the sun embedded in the center of the chorusplate worn by the chief judiciar. The heavy links of his chain of office rested on the interwoven steel and ossanite of the ancient armor, a silent promise and unnecessary reminder of the judiciar's role.

Chief Judiciar Nerilias was as tall as the Exarch was short, a stretched-out version of a man that hadn't enough room for all the extras like flesh and fat and mercy. His shaved head was gaunt, the outlines of his skull visible under gray stubble.

"...and that accounts for a total of twelve Stained recaptured or eliminated in this province in the last two weeks."

Domarik's rumbling voice brought Syl back. He and the rest of the team were standing behind Domarik, and were expected to do so for another half hour, at least. With a jealous twinge, he saw that Leon had settled deep into the sort of trance he had perfected over a decade of sitting and waiting in the legions. Meanwhile, Liora and Kass were silently exchanging glares—clearly the fallout of some argument since last night's raid.

Their Primary went on. "That number doesn't include sympathizers. The coordination with which the escapees were taken in and hidden warrants further investigation, but given the issue with Primary Gregoris's team and the unusual capabilities of recent targets..."

The chief judiciar cut him off. "We are aware of the scale of the problem, Domarik. That is why we requested your team's presence. That is why you are in this room now."

Domarik dipped his massive head a fraction, allowing Nerilias to interrupt, but Syl could see the thick muscles twitching on the side of his neck.

"A coordinated ambush on a convoy of prisoners, patrols missing, an entire Hunter team gone without a trace, and reports of more and stronger Rift-users than we've seen since the Mages' Revolt." He gave Domarik a hard look. "It hardly takes a strategic genius to see that there's more going on under the surface. My judiciars haven't been idle."

Exarch Demarhis put up a hand. "Be civil, Nerilias. You misplace your hostility."

"As you say, Father." But Nerilias's glare never left Domarik.

The Exarch sighed, the sound of a man with squabbling children quickly running out of patience. "We have a region riddled with separatist cells and sympathizers. The governor tells me there are rumors of a new pretender in the North. Our western patrols send back sightings of resurrected relics of war and rumors of the arcane warlords resurgent and fighting in the shadow of the fortress city that erupted in the last cataclysm. All of this is to say nothing of the scouting parties of the Tribes at new points along the border. If the Northern lords are restless again, if the passes don't close quickly enough, if those heathens give up on the Gates and move west in force... If, if, if..." He shook his head. "It doesn't bear thinking about. Whether the beginning of the end is nigh, or a generation off, it is coming. So, remember why we are here. We are the Vigil, and the delay and mitigation of that end is a mandate that should put you above such petty squabbling. The Emperor might have His eye to the southern campaigns, but rest assured, any failures here will be judged by Him and His Chosen."

Both Nerilias and Domarik were silent this time, but the tension was heavy in the air between those two. Syl couldn't help but despise the chief judiciar as well, despite knowing the truth of the Exarch's words. Accusations of cruelty and excessive zeal were often brandished against the Hunters of the Imperial Vigil, but that was because no one dared mention who held the leash. Their branch held too many secrets and was far too quick to summary judgments for there to be any love lost between the likes of Nerilias and the team.

Nerilias twitched a nonexistent eyebrow. "Moving on. Interrogations of detainees from recent raids have been by and large a waste of time, and the prisoners were sent onward. Those that survived. However, there were two who provided some interesting information before that point." Nerilias's iron-sheathed hand drifted northward on the map, toward a bumpy raised surface of snow-capped mountains and past them to a dark patch bordered to the north and east by mountains and ice, with blasted, red wastelands to the west. Northern Getacia. "Their reports were corroborative in concept, but hazy on detail. No matter how hard we pushed. A major attack by Northern separatists is imminent. Such an attack is almost certain to include allied Stained, considering the recent spate of incidents in the vicinity. This matches rumors passed to us by our local networks of informers."

Domarik made his lumbering thrust. "As you say, no strategic genius needed. What do you propose to do about it, Judiciar?"

Syl didn't think Nerilias had enough blood to flush, but there was no mistaking the hostility emanating from that skeletal face. Before Nerilias could answer, the Exarch started to move around the table, working his way toward them, footfalls silent on the rich carpet.

"Domarik. My son. You know what we need to do. Why pretend otherwise? This is not a time for doubts or second-guessing. We must strike at the heart of this apostasy first. It is time to show strength and remind the people of this province why they bow to the South. Unity must be reforged, from time to time."

Nerilias took over, his clipped words meant for direction, not discussion. "Within the week, you and your Hunters will head north with a full cohort and root out these separatists, these traitors, where those before you failed. You will start in Seven Rivers." Nerilias held up a hand to forestall the inevitable protest. "This is a pivotal point, and the resources allocated will reflect that. You are merely an advance force. The Twins are already on their way here, along with two cohorts of Legio Vorax. They will follow behind you." Nerilias gave his thin-lipped ghoul's smile. "I suggest you make some progress before they arrive."

The mobilization was surprising, but the orders couldn't be clearer. Domarik nodded. "Done."

"Good. But on a related matter, we have one more thing to discuss." Syl could guess where this was going. "The girl." The Exarch's words were an accusation, leveled against Domarik. Liora kept her eyes studiously focused on the far wall, while Kass looked on with a vindictive glee that she didn't bother to conceal. "Explain yourself."

Domarik cleared his throat, and Liora stirred, but Syl chose that moment to step forward, still rigidly at attention. He could weather this; Liora could not. Or so he told himself. The Exarch's eyes bored into Syl's, the unspoken question heavy in the air. Syl swallowed, wondering if he could explain this properly, even to himself.

"Your Radiance, we often take Stained into custody to send to the—"

"Not those that helped murder an entire patrol," the Exarch interrupted, a note of shrillness creeping in. "And certainly not upon the eve of what might be the start of another cycle."

Another direction, then. "I thought she could answer questions."

Nerilias snorted at that. Syl hurried to explain himself, feeling the weight of all the attention in the room on him. The damning part was that he knew they were right. Even he wasn't swayed by his own arguments.

"I know she has accessed the Rift. There's no denying that." The black eye flashed across his mind. He knew she needed to die, but it seemed important to at least delay it. "She can't be free, and she belonged in that convoy of prisoners. No doubt there. But as for the patrol? She's barely more than a child. I doubt she even helped."

"Speaking of doubts," Nerilias spat. "Are you so ignorant of your guidelines, Hunter? Is this the sort of Hunter Secondary the Vigil can field now?" His voice was poisonous, incredulous. Disbelief that anyone could be that monumentally stupid. Syl did wonder a bit himself.

"No, but... " How much to tell them? "... I had a child myself once," he finished lamely. "A daughter."

"Fascinating."

Nerilias's scorn filled Syl with an immediate, incandescent rage. He tried to keep the hate from his face and his hands still by his sides. He would have killed the judiciar on the spot, chorusplate or no, if he thought he could get away with it. It still might be worth trying later.

*You should try now. You could do it.*

Syl ignored the urge and focused on the Exarch, who seemed more sympathetic. His face softened with a level of understanding. "Then it came from a pure place. A wrong act with noble intentions is something that can be corrected. Unfortunately, it does bring up questions as to your guidance on this team."

"Your Radiance, she was her parents' child. She did as was expected of her. It was ignorance, not evil."

"No, Scyllus. Ignorance *is* evil if it leads down the same paths. Still..." Demarhis brushed his hands down his long gray-and-black beard absently. "Perhaps there is hope for her, if not the chance for freedom. Forgiveness and redemption through service to the Emperor." He nodded thoughtfully. "Yes. Perhaps you were right. This aberration is a chance for us to better understand the affliction more broadly. I would like to give our team here some time to study her condition. The eye is...unique."

Nerilias's lip curled in disgust, and Syl enjoyed the moment of triumph. Such a little victory. So temporary. Why did it mean so much, then?

The Exarch cut him down quickly. "I say might, and I mean that. Right now, I hear that she is a little hellion, spitting at her goalers and refusing food. She must accept the light if she is to ever pass through the door you have opened for her. Regardless of what the final decision may be. You may talk to her after this. See if you can convince her to cooperate. The investigation into her condition will occur either way, but she is entirely in control of her level of comfort. But either way, that's enough on that matter. Nerilias? Anything else?"

"Planning with all officers of the expedition north to Seven Rivers will begin in an hour. The rest of you are dismissed. Sol Invictus."

"Sol Invictus." Domarik smashed his fist to his armored chest in the imperial salute.

Syl and the rest of the team followed suit, bowed, and filed their way out, passing underneath the branches of the bas-relief stone trees that framed the exit. Syl's relief was short-lived as he thought about today's little victory weighed against the dangers of tomorrow. Farther north into Getacia. Again.

The Exarch's voice called after them. "Except for you, Scyllus. Mistakes, innocent or not, have consequences. Meet me in the gallery."

Syl turned once more, face a mask, and saluted again. Not quite done, then.

# THE DUTY OF HISTORY

S yl ran his fingers along the walls of the villa as he walked through the gallery. The whole place was a ruin from before the Breaking, almost perfectly preserved, despite having weathered every cataclysm since. It was built of strong lines and contained a dozen mechanisms that they knew the purpose of, and a hundred more they could only guess at. If it was located near enough to the Riftgate in Heliopolis, the flamewardens might pry some understanding from them, but otherwise, they were only more inert legacies of the past.

The Getacians had themselves a king here in this place at one point, until Syl, the legions, and a few disaffected local nobles had tipped him out of his chair and added these lands to the growing empire. He thought it odd that every place he had been with the legions or the Vigil, rulers and rebels alike were, without exception, drawn to these sorts of ruins. An instant conferment of gravitas, the authority of having been.

Syl could hardly judge. He might be from the hills and orchards of Western Helios, but the imperial capital itself? Heliopolis? One of the great abandoned fortress cities, retaken and refurbished when the Emperor returned the first time. Their Emperor? The redemptive avatar of the gods, prophesied as their recurrent savior. Sent again and again to rescue them from themselves, from the squabbling, unchanging nature of men and Stained who inevitably broke the world in conflict after disaster, despite the best efforts of the Vigil. Their best and most necessary equipment? Null collars, aegis gauntlets, chorusplate, souliron firearms, and even the dim arclamps lighting the villa? The surviving titans, airships, and cannons of Heliopolis? Animachina. Artifacts they still struggled to understand, beyond the fact that the souls of those passed on to the Rift were inextricably tied to them. The flamewardens kept them functioning and guarded the knowledge they gathered, but it was enough to know that it was better to control or destroy them rather than see them fall into unpredictable hands. Yet they were no closer to making their own, with the best they could do being a temporary infusing of spiritual energy into objects, like the trackers that had brought them to the farmhouse. It was all so old. Before, before, before. An obsession with the ancient. At least the mosaics on the walls were new. They were fitted together expertly, and the texture of the tiny tiles only occasionally caught his fingers.

Syl stepped back to examine the piece in its entirety. He didn't know how much longer he would be here and had almost no doubt it would eventually involve some level of censure. He might as well take his time. The mosaic covered the southern wall, facing toward the capital and the Riftgate there. Huddled masses reached toward the sun, which was depicted piercing the thick clouds above them and stunning the shambling and crawling creatures that surrounded them—ironspawn, chimexa, and other remnants beyond description. The mosaic might have been well constructed, but the craftsman had little eye for the details. All the figures looked more or less the same, though the Emperor and his Chosen were obvious enough. Seven figures and One, bathed in light, as if delivered from the sun itself. It was a common enough mural, and woe betide the artist who didn't include those eight.

"I see you enjoy the work. A classic depiction of the first Piercing of the Veil. I commissioned it myself." The Exarch emerged from behind one of the thick pillars to stand in front of the mosaic, slippers scuffing the stone. He barely came to Syl's chin, but his presence filled the room. The scent of incense and a soft, kindly voice couldn't hide the steel just beneath the surface. The Exarch was a man accustomed to being listened to with the closest attention and being obeyed without question. Behind, far enough away to be unobtrusive, lurked two judiciars. Nerilias's. The weight behind the words. All in gray and perfectly still, they almost faded into the background.

"Exarch Demarhis. Your Radiance." Syl shifted.

"Please, call me Father." He hadn't missed Syl's flickering glance. He waved his hand. "And ignore them. They follow me everywhere." He gave a disarming smile. "One of the perils of position. You're never alone again."

More easily said than done, but Syl relaxed a measure. If there were going to be any harsher sort of punishment meted out, this was an unlikely place.

"Vigilus Hunter Secundus, I have a question."

*Not a promising start.* The Exarch didn't turn from the wall, but his eyes drifted to the side, examining Syl, who smoothed his face to impassivity with long years of practice.

"This business with the girl... We all have crises of faith, but tell me, do you even know your purpose? I mean, really know it?"

Syl stiffened. "Of course. Father. To root out and burn the evil where we find it."

"What a banal platitude." His voice was a whip now, laying into Syl. "You're not some new recruit. I've spoken with Domarik. I know your past. Years of service after such a tragedy. And years in the legions before that. Secondary on the team. You're not an initiate like that damn girl, so don't give me an initiate's answer. *Think.* And don't embarrass us both again with such an answer. Do you understand *why* we do what we do?"

There was a sudden vision of smashing the Exarch's head into the wall before moving on to the judiciars and... Syl jerked his head, pulling his thoughts back. No. This was deserved. He had thought he was past these sorts of didactic humiliations, but based on what had happened at the farmhouse, maybe he wasn't. It was nothing new to him either way. He fought down the anger and considered his answer more carefully. His mind went back to his own why. Answering that question was easy.

"To stop them from hurting innocents."

"No." The word was like a slap, and the disappointment on the Exarch's face was a second. "You disappoint me, Scyllus. That one of our own doesn't seem to understand why the Hunters exist. Why the judiciars, bondmages, oathknights, and conduits exist. Why *I* exist. It makes it far less surprising that a new member of your team also doesn't understand."

The anger disappeared, and Syl began to worry. Worry for himself, at least a little, but mostly for Liora. Syl tensed, searching for the right words.

*You can't make him understand; you don't even know anymore.*

*It was her fault, you could tell him it was her fault.*

"Calm yourself, my son," the Exarch finally said with a sigh. "We all have our purpose and our path, but sometimes we need a guiding light too." Demarhis slowed, picking his next words carefully. "We do not send you to ruins, ritual circles, separatist safehouses, and...and families' farmhouses simply because we want to spare innocents. Make no mistake, that is an admirable goal, and you often do stop horrible acts that would have happened otherwise. But it is not the why. You know as well as I that many of those we send you after have no intention of harming others. There are some like those who robbed you of your family, massive rebel armies and Stained uprisings, but most only want to touch the river of souls through the Riftgate, the blessed Fons Anima, and use it for their own small ends. Or they are sick, or weak, and cannot resist the reach of those souls within."

He gestured Syl to the right, guiding him toward the western wall. Before them was another mosaic, fuzzy on details again, but vivid in the emotions it evoked. From a hundred directions, vague columns of men and metal and unnatural creatures converged at a central point, where the colors of blood and fire dominated. Drakes swarmed through the sky, and wyrms curled over walls, gouts of flame and light cut across the battlefield, and tall figures of fire and darkness towered above the armies they sent hurtling toward the center.

"No. The reason we send you out into the world to hunt is because those who would ignore the Emperor's decrees and pursue their own ends are followers—whether they realize it or not—of that ancient and pernicious evil. The disunity that burned the world and will do so again. The cataclysms that plunge us into years of darkness and destroyed the great old empires of the West. The ash that can still blot out our sun is the very manifestation of our own inalienable evil. It may have been the Fallen and their demons, like Zavayoth and Tharazel and Chermogar, along with their great wyrms and infernal machines that tore the West apart during the Breaking, that breached the seals, but what were those demons but men and women stained with the corruption of ages past? The fragments of evil left in the Rift will always seek the cracks in the souls of those living, and others will seek them out on their own, but it was the weakness in the hearts of men that swelled their armies and gave them power beyond anything the Rift might have cursed them with.

"It's the proof of why we need a unifying savior, why our kind can't be trusted with that sort of power. It's why I have no regrets when we must kill or imprison an 'innocent.' The penal colonies, mines, and lumber mills that dot the borders of our empire are filled with such men and women. They are not innocent. They are would-be accomplices to apocalypse, knowingly or unknowingly. They cannot be saved. The best we can do is offer lives of service to their children, if taken early enough. Boys like

Lucky, cursed, but given holy purpose in preventing the sins of their fellows."

His voice took on an iron edge again. "So, when I hear that one of our Hunters, one of our best, has started making decisions out of sentimentality, I must ask myself if he has lost sight of our vision." He stared at the great war depicted before them. "Lost sight of our past."

Syl felt as if he had to say something. An affirmation. Anything. "I understand." And he did. Perhaps his reasons for joining the Vigil were more personal, but then whose weren't? He had grown up with the same history as the rest. Years of war and months of darkness and ash. And that was only the most recent cataclysm, of dozens over the millennia since the Breaking. What couldn't be excused in the delay of those calamities' return? The Emperor had been prophesied to come, unite them each time, and protect them from utterly destroying themselves, sacrificing Himself for their sake over and over. He was here now, but even a representative of the gods needed His tools.

The Exarch studied him for what seemed an eternity from under bushy brows. "I think you might. But this isn't just about you." *Liora.* "Yes, you know already. I can see it on your face. Your sentimentality can be weighed against your years of service. A deviation, not a pattern. No such grace exists for her. You clearly care about her fate, so make her see what we've discussed here today. If she is incapable of seeing it, then we will do what we must. You know Domarik won't hesitate. He would have made a good judiciar, actually."

"Understood."

"I hope so. For the period of this expedition north, her failings will be your failings, Scyllus. If you have any doubts about her, better to cut her time on the team short now."

Syl nodded, throat dry.

"If that's too much, I'm going to offer you your own choice. This is difficult work. Not just physically dangerous, but spiritually so. It is not meant for everyone, or everyone for long."

"What are you saying, Father?"

"I'm saying that if you need, you can step aside with honor now. There is no shame in it. You've served the empire in some capacity almost your whole life. Others can carry the load."

Syl had been worried about Liora before. Now he was terrified. To be…what? Cast aside? His bonds burned away? Looking down at the runes snaking their way down his forearms, for the briefest moment, his mind flashed through the possibilities of what that life would look like. What he might be away from his service in the legions, in the Vigil, and the revenge he had held so close for all these years. Away from the power and the burdens of an oathknight, a bondknight, as they liked to complain. All he found himself looking at was an empty room in an empty house, for purposeless day after endless year. He knew how that would end, and it wouldn't take long. A shiver ran down his spine.

"No. Father, I want to serve." *Need to serve.* What else was there?

"There is no shame in bowing out now, but to continue with doubts, to hold back from what needs to be done… That would be a different matter. This is your chance, Scyllus."

"No." He put as much finality into the word as he could, and meant it. The conversation with the Exarch had been a needed reminder. A small wind for the embers of that purpose that had once burned so hot. A reminder that there was nothing else left for someone like him.

There was yet another pause, but then the Exarch nodded. "Good. I'm glad to hear it. There are too many who have forgotten where we came from. Governors and generals jockey for position while barbarians from the ice and riders from the steppes threaten our borders. All while within our own lands, separatists make noises of independence in half the provinces. And now these escaped Stained here, in a region we subdued only a decade ago. If we fail, the world suffers. It suffers like it did the last time, with a generation of war and all reaching for power in any way they can. Our failure on this endless vigil is inevitable, but each time, we can delay and preserve. But if we cannot build a better, unquestioningly united world, we cannot preserve anything. All the innocents die. So, speak to the girl. Make her see what you and I see. Let her find meaning in her suffering. Or fix your mistake." The Exarch gave a sudden, deep laugh. "Well, you've certainly woken me up this morning, Scyllus. Thank you for that. Stay here, enjoy the mosaics. There are more in the next room."

Conflicted between riding the spiritual high of the impromptu sermon and dreading his next task, Syl focused on what he could control. "From the same artist?"

Another chuckle. "No, actually. The one who made these couldn't quite get the faces right. I'm sure you noticed." Demarhis stopped on his way out of the room, thinking back. "He said it didn't matter, that it was about the idea of it. An allegory about universal values. Insisted on it. But the details matter, Scyllus, they always do. Unsurprisingly, he was later found to have helped publish seditious material. He's at one of the excavation sites now, I believe, if he's still alive. In this new world, this united world, some people don't have a place." He paused once more. "Scyllus?"

"Yes?"

"Be sure those on your team have a place. Otherwise, we will find one for them."

# OVERCAST

The blackness had been better. Waking up opened the floodgates to a level of hurt Vali hadn't thought possible. He groaned, trying to take in his surroundings. Wooden ceiling, wooden walls, and some daylight filtering in. He heard concerned voices. It was just noise. The words and their meaning were far away.

"Vali? Vali, can you hear me?"

It was Marika. He could tell by her voice, even if her face was only a suggestion. He could sense a hand entwined with his, pulling away. Maybe he had imagined that. Another figure stood behind her, vague lines suggesting concern visible even in the haze. Lucan, then.

"Course he's awake. Can't keep him down for long." Lucan's voice was high-pitched with excitement. It was overwhelming, and as his awareness returned, he couldn't help but hear the false note to it. His friend had never been a good liar. "Vali, you magnificent, crazy bastard! You broke their line by yourself! I saw it—gods-damned incredible. No one can stop talking about it. Including the captain."

Lucan's words kindled some hope, despite the pain. Vali ignored Marika's furious look at Lucan. This could still all be worth it. Sweating, he gritted his teeth, wiggling feet and moving his hands. The agony that shot down his right leg almost made him lose consciousness again. He saw the foot move though. He tried to put the good news Lucan was focusing on out of his mind. Lifting the blanket a little, he could only see bandages and heavy splints. There was the sensation of throbbing heat under all that mess. There was a bandage wrapped around his head too, but it was the leg that worried him. He wanted nothing more than to rip it all away and see what was underneath.

He grimaced, lowering the blanket. "How bad is it? Be honest with me."

Marika played with her long braid and looked off into the middle distance, round face tightening as she searched for the right words. Lucan suddenly seemed utterly absorbed in a piece of imaginary dirt somewhere on the floor, his long, fine features too expressive to hide anything. This seemed worse by far than any answer they could have given.

"Tell me." His voice cracked a little. "I need to know."

She turned to him, those kind brown eyes telling him everything he needed to know. She was only this gentle when something was wrong. "The medicus said you were lucky."

"But?"

She frowned. "But your right leg is broken, Vali. He said..."

"Tell me what he said, damn it." He sounded so much angrier than he meant to. The shooting pain from even that level of exertion calmed him down a bit. "Mari, please."

Lucan came to Marika's rescue. "Vali...they said you won't be able to walk without crutches for a few months." He had given up on the hopeful tone. "And...and he said you might never run again. Sorry."

That had to be wrong. Of course his leg hurt; he had been trampled by a dozen horses. But he was strong, he was young. And he had done the right thing! The brave thing, breaking their line. This couldn't be right.

All he could do was squeeze his eyes shut. "No. No. *No.*" Vali demanded for it to be a statement. A refusal. He could walk. He would run. The medicus had been confused. That was fine. He would show them. Vali pushed himself up on the bed, but even his arms didn't work properly. With a gasp of pain, he fell backward. Maybe just lift the leg out? He tried flexing his leg upward and nearly screamed with the pain. The sweat was pouring off him now.

"Stop. Stop, Vali! You're hurting yourself."

Once again, those gentle hands were on him, this time pushing him back down. He let them. The tears came now. He scraped them away in a fury. Already a cripple, he wasn't about to be a crying cripple too. He hated himself. For destroying his own future. Part of him hated his friends too. They were here for him, yes. But they were just happy it was him in the bed and not the other way around. A cruel, unworthy part of him insisted that it wasn't him who belonged in this damned sickbed. He was the one with a house to represent. The best fighter among them... He didn't deserve to be here. Being injured was for others. Those with less to prove. If everyone else hadn't been so concerned with saving their own skins during the ambush, he wouldn't have had to break their lines alone. He tried not to look at his friends, worried they might see his thoughts through the tears that made his vision blurry and his throat burn.

"Lucan, go tell Captain Askaris he's up. Quickly."

Lucan appeared more than grateful, slipping out the door with alacrity. Practically sprinting, Vali thought bitterly.

"What about my father?" Vali managed, trying to compose himself. "Did they tell him?" Vali's father's estate was far from the capital, but he spent most of his time in Rasovus. He had a house not far from the governor's estate.

"I'm sure he'll be here soon," Marika assured him.

"Of course. I'm sure he'll come when his business finishes for the day."

That look again.

"What?"

"Vali, you've been here three days. But now that you're awake," she added quickly, "I'm sure he'll come."

Vali lay back again. Three days. Far worse than he had imagined. As for any visit, he wasn't sure why he was surprised. His father had little use for broken things. He still had Sorin, anyway. Vali's older brother had been sent away to study at the imperial academy in Heliopolis, a gesture of acknowledgment for his father's help in siding with the empire during the campaign here. In Vali's less proud moments, he couldn't help but wish his place and his brother's were switched, and never more so than now. He knew that wasn't fair though. It was nothing but timing. It was impossible to hate his big brother, always bright and kind. He had been Vali's protector growing up, and one of both the saddest and proudest days of his life had been when they sent him off.

"He won't," Vali said.

His brother would have a court education and would serve his father's ambitions better than a broken second son ever could. His chance for distinction had been selection to the elite corps of oathknights that Captain Askaris and the men like him belonged to. The knights and shock troops of the legions. There weren't many, and every soldier of the provinces that had been elevated to that position cemented a reputation as a legend beyond their lifetime. Tarbus, who served in the corps of Praetorians that protected the Emperor's palace. Daciana, one of the heroes of the Gates, those narrow passes that separated civilization from the riders and the ice. And the most celebrated, General Lucianus of the famed Warhound Legion. Those names were a source of pride for every citizen in Getacia—at least the ones who took pride in that citizenship.

"I'm done. Done." He slammed his fist into his thigh in a fury and reeled with the pain, vision flashing to black. "By the gods, that hurt," he gasped, eyes watering with pain and frustration. Vali wanted to keep on hitting it, to push through this like he had pushed through every other damned obstacle life had thrown his way. He settled for gently prodding it, savoring the stabbing pain. "I'll never get selected now," he said, hating himself for saying it and knowing what he wanted to hear.

"That's not true," Marika said.

"Yes, it fucking is," he snarled. "I saved them. Saved them, and now I'll never get another chance. Just another cripple."

"You're going to get better, Vali. But if you do something like this again, you're going to get yourself killed. You have nothing to prove." Her voice was patient. Far more patient than he knew he deserved. He lashed out anyway.

"Why are you two even still here?"

Marika looked sympathetic, if hurt, but her eyes hardened.

"What?" Vali demanded, eager for a fight, anything.

She looked like she might hold her tongue, but then clearly decided Vali needed to hear whatever she had to say. "Seriously? You're hurt. It was a battle. What the hell do you think happens? We lost almost twenty good soldiers, and I don't think you can see that. We had to drag back Karabal's body so that he could be buried at home. We've known him since we were children, Vali. And he's gone. The only reason you're not dead too is that Captain Askaris and those two killers with him went berserk when they saw you go down. Wasn't your fault, our fault, or even really the enemy's fault, seeing as we were doing our best to kill them all. These things happen. You'll get better. I... We will both be here with you for every step."

The mention of their casualties was a sobering thought. Vali knew Karabal left behind a wife and three children. He had been a good man. But even with the added guilt, Vali couldn't let it go. "At least they died for a reason. You just said the medicus says I'll never run again. I won't even get that chance."

"By the fucking Fallen, how stupid does that sound? You're not dead; you don't get to be jealous of them. And as for the sawbones, fuck him!" She stuck her hands on her hips in a way Vali was all too familiar with. "You going to let some pisspot Helian tell you what you can and can't do? That's not the Vali I know. I know you're tough, you big silly bastard. Act like it. Yeah, life didn't go your way this time. We'll figure it out, same as we always do. And I swear, I'll kill you myself if you keep on this way."

Vali glared at Marika, whose family had served his house since his grandfather's time. Her father, the steward of House Costranis, was his own father's best friend and confidant. They had grown up together, and it would be hard to find a closer friend. That didn't make her any less infuriating. Maybe even more so as they grew older, as the edge of a new sort of tension worked its way into their friendship. Still, even holding the pain and bitterness hurt. Tired beyond tired, he let it go with a sigh.

"Damn it, you're right. I mean, fuck you. But still, you're right."

"Of course I'm right. When am I not?"

Marika's smile was a bit forced, but not as forced as the sickly grin Vali gave back. There was a lump in his throat as he tried not to think about what his leg might look like under the blanket. He could feel the odd angles where there should have been none, the suffocating immobility of splints and wraps. But she was right. The fact that he felt sorry for himself when so many had died was wrong. It didn't seem to change anything though.

"I know. I know." A bit more conviction this time. "But I need to be able to run again. To fight again."

A clear voice called back from beyond the door. "He wants to fight again already?"

A moment later, the footfalls outside materialized into Captain Askaris and Lucan. Vali tried to pull himself up, ashamed of being seen like this by his commander.

"Calm down, Vali. Relax." Askaris seemed amused by his discomfort. "I think you deserve to lie down for a bit after what you did."

Vali wasn't sure what to say. Should he say that he wouldn't have done it if he knew this was where it would end? He hoped that wasn't true, but suspected it might be. Marika and Lucan had stepped back, allowing Askaris to inspect him from beside the bed. Tanned and athletic, with a classical profile that evoked the statues of the ancients so prized in the South, their commander was the picture of Helian vitality and strength.

Around thirty, he was in the prime of his life and knew it, wrapped it about him like the heavy cloak he wore now. Vali would never admit it aloud, but he suspected part of him might be attracted to the man. He was hardly alone there. Add to that the fact that he was one of the few Helian officers or oathknights who bothered to learn the names of the Getacians who served under him, and it was little wonder half the company of auxiliary rangers would have died for him.

"Sir, I—"

Askaris waved a hand, cutting him off. "What you did was...well, suicidal is one word that comes to mind. But brilliant! Beyond brave, lad. I've never seen anything like it. Using that horse and your own body to break their line might not have been the method I would have chosen,"—he wasn't smiling, but his tone made the mocking kind, rather than cruel—"but it worked! By the gods, it worked."

Vali was afraid of what he might say, and bit back a bitter reply.

Askaris's face softened. "Don't think this hasn't gone unnoticed, Vali. You've had a rough break, but I won't forget this. In a couple months, or whenever you're healthy enough to rejoin the ranging parties—"

"Rejoin?"

Head cocked, Askaris seemed not to understand the question. "Well...yes. You're far too hurt right now. You need to heal up, get your strength back."

"What will I do in the meantime?"

"Enjoy an easy couple months! Honestly, we should all be jealous of you. Transferred to the general auxiliary here in Rasovus for the time being, but just until you're able to rejoin us. Light duty only. We want you resting up. Reports suggest that won't be the last raiding party from those horse devils, so don't worry, we'll save a few for you." He winked. "In the meantime, try not to stop any more horses with your head."

Vali nodded, not trusting himself to speak. He knew his commander meant well. Even now, those intelligent brown eyes emoted nothing but sympathy and understanding behind a veneer of joviality. It looked like he would say something more, but then he just patted Vali on the shoulder before striding out of the room.

As soon as he left, Vali sagged back into the rough bedding, the last of his strength bleeding away. He turned away from his friends, focusing outside the window to where the sun was failing to pierce the gray skies. Vali had never been, but he knew the sun still shone bright in the core of the empire, that narrow space spared both the worst ravages of the last cataclysm and the encroaching ice and ash of its aftereffects. That place where the first Riftgate emerged each time, where the Emperor and his Chosen came again and again, doing their best to shepherd humanity through each cataclysm. Getacia was a recent conquest, a far-flung, backward province of an expanding empire. The sun wouldn't—couldn't—break through the clouds, because it knew better than to waste its light here.

# BLOOD AND SNOW

The enemy had watched them, waiting, until the perfect moment to strike, hoping to catch them in an ambush again. Only this time, they were already caught, and it hadn't been wolf-cloaked warriors from the trees. It had been their own. Instead of arrows, a few choice accusations being passed about, ammunition for a final attack. The hand-to-hand fighting had been the calm but insistent guiding of their group to an isolated tent on the outskirts of the warband's camp, where guards now kept watch outside. There had been no refusing this hospitality.

Darya, Mikael, Alina, and the three other surviving members of the ambush were a huddled group of the damned. They were starting to shiver now, as the predawn chill made a last bitter pass at them before the weak sun had its brief reign. They could have been warmer if they had all bunched together, but Alina, along with Kasym, Ganzig, and Altan, kept their distance as if they were all quarantined, but only Mikael had the plague. Darya sat close to him, their bodies keeping some warmth where they were pressed together, the same way they had done as children. Before they had to grow up. Before they had to move south. Before they had to join the Thousand Tribes. This loose alliance of steppe peoples was the only chance any of them had at pushing through the frontier garrisons and fortifications of the empire into warmer lands before another cataclysm blanketed the skies in ash. The snow was already on the ground in patches. It started a little sooner each year, a little farther south each season. The meager farmlands along the borders of the passes weren't enough; they never had been. And none of it would matter when the next cycle came. They were all running out of time. Just a bit quicker for those in this tent.

Darya had managed an hour or two of fitful sleep in the frigid tent, but between the cold, the damp clothes, and the sense of dread, that had been it, despite her exhaustion. She had woken up screaming the one time she had drifted off. Something with Bohdan. She had shamefully accepted her brother's comfort then, knowing she didn't deserve it. The only consolation was that she would likely pay for that betrayal soon. She thought about telling Mikael, but couldn't bear the thought of how he would look at her. He was the strong one, the selfless one. She could at least leave him the fantasy of a kinder little sister worth protecting. Besides, she didn't want to lose the warmth next to her. The others sat mute and alone in their misery, or lay like Alina, curled up, trying to sustain themselves off their own warmth. Pretending to sleep. Waiting for the nightmare to be over.

They had struggled back to the camp, following Vels over the last three days in a haze, braving the slightly-less-dangerous swamps they had traversed earlier. When they arrived, they had been met not with tearful relief, but with cold accusations and forced isolation. Vels had said he would talk to Janbek, who led the warband, but this Sarkhan had little patience for the unsettling man that the great Arkhan had sent with them. And the Arkhan was far away, leading the bulk of the Thousand Tribes in the East, trying to push through the Gates one last time before the winter snows closed the way until the next weak spring. Janbek had ambitions of his own, and those did not involve losing scouting parties in the swamps or listening to advisors of the Arkhan, however influential or unsettling they happened to be.

Darya worried over what those ambitions would spell for them. Especially her brother. She glanced back at Mikael where he sat against her. He looked thoughtful and far away. He had tried several times already to get the guards to release them, or at least to give him a chance to speak to the warlord in private, to beg for an audience before the spectacle they all knew would come next. They had seen it too many times before not to know.

His broad frame shifted. "Do you remember the storytellers that would come through when we were children?" Mikael looked forward as he spoke, but he had clearly noticed her attention. His thoughts were miles and years behind them though. "By the dead, you were obsessed. You'd never let those poor tinkers sleep with all your questions, and daughter of the chief, they were terrified not to keep answering." He nudged her.

Mikael had never been a talker, or a reminiscer. They tried not to talk of their past, as if pretending it had never been would be easier than accepting that they had lost it. It was all so forced, but Darya could tell how hard he was trying to cheer her up, when it should have been the other way around. As the leader of the disaster, Mikael would shoulder most of the blame. She wanted to say something back, something to help take his mind off their situation.

"I remember," was all she managed.

"Do you remember your favorite story?" He coughed a laugh, and Darya felt it echo through her own back. "Oh, yes, no forgetting that. Every single storyteller that ever came through, grilled by you. A dozen different versions, and you loved them all. Confusing, if you ask me. But I guess the best stories usually are. I was never as interested, but I remember the gist of it. A cold world, with snow every winter. Hopeless." He fell silent for a time.

"And dark." It was such an easy story to remember, for so many reasons.

"I didn't forget." She heard him pick himself back up, heard it in the forced lightness of his voice. She couldn't understand how he could do it, even now. "Dark too. Ash and ice. Tough stuff. And a lot of cold, sad people, and a very sad daughter of a king. What was her..."

"Zavayoth." Darya knew he was leading her on, but couldn't help herself. And what else could she do for him now but play along? "And daughter of a god."

"Ah, yes. I forgot." She couldn't see his face, but she knew he was smiling. "Well, this daughter of a god had to watch her people freeze and starve, and her little heart broke, because her father, the king..." He waited for Darya to correct him, but she waited him out this time. "... had locked the sun away in his vaults, with all his other treasures." He shifted. "I'll say, that part always confused me. Didn't make any sense at all."

"It's a story."

"You're right, you're right. Well, poor little Zavayoth had it in her head to help her people. She begged and pleaded with her father, but it was no use. He had flying machines and magic rings and a thousand other beautiful and powerful things he told her she could take instead. King or god, you don't just give up the sun. But it wasn't all the rest she wanted, and it wasn't for herself she wanted. So, she did what any good daughter would do. She decided to steal it.

"But how? Her father's vaults were magically sealed, and only he could open them, and he never opened them at all, happy in his own miserable heart that he had the brightness of the sun, and that none could ever take it. An impossible situation. I suppose I might have given up. But she was resourceful, and brave, and with just the right amount of cruel cunning running through her bones. This was your favorite part, do you remember?"

She could feel the desperate reaching for her, the reckless appeals to their childhood, and started to understand what this was for. There was a part of her that thought maybe if she brushed it away, ignored it, then it could mean the reason he was doing it would disappear too. But she knew that for a lie.

"She built a fire," she said, barely above a whisper. She could see the others in the tent were listening too now, and she hated them a little for it. This was for her.

"So she did, so she did. Not alone though. It was a little thing at first. She put everything she had on it to burn, and it wasn't enough. A small spark in dark lands. But the truth is, when your world is nothing but darkness, it's so easy to see a light, no matter how small. Little by little, more and more people came and joined. They took everything they had, all that they had left, and threw it on the fire. And it became not just any fire, but the biggest, fiercest white-hot fire there had ever been.

"It was enough. When the king looked out on his lands, he saw the sun itself. And everyone knows nobody panics quite like the greedy. He rushed down to his vaults, certain his most precious possession was gone. But when he threw open the door..."

"She stole the sun."

The morning light at the edges and flaps of the tent was growing now, giving a bit more wan light to the space. There were footsteps outside and the gruff sounds of orders in a harsh Eastern dialect.

Mikael pulled her attention back. "Yes. And he lost sun and daughter both." The story wasn't done, and Darya knew a dozen endings from that point, but their time was. Mikael's voice became more urgent. "You know why I also always loved that story?"

She shook her head. Tried to ignore the footfalls closing in on the tent's entrance. This couldn't be happening.

"Well, first, because you loved it. I want you to remember that, Dar. But second, because it wasn't just her, but she started it. She didn't give up, and she didn't panic. She just started a little fire. That's it." He paused. "I think

I didn't understand the point though. Not really. I think I do now." His laugh was a sad one. "A little late."

The flap in front of them was thrown open, blinding them and cutting off anything else Mikael might have said. The fresh air and noise of the camp flooded into the tent behind the fur-clad riders that quickly filed in. Rough hands grabbed them and pulled them up and outside. Darya let them drag her, stumbling, into the sudden brightness. She took her cue from Mikael, who was pushed along ahead of her, and besides, she was too afraid to do anything else.

Without warning, Mikael surged against the hands that held him and muscled his way next to her. "It wasn't the sun, Darya." His voice was a fierce whisper, and his eyes demanded a promise that she didn't quite understand. "It was the fire. That was the point. It was—"

Anything else he might have said was cut off as the tribesmen pulled him back and beat him to the ground with the flats of their blades, yelling at him. They started to push them forward again, toward the center of the camp. Darya struggled, trying to stay closer to Mikael, to ask what he had meant, but the hands were inexorable. Half the warband was milling about, waiting for something. They were adrift among harsh looks and muttered curses, and Darya watched the faces around her and thought on Mikael's words. Distraction was good. Anything to keep her mind away from the truth that burned, scalding hot, at the center of her awareness, the rotting grave-stink of death looming over her shoulder.

Compared to the neat stone buildings of their childhood home, nestled in the open center of an ancient factory, the camp was a haphazard mess, stinking of the daily lives of thousands of men, horses, and barking dogs. The odors of horse dung, burning wood, and roasting meat were ever-present and long since beyond conscious recognition. But Darya knew by now that there was an order imposed on the chaos, the forces of prestige, clan, and tradition pushing invisibly yet inexorably toward a scheme of order. Where tents were placed and by whom. Who spoke to whom and in what manner. The order only emerged if one was able to step back, above the daily noise and smells of life amongst the nomadic warbands of the Thousand.

The tents grew grander and more elaborate as they neared the center, matching the armor and clothes of those they passed here too. Warriors in all their eclectic finery, looted bits of armor and bright bits of cloth wrapped amongst heavy furs. Their women, carrying their status in ribbons and precious metals, jewelry bright and shining and ringing to mark where they walked.

*Like prized cattle,* Darya thought sourly, even in her fear. It was why she had trained so hard, fought so bitterly to be seen as one of the warriors. She had seen the lives these women lived and wanted none of it. Though, if she were honest with herself, it didn't look quite so bad from her current predicament. She might be wearing the furs, leathers, and bits of plate of a warrior, but where had that gotten her? Her first chance at proving herself in real combat had gone horribly wrong. At least she had survived.

The cost of that survival put a lump in her throat, and she rubbed at her forearm again, worrying at the bandage her brother had wrapped there and wanting the pain. Bohdan's face, right at the end, would never leave her. Darya still couldn't decide if it had been a sense of betrayal, or shock that she had acted first. She tried to put the memory aside and instead focused ahead, where the warband's leader held court. One of the Arkhan's three great warlords, one of his Sarkhanae, no one could ever accuse Janbek Crow-Eye of modesty. A great area in the middle of the camp was always kept clear, surrounded by the tents of those closest to Janbek, retainers and friends from his close-knit clan.

They were superb horsemen, incomparable archers, and consummate killers. But the myriad clans and tribes of the steppes numbered in the hundreds, if not perhaps the eponymous thousand. The number of peerless riders, archers, fighters, and killers was beyond count. Janbek and his clan had not risen to their position of favor in the Arkhan's horde for their skill at arms alone. Above all, they were cunning.

One had to be here. Infighting, assassination, and political sabotage didn't cease because the Thousand sought to carve a home in warmer lands. Darya's mother had been the matriarch of their tribe until they had joined, but even in their little corner of the world, those truisms of power held. Darya remembered her words, back when she had tried to prepare them both for the challenges she thought would face them in their old lives. All those sayings about dancing on the heads of snakes and pitting your enemies against one another... Ladders of chaos and the currency of power and a hundred other metaphors she had forgotten.

That was hardly her problem now. Ahead, she saw Mikael being pushed to kneel before the small hill where the warlord and his entourage waited.

They were far past metaphor now, and she wasn't sure she could even say she or Mikael were the snakes. That would have implied too much agency. Snakes had fangs. Their tribe had gone back to the dirt. Her mother, father, friends, all dead, one at a time over the years. Her forearm burned along with her face in shame. Bohdan too. But Mikael was an excellent battlefield commander, clever and strong and quick, all the qualities so prized by the tribes. He had been elevated repeatedly, until he was leading the ill-fated scouting party.

Another shove forward, and her knees hit the hard-packed earth, scraped bare by a thousand passing feet. Darya hardly felt it. She only had eyes for the warlord above. Janbek Crow-Eye. A heavy frame sat on an impromptu throne, covered in fine armor and great swathes of bear and chylari fur, blending into the beard that swallowed his face, woven through with precious stones and bits of relics. One eye was replaced with glittering gold, part of the legend he had built up around himself. It was with this golden eye that he claimed to see the thoughts of the chieftains jockeying under him. Darya knew he was clever, but she had also heard the other story—that it had been pecked out on a battlefield decades ago when the crows had thought him dead, the real reason for the name. Now he stared down with a hungry expression. A quick wave of his hand sent the guards a few paces back and quieted some of the hundreds who had gathered to watch the proceedings. The majority of those in the camp were still going through their morning rituals, eating, praying to their respective gods or prophesied saviors—always avatars of warmth or light like Zavayoth or Tharazel—or simply not curious enough to watch the warlord's judgment.

They would watch soon though, the bastards. Darya quickly wiped at her face with the back of her sleeve. There wouldn't be long to wait. Even now, Janbek's councilors surrounded him like a flock of ravens in fur instead of feathers, fluttering about and leaning in, giving advice to the warlord. Darya suspected that they played their own dancing game, no less deadly for their soft features or pretensions to scholarship. Around them were the chieftains that formed Janbek's inner circle, a dozen men and women distinguishable by the sigils and colors of their garb, all standing under the banner of the Thousand, a great serpent wrapped around itself. Their competition was not even well hidden, and they each made passes for the warlord's ear. The ancient and wizened loremasters and shamans, ever hungry for relics from before the Breaking, kept their dignified distance. It was their robed and slightly-less-ornamented adepts that moved on the board on their behalf. Janbek waved them away too. With a sinking feeling, Darya knew he had made up his mind.

One of the lancers surrounding the throne stepped forward imperiously, calling in a roaring voice for quiet. He was hoarse soon enough.

When Janbek finally spoke, it was softly, so that finally all were silent, straining to hear his words. "Now tell me, Northerner, what task did I set before you?"

Not addressing Mikael by name was not a good sign. Darya knew he wished to stress their otherness, help any would-be friends forget Mikael's contributions during this season's campaign. Perhaps if leadership was anything, it was manipulating the base instincts of your followers.

Mikael spoke clearly, head held high. "You sent us to make contact with the Stained and separatists to the west."

"Hmm. Yes, I remember now," Janbek mused. "And tell me, how many men did I send for you to lead on this mission?"

"Two hundred," Mikael answered. He answered without hesitation, but his eyes were dead already.

"Two hundred!" Janbek exclaimed in mock surprise. There were scattered laughs around them now. He knew how to play a crowd. "I'm sure our army will be stronger again for their return." He paused. "How many *did* return?"

"Six. We were ambushed in—"

He was drowned out by the laughter of the crowd and the warlord's exclamation. "Six! What a battle that must have been. Surely, then, you ran into an imperial stronghold. Perhaps to the capital itself? Tell us, Northerner! What fortress did you find?"

Darya watched in despair, helpless, as her brother was humiliated. She knew Mikael was the equal or better of every single one of those on the hill there. Someone who had strode about the camp laughing with the other rising lancers not a month ago. Now, on his knees, he looked resigned and alone.

"It was an ambush. There was no fortress, no battle."

"So..." Janbek stretched out a hand glittering with rings and started to count on fingers held before him, voice gaining momentum. "...you don't bring back a victory." A finger down. "You don't bring back prisoners."

Another. "You don't bring back your men or even information on the enemy." Two more ticked down, leaving one, covered with jewels, a glittering accusation that he pointed down at Mikael. "Just you. That's what you bring back." Janbek exploded out of his seat, his sudden rage startling those around him. "Not enough!" he roared. "I ask for the blood of our enemies, and you bring nothing but *failure*."

The warlord settled back into his seat just as suddenly, the flush creeping from the edges of his beard the only clue to his outburst. A canny eye under a thick brow scanned the crowd. "My fellow warriors! This man has brought us shame! He thinks to call himself a leader, but leads our brave warriors only to their deaths. He promises to bring me blood, but returns empty-handed." Janbek looked across the crowd, letting the anger and muttering come to a steady simmer, a steady hand on the pulse of the gathered tribesmen. "Some of my councilors press for me not to throw away a warrior with such ability. Of such rich blood." Darya looked upwards again, thinking that she might catch a glimpse of Vels. It was not good that he had become a hoped-for sight. "What of my chieftains? Do any of you speak for this man?"

Darya looked to them expectantly. Mikael knew some of those men and women, had fought with them. There were a couple who looked uncomfortable. One who seemed about to step forward. But then, only silence.

"As I thought. Well, I think he might be of service still." Janbek quieted the rumble that came from the crowd at that with outstretched hands. He stood once more. Darya allowed herself to hope. "Our victories are built on the blood of our enemies, but he has given us none. Have you had your fill yet, brothers?"

There was an incoherent roar from the crowd, and it felt to Darya like her own blood had left her body, along with her strength. It was all she could do to stay upright. She watched all this happen from above, a horrified spectator. Mikael raised his head from where it had slumped, ignoring the crowd, and gave her a sad smile.

A rock from out of the crowd smashed into his face, sending him sprawling into the dirt. More missiles—rocks and dung—began to pelt him from the crowd. They were like animals, baying at the scent of blood. Moving in for the kill.

"Then I shall give you his!" Janbek crowed. "Take him! Bind him! And take your fill, brothers!"

Mikael had managed to push to his knees again, but already the crowd was surging forward, delighted and cruel faces pulling her brother to his feet and tearing at him in their eagerness. He struggled in vain. There were far too many. Some of the Sarkhan's men pulled the rest of them to the side, lest they get swept up in the holiday atmosphere and madcap excitement that accompanied every execution here. She was screaming now, yelling after Mikael, and struggling against the hands that held her, vision blurring with tears. She squirmed and struck at those holding her back, but they wouldn't let go.

He yelled something to her, but his last words were indistinguishable over the roar of the crowd. She was sobbing and yelling at them to stop in a voice already gone hoarse. Alina was helping to hold her now and was furiously whispering something in her ear, but Darya couldn't look away from the scene unfolding before her.

Mikael was swallowed up by the crowd, but she knew where they were dragging him. They had been camped here for long enough. On the far side of the cleared area was a stake on an oddly dark patch of ground. The dogs always came there later. That is where they would bind him. She knew what would happen next and was finding it hard to think at all, the horror of what she had seen there before suddenly amplified a thousandfold knowing it was Mikael this time. Knowing how long he would suffer.

It was unreal. A nightmare. She and Mikael had survived so much together. Their childhood on the cold taiga. Their uncertain acceptance into the Thousand. Mikael's own years of riding and raiding, pitched battles and long sieges of frontier fortresses, proving himself while Darya prepared for the same. Knowing that at least they would always have each other. This was impossible. She straightened. Yes, impossible. This was a misunderstanding, and they would let Mikael go in a moment. No, he wouldn't have command anymore. Of course not. But they would come back together and lick their wounds and continue the march south.

Everything would be alright.

Then she heard the crowd roar. They had started cutting. A peculiar noise escaped her, and she sank to her knees. It was like her soul had left her. They wouldn't stop for hours. She couldn't hear Mikael screaming yet, but she knew he would. They always did. They would scream until they couldn't. Until the crowd grew bored and left, a mass of blood and gore and flies tied to a post the only evidence there was once a person there.

Not a person. Her brother.

She needed to go to him, support him now more than ever. Struggling to her feet, Darya clawed at the hands holding her back. But then another pair of hands started dragging her inexorably backwards.

"No, my child." A soft voice. One meant for sneering and mocking and double meanings, but with a gentle undertone she had never heard from it before. Vels pulled her in an iron grip that seemed at odds with the slender, pale gray fingers that were wrapped around her arms. "You don't want to see that."

"I do, I do!" she sobbed, hysterical.

"A lie," he said. "Besides, he doesn't want you to see that."

The rest of them were apparently being spared the same fate and were being dragged to one of the larger tents surrounding the square. She could see Janbek and his councilors and officers speaking above it all, their interest already far away and beyond this point in time. She knew she hated them. More than anything. But she couldn't find the hate right now. There was only room for Mikael, and an overwhelming sense that a part of herself was being torn apart and fed to the Thousand.

She tried to wrench away again, desperate. "He needs me!"

"No, my dear. He must pass through that door alone, as must we all."

As the flap to the tent opened, Darya thought she could hear a scream behind her, but when it closed, all she could hear was the dull roar of the crowd, each swell of voices undoubtedly another cut. When she turned, Vels was already gone, and two guards stood in his place, barring the entrance. One looked uncomfortable, like he might try to say something comforting, but glanced at his companion before settling into a stiff posture. The strength had fled from Darya's limbs, and suddenly she thought she might pass out. She collapsed against Alina, whose rough hands stroked her head while she whispered gently, trying her best to comfort her.

Darya heard none of it, listening only to the ebb and flow of the mob's frenzied bloodlust until, finally, those tides fell away, leaving only the whispers of the tent and the whisper of Mikael's last words. Silence, then. A gap in her world. And in that gap, the unreasonable, inescapable belief that she was paying the price for her cowardice in the swamps. Mikael was paying the price. Darya let herself sink deeper into Alina's arms, far past anything resembling pride or shame. It was all so monstrously unfair. Where was the price for men like Janbek? The chieftains and the councilors and the warriors who made this life a living hell, beyond anything the earth could punish them with? She wanted to say she knew that they would suffer for an eternity in the icy bowels of hell beyond the Rift, but that was uncertain and far away. What was certain was that her brother was dead, and those devils in human skin were stronger than ever. There was grief, and there was hate somewhere under that, but above all, there was despair. An understanding started to crystallize, and she took strength in its revelation.

This was not a life worth living.

*I'll see you soon, Mikael.*

# THE PROBLEM

One had to question the sort of life choices that led one to prison. From the bench where Syl sat with Lucky, he stared again past the thick iron bars. They might have been on the right side, but the point still applied. The cell before them was a nicer one, as far as those went—Syl considering himself somewhat of an expert at this point—but a cell was a cell. The bars weren't going anywhere. Liora had wanted to come as well, but Syl had judged that to be an exceptionally poor idea. The girl from the farmhouse huddled in a corner, facing away from them. Wrapped in a dirty blanket, she was trying her best to fade into the background, but that eye stared out at him from behind matted and stringy black hair. Its shiny jet-black surface reflected the torches that lit this section of the prison. They called them "Stained", the mark of the other side on them in the fading of eyes and veins when they pulled from the Rift and the souls of the other side mingled with their own, but he had never seen one so aptly named as this girl. She was marked, well and truly, and there would never have been a normal life for her.

"There was nothing you could tell?" he asked, pulling himself away. "The eye? It *is* a bit odd."

Lucky shook his head.

"You're certain?"

The lanky bondmage always verged on the surly side, and now he gave Syl the aggrieved look of a professional being questioned on their favorite subject.

"Alright, alright."

All bloodhounds could sense the use of the Rift, but a few were gifted with a bit more discernment. A look at the nature of that connection and its potential expressions. Lucky was good, very good, could sense as low a signature as an infused ring across half a province, but this was not one of his gifts. And gods, he could be sensitive about it. That, and they could be territorial as cats. The bloodhound who was part of the prison's garrison here had stared at Lucky so hard when they had come in that Syl could practically see the hackles.

Inevitably, the problem before him drew his attention back. Problem... He supposed he shouldn't use that word, but damn him to hell if it wasn't true. She was a problem. *His* problem, for now. The steady thrum under his temples at least had a definite source for once. He had been trying for an hour already, and it was looking increasingly hopeless. She had ignored all his pleas for her to talk to him, to convince her to eat, to accept anything about the world she had been thrust into. Convince her to live, even if it was likely to not be for long. Even Lucky's feeble efforts had come to nothing, and hearing from someone who shared her affliction should have helped. He was at a loss.

Livia, his own little girl, would have been about this age if they had never come to his home. If the Mages' Revolt had started later, ended somewhere else. Thirteen, maybe fourteen. He liked to think his little girl would have been that same happy child into adolescence. Not this pitiful, frightened, and spiteful creature huddled in the corner with a null collar around her neck, all bones and angles. Livia would have been sweeter than this. Could have been. Took after her mother, Elena, after all. His mind circled the few well-worn memories he had of them. As always, he tried not to think of how few he really had, when it came down to it. Life in the legions—there was always another campaign season, another border to push a little farther. With an effort, he pulled himself back from the past. At the very least, he could convince this would-be suicide to not make the fact that he and Liora had stuck their necks out for her meaningless.

He tried honesty.

"I'm sorry." Syl spoke the words softly, half to himself. The girl stirred, the first movement he had seen. He was hopeful for a moment. Then she coughed up as much phlegm as she could gather and spat it towards him. It spattered across the cold stone. Syl sighed. It was slightly depressing that he considered that an improvement. At least that had elicited a response. He didn't have much time here. "If you don't talk to me, I can't help you."

That got through, finally. "Help me?" she hissed.

Unmoved, he continued. "Yes, yes. I know you're angry. You just lost everyone you've ever cared about, and the man who helped put them in the ground is here trying to tell you to eat. And part of me really is sorry. Part of me. Because I get it. But your family was going to die no matter what. They picked off an entire patrol and didn't have the grace to do it the old-fashioned way. It was only a matter of time. Our bloodhound could sense that violence from here. And then you went ahead and kept all their equipment right at the same spot, a little pile of beacons. Not smart."

She kept the blanket wrapped tight against the frigid stone walls, but she stood now, stepping across the even colder floor, chains and manacles forcing her into a clanking shuffle. He noticed her feet were bare, crusted with dirt. She had to be freezing down here. Syl would make sure they brought her better clothes. If only he could make her give up a measure of that hate for common sense and a desire to survive. He tried not to think how conditional that survival was, or what the next few days might look like for her under the attentions of the flamewardens who would examine her. It would be a chance though.

"I hate you," she hissed, vibrating with anger. "I *hate* you!" she screeched. "You massacred my family. The people that tried to help us. You killed my parents. My little brother." Tears were streaming down her face. "We just wanted to be left alone. They were innocent."

"Innocent?" Syl's face twisted in disbelief. She couldn't believe that. Her best hope right now was a penal colony, and she couldn't be caught saying things like this if she was ever going to have a shot at even that. "What about those pieces of people in the cellar? Did those belong to innocent people? You thought no one would come looking for them? If your family had turned themselves in, you could all still be alive."

There was nothing but hate and condescension on that face, aging her beyond her years. "Alive in a camp? Alive to slave ourselves to death? And that patrol?" The tears hadn't stopped, but her lip was curled back in disgust. "Mother was right. You would never stop. We escaped, and we... You followed us, like hunting animals." She could barely form the words. "We just wanted to leave!" She turned away, shuffling back to her corner.

"Listen to me. Listen to me, damn it!" He couldn't even get this girl to listen to him; no wonder they were starting to question if he had lost his edge. "Listen," he said, trying his best to keep his voice level. "This isn't something you can ignore. It's not something you can pretend didn't happen." He trailed off. "Believe me, I know. They will kill you." He was pleading with her now, but he needed this. Was it so much to ask?

"So?" she sneered. "Let them. What's the point anyway?"

"The point is that you live." He tried a different tack. "Your mother didn't seem the type to raise a coward."

She flew at him then, snarling, an underfed dog in a cage. As she stood there, trying to claw at him and cursing him in every way she could muster, it was more difficult to see the parallels with his long-dead child. He tried anyway.

Standing there impassively, he waited for her to spend her anger and energy against the bars. He understood. Syl tried to remember what it had been like. He had been unapproachable for a month, a danger as much to himself as the friends and family he had left. But this girl didn't have the luxury of a month. Eventually, the screams turned to great heaving sobs, and she sunk against the bars, face pressed into the rusty metal and tears streaking red down a shift that had long since left its white color behind.

Syl crouched down. He tried to remember the words they had told him, those lies about healing and a brighter tomorrow. They had said them so often, as if all that it took to make them true was repetition. Maybe they would work for her.

"I know what it's like to lose someone. It breaks you. It's...it's like a weight on your chest." There was so much more to say. That it was impossible to get out from under that weight, because then what would you have left of them without the guilt and grief? He wanted to tell her that more powerful than any desire to live for your lost ones was to kill for them. To tell her the truth that had kept him going. But he couldn't very well do that, so he lied. "I won't pretend to be sorry we killed your parents. But I suspect that they would have wanted you to live. Your little brother would want you to live."

*You don't believe any of that.*

The sobs had turned to sniffles, and beneath that filthy hair, her eyes were fixed on him. A little less hate in them, maybe? Syl wouldn't have bet his life on that, but at least she seemed to be listening to what he had to say. He shifted, feeling Lucky's eyes on him too, listening nearly as intently as the girl.

*Lie to her again. Tell her it will be alright.*

Syl kept his expression steady, tried to exude calm and sympathy. "I won't pretend it will be easy. The penal colonies are meant to keep you separated, and they do so in whatever way they see fit. I know that what feels like the right thing right now is to follow them through that door, quick as you can. But the easy option is hardly ever the right one. Life goes on, if you let it."

He stared at her, waiting. Patient.

But there was only silence. Not that he was surprised; he wouldn't have been swayed much either. She stared back, unmoving and unspeaking. But clearly thinking. Syl figured he would have to count that as a victory. They might find some horrible potential within her, and this would all be for nothing anyway. But he had tried. Standing up with the familiar crackle of joints, Syl turned to go. He reached the entry, felt the fresh air that flowed in when he opened the heavy wooden door. He turned, one last time. She hadn't moved.

"What is your name, at least?"

She considered him, weighing him between green and black. "Morana," she said at last. "What's yours?"

"Syl."

"I'm going to kill you, Syl."

Syl sighed. "Fair enough." At least she had found a reason to live.

Lucky stood too, belatedly, examining the girl still, as if he was waiting for something.

"Lucky. Time to go."

A shake, and he uprooted himself from the spot. Slow steps took him to the cell, not toward the door. Syl tried to be patient. He knew their task was especially difficult for those like Lucky, taken from those penal colonies at birth to be raised in the Vigil's Institute. Those children knew no other life outside of service to the empire, but the ghost of what could have been lay heavy on some of them.

"Your brother had this. Here," he said, passing something small to her. It was a little puzzle of copper loops. "You should have it. To remember."

The girl looked confused, suspicion the dominant feature after that, but that didn't stop her from snatching the rings from Lucky's outstretched hand. Syl was almost as confused. Lucky should not have been collecting things—keepsakes!—from these missions.

Syl raised an eyebrow as Lucky brushed past him toward the door.

"She needed it. It was important." He didn't look at Syl, but went to stand by the exit.

Fine. He would address it later. Time to leave on as close to a high note as he was going to get down here in the judiciars' prisons.

# THE COST OF LOYALTY

Hell was being injured, Vali decided. Injured or sick when you had so recently known strength and health. With a grunt, he rolled out of the too-short bed, pulling his splinted leg from out of the covers with weak arms.

Like the three afternoons before, he woke with a headache and a throat filled with wool, tongue stuck to the roof of his mouth. Reaching for the crutches, he wondered why he didn't just lie back on the bed. No one would bother him. It wasn't as if any of them cared. His friends visited every day, but their duties with the rangers hadn't stopped either. They would be headed back to the frontier again soon. The regular auxiliaries billeted here were gone most of the day, but they came back every night. Drink, dice, and cards provided a backdrop to their true favorite pastime. They bitched about the weather, they complained about their officers, and they moaned about any and all work they might be assigned. But they saved their true creativity for the empire and their conscription.

Vali felt like a traitor even having to listen to it, but it didn't come as a surprise. The rangers were full of Getacians, but those were volunteers, and tested volunteers, at that. The auxiliaries were scraped from the bottom barrel of the province, those whose towns and villages wanted to pass along their local troublemakers and malcontents while fulfilling their quotas. Vali didn't blame the towns, but it didn't make it any easier to stomach his new company. Not that his new comrades were put out in the least. They watched him with suspicion and ignored him for the most part. To them, any Getacian who had volunteered for the legion's rangers was an idiot without common sense at best, a traitor to their people at worst. And their people had never taken much to the idea of nobility in the way the Helians had tried to force on the province, so his father's name counted for a bit less than nothing outside of the lands he controlled.

Their commander was a severe-looking Helian officer in his mid-forties. No oathknight, but a career soldier who looked as if he had run out of patience at least a decade ago, perhaps whenever the last of his hair had disappeared. He had taken one look at Vali and told him to stay out of the way and check in with the camp's medicus daily. Unfortunately, the "medicus" turned out to also be the camp drunk, with more interest in examining another bottle than anyone's injury. Vali decided to take matters into his own hands. He would ration the meager medicine during the daytime and toss and turn in his bunk in a sweat while the soldiers conducted their drills and daily tasks.

Strapping his belt on, he wondered why he bothered carrying the axe and short sword around camp. It was a sick joke—the cripple pretending to be a warrior. The weight and the hafts made doing everything on crutches a bit more awkward, but they were a comfort, and leaving them behind felt too much like giving up. Hauling himself up on the crutches, he moved toward the door through the narrow space between bunks. They would be back soon. Time to go.

As he crabbed his way forward, one of the sticks caught on a nearby post. With a sickening lurch and an undignified yelp, Vali tried and failed to catch himself. He fell in a pile of sticks and limbs, lying there for a moment. He wanted to scream. To cry. To do anything but drag himself around this damned camp under the scornful watch of men he knew he was better than. *Had* been better than, he corrected himself bitterly. Now he was nothing but another mouth to feed. Another resentful Getacian taking a billet in the sprawling camp for the legions.

Hauling himself to his feet, he pushed himself out of the low door and steeled himself for another long night of dragging himself around the camp. Wrapping strong hands around the supports of the crutches, Vali supposed he should be grateful for what he had and remember how much worse it could have been, but all he could think about was what he had lost.

"Doesn't matter," he muttered. "Doesn't matter." A little louder this time.

He would recover. Had to. Vali resolved to go farther this time. As far around the billets of the rangers as he could, past the neatly ordered rows of long cabins for the imperial legions. Past the billets for all the other auxiliary regiments. The short, grim hillmen of Ilkyani, famously jealous of the rich veins of ore in their mountain ranges that now fueled the imperial war machine. The suspiciously gregarious, dark-skinned and golden-eyed cavalry outriders from the plains of Moeselia, who would steal—"permanently borrow," if you asked them—the shirt off your back if you turned it toward them. Even a company of the willow-slim archers with their slightly pointed ears from the faraway lakes of Salkassar, elegant and haughty, and looking entirely out of place among the harsh lines of the military camp. A dozen peoples, half with far-fetched origin stories from before the Breaking. He knew them all by now. A tour of the empire in miniature. Lucky him. Only one he'd be getting at this rate. The only ones that weren't here that he wanted to see were the Voraxians, the massive soldiers that served as the personal elite to each of the Chosen and made up the core of the Emperor's Praetorian Guard, alongside the elite skyborne warriors of Legio Alaris. Today he would push himself all the way to the edge of the camp's rise, where he could see the Exarch's estate perched on the hill opposite, overlooking the provincial capital.

What was the point though? Going through the clean and disciplined camp of the actual legions and coming back to the poorly built, littered structures of the Getacian conscripts was torture enough. And he still couldn't bring himself to walk past the simple, clean huts of the rangers, where all his old comrades would be laughing and preparing for another day. The part of him he hated, the one that told him he had never belonged there to begin with, told him that he would never be there again. So, the Exarch's estate? Where the priests and oathknights of the legions and Vigil stayed? What did he think staring at the walls and pillars of that place would do for him? It would be yet another reminder of the future that he would never have. Maybe he meant to go there to look at the prison squatting ominously below the estate, to remind himself that no matter what, at least there was always someone to look down on, someone whose pitiable circumstances always made you a little more grateful for your own.

Laughs and grumbling voices sounded nearby, growing closer. Vali hurried out into the camp, fast as he could. He might not know where he wanted to go, but he was certain where he didn't want to be.

It was bitterly cold in those dark hours where the only movement was that of those luckless guards who had been assigned the middle shifts, and the only sound was the wind through the camp. Sitting on a rock at the perimeter, Vali was covered in sweat, face flushed with pain and effort. It felt good. He stared across the way to where torchlights twinkled through slits and on walls of the estate and prison. Trying to distract himself, he thought absently about what it must be like, suffering hunger and thirst in that prison and knowing that barely a stone's throw away, the elite of the empire ate and drank the best the province could provide. One would need windows or an active imagination for that, he reflected. Perhaps a closed cell was a mercy. Suffering was difficult enough without constant comparison.

Regarding his own suffering, the sweat was starting to cool now, and he was quickly going from too hot to too cold. It would be best to start back soon. The thought of struggling back through the camp to his hard cot made his gut clench, but he picked up his crutches and levered himself up, picking his way carefully as he could back to the packed earth inside the low wall of scattered stones. Only the imperial legions themselves bothered with a true wall, an encampment within an encampment. Here, the "wall" was a low pile of stones, barely waist-high, followed by a low ditch and stakes. More of a courteous reminder to stay out, or stay in, depending on your station.

A pair of torches moved closer, completing their portion of the massive perimeter of the combined camp. As the light thrown started to blind him, Vali stopped where he stood. It was the same short, surly, bearded pair from earlier. Ilkyani, he thought. They saw him there, in the middle of the night, armed, with crutches at his side, and didn't care enough to ask why or how. Not that he had bothered to do more than nod the last time. Ships in the night, each lost in their respective misery.

Soon they passed, and Vali was left in darkness again, vision readjusting. Before him stretched the long path back between the practice yards, tents, and barracks, all the way back to where his new comrades-in-arms waited. Sitting back against the rocks with a groan, he decided to stay a little longer. It wasn't as if he had anywhere to be.

He hadn't been there longer than ten minutes when he heard the footsteps of the guards coming back his way. Frowning, Vali wondered if they had decided to roust him from his own night watch. Couldn't those bastards mind their own business? It was the one thing everyone here was good at. A little pleased to have a new target for his frustration, Vali pulled himself around to face them and give them a piece of his mind.

... And froze.

There were no torches. No pair of guards. If his eyes hadn't been so adjusted to the night, he might have missed them. A dozen—no, at least a score of men were perfectly still, stopped in the act of crossing over the perimeter, like some tableau in a court, depicting the moment of the crime. All still and staring at Vali. They must have heard him shift to face them.

There was an eternity of silence as they faced each other. With the looks on their faces, the time, the place...with everything, it was immediately clear to Vali that he was seeing something he hadn't been meant to see. The only remaining question that really mattered was what the consequences were of seeing it anyway.

One of the figures finally broke the tension, whispering instructions and pointing toward the estate. The group went back into motion, while two figures broke from the rest and joined their leader in approaching Vali. They came on slowly, like one might approach a skittish dog. The man in front was tall and thin. As far as Vali could tell in the dark, all of them had their faces smeared with dirt or ash, and their eyes and teeth were all that seemed visible against the night. Tense and feeling the disability of his injuries more than ever, Vali wasn't worried about the cold any longer. Sweat started to bead across his brow.

"What are you doing here?" the man in front asked, calm as if they were all met together at the tavern.

"What the hell are *you* doing here?" Vali countered.

"Ah, good. A Getacian lad. Get back to your barracks and pretend you never saw any of this, aye? Naught but an odd dream. Good?"

"No, not fucking good." Vali fought to keep the hysteria out of his voice, but he could already see the two other men reaching for their sides. His own hand started to drift across to where he had propped his axe. "What's going on?"

"Ah, ah, ah. Let's not have anyone lose their tempers. Lads?" He gestured sharply to the two behind him, who stopped reaching toward their sides. But they didn't move their hands away from the weapons either. "All Getacians here tonight. We're on the same side, didn't you know?"

"And which side is that?"

Vali couldn't see sharp details in the darkness, but he could sense the frown.

"So, it's like that, eh? You one of their dogs? I'll tell you what. Your kind understands self-preservation, I'll give you that. I propose a trade. You keep it nice and quiet, no barking, and we won't put you down. Don't complicate our lives, we won't end yours. Fair?"

Vali wanted to say something, do something. But what could he do? Leg broken against a group? Even if it were just these three, he was dead. He kept his silence.

"Good dog. Maybe they'll take you with them when we kick them out." He spat. "You better hope like hell they do. There's a reckoning coming."

The man turned to go, his companions backing away slowly, still facing Vali. Now that he knew what to look for, he could just make out the gray and white strips of cloth tied around their upper arms, little tassels of the old Getacian banner's colors. They might be using the cover of darkness, might be sneaking about, but those bands told him everything he needed to know. You didn't wear a uniform, even a simple one, unless there was a heap of other bastards ready to put it on beside you.

For his own part, Vali was seething. His chest was tight, and he could barely see straight from the anger. Here he was, wounded from defending their borders and their people from the savages that would like nothing better than to rape and pillage their way across the valleys and hilly fields of their home. Ensuring that Getacia was part of the empire, their only hope against the next cataclysm. And then there were these short-sighted cunts who guaranteed an imperial patrol in every Getacian village, spreading their strength thin. These faux patriots who would drag their people back into the past for their own advancement, all under the guise of independence. The independence to fall under the yoke of the Thousand Tribes or squabbling Stained.

"Fuck you."

The men paused.

"Careful, boy," their leader drawled, still turned away. "Don't be an idiot."

Vali knew he was right. They would kill him. This was not the smart move. He didn't care.

"Raise the alarm!" he shouted at the top of his lungs, pouring everything he had into the cry. It sounded shrill and unreal in the quiet. "Invaders! Raise the alarm!"

It was all he had time for as the trio rushed back at him. One of the men yelped, struggling to right himself as he tripped on something on the broken ground between them. Vali lurched forward, twisting to hurl a rock at one of the oncoming men. Another cry, a lucky throw. He grunted with the pain of the exertion, stumbling back onto the perimeter wall. He drew the short sword.

The third man was on him now, and Vali could hear the other two picking themselves up. He might have been imagining it, but he could have sworn he heard a commotion from the nearest part of the camp. Hopefully this wasn't all for nothing.

"You gods-damned traitor," the man snarled as he struck at Vali with something heavy.

A mace, he realized as he knocked it to the side and cut at the man's legs from where he leaned with his back against the rocks. Missed. Vali's right leg was screaming at him, but it was distant as the threat of more than broken bones loomed inevitable. The other two finished the semicircle around him now, edging forward. A couple more ran up from the group that had mostly crossed over the wall by now, but their leader waved them away.

"Go! Stick to the mission. We've got this one handled. Go!"

They closed in now, points of weapons flickering in, and Vali doing his best to watch them all at once. It was so hard to see them all in the dark.

"You're going to die now," one hissed.

The first voice spoke up again, almost sad. "Didn't have to be this way. You're a brave lad. Can't for the life of me understand why you would die for those slick black-and-golds."

He paused, listening. Vali heard it too. Shouting in the distance. Someone had heard him. At least he wouldn't die for nothing. The man grunted, and they all advanced for the kill.

The man on his left feinted forward. Vali saw it for what it was. Waiting, he saw from the corner of his eye the one on his right dart forward with a short sword, aiming for his neck. A vague explosion of movement in the dark. With a desperate burst of effort, he slipped under the thrust and jammed his short sword under the man's rib cage. Perfectly struck. Maybe he had a chance. There was a soft exhalation of breath, a sound of disbelief, and then the man collapsed forward, dragging Vali down under him.

Snarling, Vali pushed frantically at the corpse he had just made, writhing underneath the weight. The pain in his leg was unspeakable, penetrating even the adrenaline surging through him.

"You want to make noise, fine. See where that gets you, dog."

A blade thrust out of the dark and pushed into him, a fiery brand in the side of his chest. It hurt worse on the way out, and Vali curled around it like a dying spider. The pain made his leg feel like a bruise, and he didn't bother holding back the tears as the men ran over the wall. There was no one to see, and it didn't matter anymore. Soon, nothing would. He had never wanted to die, but this seemed an especially pointless way to go. It didn't feel like a noble sacrifice. Felt like nothing at all. He could feel the warm wetness spreading over his hand that he had pressed to his side, mixing with the blood that seeped over him from the man on top. Heaving at the weight was useless and made him cry out. Already, the edges of his vision were fading away. And he was cold again, so cold.

Why was there a man on top of him again? It all seemed a little confusing now, and Vali wondered why he couldn't move anymore. Slowly, his muscles relaxed, and his breathing slowed. It was finally warm again. The sword slipped from nerveless fingers. And right before the darkness took him, he thought he could hear the most beautiful but unexpected thing.

Bells.

# BAD DREAMS

Staring up into the green and black of her eyes, Syl could feel the knife at his throat, a cold promise.

"You killed my family. I'm going to kill you, Syl."

The protests died in his throat as Morana's face became a dozen, a hundred faces, most half-forgotten, buried in his subconscious. Bloodied, bruised, collared, ages and features blending together into an amalgamation with one defining, shared characteristic: accusation.

"You killed me."

"You killed my boy…"

"My mother…"

"…to a prison at the end of the world."

Half-forgotten was the best he could do.

"Why? Why? Why…" The question echoed, louder every time, until the word itself dissolved into a meaningless clang, metallic and urgent.

Bells.

Sweating, Syl ripped at the blanket that wrapped around him, holding him down. Bells. He hadn't imagined it. From the barracks and legion's camp across the way, the unmistakable tolling of bells rung in alarm. No steady cadence marking the hours, but a frantic clatter of men rending the night, desperate for their noise to wake their fellows.

Free now, Syl reached for his sword and then quickly dressed. There were no noises he could hear in the villa. Sturdily built and sprawling, he knew that meant less than nothing. Syl could feel that familiar heat filling his veins as he pulled from his conduits and crept to the door, all senses straining for something, anything, that might explain the bells.

Nothing. Only those distant peals that told him the silence was a lie.

No one survived years as a Hunter without natural and practiced skills of stealth, and Syl employed all of these as he steadily checked on the team.

Most were already awake. He ran into Lucky on his way to Domarik's room, already up and sliding along the shadows of the walls. When he grabbed Lucky's shoulder, the bloodhound jumped and stared with startled, wide-eyed reproach back at Syl.

"Can you sense anything?"

Lucky shook his head.

"Positive?"

He didn't deign to respond.

Before long, the entire team was in the hallway, armed and awake, but unsure of where the threat might be. The bells were accompanied by the distant din of fighting now, that unmistakable clamor of clashing metal and men.

Domarik took charge. "Leon, Kass, Liora, to the prisons. Check on Nerilias. Now. Syl, Lucky, with me."

"Where are you going?" Leon asked.

"Exarch. If the judiciars don't need your help, rendezvous with us at the Exarch's quarters. We'll figure it out from there."

"What's happening?" Liora asked.

"We'll know soon." Syl had meant it reassuringly, but his impatience bled through.

"Go." Domarik didn't bother waiting for a response and strode toward the Exarch's quarters on the other side of the estate. Lucky and Syl followed as he increased his pace to what was an eerily quiet lope for such a huge man. Syl would hate to be the first one to run into Domarik.

They covered the distance in minutes, even with frequent stops at turns and doorways, standing in perfect silence, straining to hear or see any sign of something amiss. There would be enough issues if the attack was only on the camp, without enemies in the estate itself. Syl began to suspect they were wasting their time and should regroup to assist with whatever was happening in the camp. Then they found their first sign.

A judiciar, slumped against the wall, as if lost to drink and sleep, due for a bitch of a hangover and extra duty in the morning. He looked almost peaceful—as peaceful as a man could look with his lifeblood painting the front of his gray uniform black. About as clear a sign as they could hope for.

Domarik looked at Lucky, who shook his head again, some nervousness beginning to penetrate his blank features. If they were Stained, then they knew better than to draw from the Rift here. Sharp objects, blunt instruments, and surprise, then. So, either separatists, or very clever Stained. Syl frowned down at the body. Considering recent reports, maybe both.

They redoubled their pace, trading caution for speed now. It might already be too late. They passed more scenes of struggle, guards who hadn't been as utterly surprised as the one earlier. More bodies lay beside them, where the invaders had left their own behind, white and gray cloth bands around their upper arms. Separatists. The mosaics passed in a blur. There was no possible doubt as to the target, with a route that didn't deviate from the most direct way to the Exarch's quarters. They were sprinting now. There might still be time.

Rounding a final corner, Syl burst through the doorway into the Exarch's outer office. The screams and shouting took shape and revealed a frantic fight in the dim light. No time to think. There was enough light to tell friend from foe. Syl immediately lunged forward, thrusting his blade home through one of the intruders that was hacking away at a guard's shield. It pierced the leather armor, parted the chain rings below that, and its momentum stuttered as it punched through the other side.

*In the fight again. Finally.*

Syl twisted the blade and ripped it back out. Felt the fine spray, the clarity. This was easy to understand. To his side, Domarik cleaved one nearly in half, his longsword not quite pushing through, but throwing what was left of the man against the wall in a ruin. He moved on to the next one, cold, furious, and massive, silent death in motion. Lucky was smart enough to stay crouched in the shadow cast by the larger man's swings, watching for any sign of a Stained. The pain was gone from behind Syl's eyes in moments like these, as everything moved a little slower and took on the crystal-clear quality that always came for him when he fought. It was as if this was all a story he had heard a long time ago, the next part not quite remembered, but its shape inevitable.

On instinct, he turned to the corner of the room. And there it was. Syl could feel the pressure around him, building. Motions became more difficult, and the tattoos that ringed his body burned faintly as the flow of the Rift through those conduits fought to keep the Stained, wherever he was, from turning him inside out, or whatever horrible way he would have died without the extra protection. With an effort, he wrenched his gauntlet up, engaging it and further dissipating some of that lethal arcane energy.

"There!"

Lucky was pointing to a corner where two men were hiding behind a pillar, separate from the chaos around the table. The shouted warning immediately drew their attention, and Syl could feel the pressure lessen as whichever was the Stained directed his violence against Lucky.

A mistake. Their last mistake. Syl sprinted toward their corner, dodging around the remaining fights. Lucky wouldn't last long under that pressure, but he wouldn't have to. In the faint blue light of the dimmed arclamps, Syl could see their panic as they saw him coming. Throwing himself forward, Syl slid into the second man's knees and cut the first man's legs out from under him as he passed. The one he smashed into tumbled with a cry, and Syl followed, twisting around to smash the pommel of his bloodied sword into the man's forehead. The Stained bucked, and Syl brought the pommel down again, stunning him. Syl readjusted. Reached back a little further this time. Aimed. Brought it down again.

Once more. A gasp.

Twice. Eyes rolled.

A third. The skull cracked.

A fourth, a fifth, a...

"Syl!"

Coming back to himself, Syl looked down. Under his gore-covered hands was nothing that could ever be mistaken for a man. Bone and gore and the pommel of his sword dented from impacting the stone floor. Turning, he could see Lucky frowning at him with concern. Syl flushed.

*What the fuck is he looking at? He should be thanking you.*

He pushed the bloodhound out of his way. Domarik was helping the Exarch to his feet, who looked as if he had been inches from death. His face was bloodied and haggard, arm held at an unnatural angle. They had made it in time. Barely. He was injured, but not dead. Injured and in a towering rage.

The whole room held its collective breath, Syl, Domarik, and the few remaining judiciars seeing what was written across those features.

"These...these..." The Exarch could barely form the words, spittle sticking to his beard as he hissed out the words. "These *animals. Me!* These animals try to kill *me* in my own home."

There was noise at the entrance to the room. A new group arrived under those interwoven branches of stone. The Exarch's head swiveled to where

Nerilias stood, a gaunt skeleton, features made more deathlike than ever in the deep shadows. "You! How...how..." The Exarch's anger was beyond words now, face scarlet with fury.

The chief judiciar didn't seem to care, face impassive as ever. Syl felt a flash of disappointment at seeing Nerilias alive and well. It was never the ones that deserved it who got unlucky. The judiciar bowed and then pushed his way between the surviving guards. Behind him, Syl could see the rest of his team, faces nearly as grim as Nerilias's.

"Permission to send a pursuit party, Father."

The Exarch placed a hand on the great table to support himself, not seeming to notice the puddle he placed it in. The rivers on the map ran red, and the glaciers were eased along with viscera now.

"Pursuit? There are more?"

"This was one of several attacks. Reports detailing the full extent of the damage are filtering in. We know that the governor was assassinated, multiple local officials reported missing. And..." There was the faintest twitch of a muscle on the side of Nerilias's head. "...the prison has been emptied."

*"Emptied?"*

Syl understood the Exarch's shock. The prison here wasn't for thieves, murderers, and tax evaders. Those thick walls held the political prisoners of the province, the dissidents, the rabble-rousers, and the would-be warlords. And a certain Stained, who had only just found a reason to live. His breath caught.

"Emptied." Staring straight at Syl now, Nerilias continued, voice dripping with accusation. "As far as we can tell, the first cell they went to was the girl's. They are all gone though. There might yet be a chance of catching them. Most likely path is—"

"Then what are you standing here for?" the Exarch screeched, throwing his hand to the door. "Go!"

With a gesture for the team to follow, Domarik fell in behind Nerilias as he left.

"No, not you, Domarik. Not you. Send your bloodhound with them. The rest of your team stays. And the rest of you—out!" Noticing the stickiness of his hand, he let out a growl of disgust as he wiped it absently on his robes. "This whole place is going to need cleansing," he muttered.

The map room was empty now, but for the team, sans Lucky, and the Exarch. And a dozen leaking bodies. The adrenaline fled his body now, and Syl's hands started to shake, the one sign he could never control after a fight. Clenching them reflexively, he couldn't help but think of Morana. Why her? And why wasn't he more upset about her escape?

"Is something amusing, Hunter?"

Startled, Syl realized the Exarch was staring straight at him, talking to him. He wiped away the treacherous half-smile that had made its way to his lips.

"No, Exarch."

"Oh, well, that is excellent. I would hate to think you find this amusing. Don't think it's been forgotten why that girl is alive in the first place."

Syl said nothing. Silence and obedience were his best defenses now.

Another shuddering breath from the Exarch, a visible effort to compose his emotions. With an eerie quickness, the unstable head of the Vigil in Getacia disappeared, replaced by a battered, fatherly figure, concern written across kindly features.

"I've kept you back because there is more bad news."

Domarik's displeasure and disbelief were a low grumble.

"Yes, more than this catastrophe here, or the governor, Emperor guide his spirit to the Rift. Earlier tonight, only hours ago, a messenger arrived. Urgent enough to see me woken. More than half the northern districts of Getacia have fallen to a coordinated attack. A new pretender is making a bid for the old throne at Nordea Kerest. And that is half the districts that we know of. We are largely still in the dark regarding which garrisons have turned, been slaughtered, or have been able to hold their positions. Lines of communication are almost utterly broken. We were fools to think they wouldn't attack here as well. I blame myself. Not that there isn't enough to go around." The room was quiet enough they might all have been dead. "Not only that, but we have confirmation of a successful uprising at one of the largest penal colonies, the Bal Maru fortress city excavation site. Once again, one that we know of. I thought to wait until the morning to tell you, but clearly their plans didn't end there."

"In response?" Domarik had a way of asking the right questions with the fewest words.

The Exarch nodded slowly, cradling his broken arm. "Yes. Obviously, this is no longer a simple matter of investigating missing patrols or escaped prisoner convoys. The Twins have already committed their legions to an expedition north. You will still be ahead of them. According to our messenger, Seven Rivers remains firmly under imperial control. Help to keep it that way. Investigate. It will be a staging point for the pacification efforts, and would be a natural stopping point for any escapees or rebels crossing the Severan Mountains this late in the season. Find out how far the rot goes. When the legions arrive, while they focus on smashing the spirit of the separatists before this infection has a chance to spread to any remaining districts, you will do what you do best."

"It might not be enough."

"I am aware. That is why we have already requested the reinforcement of six legions from the south. They, along with two more of the Chosen, should be here within weeks."

There was a stunned silence in the room. Syl surprised himself by speaking. "There hasn't been a mobilization like that since..."

"Yes. The last campaign here. At least some of you have experience from those times." The Exarch looked at them all in turn. "The ground is shifting beneath our feet, and we must be ready for unfamiliar territory. It will not be the same as back then. Your faith will be tested, I think, in the coming weeks. That brings me to my final point. One that you likely suspect by now. The Emperor has spoken, and the Pentarchate concurs." He paused, nodding again as if to convince even himself. "A second Riftgate has opened. The cycle has begun. Our watch is over."

The silence in the room was absolute, with only the suddenly distant sounds of frenetic activity on the estate drifting through the door. There was a sense of unreality to his pronouncement. They all knew what this meant, the slow confirmation of suspicions that had grown over the last few days, especially ever since the farmhouse. They were the Vigil, the watchers for the end. For any doubts any of them ever had over what they had to do, there was one thing they always knew to be true; that one day, the watch would be over. Yet knowing something for a possible truth and watching it unfold before you were very different things.

"Our watch may be over, but the war has only just begun." Demarhis's face was grim. "We have fought to delay this beginning as long as possible, but that does not mean we cannot delay it still. The *Vox Caelorum* speaks of cataclysms held at bay for a generation or more. Our mandate stands. Nothing has changed, though we will avoid word of this spreading for as long as possible to avoid panic. Along with the legions, you will cross the mountains and do what you always do. The emergence of another Riftgate will come with the chaos of hundreds of emerging Rift-users. You must be there first. Scour the countryside for Stained, and eliminate those we cannot use. Collar those we can. Healers. Conduits. Bloodhounds. As for those who have escaped, there will be no prisoners this time, no rotten apples to spoil the bunch in another camp. Your ultimate goal is that northernmost penal colony, the excavation site of an old fortress city, and the most likely locus for this new Riftgate. You will not be alone and will work closely with the generals under the Twins. They will secure the site, but your task will be to eliminate any and all Stained that have made pretensions to its ownership. Capture their leadership, if you can. We will also settle for their heads. Domarik, you will be provided with the necessary details. You leave within the day."

There was nothing else to do but salute and try to leave that room. Perhaps it would make more sense in the light of the morning. The recurring disaster of their world approached again, but Syl found—far quicker than he expected—that the Exarch had been right. It all felt the same still, and knowing their role in helping to delay that end and preserve what made it through was a comforting purpose. And in the meantime, there were preparations to make, gear to pack, and plans to coordinate. Life went on, same as always, cataclysm or no.

As they left, the Exarch's voice arrested their exit. "One last thing. The girl. If they cared so much about freeing her, then she is undoubtedly a tool in their plans. It is beyond unfortunate that the flamewardens did not have time to examine the nature of her affliction. Likely far more powerful than we credited her for. I have my suspicions. If I am correct, she is not the sort of weapon we can afford falling into our enemies' hands. If Nerilias and the others catch her, all the better. But no matter what happens, she dies. It will be chaotic in the North. There will be competing priorities. But hear me now: she dies."

There was one last salute as all on the team acknowledged his orders. But Syl knew exactly who he was speaking to.

# BAD HABITS

He'd heard you could get used to pain. Groaning, Vali thought whoever said that hadn't experienced very much of it. Emerging from blackness to be birthed into a world of pain, weakness, and too-bright light. There was a shout. Shuffling feet. People moving into a room. Had everything that had happened since the ambush with the riders been some sort of fever dream? No, he thought with a frown and a twinge of pain in his chest. He tried to reach for it, but someone pressed his arm back down. Not a dream. No dream had ever hurt this much.

A cup of water found its way to his lips, and Vali sucked greedily at it, only now realizing that he wanted nothing more in the world than more of that. They took it away too quickly. This was all awfully familiar. Was he doomed to spend the rest of his life waking up injured, stumbling from one near-death experience to the next? They wouldn't be writing any stories about that. He surveyed his surroundings. He had expected the wooden and woolen chambers of the medical barracks. Instead, blocks of cool marble reflected the morning light from an ornate window garlanded with flowering vines. It *was* like a dream. Turning from the window and the light clouds that promised a rare clear day, he saw the rest of the room.

Vali panicked. His heart leapt in his chest as a half dozen of the province's most powerful men and women finished filing into the room. They were all staring at him. Was he being punished for failing to stop whatever happened last night? For a third and final time, he prayed that this was all an absurd dream. Better to be unconscious than have these men and women looming over him expectantly.

Then he saw his own father in the back of the group, a sly grin on that broad, ruddy face. Vali relaxed a fraction. His father was here for him. He had known he would come.

"He's awake." The man's bruised face was new to Vali, but there was no mistaking the robes, disheveled as they were. This was the Exarch, the most powerful figure of the Vigil in the province. The most powerful person, bar none, according to his father. "I owe you a debt, Valerek, my son." He didn't bother introducing himself, instead waving his arms to encompass the rest of the room. "We all do."

Vali tried to make out who else was in the room through the fatigue and mental fog. The Exarch, Captain Askaris, and his father were all obvious. The rest were a few high-ranking members of the legions and the Vigil. There were a couple of robed figures in the back, more simply dressed than the Exarch. Priests? Vali knew a couple through his father, but he couldn't understand why so many important figures were in this room.

The room was still silent, waiting. Waiting for him, he realized with a start. A cough and a nod were what he could manage. "Of course, sir," he croaked. Even that hurt.

"*Your Radiance,*" his father mouthed, frowning slightly.

The Exarch didn't seem put out with the missed title. "You've been injured. Again, I hear. And this time, your actions saved countless lives, my son. When they found you, you were half dead—but then again, so was I."

Vali fought to keep the skepticism from his face, lying in bed, covered in bandages. The plump man looked like he'd had a rough go in the training square, nothing more. The few bruises were the faded yellow of weeks past. But little facts started to connect through the fog as he registered for the first time what the Exarch's appearance meant. Those men had meant to—tried to—kill the Exarch. He started to grasp the scale of what must have happened last night.

"Today has been filled with the steps we need to take to ensure this never happens again, but I asked to see you when you woke. I want to thank you as best I can, in two ways. The first is to get you on your feet."

With a fluttering of fabric and the faintest smell of incense and cedar, a bondmage swept forward from behind the Exarch. Lines of white and gold threaded themselves everywhere in smooth patterns on her robes, whorls and vines spreading and intersecting in a hypnotizing kaleidoscope. An enormous hood covered her features, with a mask over her lower face. As she grew closer, Vali caught a glimpse of the face underneath. He couldn't help but flinch backwards, pain forgotten for a second. Noticing, she adjusted the fabric, pulling it lower over her head with pale, delicate gloved hands. It had been so quick. He must have imagined it. But Vali knew he hadn't. He had made eye contact with her for a second—and looked into nothingness. No pupils, no iris, nothing. Perfectly and perversely white. Pure in their emptiness, where there should have been life.

The room had taken on a solemn and expectant atmosphere, believers waiting for a miracle. They watched hungrily as the woman prodded at him, ignoring his muted grunts of protest. She seemed intent on finding the direct points of injury. With an impassive slowness, she continued to inflict pain on Vali. Gritting his teeth and smelling the stink of his own sweat, he listened as the Exarch continued.

"This is a healer, Vali. My healer, in fact, and one of only a few in all the empire. She has already had to tend to me this morning."

Vali's surprise was interrupted by another prod. Staring up at her and then at the silent group watching, he understood why no one had left yet. Using the Rift to heal others directly was a gift so rare as to be near mythical, in the same category as volseers, telepaths, and riftwalkers. The accelerated healing of oathknights was a pale shadow of what healers were rumored to be capable of. Looking at the Exarch, he wondered why one man might have his own, and how often such a gift would have been in demand.

"I cannot sufficiently express the exception we are making for you, my son. But such loyalty deserves recognition—yours, and that of House Costranis, a steadfast ally in these uncertain times. And your work is far from over. The empire has need of you yet." He turned slightly, acknowledging Vali's father, who sketched a short bow. Vali could see the smile he suppressed, even if many of the others in the room looked distant and troubled. "Has need of all true friends in these lands. We enter dark days, but there is always light at the end, however far it may be. Remain still and let her work."

With a flush, hope rushed in. It was as if he were healed already, and whatever the woman was doing would simply formalize it. Earlier despair and self-pity belonged to a distant past self that he had little use for. Of course his bravery was being rewarded. He was meant to be whole, not doddering around camp like an old man at nineteen.

Shifting his attention to the healer, Vali could feel the room grow warmer by degrees, a faint shimmering haze distorting the air around the woman. Then a searing heat flooded through Vali. He gasped. It was like drinking spirits in winter, like approaching a fire on a snowy night. Warm sun and sex and a spring breeze. The feeling flooded him, increasing rather than decreasing in intensity. There was pain too. He could feel an intense itch and crackling around his worst points of injury. So, almost everywhere. But he gloried in the sensation of the pain, because it was inseparable from the greater feeling of...rightness. And strength. So much strength. He wanted to run, to sprint.

Vali started to lift himself out of the bed, suffused with energy. Effortlessly, the healer pushed him back down. He let her. That was fine. Everything was fine now. He could see the strata in the stone above him, every grain and cobweb in impossibly sharp detail. He could hear his heartbeat, fast and strong. The healer's heartbeat, slow and steady. Her eyes faded even more into nothingness, and delicate veins of white traced their way across what little he could see of her face. Was this what it was like to pull the Rift through a conduit? To be an oathknight? He looked to the door where his commander stood. Was this how he felt all the time? How could he ever have thought to compete with Askaris? Against any of them? He laughed, overcome with the joy of it, the warmth of that fire in his veins.

And choked on the ashes of it.

As quickly as it came, the feeling fled. It was like the sun had been plucked from the sky, and he was blind again, a worm wriggling through the dirt. His gasp this time was one of panic. He reached out in the only way he knew how, trying to grab the bondmage. Not yet! He wasn't healed! A little more, and he would be whole again. She brushed him aside like one would a greedy child and turned, swirling robes reflecting the light. She waited until the Exarch gave a terse nod before sweeping out of the room on silent feet.

The world was faded again, its usual self, but Vali flexed his limbs and found that everything worked. More than worked. There wasn't even the hint of stiffness or soreness to point to a week in bed, much less being trampled half to death and stabbed besides. There was a collective sigh as Vali swung his legs out of the bed and tested them, placing his weight gingerly, and then with more confidence—the reward of faith well placed. The Exarch watched, allowing the crippled to walk again. But there was still a province to run.

"It's good to see you walking again. You've a lot more of that to do soon. As for the second reward for your loyalty, I'll leave you with your commander to explain that. Unfortunately, other matters demand more attention than I have to give today. But I can promise your actions won't quickly be forgotten. You're an example to your countrymen."

Most of the people in the room shuffled out after the Exarch, all giving nods of respect to Vali, who stood, bewildered by the turn of events, and a bit overawed by the braid and badges of so many high-ranking officials in one room. Eventually, only his father, Captain Askaris, and two black-clad oathknights remained. His father approached, all smiles and approval. He was happy to see him.

"You did well, my boy. Did me proud. Did our house proud. I wish your mother could see you now." His hand was firm and comforting against Vali's shoulder. "You found your moment. I knew you would rise." He squeezed once more, leaning close to whisper conspiratorially, "But there is so much further to go." He winked.

Vali couldn't keep the broad grin off his own face. He wanted to ask him why he hadn't come earlier, but his father was a busy man. Busy and distant and cold, but so warm and proud when it suited him. And Vali couldn't help but enjoy basking in that glow. He thought his brother would be proud of him too, and that made it all the sweeter.

"I've business to attend to as well, I'm afraid. Those separatists have stirred up a hornet's nest. All sorts of reports." His father's smile faded into something a bit more troubled. "Let's just say you couldn't have proven our family's loyalty at a better time. Assassinations, prison breaks, and reports of worse from past the mountains."

"What happened last night? And what do you mean? What happened in the North?"

"Ask them. You'll find out more soon enough, I'd wager."

Vali tried to reach for his father as he turned to leave, but he shrugged his hand off, fixing him with a last hard stare. There was an emphasis there, for words meant to be remembered. "I've got to go, but I'll see you soon enough when you return. You're heading for some treacherous and dangerous paths. So, prepare. Remember all the lessons I've taught you. Know the terrain and see the lay of the land. Be cautious and never too proud to learn. And when you find your moment again, seize it without hesitation. I know you'll bring honor to our house."

With that, his father was gone again, too soon, leaving Vali with Captain Askaris, cheerful as always, and the two Vigil oathknights, who watched his father's leaving form darkly. They turned their attention to Vali.

Askaris waited until his father's footsteps had receded down those stone corridors before smiling brightly at Vali. "Well, that was emotional."

Flushing, Vali shrugged. The whole morning had been a bewildering experience, and he was still riding the high of going from bedridden to healthy in seconds. He pumped his knees and flexed his wrists, feeling the strength in those arms. They wanted a sword—or an axe, or anything—again already.

"Feeling better?"

Vali didn't say anything. He looked at Askaris with a jealousy he wasn't sure he concealed all that well—or wanted to conceal.

Askaris chuckled. "I know."

The oathknights still watched with cold, neutral faces, in sharp contrast to Askaris's cheerful patience. He tried to break the awkward silence. "What's this second gift, sir?"

"Ah, yes." The captain cleared his throat, glancing toward the two in black, who stared unblinkingly at Vali. "The Exarch and your father mentioned a few of the details, but the ground is shifting under our feet here, Vali. Looks like the separatists in the northern districts have made a go at it. Probably allied with some Stained. Prisoner revolts at the border, and local garrisons slaughtered."

"What? How many towns?" Vali couldn't believe what he was hearing.

His disbelief only grew as Captain Askaris finished outlining the scale of the disaster. His life and death struggle, even his part in saving the Exarch, had all been a footnote to the events of last night. His forced cheer couldn't conceal the gravity of the words or the exhaustion in the bags under his eyes. Vali noticed for the first time the din of shouted commands outside the window, the sounds of preparation.

He wondered what today might have looked like if he had never raised the alarm last night, had turned a blind eye to the men crossing to this estate. His part might have been a footnote, but no doubt an important one. Unconsciously, he flexed his muscles again, reveling in the strength he could feel. Things certainly could have been worse. For everyone.

"Are we heading north, then?"

"Not us, no. The rangers are still needed on the borders, now more than ever." There was a troubled look on the captain's face, and it looked as if he was about to say something more. After a quick glance behind him, he forced a smile back on. "But you, you brilliant idiot, will have a chance to injure yourself heroically again." Vali couldn't help but mirror his captain's grin. It really was impossible not to love that man. "It was discussed this morning. You will accompany the expedition north, as an augment to..." Here he pointed out the oathknights with a theatrical flourish. "... one of our dauntless Hunter teams. They will be part of the campaign to secure the North and recapture a key excavation site at Bal Maru. And besides, word will get out that you were the one who raised the alarm here. Right now, it would be best to have you as far from the auxiliaries as possible. Moving up in the world, lad."

"As in..." Vali's voice caught.

"No, no, let's not get ahead of ourselves. But close. Consider this a final trial. Acquit yourself well, help them and the legions bring order back to the northern districts. When you return...let's just say there is an opening in General Lucianus's personal guard."

The hunger was naked on Vali's face. Finally. So close, with a clear goal in sight. He took a deep breath and nodded. "I'm ready."

"Well, that's good to hear." Askaris laughed. "But these two need to give the final stamp of approval. Meet Hunters Scyllus and Kassara, two from the team. They have a few questions. Answer them to their satisfaction, and you'll be accompanying them."

"And Marika? Lucan?"

Askaris gestured again to the other two. "A question for them. They'll have a place with me, if not. I'll leave you three to your conversation now, but I wanted to say it's been a privilege serving as your commander, Vali." He came forward and gripped Vali's hand firmly in his. "It can be tough working with you grim bastards up here, crawling through the muck, but you're one of the good ones." With that, he gave one last squeeze and a nod before leaving the room.

Leaving him with the oathknights. They stared at one another. The man, Scyllus, was a decent bit shorter than him, with none of the bulk that really made people feel as if Vali was looming over them. The Hunter had more the look of a sleek hunting dog, gray eyes bored, but missing nothing. His hair was short, the sides barely more than stubble, and his face looked like he had taken a very long and painful time to learn to shave. His companion, Kassara, was built much the same, but that was where the similarities ended. The luxuriously plaited and lustrous hair, the wry twist of the lips, the way she held herself, the sharpness of that pointed chin, those haughty brown eyes and honey skin... It was a face Vali could get lost in. He coughed, suddenly aware of how long the silence had stretched and trying to look anywhere but at her.

The man, Scyllus, finally spoke. "So, what's wrong with you?"

"What?" Vali sputtered, too surprised to be offended.

The woman, Kassara, started to circle around him, and Vali tried to watch her from the corner of his vision, more uncomfortable by the moment.

"Did you not understand him?"

"I did, I just..."

"Answer him, then."

"There is nothing wrong with me," he managed through gritted teeth.

Scyllus was circling the opposite direction, not bothering to look at Vali, appearing lost in thought. "What would you call it when a crippled boy tries to fight three men at once, Kass?"

"Arrogance," she bit out. "Stupidity."

"I saved the Exarch's life!" Vali protested. This was like a bad dream. He had been given everything he had ever wanted, and he could feel it dissolving between his fingers. There had to be a way to convince them, but he didn't even understand their objections. "If I hadn't raised the alarm, he'd be dead."

"Maybe," Scyllus conceded with a nod. "Maybe not. But either way, you couldn't possibly imagine a better way to raise the alarm? One that might not involve the equivalent of slamming your head into a wall to get through instead of climbing over?"

Vali gawped, unsure of what to say. Everything he had done, all the heroism of his sacrifice was suddenly painted as stupidity. Could he have waited until they crossed to raise the alarm? Wouldn't they have just come back for him? Second guesses and self-doubt suddenly flooded in, hot and fast, washing away any of the self-satisfaction and pride of a minute ago. "I did the right thing," he muttered lamely.

"The right thing?" Kass jabbed him in his ribs, hard. He flinched. "What about the smart thing? Would it be too much to ask for both?"

"If we wanted brutes, we could have stopped by the local tavern," Scyllus said from his opposite side.

"Are you brutes? Is it true what they say about you Gets?"

"No, it isn't..." Vali started, before catching himself. He looked at them both, seeing that they were watching for something. Pushing, with their accusations and slurs. He thought he understood. These were not questions meant to be answered. He waited, silent, seething.

Scyllus let the silence stretch before he pushed the knife home. "Bravery is good. Loyalty even better. And we can use killers, no doubt. But violence is only a tool, and bravery is the fool's pride. So, tell us now. If you don't understand what we are saying right now, if you can't swallow your pride, if you can't look for the smart way through, say so now. Stay here. Because if you compromise our mission in any way, you had better hope your mistake is fatal. Otherwise, we will fix that."

Fury flared in Vali as he stared at the dead-eyed Hunter, but much of that was directed at himself. There was plenty to go around.

"Do you grasp what we are saying? Can you find room in your thick head for this new information?"

Vali's jaw clenched. "Yes."

"Good. As far as your friends go, if they can grasp this same lesson, then we can use them too. Consider whether they can or not as a reflection on you, and decide for yourself if we can use them."

They started for the door, apparently satisfied.

"When do we leave?" Vali managed.

"Tomorrow, first light." Scyllus turned back, seeming to look through him. "Dress warmly."

Vali watched them go, his success and the opportunity suddenly bittersweet. Still, these next few weeks could determine the rest of his life—whether he would become an oathknight, whether he would make a name for himself. He could put up with asshole Hunters and the cold for however long it took. Grabbing his belt from beside the bed, he gripped the familiar haft of the axe, firm and comforting under the hand. It was easy to put up with so much when you had your health and your strength. Time to go north.

# TRY, TRY AGAIN

Darya found herself in a fog. Time passed and was barely noticed. She cried, then raged, then cried again. Alina tried to comfort her as best she could, but even her clumsy attempts only reminded her of Mikael. Mikael, her brother, her best friend, her protector. Gone. Forever.

While Darya mourned, she knew the others were only trying not to think about whether they might be next. She hated them for it, more than she already hated herself for not fighting harder for her brother. For all the excuses she made for herself, she knew that if their places had been switched, there would have been nothing but death that would have stopped him from trying to save her.

Alina had fallen asleep, and Darya lay curled in an exhausted ball beside her, dry-eyed and out of tears. As day passed into night, she had even managed to fall asleep, exhaustion of every sort finally overwhelming her grief. Now, blinking open crusted eyelids, she woke in a state of profound displacement. Woke, as always, under the comforting sky of hide tent walls, but with a deep sense of wrongness, the knowledge that there was something she should remember.

*Mikael.*

It hurt like seeing it happen again for the first time. Darya wondered whether if she lived, if this was what it would be like every morning. Any sense of contentment or peace long gone, replaced anew each day with the crushing reminder of what had been lost. There were those that said the spirits of the dead only left their bodies and became part of the tapestry of the Rift between all the worlds. That you might hear them, if you but listened close enough. Darya listened, but there was nothing. Only the faint sounds of people meeting another day, same as yesterday, as if nothing had changed. And why was she surprised? The Breaking had cut the other worlds off from their own; perhaps those souls were behind the same walls, battering against them like the Thousand against the empire.

There was movement outside, and inside the tent, they all stirred, hoping to finally learn what was to become of them. Or for food and water, at the very least. Instead, a tall, burly figure swept the flap aside and swaggered in. His nose wrinkled as he surveyed them. Darya knew this one. A chieftain, Taharuk, from one of the tribes east of her own—though that included almost all of them. He had been in that inner circle by the Arkhan. The ones who had helped push for her brother's death. She shrank from that gaze, on a face that looked as if it had been chewed up and spat out by something even meaner and uglier than him. A missing ear, sagging jaw, and bald patch on the side of his scalp all told the story of a life spent killing and narrowly avoiding being killed in turn. Behind him was another man, handsome, smaller in a rangy way, hair grown long, and clever eyes that expressed a measure of sympathy for those in the tent.

"Listen up." Taharuk needn't have bothered. All attention was fixed on him. Darya was grateful to have a distraction from her grief. "As useless as you are, Janbek has decided to give you a second chance. At the insistence of the Arkhan's prophet." He looked uncomfortable, eyes checking the corners of the tent, as if he expected Vels to be hiding somewhere in the shadows. It was odd to see such a rough man so discomfited by someone not even present. Darya didn't blame him.

Taharuk cleared his throat, contempt covering any earlier lapse. "I'll be taking my men and some others besides west, over the mountains." He gestured dismissively to the man behind him. "Serik here will be bringing his men. Kursagai too. 'Why,' you ask? Excellent question. Vels says these...these Stained and Getacians are still worth meeting as potential allies, even if your"—and here, he pointed accusingly at Darya—"idiot brother got a couple hundred other idiots killed trying already. We won't be making his mistake, trying for the easy southern passes and looking to cut through those swamps. Our path lies straight north and then west, and I don't fucking care how high or how frozen the peaks are. Now, that chance I have been ordered to offer you. You can come with me, have a chance to redeem yourselves, maybe, or...you can accept exile and never show your faces anywhere the Thousand might roam. And believe me when I say this: I do not want you. If you come with me, you will get the dirtiest and most dangerous tasks on an already dirty and dangerous mission."

There were shared glances within the tent as Taharuk sized them up again.

"If you're coming with me, we leave today. If you don't follow me out of this tent—which, again, I sincerely hope you choose not to—it will be assumed that you have chosen exile."

With a glare and without another word, he whirled, stepping out of the tent and pushing aside the other chieftain. Jaw clenched, Serik followed him, clearly an unwilling junior partner in this little endeavor.

Perhaps they had all lain in the tent for too long. Not a one moved. Then, all at once, there was a hurried unfolding of limbs, a scrabbling to feet, and a general rush for the flap of the tent, as if only the first would have a chance to take Taharuk up on his offer. All but Darya. Sitting there, it was as if her whole body had been filled with lead. How could they expect her to just...forget? To go out again on the same mission that she had barely survived, that had killed her brother, even if he had made it back to camp? A shudder rippled down her spine, and she couldn't seem to get her mind to work. There was nothing but a dull resentment as she watched the others practically fight one another to be first to follow Taharuk. Faithless, fickle, only concerned with their own survival. Happy it was her brother who had died and not them. And who was Darya to blame them? She had seen what she was willing to do to survive, and the grief hadn't entirely displaced that guilt. It was all too much.

Alina had sprung to her feet too after the chieftain's speech, but she stopped now, seeing Darya. "Get up. Come on." Alina grabbed Darya under the arm and started hauling her up. "We can't stay here."

"But I can't."

"Can't what?"

"Can't go with them. They're...they're...animals."

Alina let out a quick bark of a laugh. "Yes. But you've got no choice." Darya was standing now, gaze unfocused, but Alina grabbed her face and stared at her until Darya had to meet her eyes. "*We* don't have a choice. And you know it. So, come on. We can deal with this later."

Darya wasn't sure what "this" was, but she let herself be dragged from the tent. She still didn't think Alina was right, but then again, she knew she didn't have the right answer either. At least one of them was sure.

It was late afternoon now, and the four other survivors swayed in their saddles, but the spark of hope Darya had seen in their eyes as they followed Taharuk was long gone. Hope had a way of shining a flattering light on even the most straightforward statements. Darya wasn't surprised to find that Taharuk had been telling the truth; they were neither wanted nor needed, and were treated like it from the moment they set off. A group apart. The other warriors studiously ignored the five of them. It was as if they were dead already and were haunting these living men and women. And other than Alina, the other survivors—Altan, Kasym, Ganzig—seemed intent on acting as if Darya didn't exist, as if they could claw their way back to the living as long as they pretended they didn't share her fate.

Alina kept close to her side, and for that, Darya was grateful. A tribe down to two. Darya didn't think that counted as a tribe any longer. The heavyset, sullen woman's cynicism that had been so like a weight around the neck in happier times was a shield against the grief that did its best to reduce her to a blubbering child at every step farther away from the warband's camp. Where they had thrown what was left of Mikael to the dogs. It helped that there was little time or room for mourning.

This time, five hundred horsemen accompanied the five of them who had survived Sarkhan Janbek's disappointment, the majority from Taharuk's tribe, but sizeable amounts loyal to Serik and another chieftain, Kursagai. There was a scattering of other small groups to leaven the force, lonely handfuls like her own. Taking all the outcasts together, it made it more like four tribes than any sort of united warband, all under Taharuk's leadership.

As for their own miserable group, Darya tried to wrap her mind around the inexplicable intercession of Vels on their behalf. Even now, beyond her understanding, that eerie figure rode only a few paces behind her, looking into the distance. He never strayed far either. Like a jealous farmer protecting his prized dairy cow, she thought sourly. His investment. There was only one question: why?

He seemed to feel her examination and turned slowly, the mocking smile that hardly left his face making her uncomfortable enough to turn away. It was the eyes, she decided. It was the eyes that were...inhuman. The teeth too, perhaps. Too many, or too white, or just too often used. It was hard to trust anyone who smiled that often. Or maybe it all had to do with the terrifying and unsettling reputation he had built as the Arkhan's prophet—a reputation that hardly matched his outward appearance. Now, long fingers strummed restlessly and endlessly across the front of his saddle. He wore a long black coat and sturdy riding boots. And the bandages, of course. Those seemed more like his skin though, and it was almost impossible to imagine what affliction might exist under all that.

Looking forward, she saw only the endless rolling hills that disappeared into a thin line of snow-capped mountains in the distance. Darya decided to try starting a conversation with Vels. Why not? Anything to keep her mind occupied.

"Why did you speak for us? Why save us?" she blurted before she could talk herself out of it.

Vels hadn't looked away and still stared at her. On her other side, she could feel Alina start, surprised that she had engaged Vels in conversation. She would listen though, that was certain.

"Would you rather I hadn't?"

Darya opened her mouth to answer, and then closed it, considering. The horses' hooves were a steady beat against the rocky ground, and the conversations of those ahead floated back on the breeze. There were more trees around them in this hilly country, but there were fewer on the old road, and they weaved around these brave settlers. The ancient roads were still the fastest way anywhere.

"I'm...I'm not sure. But why did you do it?" she finally answered.

Vels cocked his head. "Really? There is nothing you can think of living for? I thought better of you, girl."

The kindly tone from back in the camp was a distant memory. Probably she had imagined it. This was the Vels she knew—more or less impossible to talk to without feeling a fool. For someone who always drifted around the camp, he had found his way to their section far more often than any of them had been comfortable with. Back then, she had assumed he was interested in Mikael, a rising commander in the warband. He would come and listen and talk and mock, always with damn peculiar questions about their past. Now? Darya could not figure out what he wanted for the life of her.

Darya tried a different tack. "Where do you come from, then?"

"Far from here."

"How old are you?" "Older than you."

"Why can't you answer my questions?" she exploded.

"I could." As her expression darkened, Vels laughed, clearly amused at her frustration. "Persistent, aren't we? Haven't you heard it's bad luck to talk to me? Your children will be born twisted, and you'll have nine years of bad luck, and your sword will freeze in its scabbard, and... What else do they say? I lose track."

"They say you can't be killed. That you can kill with a word," she said softly. And then louder. "And anyways, I don't want children, and how much worse could my luck get?"

"Oh, it can certainly get worse. I find that people consistently overestimate their own troubles. Those who believe their lives couldn't get worse simply lack imagination."

Darya could hear Alina spitting over her shoulder, trying to ward away the evil of the man's words. She persisted. "And what about the first part? That you can't be killed? That you can kill with a word?" She spoke with more confidence now that he was actually answering her questions, even if it was with riddles and questions of his own.

"Can't be killed," he mused. "Anything and anyone can be killed, Darya. Just because someone fails to do something doesn't mean it's impossible. And as for killing with words? Please, there's nothing simpler. You've seen it done yourself."

*"Take your fill, brothers."* Darya shivered, the memory threatening to overwhelm her again. She wanted to vomit, to remove the grief somehow, to...to stop being. Anything to forget this pain.

Vels inspected her with a critical eye. "You'll need to be stronger than this, girl. If you want to survive what's coming, at least. Or let it consume you. Do that petty warlord's work for him, and let what happened to your brother destroy you." Darya looked down, tears threatening to spill again. "Look at me," he snapped. Darya raised her eyes to meet his. "You could do that. That would certainly be what some want. Or...you can heed what your brother would want for you. Is that so hard to imagine? Or do you know, and you are just too much of a coward? Too weak? Mikael's little sister, worthless without her protector?" He leaned in from his saddle. "This world is a harsh place, make no mistake. This loss will define you, but you get to decide how. So, decide. Quickly."

Darya didn't want to think about what he was saying. But there was too much of what she recognized as sense in his words. "Why do you even care?" she finally asked, quieter.

"Hmmm..." Vels relaxed back into his saddle. "A good question for once. Sometimes I ask myself the same thing. The closest I have come to answering that is, when you have seen as much as I have, lived as long as I have, you go through stages. First, you live to watch your dreams wither, and you see that even your successes are temporary. There is an eternal appeal to despair. But then, after long enough, time has a way of building an appreciation for the immortal, foolish, beautiful optimism of hope. For potential. And Darya, you have such potential. Mikael's little sister? I have no use for her. But Darya? A woman who has chosen her path? I think we might speak then of her future."

He dug a bandaged hand around in his coat and produced a small, glinting coin. "In the meantime, take this." He tossed it to Darya. She snatched it out of the air and looked at it in confusion. It had been Mikael's. A rare piece of metal from a piece of history too ancient for them to understand the face or the letters. Dead kings and promises. A trinket. There was a new symbol carved into it. "I managed to grab it. He would have wanted you to have it. Good luck, call it."

Vels turned away slowly, leading his horse away from the column. To where, Darya had no idea. As he went, leaving her confused and angry, he shouted behind him. "A bright future, Darya." A pause as the distance grew. "Think! We will talk."

Darya turned to look at Alina, overwhelmed. She gripped the coin tight in a sweaty palm.

The other woman shook her head. "That's what you get for talking to that madman." She spat over her shoulder again. "But he was right about one thing." Alina gave Darya a meaningful look. "You have to decide."

Alina spurred forward without another word, catching up to the rest of the warband as they continued along the scattered remains of the road, leaving Darya alone and lost in thought. She looked around her, to the hills and forests, and wondered what a life out here might look like. Tonight, if she wanted, she could leave. Alina might even come with her.

The calls of small animals broke the quiet, and the wind blew along the road, forcing Darya to pull her coat a little tighter. She knew what that life would look like though. Hunger, cold, and sickness. A slow crawl to a painful death.

Ahead, the warband kept its steady pace. In a few hours, they would call a halt and set up the watches and the small fires that would do their best to fight back the late fall chill. Even the thought of those fires warmed her a bit.

That settled it. Spurring her horse forward, Darya considered Vels and Alina's advice. She knew they were right: she had to decide. But there was nothing wrong with one more night of relative comfort, wrapped in her bedroll, by a fire, and with guards around them. She tucked the coin away. She could decide later.

# PART II

*For the Five Undying, for their benevolent hands, which stretch to the darkness before, a chain unbroken, for the saviors and the destroyers, our bastions against the void eternal!*

*Can there be any doubt as to the perfection of the plans of the divine? For when operating on the basic premise that all beings and worlds act in their own self-interest, supplemented with a standard interpretation of recovered prophecy, we are left with the inescapable conclusion that aggressive, exclusive access control (paired with an effectively managed extractive resource plan) remains the only viable cycle decision.*

—Andwen's Prophecy:
"A Closer Examination of Fate and Strategy, or, a Rejustification"
(Caeloran Collegium, Thirteenth Centurial Synod, Submitted Works and Selected Essays)

# QUESTIONING

Syl watched the water gather itself, pulled from the spreading mold that covered the stone ceiling by some invisible force. It coalesced, and fell. Again. Onto the prisoner sitting before him, who jumped in surprise. They were running out of time. Syl tried again.

"How do you know Pilar, originally of Andovus? Darian, same family name?"

"Who? Oh, them? They are neighbors. Just neighbors!"

"Where were you yesterday evening? Why did you participate in the murder and attempted concealment of three imperial legionnaires?"

"I ... I never... What? Three legionnaires?"

"Yesterday evening. Four the night before that. Focus. Now."

A swallow. "Yes, yes. But I told you already, I was home! Ask my wife. Ask anyone."

"We have. That's why you're here."

"I..."

"When did a girl, approximately five feet tall, black hair, left eye blackened, pale skin, pass through here? Why did you help shelter her? Who was with her? How many, and how armed? When did they leave? In what direction? How many days ago?"

Mouth open. No words. Utter confusion. A consummate actor. Most likely.

Another drop fell.

The same questions, the same answers. Syl supposed that made sense. He rubbed at his temples, trying to ease the pressure, and let out a long breath, hoping some of his frustration might leave with it. All it did was cloud in front of him, smoky in the cold underground of the city's prison. Seven Rivers might have been the largest city of the largest district of Northern Getacia, a beautiful town of streaky granite and composite built atop and from the bones of a city from before the Breaking, but prisons didn't change much. The massive dam that formed the southern half of the city, the dwellings carved into it as far as the poor of the city dared ascend, the series of locks inside and outside the city walls that led farther into the north along the eponymous waterways—all that was far away right now. He might as well have been back in Rasovus, trying to convince that gods-damned girl to live. And now here he was, stuck hunting her, even farther into the sun-benighted, barbaric, and above all, fucking freezing province that he thought he had left for good all those years ago.

Gods damn it all. What a joke. It ought to be the official motto of the Vigil that no good turn went unpunished. You stuck your neck out for one vindictive little witch—once! In a decade!—and you spent the rest of your life cleaning up the mess. He needed to be out there hunting down real threats, not spending his days questioning merchants. This was a job for those secretive little sadists, the judiciars. Never around when you actually needed them.

And yet, Syl couldn't deny his own role. A second Riftgate open, the slow, slow spiral into another cataclysm begun, and the weakness in his resolve a stain at the very start of it. He might die before another fortress city erupted, plunging the world into darkness again, might help some semblance of the empire survive the ash and ice once again, but he couldn't shake the feeling that there was responsibility in there somewhere, and that he needed to fix his mistake. Grinding his teeth, he could feel the headache building in intensity, like a storm with nowhere for the pressure to go. The man in front of him shifted uncomfortably and cleared his throat, clearly nervous, and growing more nervous by the minute.

Syl glowered at the fat merchant, as if he were the one to blame for this whole situation. A gibbering mess, anxious and eager to talk, but about all the wrong things. Heavy jowls and a fashionably cut beard under dark brown eyes that oozed desperate, frightened, and confused honesty. Still being dressed in his sleeping clothes did nothing for the man's confidence. An intentional choice. You don't grab someone from their bed and then let them change. Supposedly useful. Yet here they were, repeating the same questions and answers that had been asked and answered in circles for an hour now.

Another drop splattered against the man's balding forehead.

*Nothing learned, no better off. And now you can't even remember his name.*

*Not that it matters.*

It had been a long night, with three others dragged here from their houses before this one. Four the night before. He needed sleep, but for every little fish they nabbed, a few more soldiers, a couple more imperial citizens went missing. The legion cohort that had marched over the passes with them had become infected with the paranoia that had—perhaps justifiably—seized the garrison headquartered in the barracks beside the prefect's estate. They didn't leave their barracks in groups smaller than a squad anymore. Apparently, the murders had only accelerated after their arrival. Despite all the sleepless nights, they weren't working their way up the chain fast enough. Not to mention the fact that there hadn't been a single word about an angry girl, black-haired and -eyed or not, much less any sign, even though Syl felt like he had personally broken down a quarter of the doors in the city. Not hide nor hair of any Stained. Just a bunch of pissed-off and disgruntled Gets.

Liora bent down to place a hand on his shoulder and whispered in his ear, "Could be he doesn't know anything? The last one could have been lying."

He shivered involuntarily at the closeness. In irritation, he suspected. She was always questioning, undermining. Last time he'd listened to her had been a disaster. He'd be damned if he let her put either of them in that sort of position again.

"That's not how this works," he said, loud enough for the merchant to look at him with even more concern. If that were possible.

Liora withdrew—suitably chastened, hopefully—but the problem remained. Namely, that she might be right. Their methods weren't foolproof. Still, one had to be thorough. Some of the best liars Syl had ever known or found had those broad, honest faces. They would tell you over and over, oh so sincerely, how they didn't know anything about that— *"Oh, wasn't that awful, how could I have anything to do with that?"* They would tell it to you, and tell it to you, so sincere that it really was the truth, and you believed them. You felt ill that you had suspected someone like them. They told you their truth through their teeth, right up until you opened the closet, the cellar. Whatever dark, filthy, hidden corner they kept that part of themselves locked in, and you saw them for the monsters they were.

Syl wasn't sure, but it always seemed like those liars, the really good ones, were always a little proud then, maybe a little embarrassed. A little grin, like, *"Oh, you got me, didn't you? But I had you going, didn't I? You believed me. They always do."*

He thought about it though. What were the odds this idiot really knew anything worth all this? He could let him rot in the prisons for a bit; there might not be a need for Leon's work.

*And if you're wrong?*

*As if that matters either.* A laugh.

Syl steeled himself, grimacing. He might not enjoy this part, but he had a job to do. He spared a quick glance to where Leon sat, toying with the knives and vials of acid on a simple worktable. It wasn't as if he could count on Leon to patiently sit through the life stories of these bastards. He would probably need him soon though. Liora and Vali stood behind him, each learning in their own way, both exhausted after a night of snatching others from their beds.

His attention returned to the man seated before him. "One more time. I'll keep it broad. Who else here has been working with the separatists? Have you had any contact with Stained of any sort? What do you know about the recent murders?"

"I promise, sirs, really, I swear! On my life, I've not seen one, never have. Wouldn't know it if I had. I'm loyal as they come!"

Between that stutter and the thick, thick accent of these northern districts, Syl was only fairly certain he'd understood. It was like they all talked with rocks in their mouths. He turned back to where Vali hovered.

"The same."

Back to the prisoner. "Slowly, when you answer. Please." No reason not to be civil. "Listen..." He paused, trying to remember. "What's his name again?" he asked behind him.

"Kipre," Vali supplied.

A quick lad, that one, for all his scowls and bulging muscles. Syl had to admit they'd been lucky to have the Getacians attached. Not that he would ever tell them that. "Thank you. Listen, Kipre, you need to help me help you. Do you understand that?"

Kipre bobbed his head, sweat on his pudgy forehead, despite the chill of the stone cell. The ceiling rained on him yet again, and another drop joined the sweat.

"Good. Good. Well, you haven't helped me at all yet, Kipre. Give me something. Who recruited you. Who you might know. Any plans you know of…anything. We know that there are more of you, we know that you have been killing the local soldiers and civil servants, and we know a certain wanted individual passed through here on her way north." *"Know"* might have been a strong word. "And before you start telling me that you have nothing to do with any of that, I want you to remember that you wouldn't be sitting here if someone else hadn't given us your name. This is not us deciding if you were involved. This is you deciding how harsh the consequences will be. Whether you are willing to help yourself or not. The man before you made the right choice, and so you sit here, where he sat. Think on that. Again."

Kipre's eyes only widened. There was no trace of deception there. Syl despised himself, seeing what was reflected there. What if the last prisoner had just named names? Those he hated, or maybe just those he could think of. People would say anything for the pain to stop, an inconvenient fact recognized even by the Vigil's judiciars. Not all confessions were equal. Part of himself was screaming at him to stop, wondering how he could treat these people, anyone, like this. But that wasn't the only voice in the back of his head. Besides, the pounding behind his eyes was worse than ever. Pain left very little room for empathy.

*"I had you going, didn't I?"*

Instead of answering, Kipre started to break down, a stream of words that Syl barely kept up with pouring out of him, all directed toward Vali, who listened, almost as wide-eyed as the prisoner.

Leon closed the dam. Striding forward, the scrawny man delivered a deceptively powerful backhand strike that sent Kipre sprawling out of his chair. Syl heard something crack. Leon went back to his table while the merchant gathered himself on the floor, blood leaking from his nose.

Syl stretched backwards toward Vali. "Well?"

A worried look. A glance to Liora, as if for support.

"Don't fucking look at her; look at me. Tell me what he said."

He shrugged, clearly uncomfortable down here. "More or less the same."

Another sigh, longer and more heartfelt this time. Syl really hated having to resort to this. What an awful position this bastard was putting him in. He glared again at the prisoner, who was shaking now, but had managed to pull himself back into his chair. His eyes were making darting motions towards the door of the room. Kipre had undoubtedly heard rumors of the others who had sat here before him.

Leon raised an eyebrow. A question. They had all gone through this enough that the order of things had become a pattern. A horrible, awful pattern. Syl's stomach knotted as he nodded.

Leon strode forward, grin stretching a bit wider. He had been so patient, after all.

"Wait, wait, wait!"

"Yes?" Syl asked, hopeful.

Kipre spoke slowly, taking care to enunciate his words. "This is Getacia, yes? We are in the empire. I am a citizen. You cannot torture me!"

Leon started chuckling, pausing a step before the man. Kipre looked up at him, a nervous smile taking root there. Maybe it was the good sort of laughter?

Syl couldn't understand how he could possibly believe that, but hope was a powerful drug. He made sure to crush that little spark underfoot. "No, you moron. You want to be a separatist? Have an independent Getacia? Today, and today only, we grant your request. We are no longer in the empire, and you certainly aren't a citizen." Syl frowned. "And what in all the worlds made you think that we can't torture you?"

He could see the light die in Kipre's eyes. Suddenly, he lashed out at Leon with one arm while lunging forward, a desperate last attempt to escape. For such a fat man, he moved admirably quickly. Leon knocked the hand aside and brutally clotheslined Kipre back into the chair. Kipre gasped for breath as Leon pulled him back before he tipped over.

Same questions, same answers, same patterns. It was like a bad dream. A play he had seen too many times. One that had been entertaining once—exciting, even. A third sigh. Even Syl thought that the last one might have been a bit self-indulgent. He could recognize the signs. There was nothing more pitiable than self-pity. Melodrama was for children and actors. He was a professional. Time to work.

"Bind him."

Vali was already moving forward, rope in hand. There was the briefest struggle, but with the rest of them there, it was a foregone conclusion, like a rabbit struggling against wolves. So much energy expended for so little result. Eventually, the rabbit was trussed and staring at Syl. No, not a rabbit. Syl could see the hate now. And if he looked a little harder, he thought he could see a small smile of resignation.

*"I had you going, didn't I? You believed me. They always do."*

"You and your kind are a stain on the world, and I pray to the gods you never know peace. May you never know the peace of the Rift and pass straight into hell." Kipre's voice picked up speed, the air of a long-thought-out curse or prayer dissolving into incoherence as Leon closed the distance. He scrabbled backwards in his chair. "May everyone you ever love die screaming and burning and choking on ash and ... *you!*" He bared his teeth at Vali, spittle flying as the hate became hysterical. Syl could hardly understand him anymore. "Traitor, cur, faithless, a thousand deaths would be too—"

Leon's fist shot forward into Kipre's nose, cutting off the stream of invectives. Sputtering and dripping blood onto his nightclothes, he tried to compose himself, a deep, shuddering breath ending with him coughing on his own blood and mucus.

"You won't be getting anything out of me," he managed. "I won't talk."

"Yes, yes, I'm sure you won't." Syl nodded to Leon.

The cutting began. He talked. The answers started to change. Syl hated this—this whole process, the pattern, Kipre, Leon, himself. He even found room for Vali and Liora in that boundless hate. Their judgment hung above him, a silent jury. They thought that somehow they were above this, as if this didn't need to be done. He forced himself to watch. Another reminder that it was the old Syl who had gotten them killed. The trusting one. The one who saw the honest face in his neighbors. The one who let memory become weakness for a Stained that needed to die, and the mercy that would see their world drown in ash again. Let this be another bitter lesson, a medicine that had to be taken regularly. Never again.

Another drop fell, diluting the blood.

---

What was left of Kipre wasn't smiling anymore. They had a few more names, and the city of Seven Rivers held a few less secrets for them. Those answers would see them knocking on more doors tonight, working their way up the chain as fast as they could, before whoever was at the top had a chance to try to slip through one of the gates. It was a good thing that they had marched north with a full cohort. They had enough soldiers for their nightly raids and for a suitable security plan. None of them had the greatest trust in the local garrison. All the loyal ones, the dependable ones, were being picked off each night.

It didn't help that the city here was as difficult to search as it was possible for a city to be. The pretentious, sprawling manses of the traders—ambitious risers who made their living bringing goods back and forth over the mountains, using the rivers that spread northward in every direction from the massive dam and locks of Seven Rivers itself. The cobbled-together houses that lined those waterways, the homes of those who helped those merchants make good on their promises. And all that to say nothing of the absolutely mad tendency of the city's poor to carve their homes into the dam itself, which hung above the city like the hand of the god of the mountains, chipping their tenements a little higher every year. Hopefully not too deep. Syl wasn't afraid of heights, not exactly, but he considered it prudent to respect them, and their night raids up those windy scaffolds had been harrowing.

Nothing like the imperial capital, Heliopolis. Clearing it out had been the first true act of the Emperor a dozen cycles ago, and the effort and crowning achievement of a generation. It was a shining beacon of hope, bright towers reaching higher than anything even the best engineers could build today. Compared to Heliopolis, this place was chaos, a city grown too large for its walls and spilling upward and outward.

Syl would be happy to leave this city, but not as happy as he would leaving this room. They had all been working on their separate leads, but Syl would be overjoyed to never see this prison again after the last few days. It made the passage through the mountains, dragging disagreeable mules through early snowdrifts, seem like a pleasant memory of a holiday. The following legions would need to come quickly if they wanted a chance of making it through before the winter. It didn't matter how high the walls of Seven Rivers were, or how defensible the garrison's commander assured them it was. Being marooned in a rebellious province without support held very little appeal.

Regardless, they were done here for now. Syl, Liora, and Vali made ready to leave, but Leon pulled a chair closer to the man, crossing one leg over the other and tapping his own cheek with the bloody knife, like an artist wondering where to put his brush next.

"Why don't you just put him out of his misery?" Syl asked. There was no one he had been with longer, but Leon still found ways to disgust him occasionally. Something had broken in him long ago, or maybe had never been there. Which made him wonder all the more why Liora was staring at him, looking at Syl as if he were the one with the knife.

"Oh, you know there's always more. I don't mind. I'll stay."

Syl shook his head, motioning the others toward the door. Leon could stay down here if he liked. And if he was honest with himself, he wasn't sure who the show of disapproval was for. Leon could be a ruthless, bloody-minded savage. But—and Syl knew this was why he always appreciated having Leon on the team—he was probably right. There was always more. Someone had to get their hands dirty.

# A PRIVILEGE

V ali suspected that he had mastered the art of invisibility. It seemed the only explanation. After traveling through the passes and asking a few cursory questions, the Hunters barely seemed to acknowledge their Getacian companions' presence. They assigned them guard duties more out of politeness than anything else, Vali thought. If they were lucky, they had the opportunity to serve as a mostly unnecessary translator and witness the team's real work. It had been Vali's turn last night, all through this morning. His lip curled as he marched up after Syl and Liora, leaving the psychopath, Leon, alone with that poor merchant below.

The Vigil, the judiciars, the Hunters—hell, even the torture itself... Vali knew the empire depended on these tools. Unity depended on these tools. He told himself that there was no time more appropriate for their application than now. They had caught and interrogated at least a score of traitors in half as many days, and the air of anticipation lay heavy over the whole city, like the early morning fogs that descended from the mountains, spilling over the lip of the dam in waves. However, knowing something was necessary and seeing it, being part of it, were very different things. He was looking forward to returning to where the fight was a bit more straightforward.

At the entrance to the prison, off to the side of the garrison's main barracks, Vali split off from the Hunters to join Lucan and Marika where they stood huddled against the morning chill around a small brazier. They nodded to him morosely as they pulled their cloaks tighter and stamped from foot to foot in a vain attempt to keep warm.

"Ho, Vali." Lucan made room for him.

"Mari. Lucan."

What else was there to say? He pushed in between them and started to warm his hands while surveying the town as it came alive, another morning dawning, and all grateful that they hadn't been the ones taken from their house in the middle of the night. His newfound power of invisibility was less perfect with the townspeople. They would glance their way before looking away quickly. There had been a couple friendly overtures at first, before the team had started working their leads. Now the people here had learned to avoid this area, skirting around and taking side streets. The bridge by them, once one of the main thoroughfares of the city, was practically abandoned. If any had no choice but to pass by, they did so quickly and with eyes lowered.

Vali didn't mind. He alternated between being embarrassed working as an attachment to the team, and disgust and frustration with the townspeople. There were some from the South, but most of the Getacians here came from Northern clans and had never taken well to imperial rule or customs. It was easy to look down on them, but he knew that was how most Helians saw all Getacians. Pale savages, too stupid not to build directly into and from the ruins left behind. It pained Vali to see the casual defacement of the reliefs that ran up the dam and along the great walls, scenes of wyrms and armies and battles chipped apart to add heft into the concrete mixes poured into all the new houses. "House Costranis" itself was his father's own attempt to Helianize their own clannish origins, though it would probably take the sort of torture they'd put Kipre through to get him to say that aloud.

"The captain really fucked us on this one, eh?" Lucan joked, grinning at Vali through the wispy beard he had decided to cultivate.

Vali knew Lucan was trying to cheer him up. His mood had worsened every day here, waiting and watching. He didn't really feel like being cheered up. A chance to prove himself, indeed. It would have been better to stick with Captain Askaris's unit, ranging the borders.

Vali grunted noncommittally.

"True, true," Lucan said. "Such a way with words, Vali." He pointed to where a group was passing by. "At least you're not one of those poor sops, eh? Might make me a shitty person, but always cheers me up to see someone having a worse go of it than me."

Vali watched as the small group passed in front, a squad of guards herding along three haggard-looking men and a woman to the city's central square. He recognized one from the night before, now limping along, bound and looking half dead already. Already, he could hear the anxious murmuring in the distance as a crowd awaited what had become a daily spectacle.

"Nothing like a hanging to bring people together," Marika muttered.

"Yes? And what would you prefer?" he asked, rounding on her. She'd been like this the last few days. Didn't matter that he agreed with her cynicism and disgust; that only made it worse. "What should we do with the people that try to rebel, Mari? A slap and a warning?"

"There's always prison," Lucan added cheerily.

"Nah." Vali shook his head. "We were young, but don't tell me you don't remember what Getacia was like before the empire. Constant clan warfare and every asshole with an inkling of ability to pull from the Rift thinking to make himself some warlord sorcerer. Didn't matter that all they got was a trickle this far from Heliopolis." He got even angrier as he could feel himself mimicking his father. Was it his fault the old man was right? "Fucking disaster is what it was. That's what these bastards want to bring back."

"And all *I'm* saying is maybe there is another way," Marika said. "Think for yourself. Gods, I swear you sound thicker than usual when you parrot your father. And don't talk to me like that. You're being an asshole yourself."

Vali was still angry, but she looked hurt, and it broke his heart to see it. There had been something unspoken between them for the last year or so—unspoken and unacted upon, which had made their comfortable childhood friendship strained and awkward. She was right about him being an asshole though.

"Look, it's been a long few days with the team," Vali said with a sigh. "But you know I'm right."

"Maybe," she said, relaxing, if not totally convinced. Apology hopefully accepted.

"It will be better once the legions get here," Vali added. "We can get out of here and head north."

"I won't be sad to be done with this skulking about," Lucan said, clearly happy for the argument to have stalled. "Still, don't fancy facing any actual Stained. You hear about the ones they took down right before we came along?"

"Yes, yes," Vali said dismissively. He didn't entirely believe Leon's stories. The wiry man struck him as a stranger to mental stability and constantly looked as if he was in on a joke on the rest of them. "Point is, we know fighting. Good at it, even. And..." he said, sparing a look toward the square where cheers had started, "... it's a lot cleaner than this business."

Marika looked at him thoughtfully. "We'll see, I guess."

Vali wasn't sure at all what she meant. He settled for an awkward nod, hoping that was the end of that.

Thankfully, their shift was at an end. He could see their replacements wandering toward them, late as always. Members of an auxiliary unit from the Far South, desert dwellers stranded in the snowy North as part of the cohort accompanying the team. Yet in some ways, they were far more like Vali and his friends than the locals. He could see the disdainful glances they directed at the folk who gave them a wide berth as they made their way down the broad street.

Vali waved at the incoming squad. "Let's go," he said, turning away.

Lucan was just as eager to leave, but Marika stood there, listening to the distant clamor. "I'll catch up," she said, walking toward the square as if in a trance. "At least one of us should watch."

Vali looked to Lucan, who shrugged. "Be careful," he called. And what was that about watching? There would be a crowd already. Maybe...

"Do you think she's still mad at me?" he asked Lucan. "Should I go with her?"

Lucan smiled tightly before throwing a lanky arm up around his shoulders and pulling him away. "Vali, it's a lucky thing you're a good-looking bastard."

# MISSING PIECES

"The problem with our search thus far is namely that we have found nothing." Domarik surveyed the map of the city before them on the table in a clinical way, a medicus who understood his patient was dying, but couldn't quite figure out why. Those dark gray eyes popped up to look at each of them in turn, sandwiched between scrunched brows and the delicate lenses precariously perched on that mountain of a nose. "Murders of patrols have not stopped. No Stained have been found. And most damningly, we have failed to determine the mechanism by which they have transported runaway prisoners and arms shipments to the far northern provinces. So," he asked, splaying his fingers on the map and causing the seams to stretch, "who wants to tell me why we're failing?"

Syl cleared his throat. As Domarik's Secondary, the blame was coming his way sooner or later. Domarik was not the sort to cool down or get over it; he might as well get out in front of this storm that had been building all week. "Domarik, over the last two weeks here, we've made inroads on three distinct, well-organized separatist cells. Over twenty-five individuals arrested and interrogated, five safehouses found, and four caches seized. We—"

"I didn't ask for an inventory, Syl. Twenty-five, twenty-five hundred—I do not care. What about last night? Anything new from the interrogations this morning?"

"They didn't know anything," Liora said with too-obvious self-disgust.

"They didn't know *much*," Syl corrected, catching Domarik's look. *Damn her, couldn't she at least look out for herself a bit? Was that too much to ask?* "A few more potential conspirators for us to track down and check in on tonight."

"So, nothing."

Syl didn't bother correcting him. Domarik was in one of his moods. He had been hunting down Stained for twenty years, had dedicated his entire life to the Vigil, and still seemed to reach an existential level of frustration when their investigations stalled. Syl had never asked about Domarik's past, and it was difficult to think of their Primary as anyone but the brutally efficient man he was today. It was impossible to imagine people like Domarik as children. The fact that a second Riftgate had opened and the slow march to the next cataclysm had begun was reason enough for them to all be on edge, but Domarik was obsessed, sleeping even less than the rest of them, poring over maps and leading most of the raids personally.

"These small fry don't matter. What matters is the *how* and the *what*. The *how* being how this city continues to operate as a smuggling hub in the province under the watch of the largest imperial garrison north of the Severan Mountains. And the *what*," he said, rumbling voice growing in accusatory volume, "is that the same imperial garrison cannot move about their own city safely, and so has settled on retreating to and defending their own barracks, as if already under siege."

"Vigilus Hunter Primaris, my men have been on constant patrols in the city," Captain-Major Beharis protested. The thin officer and commander of their accompanying cohort stood almost at attention, too-big ears on full display with his winged helmet tucked under an arm. "There is only so much I can do regarding the garrison and its commander," he finished lamely.

There were some legion officers who would have tried to buck for control and would have assumed that a title like *Vigilus Hunter Primaris* surely fell somewhere among the many titles littered underneath *Imperial Legion Captain-Majoris*, but Captain Beharis did not suffer from such a misapprehension. A month crossing the mountains and working with the team in the city had only seen his posture relax from "ramrod attention" to "almost at attention."

"Relax, Captain," Domarik said. Beharis nodded in grateful agreement, not relaxing an inch. "We appreciate your efforts. The pace of operations here would have been impossible without your soldiers. I'm not meaning you. That blowhard in command is the issue. One of the issues. Colonel Gralinis." Domarik clenched his fists on the table as if it were Gralinis's wobbly dewlap between them. With an effort, he unfolded them. "Without full control of his garrison, it's like fighting missing an arm. And he's only half the problem. Gralinis couldn't keep putting us off if the prefect wasn't supporting him, and that's the only man here who can claim a level of authority to compete with our charge. And all he wants to do is stick his head in the sand until the Twins arrive. Kass, any headway with the noble houses here? Any of the prefect's hangers-on?"

Kass gave what could only be described as a luxurious sigh. Syl wasn't sure what separated it from his own, but there was an indefinable something there. "Domarik. Fearless leader. My father's name only goes so far. I exhausted any true social calls the first week here. 'Oathknight' doesn't hold quite the same sway as 'minister's daughter and heir,'" she said bitterly. "Now I'm inviting myself to their houses for more polite versions of interrogations. Not that they answer much. Lots of talk, lots of excellent tea and delicious little foods, very little in the way of substance. They're all so tiringly nervous."

"And the imperial officials?"

"Hmm. Yes. By the by, it's going to be a while before I forgive you for assigning me two weeks of talking to bureaucrats. Less talk, far worse refreshments, and even less substance. For all the prefect's senile affectations, he appears to have an iron grip on the apparatus here. They do as he says and toe the party line. Don't know how he managed it, but I get the distinct impression that more or less all of the officials here are out-and-out *centrists*." She spat the last word out and shuddered.

"Are you done?"

"I do believe I am."

"So, no progress?"

"That's not fair, Domarik," she pouted. "You're going to hurt my feelings. Unlike Syl, our brave and indefatigable Secondary, I have those."

Domarik ignored her. "Lucky? Anything?"

The young bondmage had been unconsciously fidgeting with the medallion underneath his shirt. He dropped it like he'd been burned and looked up at Domarik. "What?"

"Lucky. Pay attention, damn it. Have there been any arcane signatures in the city? Or anywhere that might be helpful to us?"

"There are quite a few to the north," Lucky said hurriedly, caught off guard and in the crossfire. "Sir. Almost every day. For two straight days when we first arrived, there was a cluster of signatures at..." He scrunched his face, searching for the information. "... north-northeast by the compass.

Yes, that's right. But definitely outside the city. Hard to tell exactly how far without starting to follow the afterglow right away."

"Lucky, that is not very helpful." Liora looked genuinely disappointed.

Given enough time to recover, Lucky's face underwent a distinct transformation. Lucky, the eager-to-please bondmage, could only be found for moments at a time. He shrugged, his usual sullen exterior pulled back over his earlier startle. "Sorry."

"Most useless bloodhound I've ever met," Leon said to the ceiling from where he lay on a couch.

Domarik rounded on Leon. "And do you have anything better? Syl and Kass have produced nothing. Meanwhile, you've been running your side investigation—gods know why I let you—into your would-be criminal peers on this side of the mountains. Have you come up with anything? Or do you just want to keep sitting there?"

Leon straightened a bit from where he had sunk into the luxurious furniture that nestled against the wood-paneled walls of the study, driven by some atavistic impulse from a decade in the legions. Quickly, his own nature wrested control back, and he slouched even further into the cushions.

"You really are a dick when you're angry, Domarik."

"That's 'Vigilus Hunter Primaris' to you. Do you have something to report or not? And would it kill you to show some professionalism?"

"It might, it might." He imitated Kass's sigh. It was impressively close.

"Leon," Syl said. Leon could be frustrating at the best of times, but having Captain Beharis in here to see how dysfunctional one of the supposed elite Hunter teams could be up close was rubbing him the wrong way.

"Syl," Leon mocked. But he stood up, pushing his way into the circle around the table. "Fine. As it happens to be, you're lucky I'm the sort of professional you need. Unlike Lucky. Between raids, interrogations, and helping keep track of those brain-dead Gets, I've found time to build some contacts," he said, with the saintly air of the long-suffering. "Long patrols through the whorehouses, grueling surveillance missions in the taverns, and bloody dice battles. It's been rough going. But!" he exclaimed, holding up a finger to forestall Domarik. "All that self-sacrifice has paid off. I've found out how they've been moving the shipments out of the city. After a few well-placed—"

"Leon." Domarik gave a long exhale. "Why didn't you mention this at the beginning of the meeting?"

"And rob myself of this moment?"

"It's called building tension," Kass said with approval. "Good job, Leon, you magnificent little pissant."

"Thank you, Kassie, you bitch. Anyway, before I was interrupted... You know how they've blocked the tunnels here from that northern fortress city, Bal Maru? No need to answer, Gralinis wouldn't stop bragging to us about it when we got here, we all know. Well, he's not wrong, but there's a channel."

"Shit," Syl said.

"What does that mean?" asked Liora. Most of the others looked confused as well. Only Syl and Leon had ever had to fight down there before.

"It's like an underground canal," Syl explained. "Most of the passages down there are dry, mostly, but there are some that are filled with water. Some look like they were made that way, and others... Well, our best guess was that they were normal passages that got flooded when upstream points were damaged. Bad idea to be down in those when it rains. Suppose it's not surprising, here of all places."

"How do they use this channel?" Domarik asked. "And why do they bother? Considering the number of cells you've found, surely it would be easier for them to bribe the guards or have their own people on duty."

"According to them, there are a few wells in the city that they've modified—made? No idea, doesn't matter—to reach the channel." Leon started using a small piece of charcoal to mark points on the map, making a rough line that went from near the dam to the wall. "They send the goods that way. People too, maybe? As for why the channels? Maybe it's easier? Gods know there are enough waterways up here to divert." He shrugged. "There's a reason I'm not in charge. I've done my job."

Domarik had taken off his glasses to rub at the bridge of his nose. "Good work, Leon."

"Thanks, Boss." Leon positively beamed.

"Captain Beharis, let's have men down there to block these wells off by this—"

"Domarik," Syl interrupted. "Wait a moment. Leon, who are they sending the shipments to?"

"Whoever pays them, I assume. Other upstanding citizens farther north, separatists... I imagine it's all the same to them. Most of the friends I've bought here aren't political. Just opportunists who don't like taxes and don't mind dabbling in a little light human trafficking. My sort of people."

"Lovely," Liora muttered.

"Domarik," Syl continued quickly, "we can block them off now, but that's always an option. Better to watch first. Surveillance will tell us even more. Some well-placed follows wouldn't hurt either, if Beharis here has some people suited for it. Besides, it's too late to stop anything important they might have been sending along to the separatists. We'll keep pushing on our end and see if we can flush anything out before the legions arrive this week."

"None of this is a good enough argument against sealing them off."

"I have another idea for once the legions get here."

"Which is?"

The last war up here had been awful in so many ways, but there had been some fun times. It wasn't his fault that he found masterfully engineered arcane explosions fascinating, even if the flamewardens, that order of relic priests, was murderously jealous of their secrets. Syl couldn't help the flare of excitement. "How many flamewardens do you think are coming with the Twins? I think it might be appropriate to send a gift north to let them know we're coming."

# PRACTICE MAKES...LESS AWFUL

In the golden-reds of the late afternoon, sweat dripped from Vali's bare torso, steaming in the cold air. Across from him, Lucan wasn't grinning anymore. That would have required too much energy. His thin chest heaved, the point of the wooden practice sword facing Vali wavering in the air like an old man's accusing finger.

It cheered him up to no end, knowing he still had the edge between them. Lucan had the reach on him, but Vali had everything else. His breath steadied, the point held true, his grip tight, but not too tight as he prepared for their next exchange. To put his friend back in the dirt again. The expression of all the little lessons ingrained by his father and a half dozen tutors over the years. It wasn't Lucan's fault he was about to lose again. It was theirs. And the fact that he had half a hundred pounds of muscle on Lucan. That didn't hurt either.

They started to circle again, wary, feet placed smoothly in the cleared patch of the great house's yard where they stayed with the team. Vali had never even seen the family that had "volunteered" their house, but he had to admire their taste. The house had a wonderful courtyard, pine trees rising above the walls and blocking the sounds and sights of the city beyond. Their breathing echoed off the walls and made the space seem smaller than it was. Marika was seated on a chair nearby, coat unbuttoned and a surly expression on her face as she sipped at a skin of wine she had found somewhere. She had been like this since the hanging, and Vali was tired of trying to figure it out.

Ignoring her, Vali chanced a glance upward, toward the balcony where some of the Hunters had taken to watching them. He saw Syl, Liora, and Kassara this time. Again, Vali caught himself staring longer than necessary at Kassara. Kass, they called her. With her tanned complexion and those long, dark tresses, Vali couldn't help himself. She smirked at him, and Vali felt an idiot's grin come to his lips as she looked down at him. With an effort, he pulled his attention back to the bout—and immediately saw why she was amused.

Lucan lunged forward, closing the distance. Any thought of treating his opponent's distraction as an unfair advantage had disappeared some two or three blows before. With an undignified squawk, Vali threw himself backward, rolling awkwardly and trying to meet Lucan's furious onslaught. Within the space of a set, Vali managed to recover. Furious and embarrassed now, he whipped his practice blade in looping arcs and brutal jabs, eventually landing a breath-snatching thrust to his friend's midsection, but not before Lucan had caught his left leg with a glancing blow.

"Unnngh."

"Sorry about that," Vali said, helping Lucan up. He wasn't sorry. Glowing with the victory and proud of his recovery, he glanced up to their impromptu spectators, where Kassara flashed him a brilliant smile.

"Sloppy."

Also from above, a simple statement, brutal in its summary judgment. Annoyed, Vali looked over to where Syl stood, preparing to leave.

"What did you say?" Vali demanded.

"Did you not hear me?" Syl asked.

Thrown off, Vali looked to his friends for help, but found none. "Yes, I heard you, but—"

"Then why did you ask?"

Something about this man consistently enraged Vali. He was shorter, slighter, and even—Vali knew he was being vain here—less handsome than him. But every time he was around, he made Vali feel especially worthless, the village idiot who was inexplicably allowed to wander, inflicting his stupidity on all and sundry.

It was Marika who came to his rescue while he was thinking of a thoroughly uncivilized response. "Then show us," she called, not bothering to move from where she slouched.

That gave Syl pause. He considered them.

Feeling the wine, Marika pushed her luck. "If you're going to tell us how bad we are, then at least help us be better. Or do you just like to talk shit?"

Syl nodded, reaching a decision. "Fair enough." He vaulted the balustrade and landed with an eerie softness in the yard. "Who's first?"

There was another moment of hesitation before Vali spoke. "I am."

He stomped forward, shrugging his broad shoulders and hopping foot to foot. He shook the acid out of arms corded with muscle. They always told Vali he was built like one of the many gods. He always liked to imagine it had to be one of the gods of war. Time to show this arrogant bastard why. Show Syl why Captain Askaris had recommended him for this mission.

---

A few minutes and more bruises than he could count later, Vali once again found himself on the ground, spitting blood. The rivers of sweat had long ago turned into a flood. He was covered in lumps and sweat and dirt. Groaning, he pulled himself back to his feet.

Syl watched, impassive as ever. A single line of sweat worked its way down his temple, catching the dim light of the setting sun. It was the only sign of the systematic beating he had been administering.

At least Vali knew why the contest had been so unequal. Syl had taken his shirt off as well, and it had been a transformation. Almost every bit of the Hunter's skin was covered with intricate runes, whorls, and arcane patterns, chasing one another around in a design beyond Vali's perception. Small comfort against his aching sides, but it helped. He remembered what it had been like to feel suffused with strength, with the world around him taking on new details and a richness of sensation that left what he saw now feeling drab and lifeless.

"This isn't fair," he said.

Syl looked bored. "I agree. You're awful at this."

"No," Vali snarled. "I mean you're an oathknight. You're channeling. Everyone knows it's impossible to beat someone channeling one on one."

There was a sparkle of amusement in those gray eyes now. "Really? That's good to know—I'll tell that to the next person I fight. The next competent one, at least."

Lucan let out a chuckle at that one, but Vali glared him into silence. His friend was enjoying seeing him put in his place a little too much.

"And besides," Syl continued, "I'm not using that right now. You're just not as good as you think you are."

Vali blinked, stunned. "What do you mean?"

"I mean, my thick friend, that I am not using anything extra right now. Do you think we can wander around, using that power for no reason all the time?"

"Well...yes. Don't you?" Vali knew he would. Why would you ever let go of that feeling, even for a heartbeat?

A real laugh from Syl. That was so rare, it made Vali smile unconsciously, a bit nervously, before forcing a frown on again. He despised himself for how much he craved this man's approval.

"Gods, no! That would burn me up." Syl unconsciously traced a finger along his arm, following the patterns. "Not to mention the poor bastards back in Heliopolis providing the juice." His voice turned serious. "It's something that should only be used when needed. Power always comes with a price. Or at least, it should."

"What's the price, then?" asked Marika.

"It's arcane energy from the Rift, but at the end of the day, it's still just energy. There's only so much the body can use at once, and it takes a toll over a long period, both on us and the conduits. It's the same for the flamewardens and their tools."

"What toll?"

Marika was persistent, and Vali wasn't sure if he was more appreciative of his luck at having her as a friend, or the break her questions were giving him. He focused on catching his breath, leaving the questions to the curious. Vali knew what he needed to know.

"It's... There is supposed to be degeneration. We age faster, for one."

"Degeneration of what?"

Syl frowned. "You've got a lot of questions."

Marika shrugged, not disagreeing.

From above, Kass was watching, in that bored cat way she had, body melting around the railing in a way that defied examination or physiology. And Vali should know; he had been examining her physiology at every opportunity that presented itself. She butted in now.

"Don't you know, my precious naifs? Syl's a simple soldier at heart. One of the Helian legions' finest," she said, puffing out her chest where she lay and deepening her voice. "Good, wheat-fed stock. The iron core of the empire." She blew out all the air noisily. "Gods, my father would have killed to have a couple of Syls in his retinue, always scowling about behind him. But it's not his fault. No one *really* knows. Or at least, none of us. It's not as if the judiciars go about telling everyone their deepest, darkest secrets. That's supposed to go the other way around. All they tell us is enough for us not to burst our little hearts out, or those of the conduits bonded to us. They do seem to care about the second part a little less. Saw it happen once in training," she mused. "Six conduits bleeding out of every orifice you can think of when their oathknight tried to pull a little too much. Disgusting."

For this whole speech, Syl stood very still, eyes closed and breaths coming deeper and steadier with every second. Little prayers to one of the deities of patience. Despite his increasingly undeniable attraction to her, Vali had no doubt that Kass was one of their greatest proselytizers.

"Are you done?" Syl asked.

"I forgot, you never did like to be shown up. Yes, my darling Secondary, I am done. This was getting boring anyway." She unspooled herself and drifted back into the house. "Have fun!" she called behind her. "And don't be late! Domarik would kill you."

Syl waited until she was gone to cross to the middle of the courtyard. He used his own wooden blade to lazily flick Vali's across to him. Vali snatched it out of the air, eyes never leaving Syl. He settled into his ready stance, despite the ache in his legs and back and...well, everything.

"Back to something useful. Though maybe it will help you understand. Earlier, that was just me. Do you think you're some sort of master swordsman because you can chop up some barbarians or beat on your friends? The bonds only amplify what you can already do. It doesn't fix poor technique, bad habits, or"—he walked up to Vali, poking his feet into position until he grunted, satisfied—"or shoddy footwork."

Vali was frustrated, but this time with himself. Damn him, but Syl was right. He had become complacent. *Never be too proud to learn.* His father's words came back to him. One of his favorite aphorisms for him and Sorin.

"So, teach me. Teach us," he corrected. Vali swallowed. "Please."

Syl eyed him wryly. "That looked like it hurt."

Vali couldn't tell if he was talking about the last blow or his request, but he couldn't help laughing. "A little bit. Will you teach us?"

"What do you think I've been doing?"

"Beating the shit out of him," Marika interjected. Was that smugness Vali heard in her voice?

Syl snorted. "Alright. Alright. Maybe we can include more talking next time. But the beatings will continue until technique improves." He squinted toward the clouds, where the setting sun fought through. "Gather around. All of you this time. There's time for a couple more beatings before this evening's dinner with the prefect, I think. Which, by the way, you're invited to. Apparently. All of you. Which means you're coming."

"Thanks?" Marika said, summing up Vali's feeling about that invitation nicely.

As for him, he set his feet, preparing for another onslaught. Night raids and torture and getting beaten by surly Hunters...and now dinner parties. It really was a long road to knighthood.

# FIRESIDE STORIES

O nce upon a time, Darya heard a story. It had been a good one, as far as stories went. It had possessed all the right parts. A brave hero, a beautiful love to be saved, and a terrifying monster to overcome. Powerful weapons, loyal companions, and wise old men helped the hero along his journey, a noble horse carrying him far and wide and even beyond mortal lands. She remembered loving that story, sitting cross-legged and wide-eyed around the fire with the other children, even if she couldn't remember all the details.

It had all been a steaming pile of horse shit, Darya decided.

All the details had been missing or were wrong. Shivering, she pulled her blanket tighter around her where she sat, huddled with Alina. Relics? Magical swords? The coin tucked close to her skin was more misery than it was worth, and no gifting spirit appeared when she rubbed it between freezing hands. Not that she could bring herself to throw it away. More than anything ancient, it had been Mikael's. What she really could have used right then was a magic blanket. The stories forgot to mention that after a few days in snowy mountain passes, a damp, patchy fur cover caused more misery than it was worth.

The brave hero? She had loved pretending to be the hero, and some-times—though Mikael had made fun of her—the beautiful damsel that was in constant need of rescue. It would be nice to be rescued; she still agreed with that in the strongest terms. But she hardly felt heroic, and certainly didn't need to see a reflection to know "beautiful" would be a stretch. Perhaps a hero would settle for a dispossessed chieftain's daughter with windburned cheeks and a dripping nose?

Probably not. Darya had never heard of a hero rescuing one of those.

As far as loyal companions? She furtively surveyed the woolen and fur lumps that dotted the snowy ground between the horses, all sheltered behind and beneath the closest thing to cover they had come across since they had shaken off the snow this morning. The wind howled in eddies into their cove, battering them and reminding them all that it would have them again the next day. Lonely howls in the distance kept even those who might have slept through the night awake. In principle, Darya was fascinated with the idea that corners of the world were filled with all manner of creatures from worlds beyond their own—remnants like drakes and arachni and koronae, along with countless other leftovers without names from the Breaking. Her fascination preferred a level of distance, however, and those howls were a bit too close. There were enough threats close at hand.

Red-rimmed eyes stared jealously at neighbors with warmer clothing, and more than one scuffle had ended with bodies in the snow, the frictions between tribes brittle-hard in these cold mountains. Loyal in a fight against outsiders, maybe. The bowlegged steppe tribesmen were, by and large, a leering, insular, vicious lot outside of those instances. The only reason the great Arkhan had been able to unite the fractious and treacherous chieftains was due to their common threat: freezing to death on the steppe plains, which yielded a little less grass each year, and a little more snow. The next cataclysm was always coming, sure as the Fallen that still roamed the Middle Lands, and if they were on the wrong side of these mountains when it arrived, there wouldn't be enough of them left to make ten tribes, much less a thousand.

And wise men? Darya spat, but there wasn't enough saliva, and the spittle dripped down her face. Stiff, gloved mitts wiped it away, scraping her raw face with the frozen residue of the last few times she had done the same. Vels. Fucking Vels. Saved her, mocked her, promised answers, gave mysterious riddles, and then disappeared, leaving her to freeze to death in the mountains. She would have loved to trade her wise old man in.

Darya refrained from thinking ill of her new borrowed horse though. Noble steed the hardy little gelding was not, but he looked miserable enough up here without her judgment. Anyway, she would need his help again tomorrow.

Alina shifted, and Darya couldn't help but resent it. Any movements disturbed the tiny, fragile pocket of body heat they were managing to maintain.

The larger woman stood up, shaking off some of the snow. "I've got to take a shit."

Darya nodded numbly. The stories really missed quite a lot.

Alina marched away through the snow from the dim light of the small fires that came from the center of the encampment. They all had fires the first few nights, but there was nothing more to burn up here. Darya knew sleep wouldn't come easily or at all with how cold she was. The last few nights had been fitful, half-waking nightmares of exhaustion. A few hours to stiffen up before Taharuk called the march again. After a week straight of wandering these damnable mountains, the last two mornings had seen some of those fur and woolen lumps returned to the landscape as the warband moved on. Spring food for whatever lived up here. Already, Darya thought she could point out a few that wouldn't be able to drag themselves up, shivering and beyond sense. No one moved to help them. Darya couldn't judge; there was nothing she could do either. She could just as well be one of those lumps tomorrow. She had been delaying her decision, moving in a fog of grief and misery, but it was looking more and more like the mountains were going to decide for her.

From the center of the camp, another bundle started moving toward her. She watched apprehensively as he came closer, the gap-toothed grin on his grizzled face clearly meant to set her at ease. It did not.

He spoke the Common tongue, but his speech was thick with unfamiliar words, symptoms of a world broken apart for too long. And more than a little alcohol. He reeked of the fermented mare's milk that was one of the more constant aromas in the camps. Darya thought that the weight could have been replaced by more food, but everyone had their own priorities.

"Cold!" He rubbed his crossed arms, smiling before suddenly sitting down next to her. "I'm sorry about your brother. Really! Such a shame, what they did to him." He touched two fingers to his forehead, eyes closed.

Darya was profoundly uncomfortable, but wasn't sure what to do. She looked anxiously back into the darkness. Where was Alina?

"Thank you?" she managed.

"Yes, yes. Very sad. Now you are alone," he said.

"No, I'm not alone," she insisted. "My friend is here. She'll be back soon."

Darya looked around nervously, hoping that perhaps one of the other survivors from their shunned group might at least pay attention. She had come to know some of the others who had survived the ambush at least a little. Altan, Ganzig, and Kasym had all been at least willing to speak with her since. But none stirred. Kasym looked up from under his hood, but didn't move. The others kept their heads down, uninterested beyond their own misery.

"My name is Erbol," he continued, giving no sign that he sensed her discomfort.

"Thank you."

Why had she said that? Darya knew she needed to go.

She unwound numb limbs to stand, but a wiry arm shot out of the furs around Erbol and grabbed her own forearm with fingers that dug painfully tight. He was small, but surprisingly strong. He dragged her back down and drew a small, curved knife that he tapped against her cheek.

"Sit. Quiet."

Darya was too stunned to speak. She knew she should cry out, lash out, do anything, but found herself frozen, one of those that couldn't rise, even when their lives depended on it. It was as if she watched from above, some impassive observer. No, not impassive—horrified. She could watch, separate from the experience, as rough and clumsy hands started to paw through her and Alina's meager packs, pulling out the thin and already too-light bundles of wrapped meats and even that last little block of cheese she had been saving. It wasn't much, but every ounce meant another mile, a chance to make it out of the mountains. And she watched, prey-still, as he shifted to dig even deeper, a greedy child checking to see if there was more.

In those seconds, she imagined a hundred scenarios, vivid in her mind. She tackled him, beating at him with her small fists. She pulled her knife out and stabbed him in his side. Gouged his eyes, bit his face, slashed his throat—a thousand violent options spread before her, the endless branches of the world's worst tree. But at the end of all of them was the same thing: her beaten, freezing in the snow. Stabbed, leaking lifeblood draining away what little warmth she still had. Dead, dead, or soon to be dead. Why could she do something so awful in those swamps to save herself, but now was paralyzed with fear? If only her brother were here, or Alina. If only she were stronger, or braver, or anyone but herself. Instead, she did nothing, hating him, but hating herself even more. He was strong, and she was weak, so he took what he wanted. It was the way of their world. Darya could only hope that it stopped short of her life and that maybe someone else would intervene.

Even hoping for it, what happened next surprised her.

A fist came out of nowhere, sending Erbol flying back into the snow with a croak. His knife disappeared into a drift.

Alina. She had come back. Darya couldn't think of a time she had been happier to see someone.

Erbol tried to stand, but Alina was bigger and built like a wrestler. She was on him, pummeling his face, not giving him a chance to recover. Her face was impassive, as if this were only another unpleasant task that needed to be done. Some of the faces around them peered from their coverings in curiosity now, but they seemed as unwilling to involve themselves as before. Darya tried to stir, but found herself rooted there, watching the violence unfold from some separate, safe place.

Alina finally stood up, letting him free. Erbol scrambled to his feet, cursing, spitting pieces of a tooth out, and Darya seemed to return to her body, shaking and sick to her stomach. She was too shocked to say anything as Alina stood watching the man until she was sure he was gone. Good-natured laughter came from the group he returned to.

"What the fuck was that?" Alina hissed, standing over her.

"I don't know," Darya stuttered. "He came over here and started talking and..."

"No, I mean, why didn't you do anything?"

"What?"

"You just sat there! That little bundle," she said, pointing accusingly to where the foodstuffs were scattered, "is all we've got. That's your life right there. More importantly, it's mine. You can't just let people..." She struggled to find the words. "... you can't just let them take it. And they will if you do nothing. Now I probably can't go more than ten feet from the packs without someone else trying it."

"I..." Darya trailed off. She *had* just sat there. Why hadn't she moved, screamed? Done anything?

Alina leaned down, sweat glistening on her forehead under her hood. "Your brother is gone, Darya. *Gone.* He isn't coming back. He made me promise to take care of you way back, before he died, but I can't always protect you. I'm sorry I didn't stop for you in the swamps, but I can't go back and change that. That's on me, but you managed to survive then." Darya couldn't look at Alina, afraid she would see what that survival had cost. "What's different now? Because I sure as hell can't protect someone who can't seem to decide if they even want to live. I need you to *wake up*. These people," she said, glancing around, "they want to live very badly, and they can sense weakness. They can smell it on you."

"I'm sorry?" Darya tried. She still felt half out of her body, and Alina loomed over her, hands braced on her knees and blood spattered across her knuckles.

"I don't fucking *care* about your sorry's, Darya, and neither do they. Can you at least promise me you will stand up for yourself next time? For me, if not for yourself? It's my life too."

Darya wasn't even sure what to say. She sat there, unmoving, right where she had been when Alina left. Alina examined her for a minute longer before grunting, satisfied or dissatisfied with what she saw there and settling back-to-back with Darya again. Somehow, there wasn't nearly the warmth from earlier. A comfort though. When you were out in the cold, you'd take any warmth you could find.

It should have been her brother though. With that little intrusive thought, the warmth was gone, and all she could think about was that morning more than a week ago. Mind stuck in place again. When they had murdered him, and she had done nothing. Had taken their first offer to be part of the Tribes again. Had sat there while one of them tried to take even more from her. She had killed someone who had only tried to help her, and now she couldn't even defend herself against those who actually wanted to hurt her.

Staring back toward the center of the camp, Darya knew that she hated them. Taharuk. Serik. Kursagai. All the chieftains who had laughed along with Janbek as he sentenced her brother to death as an example, as entertainment. Erbol. The rest of them. These...savages. They didn't deserve to live.

One of the tribesmen sitting there made eye contact, and Darya looked away hurriedly. But what could she do against all of them? They would take anything she had left to give and leave her dying in the snow. There was nothing she could do.

*You could kill yourself. Follow Mikael.*

There were no self-pitying tears, only thoughtful consideration. The decision had to be made at some point. She could. See if the stories were true, the warm currents of the afterlife in the Rift. Maybe it was true, and if it was, maybe they could find each other there. Leave this all behind.

Alina would be better off without her, and perhaps the other members of their group could be accepted more easily without the living, breathing reminder of the leader of their failures.

*"Or...you can heed what your brother would want for you."*

Vels's words echoed in her head. Maybe her wise man had his uses, even if he was nowhere to be found. Could she honestly say that Mikael would want her to give up? Attractive as it was right then, she knew that's what it would be: giving up. No, she didn't think so. What would he want for her? Safety, yes. A home, yes. But how? She didn't know, but she knew that death wouldn't bring answers either. And it wasn't as if she didn't still have the option. Not just yet. Later, maybe. She pulled the blanket tighter again, focusing on the steady pressure of Alina's back against hers, grounding her.

Once upon a time, she had heard another story, a darker story. It had been good too, as far as those stories went. All darkness and dread and despair. Monsters that couldn't be overcome, and gods and goddesses of winter, death, blood, and revenge. Cowards and villains and victims composed the cast of those stories. She rubbed at her forearm again, the poison of that wound still festering in her mind. Darya knew that the first story was full of brave, selfless people, the sort who would do the right thing no matter what. She thought she knew which story she was in, and she had the increasing, despairing suspicion that it was the only story she deserved.

# A SIGNAL

An eternity and a half later, they stumbled from the high passes into foothills. It was unreal finally being out of the mountains, and there was a sense of wild, disbelieving joy in the simple fact of being passably warm again. It was as if Darya's veins and limbs had finally remembered how to work, and strength and warmth coursed through everything, the way it was always meant to. Physically, she found herself recovering from the ordeal even faster than Alina, which was a nice change of pace. Occasionally, like now, it was even pleasant enough of a feeling to block out all the other worries.

Darya and Alina stood with several others, surveying the valley before them while the rest of the warband prepared behind them, below the crest of the hill. It was a beautiful vista. Rolling hills, dotted with little clumps of trees too organized to be anything but orchards and larger, neat patches of tilled earth. All radiating out of a town of wooden structures with a few buildings of stone at the center. It was a long way off yet, but the woodsmoke floating above the buildings was visible, an alluring promise of food and warmth. Too alluring for the warband. Taharuk had announced that they would be taking the town, along with anything in it. A sturdy-looking wooden palisade surrounded it. It wouldn't be enough.

"What if they're rebels? Or they know where the Stained are?" Darya asked. "Couldn't we just ask them for supplies? Aren't we trying to make an alliance with them?"

Alina shrugged. "Who cares? It's warmer here, and they have food. Who cares if they know about any Stained? As far as rebels, I don't see any soldiers, so I think we're good. Taharuk said that we're far enough out, they probably aren't involved at all."

Darya nodded hesitantly, unable to find anything specific to disagree with. Alina, practical as ever. Taharuk, as persuasive as ever. It would certainly be nice to have more food again, there was no denying that. Anything would be better than what they had been able to hunt in the foothills as they had worked their way west at a lazy pace, gathering their strength again. Theirs was an easy lot to convince right about now, and the other two leaders had agreed with Taharuk.

Still, to Darya's mind, "probably not involved" seemed a very low bar.

She sniffed the air and could have sworn she smelled the woodsmoke that drifted on the breeze toward them. Imagination, or hope, maybe—it was too far for that. In the background, the sinking sun gave the whole scene a peaceful, pleasant feel, and despite her concerns and the coming violence, Darya couldn't help but be reminded of better days.

"Feels like home, doesn't it?" she asked on a whim.

Alina considered for a moment, thoughtful. "A little, I guess. Before we couldn't grow anything. You were so young then. Do you even remember?"

Darya felt a flash of irritation. Alina was only five years older, but constantly sought to remind her of the gap. As if it gave her more of a right to their past.

"I remember," she muttered.

Ignoring or not noticing her mood, Alina continued blithely on. "It used to be so peaceful up there. But then the snows came earlier, the ice left later. Year after year. Hard to be peaceful when you're hungry."

"I remember."

Alina turned to her, concerned, misinterpreting the reason for her tone. "You know none of us blamed your mother, right? She did the right thing." She spared a look for the riders around them. As usual, Altan, Ganzig, and Kasym were nearest, not wanting to be near Alina or Darya, but not welcome anywhere else. "These 'Thousand Tribes' are a glorified bunch of savages from the steppes, but it was the only choice."

"I know," Darya insisted.

"Yes, yes. You know, you remember. Got it. Don't be such a bitch. I'm trying to be nice. All I'm saying is, remember why it was the right choice then. It still is the right choice. The ice is only going farther every winter, and the only way to push south is through the empire. And the only way to beat them is with numbers. Lots and lots of these bastards. Maybe some Stained to help, if Vels isn't full of shit." She gestured toward the main group, which was huddled in the trees, hastily planning with Taharuk. Low voices came from the circle of war chiefs, as Serik and Kursagai did their best to exert their own influence. Vels was still nowhere to be found after disappearing before the crossing.

Darya opened her mouth, then decided to close it. She wanted to say she knew, that she understood what Alina was saying, but thought she would stay silent this time. And she also looked back. Ever since the incident in the mountains, she had been on a constant, tiring guard, never letting Alina out of her sight. Among the trees now, and with some food in her belly, there were even moments free of the crushing reminder of her brother's absence. Time to think. To realize that all that vigilance meant something more than habit, that killing herself didn't hold quite the same appeal as it had. She did want to survive.

"You were going to say you know again, weren't you?"

Darya's face flushed.

Alina chuckled before growing serious again. "Yeah, you know, but you don't really believe it."

"What do you mean?"

"I mean, you keep acting like somehow this is all temporary. Like you're above everything that happens here. You can't be. I can't be. We aren't back in our home, and we never will be. Our only chance is here, with them."

Darya turned away, toward the village, where the setting sun set the thatched roofs flashing golden-bright. Little flickers of firelight already shone through slits and windows in the wooden huts and at intervals around the palisades. She didn't want to let Alina see the tears that gathered at the corners of her eyes. Couldn't she understand? They had killed Mikael. Knowing she wanted to live only made it harder, not easier. Letting go would have been simple.

Alina's hand shot out and roughly grabbed her chin, pulling her face-to-face. "Listen to me. By the fucking Sun, stop acting like a child. I have no idea how you're still this soft, even growing up spoiled by your mother and brother." Darya tried to turn away, and Alina yanked her back. "Listen, damn it! Learn from their mistakes, Darya. You think I like this any more than you? That this is the version of me I want to be? No. But I've accepted who we need to be now. If you can't also learn from these assholes, learn some of that ruthlessness, lose some of that baby fat and self-pity, you're dead, and probably me with you." She studied Darya, one hand firm around her chin, before gently wiping away the tears with her other.

"Am I interrupting something?"

The clever one, Serik, was looking at her and Alina with something like amusement. Darya knew the rumors that had started to circulate about the two of them and was in no mood to discredit them. Anything that would provide her some protection was welcome. But Alina hurriedly released her and turned her full attention to Serik. Their fellow outcasts were also listening intently. This was the first time any had come to address them.

"What is it?"

"We've got a job for you lot. My idea; you can thank me later. Call it a way to work yourselves back into better graces."

"Better graces?" Alina's lip curled.

"Whose better graces?" Kasym asked carefully.

"Shouldn't matter to you," Serik said. "Step up is a step up, no matter the direction. Especially when you're up to your eyeballs in horse shit. But shut your fucking mouths and listen to me, because this isn't a request. You see that town?"

"That one over there?" Alina asked, pointing behind her.

"Yes, that one." Serik's face darkened as he realized she was mocking him. "Keep that sense of humor, you're going to need it. Let me break it down simply, since it seems like you need it. That town—yes, the one over there—has a wall. Horses don't like walls. But this wall has an opening. An opening that is currently closed. You will open it. Is that clear enough?"

"Are you trying to get us killed?" Alina retorted.

"That's impossible," Darya breathed at the same time.

"No, and no," Serik continued calmly. "Not impossible, and I sincerely hope you succeed." He winked. "Not that there isn't a backup plan."

---

Darya hadn't known she could hold her breath this long. She was crouched in the wet dirt, in a small depression in the earth short of the walls. Alina was pressed close on her right, eyes glinting faintly in the dark. On her other side was Kasym. Or maybe Altan. She was too concentrated on the barking they could hear from the dogs inside. Darya still couldn't believe the idea she had suggested when the five of them were planning this. This...this suicide mission. It was like a bad dream. Any earlier reservations were far gone, and Darya had come to the conclusion that she would really like to see the morning. If they were caught, knowing the warband would take the town would be scant comfort.

"You're up."

Alina's harsh whisper was practically in her ear, and Darya started. The night was cold, and the damp earth didn't help, but she couldn't stop sweating. Her bow was strung and slung over her shoulder, along with a quiver stuffed with wool to silence the arrows. She wiped her hands on her coat, preparing herself.

*Stupid, stupid, stupid.*

It was rapidly becoming a personal motto. Darya wished she had something else to tell herself, something encouraging, but she couldn't, for the life of her, figure out why she had spoken up during their planning.

*"I can climb the wall."*

She closed her eyes as hard as she could, hoping she could somehow turn back time and slap the words out of her own mouth. No. Nothing. Still in the dirt. Upset and inspired and all out of sorts after Alina's little speech, she had wanted to prove something to her, to the others. Maybe to herself. And as the lightest, and best with a bow, it was probably going to be her no matter what. Better to volunteer.

*Idiot.*

Wiping her hands one more time and trying to ignore the chalky taste in her mouth and the watery feeling in her guts, she tightened her grip on the rope and grapple and sprinted for the wall, trying to close the distance as fast as she could. Darya mouthed a silent prayer to her ancestors as she ran. *A little help would be nice.* She half tripped as she tried to come to a stop and slammed into the wall. She closed her eyes and winced, wondering if she should just kill herself now and get it over with. She waited, listening. There was only the occasional distant voice and low barking of dogs fighting on the far side. Thank the dead for that. Sending Ganzig to the other, upwind side with a bloody cut of meat had been her idea too. Enough to draw the dogs in that direction. He was probably waiting in view of the gate now, like the rest of them. Waiting on her.

Letting out another breath she hadn't known she was holding, Darya readjusted her grip on the grapple, studying the top of the wall, where the uneven cuts came to jagged points.

*Throw the grapple. Climb the wall. Open the gate.*

Simple.

Darya repeated the steps in her mind, trying to encourage herself. It was nothing. Like climbing a tree or a rock face with Mikael when they had been children. Darya pushed those memories out of her mind and focused on the tasks at hand. Get over the wall, open the gate, and hold the entrance with the rest of her group. All they had to do was hold until Taharuk sent the warband through from where they were huddled in the tree line, waiting for their signal.

Her first throw was embarrassing. Darya stifled a yelp as she dodged out of the way, and the heavy grapple thumped into dirt next to her. Glancing back into the dark, she couldn't see her companions, but could only imagine Alina's frustration. She was proving something, that was for certain.

The next throw was perfect. With a clank that was physically painful, the grapple settled into place between two of the massive trunks. After a quick pause, Darya gave the rope an initial, hesitant tug, before leaning her whole weight on it.

Good enough.

This was the dangerous part, she told herself. Of many other, equally dangerous parts.

Using the rope, she scrambled up the side of the wall and the fifteen feet—twenty? It seemed high—of the sheared logs. Before she knew it, she was at the top, hands grasping for purchase on the weathered wood, slippery with age. She peeked over the top.

Darya wasn't sure what she expected to see, but the town was more underwhelming up close than it was from a distance. Up close, the great houses were squat, poorly fitted wooden huts. The area of packed and cleared earth between the houses and the wall was scattered with rubbish and reeked of rotting food and every sort of manure. She looked down. Burning Sun, even the wall was shorter than it had seemed before climbing.

More importantly though, she couldn't see any people or dogs. It was awkward, but she managed to haul herself over the edge with a minimum of splinters and stifled curses. On the other side, she dropped to the ground in a crouch, fumbling for her bow as soon as she balanced herself. Bow in hand, arrow fitted to string, and no one in sight, Darya was feeling a bit better about the whole idea. Maybe Serik would even be impressed.

*Throw the grapple. Climb the wall. Open the gate.*

Just one more step. Easy. Moving as silently as possible, Darya crept along the wall, trying to keep to dark patches as she worked toward the gate. Already, she could see the heavy bar holding it closed. Ten paces away now. Too easy. She started to grin, thinking of the look on Alina's face when she opened the gate.

"Hello?"

Darya's daydreams vanished. She stared back at the old man who leaned forward out of the door of one of the huts, trying to make out her features in the flickering torchlight. Darya was fairly sure she wasn't allaying his suspicions with her frozen posture, wide eyes, or the bow in her hand.

Clearly reaching the same conclusion, the man bellowed something in a cracking voice, a warning for the rest of the town. At the same time, Darya darted for the gate. This was her only chance. Adrenaline pumping, she practically threw the beam out of its place, barely a second to wonder at how easily she had managed that. A small whimper escaped as she heard answering shouts and barks behind her. *Please let them be close.*

Before she had a chance to crack the gate open, Alina and Kasym burst through, with Altan and Ganzig close behind.

Darya turned, her job done. Well, almost done. In all her preparations and rehearsals in her head, she had left out something—the fourth step.

*Give the signal.*

She saw the nearest torch and darted towards it, but suddenly, there were a half dozen or so men running toward them. In the half-light, they were raging, deadly shapes. On instinct, she paused, drew the string back to her cheek, and let fly at one of them in the middle.

Down.

The rest charged forward, meeting their own little group in a snarling, swirling mess. The townsfolk had clubs and spears and at least one short sword that Darya saw cutting through the air in a glittering arc. Alina and Kasym were possessed, screaming and fighting at the front, while Ganzig and Altan were giving ground before another two. With their group's heavy furs and the lighter clothing of the defenders risen from sleep, it looked more than anything like farmers fending off an attack by enormous beasts from beyond the edge of the map. Darya suspected that was exactly how they saw it.

*The torch!* She needed to signal the rest. They were across the cleared fields, hidden in the woods. She could already hear the sounds of the rest of the town waking up. They would be dead soon if she couldn't pass the signal. Darya let another arrow fly, taking one of those rushing toward them right below the nose. He went down to his knees with a wet, confused grunt, frantically grabbing at his face.

"Signal!" Alina roared over the chaos, spittle flying, hacking and slashing furiously at two men who were trying to close into her guard.

Darya sprinted for the nearest possible source of fire, a stone brazier on the ground. With a cry of triumph, she pulled a brand out and turned to wave it toward the dark beyond the gate. That cry quickly turned to panic as she was tackled from behind. She hit the ground hard. There was dirt in her mouth and a dizzying impact from her head bouncing on the ground. Darya lashed out behind her. She felt the flaming brand connect and heard a roar of pain and anger as the man let go of her. A lucky hit. She rolled over, seeing the man grasping at his face where she had hit him with the burning wood. He scrabbled to find his knife from where he had dropped it, half-blinded by the burns and ash.

Darya threw what was left of the wood at him and turned back to the brazier, the frustration boiling over even the panic.

*Give the signal. Just a fucking signal. Will no one in this cursed world give me a Sun-damned moment? I'll give them a gods-damned signal.*

Darya didn't waste a breath. She plucked two more pieces of burning wood directly from the flames and flung them onto the nearest roof, one after the other. She stared at them lying on the thatch, willing it to catch and praying it hadn't rained here recently. Behind her, the sounds of battle faded away, and she was utterly by herself, for the first time in forever. Only her and the fire, guttering against the damp thatch. Almost out. *Please, please, burn!* It seemed like she could feel it, trying and failing to catch, sparks spending themselves in effort after effort into their smothering surroundings.

Darya prayed with the sincerity of the moment. For herself, for Alina. For Mikael. This might not be a life worth living, but she wanted to live, just a little longer. *Decide? I've fucking decided, damn them all. Now, burn!* She rendered herself down to nothing, a spark herself, a need, an imperfectly pure desire to be. Darya poured herself out and felt something fill the gap, that wonderful warmth and strength that had been hovering at the edge of her awareness ever since leaving the mountains.

*Burn!*

There was a gust of something, and it was as if the fire answered her, blazing with new life. A prayer answered for once. Darya didn't bother to keep watching. One prayer had been answered, but the gods helped those who helped themselves, above all. She drew her shashka, that short, slashing blade, and rushed at the man who was struggling up from his knees and scrubbing ash from his eyes. With a screech, she slashed forward with a strength that surprised her, cutting through the fingers he held up to stop the blade and deep into his face.

Another moment clawed back.

Turning, she could see the fighting growing more desperate as Alina and the others were forced back, almost to the gate itself. Darya picked up her bow from where she had dropped it, and taking a knee, started to methodically pour arrows into what was rapidly becoming a crowd. She wanted more than anything to run to Alina, to fight next to her, but knew the best way to help would be to kill.

Intruding past the pulsing of her blood was another sound. She chanced a quick glance backward. The thatch. Thank all the gods, the Sun, and the stars. Any and all ancestors who were listening or watching. Darya threw up thanksgiving in every way she could think of as her heart soared with the first bit of hope she had enjoyed since her brother was executed. She *had* decided. There was a thrill in that. There was no doubt what she wanted right then: to survive. She could learn from them, do whatever it took. She might live today. Alina might live today. If they could hold out a little longer, she would learn all the lessons she had to.

Darya could hear the hoofbeats now, like an invisible cavalry of demons from the dark, from the ground itself. But so could the townsfolk. Pale faces twisted up in fury and desperation. Ganzig screamed horribly. Darya saw a spear sticking out of his side as he collapsed, still screaming, still waving his sword wildly like a broken puppet with its strings tangled. The defenders swept over him, silencing him, sending him down through the last door and to the Rift.

Alina took a cut across her front with a grunt, no breath left for anything else. She backed up, a furious whirl of fur and steel by Kasym and Altan.

They were slowing now, their energy spent. A group of the townsfolk had noticed Darya and were spreading out, working their hesitant way toward her in spurts as she shot arrow after arrow. They were ducking and weaving, taking advantage of when she would have to switch her aim or pull forth another arrow. She was almost out. Fingers and arms worked their terrible magic, years of practice bringing down man after man in a process that her mind was hardly part of anymore. Never enough. Not fast enough. It was horrifying, but in a detached sort of way. A terrible joke. They had succeeded. Done everything right. Been resourceful, planned well, fought bravely. And for the first time since her brother's death, she *knew* she wanted to live. And they would die, seconds from salvation. The warband would take the village, easily killing the defenders who had slaughtered them. Maybe they would honor their sacrifice? More likely they would laugh. There was a complex hierarchy to the Thousand, that amalgamation of tribes, but always there was the bottom: the dead. If not an ancestor, then worthy of neither pity nor respect. Nothing but a reminder of one's own life and a reason to celebrate another little victory in a harsh world.

Darya wanted to run. It wouldn't have helped. The men were paces away now. She let the bow drop and picked up her blade with shaking, sweaty hands. Maybe deciding wasn't enough? Life had a say as well, after all. She couldn't even hear her own thoughts anymore over the hammering of her blood through her ears.

No, not her blood. There was a burst of movement in the corner of her perception, and the world exploded into another scale of violence entirely. The defenders whirled, knowing their chance was gone, but not willing to stop fighting for it.

Taharuk and Serik led the charge, Kursagai right behind, rolling over the defenders with a laughing madness, glorying in their invincibility born of being horsed above scattered prey and at the head of nearly five hundred whooping raiders. More torches were thrown, and Darya saw more graceful arcs of fire as more of them made their hungry homes on the roofs. She never thought she could be so glad to see buildings set on fire. Or to see those three at the head of a charge.

Stumbling over to the others, Darya could hear the cries of panic and of delight spread through the town as the charge quickly turned into a rampage, many of the defenders dead already. Now, counting the number of dead around Alina and Kasym, who had collapsed to the ground, Darya frowned. Surely there had been more?

Darya reached a hand under Alina's muscled back, meaning to help her up, but instead, Alina fell backwards, choking.

"No! Alina, what's..."

The choking turned to burbling, sputtering laughter, spit-flecked and hysterical. "What a fucking disaster." Alina laughed again, eyes bright and chest heaving, still trying to recover from the fight. "Alive, though! Alive, Darya!" She looked around. "Kasym! Altan!"

Kasym was smiling now too, a tired thing, but a member of their tribe now, brought close in their visit to death's cold doors. Or maybe just for want of better options. Altan looked half-dead himself, catching his breath on hands and knees and dripping sweat and blood. Ganzig was another bloody pile among the rest, distinctions lost. Darya spared him a glance, a glimpse of what might have been. The others didn't bother.

"What now?" Darya asked.

Alina kicked her leg out, toppling Darya. She fell with a squawk and a thump onto the blood-soaked ground. "You're alive. You enjoy it for a second, Darya. Sun above, it's like you want to be stressed. Sit here. Go kill someone. Find someone to screw. Search for some food. Or keep the dead company here. Do whatever you like. That's the whole point." She started laughing again. "Well done with the brand, by the way. I didn't think thatch could catch so quickly."

The brand in question was somewhere in the roiling smoke and roaring fire that had been the roof.

Frowning, Darya thought back to that moment. Alina was right. What exactly had she seen? She held up her hands. And where were the burns? She had pulled that wood directly from the fire.

Kasym grunted in agreement before pulling himself up with the help of one of the spears lying around. "Well, I for one know which option I'm *not* choosing. I've had my fill of fighting for the day. And I've never been one for sitting." He winked at Alina. "Only a couple options left."

Alina guffawed, nearly choking again from her position stretched out on the ground, heedless of the dirt and the blood alike. She was staring up into the heavens, stars disappearing in the surrounding ring of fire. "I always knew you had a sense of humor buried somewhere, Kasym. But you're right, that sounds lovely."

Kasym blinked. "It does?"

Alina stood, a slight groan giving away the pain in that effort. She walked up to Kasym, slowly and sensually placing a hand on his cheek, while Darya pulled her attention from her own hands to watch in confusion and the faintest disgust. And perhaps a little curiosity. Even Altan was interested enough to pull himself away from his own misery long enough to look up.

"It does. So, why don't you go find us some food?" With a chuckle, she slapped his face full-on and turned to wander deeper into the town, ignoring Darya's laughter and Kasym's curses behind her. "Idiot."

# COMRADES IN ARMS

The small empty dishes were taken from the long, mirror-polished table, and bowls of soup placed in their stead, all with a speed and coordination that was a magic of its own. The prefect's staff would have given Syl's team some competition when it came to a synchronized operation. Rich carpets, fine wooden panels, and a sparkling chandelier all added to the impression—carefully curated by Prefect Antinius, no doubt—of wealth and taste. The riot of colors in the room were even more shocking after so much time spent creeping around in the dark and squatting in this same prefect's interrogation chambers. The walls themselves were covered in paintings. Some were masterful, as far as Syl could tell, and some bore the signs of an amateur imitating the masters and hoping their proximity might help them all blend together. It didn't, he noted. Adjacency only highlighted deficiency.

The guests themselves were no better. Peacocks, all, and just as useful. From the prefect at the head of the table, to the too-loud, would-be nobility at this ass-end of the empire, they all competed with one another in subtle jabs and less subtle exaggerated anecdotes of their own exploits in the last war. The prefect in particular was the unwitting recipient of much of Syl's ire. To all appearances, a kindly if distracted-looking old man with a well-trimmed beard and paint-stained fingernails. It was his inaction that enraged Syl. That self-important career politician was more concerned with his authority and any potential trespass of its bounds than the fact that he was rapidly becoming the jealous ruler of a sinking ship. Plus, the paintings really were execrable.

Syl and the members of the team were the ones trapped and surrounded this time though. Dressed in simple, practical, black high-collared uniforms, they were hemmed in on all sides by expectation and stuck here thanks to the insistent invitation of the prefect. Ostensibly to celebrate the fact that the Twins would be arriving within the week, according to the messengers they had sent forward. They would celebrate then, and only then, if Syl had his way. And not even then, to be honest. He didn't like the feeling of being so isolated within a province in revolt, with the first sign of the cataclysm barely more than a week's ride to the north. Despite the high walls and cohort of legion soldiers augmenting the local garrison, their situation felt precarious.

Then there were the Getacians, looking even more out of place than Syl's fellow Hunters. At least Marika and Lucan seemed to be making an effort to enjoy themselves, taking advantage of the fine spread. Lucan looked grimly determined to find out if and when the servers would stop filling his cup, and Marika seemed inclined to follow suit. All to poor Vali's consternation, who sat stiff-backed and awkward in a chair too small for his bulk. He sat across from Syl, next to Kass. She was already torturing the poor lad, fluttering her lashes, making eyes, and laughing at his stumbling attempts at conversation. Like putting a lamb next to a tiger.

Next to Syl sat the local garrison's commander, Colonel Gralinis, who had inexplicably chosen him as the primary victim of his conversation. This whole dinner was an undeniable waste of time, and this windbag before him was the definition of a waste of breath. They needed to be out there, on the streets, killing and questioning their way through the cells of separatists that riddled the city. Syl stabbed his spoon into the soup and bared his teeth in a facsimile of a polite smile as the commander droned on at him.

"...so it really did come as quite the surprise. These Rift-damned Gets up here..." He gestured placatingly to the place where Vali and his friends sat. "Beg your pardon... These *Getacians* have been a restive lot since the last campaign up here, but... Say, did I tell you I served under the Leveler for that campaign?"

"You mentioned it, yes."

"What am I saying, of course! You were up here as well, weren't you? Under the Leveler as well? Or the Angel?"

"Under the Leveler."

"I'll be damned, we are practically brothers-in-arms!"

"Practically."

Syl looked across to where Leon and Liora sat, desperate for rescue. Liora somehow managed to look better in their plain uniform than any of the noblewomen strutting in their finery and jewelry, but her attention was far away. She sat poking listlessly at the soup in her bowl, mind still stuck in the prison, he suspected. Not that Leon was any more help. With a sly grin for Syl, he goaded the useless old man on.

"What was it like?"

"*Bastard,*" Syl mouthed. Leon made a shushing gesture.

"Oh, Emperor be good, it was glorious. Eh, Syl? What's that short for, anyhow?"

"Scyllus."

"Unusual, yes? A fine name though, a fine name. Anyhow, this campaign—what a time!" Gralinis stopped talking for long enough to slurp down another mouthful. Even his slurping was too loud. "Don't get me wrong, we were having a hell of a time by ourselves, until they brought another Chosen, that blessed Angel of the Gates, from her perch. Lot of bloody battles and thoroughly boring sieges. Say, what unit were you in?"

"Tunnel hounds."

"Ah." Gralinis had a look of polite shock on his face. "Ah, I see. Tough going down there, eh?"

The fine meal and all the guests disappeared for a moment, and suddenly Syl was back in those tunnels, crawling terrified along those ancient lines that crisscrossed this half of the province, grasping roots of the northern fortress city of Bal Maru. Hand-to-hand fighting in the dark, praying it was just Getacians they ran across. Hoping they hadn't strayed too close to the abandoned darkness of that poisoned city, hoping that the rusting ironspawn stayed dormant.

"It wasn't boring."

"Hmm, yes, I see."

Leon, who had served with Syl in those endless tunnels, was enjoying the officer's discomfort. "What were you doing, sir? Manage to burn a couple villages? Or just got really good at counting and confiscating after those boring sieges?"

Puffing up his chest, Gralinis stared down his nose at Leon, like he might at a small dog that had pissed on his boot. "There is absolutely no need for such rudeness. Not all of us were grubbing around in the dirt. I was there at the Battle of Nordea Kerest. That ended the war, you know."

"I know that a charge by those massive Legio Vorax bastards broke their lines, and our 'allies' decided to come down on our side after that."

Leon nudged a distracted Vali beside him, pulling the lad's attention from his staring at Kass. Syl suspected Vali thought he was being subtle. "We have one of their spawn here tonight. Vali here—well, his father—was one of those indecisive clan warlords. Excuse me, staunch and noble allied houses."

Their half of the table descended into a profoundly uncomfortable silence, all glaring at one another, except for Leon, who tucked noisily into the soup before him. Most of the men and women had only had their blood retroactively upgraded to "noble" after a similar decision.

"Great soup, by the way."

"What about the tunnels here?" Liora cut in. "You mentioned them when we first arrived. Are any still active?"

Vali hadn't stopped staring in confused outrage at Leon, but the rest of the table was happy to shift their attention.

Looking grateful for the change of subject, Gralinis's face lightened a bit from the worrisome shade of red it had taken on. "Never fear there. We were thorough. Few enough reach this far from Bal Maru, and we collapsed those that did years ago. Oversaw the whole operation myself. Didn't even have to use flamewardens or their sunflares, only the strength of our backs and a few good tools."

Syl found it ludicrous to imagine Gralinis holding any sort of tool, except maybe in confusion. He'd known too many high-ranking officers like this one not to know better. Getting your hands dirty was for captains-minor on down. The lower, the dirtier, of course.

"Then how are these separatists able to so easily move about your city?" Liora asked.

The redness returned with a vengeance. "Well, I mean...there aren't so many, and we remain firmly in control here, as you can see. I can't speak to what my colleagues north of here were doing with their garrisons, but we keep a tight rein here. It certainly isn't the tunnels."

Syl gave Liora a nearly imperceptible nod, thanking her for the change in direction. This was useful, not a rehashing of old glories or recriminations for actions taken almost a decade ago. There was plenty of blame to go around now, and Liora was striking to the heart of the matter. The channel that the smugglers were using was a problem, and Gralinis was isolated, even if only by a few dinner guests, from his protector, the prefect, who was distracted at the head of the table.

"Then is it that they are able to organize in front of you? There have been a total of twelve of the local garrison and five of our own cohort's soldiers that have been killed since we've been here. You hang half a dozen every day, most of which we find for you, and still, that hasn't stopped. How are they moving around, then? In broad daylight? They don't need the tunnels?"

"That's not at all what I'm saying," he sputtered. "This is not some peaceful southern province, filled with vineyards and happy subjects. These Gets are a thoroughly disagreeable lot." He didn't bother correcting himself this time, nor did he catch the embarrassed discomfort of the Getacians at the table at the repeated use of the slur. "The fact that we have suffered no coup, no overthrow, and the fact that the prefect remains safe is a testament to our efforts."

"Perhaps," Syl said.

"Perhaps? *Perhaps?* I'm not used to having my honor questioned by the likes of you." He was sneering now, jowls quivering, any pretension of politeness long gone. "Tunnel hounds, indeed."

"It's not your honor we're questioning." Liora was warming to the script.

"Only your competence," Leon finished cheerily. Another slurp.

"Or perhaps your loyalty." Syl held up his hand to forestall another outburst. "Before you speak again, remember that rank means very, very little right now. We are here representing the Vigil. Reporting to the Exarch, and through him to one of His Chosen, and after that, the Emperor Himself. So, no more righteous indignation, please. It's tiring. We have found an...offensive number of separatists cells working under your nose in this city. Now, the Twins will be here in less than a week. There are two kinds of reports they might hear from us. In the first, a loyal garrison commander did his best against the rising tide of insurgency, and with our help, ensured that their legions had a secure staging point to retake the northern districts. In the second, an officer allowed the seeds of sedition to grow in the city under his protection, either through disloyalty, or more inexcusably, through incompetence. Do we understand one another...sir?"

Now, the scarlet trim of Gralinis's uniform had gone from seamlessly blending in with his face to a stark border between his marks of office and the bloodless skin above them. Those around them were studiously ignoring the exchange, at least on the surface. Their conversations were fluff, and every ear was clearly bent toward the commander's humiliation with greedy eagerness.

"Yes...yes, of course. You must excuse me," he stuttered, forcing the words out between bobs of his head. "I am here to help. At your service." His eyes darted to the head of the table, where Domarik and Prefect Antinius were deep in their own animated discussion, no doubt a rehashing of previous arguments over jurisdiction and authorities. There wouldn't be any help for the commander coming from there—not right away, at least. Syl pulled his attention back.

"Good. Good. I'm glad we finally understand each other. There seems to have been some confusion the last few days, a lack of cooperation from some of your men." Back to the questions. "Perhaps you can explain to me again, thoroughly, why your prisons were empty when we arrived. Why we have multiple suspects who have corroborated the fact that there was—hell, might still be—a massive, coordinated, and centrally organized smuggling effort to move renegade Rift-users and other escaped political prisoners further north. Why we, two weeks later, are having to work our way up the chain of not one, not two, but three separate and distinct cells of separatists in your city." Syl held out his hand expectantly. "Begin."

Ambushed, Gralinis looked from Syl, to Liora and Leon, and back to Syl. "Surely you can't think I have something to do with anything that happened up north?"

"Not what I'm saying."

"Interesting where guilty minds jump to, isn't it, Liora?" Leon asked.

Liora was clearly uncomfortable. She really didn't enjoy inflicting pain, verbal or otherwise. Syl again wondered how she had found her way to the team. But she played her part.

"It is, it is."

*She still doesn't understand. She will.*

*You only need to learn that lesson once.*

Gralinis spread his hands on the table and leaned forward, the picture of desperate earnestness. "You *must* believe me. We had seen nothing like what happened up in those cities here! No reason to distrust those living here. There hasn't been anything! Clearly, they know they would fail in any attempt. Of course, it's wonderful"—he choked over this word as it stuck in his throat—"positively wonderful that your team is here now. Our regiment is here to keep the peace; the peace has been kept! If there has been..." He swallowed. "... any failure, I humbly apologize. I'm a simple soldier," he finished plaintively, stopping himself before reaching out to Syl, trying to appeal to their shared service.

Sweat trickled down the sides of the colonel's head as he swallowed, waiting for a reaction from Syl. Staring into those frightened eyes, Syl wanted to believe him, that he was just a man placed beyond his capabilities, thrust into a situation he was not equipped for. Never assume conspiracy when incompetence will suffice.

*"You believed me. They always do."*

An idea took shape.

"Very well. But we will expect absolute compliance in the future from any and all of the soldiers under your command, is that clear?"

Jowls shaking, Gralinis bobbed his head energetically. "Of course, of course!"

"Good." He spoke just loud enough to ensure the others listening would hear him. A trap wouldn't work without bait. "We will begin with a search of your garrison's barracks first thing tomorrow. You will also provide a list prioritizing our interrogation efforts when it comes to your officer cadre." Tonight, they would set watchers to see if any rats tried to escape. "As for yourself, hopefully there will be no need for more...in-depth questions, sir." Syl smiled at the commander as he dug his spoon into the soup and slurped noisily. "And Leon! You were right. The soup really is quite good."

and teasing him in ways that he could have sworn were flirtatious, but he knew better. He was doing his best not to make a fool of himself. He was also fairly sure he was failing.

"How old are you, anyway?"

Another question. He swallowed, and his resolve to be unaffected vanished under her attention. "I'm... Well, I'm nineteen. Almost twenty," he added hurriedly. Why had that number felt so much larger whenever anyone else had asked?

"I'm sure you are. So young. And so big!" She squeezed his arm with those slender fingers, almost painful with the pressure. "All these muscles, Vali—you must work so hard."

He coughed. "I do?"

"Yes, you do. I'm sure training with Syl can only help, dreary sop that he is. Work is all he knows." She winked. "Maybe one of these days, you can train with me." It wasn't a question.

Vali thought he might choke, he coughed so hard this time. People were looking at him with mild concern as his face flushed another shade redder. "Maybe?"

With a gentle laugh, she let go of his arm. "Maybe. Though I'm not sure your little friend would be quite so happy about that."

Marika had turned her attention away from the wine to stare with worrying intensity down the table toward them. Vali wasn't sure what her problem was; she wasn't the one stuck up here with the team. He did his best to ignore her.

"What...why...are you..." He struggled to come up with something, anything to say. He hadn't wanted the conversation to end just yet, but now he had trapped himself. Kassara stared expectantly. Vali begged his brain or at least his mouth to come up with something. Every second of awkward silence undoubtedly further cemented his status as a bumbling moron in her mind, and most definitely in his own. He panicked, and the real, so-far-unasked question he had for every member of the team came blurting out. "Why did you join the Vigil? Become an oathknight? Hunter, I mean."

Lucky, on her other side, went very still.

For Kassara's part, the teasing, playful look was gone as quickly as if it had never been there in the first place. "What a rude question," she snarled. Vali had followed Lucky's example of perfect stillness, hoping it would help. It didn't. He had wanted her full attention, and now he had it. "Rude and so, so stupid. Don't *ever* ask me that again, boy."

"I'm sorry?" Vali wished he could claw himself out of this state of confusion, but he only seemed to be digging himself deeper.

"You should be," Kass said, with forced levity, a shadow of her usual teasing returning. "But it's fine." She breathed away the rest of the sudden anger, visibly composing herself. "I made that decision for the same reason most of us make most decisions. Same reason you and your insufferably rustic friends are here. Because when it came down to it, I didn't really have a choice."

Even Liora was listening intently now, head cocked and hazel eyes fixed on them. This was not the Kass any of them were used to, and it was gone quickly enough that Vali thought he might have imagined the whole thing. The mask was back on, whole and entire, smile reaffixed.

"So young, and so very stupid! You've got to learn someday, but don't you know it's poor dinner conversation to ask about someone's past? It never gets shorter, and it's invariably filled with enough embarrassments and disappointments that no one needs another to point them out. You can talk about the weather, of course. Gossip if you're a woman. Other people's pasts are fair game. Naturally. And apparently," she said, gesturing to the commander, who was still droning on, "war stories about yourself for hours, if you're a man. Or Liora, I suppose." She tilted her head conspiratorially toward Vali, voice more than loud enough for the other Hunter to hear. "You really should see her records. Danger, impossible odds, lone survivor... Quite gripping stuff, really. Lots of shiny medals, naturally. But I daresay she won't be shouting about them to any and all who will listen. Unlike some."

As if to prove Kassara's point, Gralinis increased the volume and animation of his story, something Vali hadn't thought possible, until everyone on their half of the table was part of the conversation, willing or not.

"...so, it really did come as quite the surprise. These Rift-damned Gets up here..." Gralinis gestured apologetically to Vali. "Beg your pardon... These Getacians have been a restive lot since the last campaign up here, but... Say, did I tell you I served under the Leveler for that campaign?"

Flushing a deep crimson, with shame now piling on confusion, Vali fought to keep his clenched hands on the table, resisting the urge to leap across and stab the officer in his flabby neck. It was nice to have a target for his embarrassment.

A leg bumped his under the table. Kassara. It had to be. She was utterly engaged in the conversation continuing between Syl and Gralinis though. An accident. After his question and that wonderfully awkward interaction, he wanted to try talking to her, to say anything to make up for an offense he didn't even understand, but he wasn't sure where to begin. Vali stewed instead, only half listening to the conversation. More talk on tunnels, sieges, and battles. There would be more than enough of that soon enough, hopefully.

On his other side, Leon cut in. "I know that a charge by those massive Legio Vorax bastards broke their lines, and our 'allies' decided to come down on our side after that." Leon nudged Vali. "We have one of their spawn here tonight. Vali here—well, his father—was one of those indecisive clan warlords. Excuse me, staunch allied houses."

With every word, Vali's disbelief and anger grew. The empire's campaign would have failed if it weren't for his father and the other loyalist houses that came down on their side, and now this vicious little rat wanted to put their name in the mud.

"Wait just a damn minute..." Vali started, ready to tear Leon's head off.

Suddenly, he cut off, voice choking and strangling another cough before it could escape. The sensation was unmistakable: there was a hand placed firmly on the inside of his thigh. Leon? Thank all the gods, no. He looked to Kassara, who to all appearances still watched the conversation with rapt interest. Her eyes sparkled though, daring him to react. The flash of vulnerability earlier seemed a hallucination. Maybe a trick? The hand traced its way a little further up, up, before disappearing as suddenly as it had come, leaving Vali confused and sitting far stiffer than he had ever been before.

Any concerns about standing out were long past, and Vali focused on keeping his composure as he sat, sweating, trying to at least pretend to listen to the conversation. Something about loyalty, the lack thereof, and consequences. It was hard to keep track, and mostly repetitive anyway. The rest of the dinner passed in a warm, confused blur.

# HAPPY MEMORIES

S yl was dreaming.

Sometimes, when dreaming, even that ephemeral nonsense world would seem perfectly concrete and true enough that he would wake smiling or screaming. Syl had found though that even if it did seem real enough, if he dreamed the same dream enough times, his mind could recognize it. The wrongness of that utter familiarity. A cycle repeated, a wheel going nowhere.

Syl knew his mind wandered far every night, but he had dreamt this particular dream often enough to know its shape. It wasn't a good dream, not exactly, but not a complete nightmare either. Somewhere between, with a little of both.

"I missed you."

His wife, Elena, stood there, like she always did. The details of her face were fuzzy. He ignored the pain that brought, like he always did. Syl wanted to say he had been here a few nights ago. That she couldn't miss him, she wasn't real. Not anymore, at least. Dust and memories. Syl wanted to tell her this was ridiculous and that he was tired of these absurd dream-nightmares.

But he didn't.

"I've missed you too," he said, and meant it.

There was a hint of a smile that was lost in those blurred features, a statue left outside for a few hundred years. It had been less than ten; that hardly seemed fair.

Another presence, felt more than seen, took hold of his hand. Livia. A little hand that was swallowed by his, even as it pulled him along, following her mother. Syl couldn't look down, knew what he would see already, and that he would have to see it again soon enough. That wasn't his little girl. Not anymore.

They walked down, down the turret-narrow staircase, spiraling further into the dark. He didn't mind. Somewhere between the tunnel fighting of a lifetime ago and all the prisons, bolt-holes, and hiding places his current work sent him, the perfectly human fear of dark underground spaces had lost almost any grip it might have had on him. For now, he could pretend they were together. Syl had found that as long as he didn't look too far ahead, he could savor the moment, even if it was tainted by knowing the aftertaste already. He tried to stop them on that stair. But he always did, and as always, her reply was the same.

"We can't stop here."

"Why not?"

"This isn't where we belong."

The little hand pulled at him again. They continued, two and one. Before long, they came to the place it always ended. The ruined house, burnt down to ashes, the whole village erased, depopulated.

He pulled up short. It was different this time. No house, no village, only a massive open space. A sepulcher? A temple? No, neither of those fit, not exactly. The space was old, no doubt about that. Ancient beyond ancient. The ritual sanctums at the core of Heliopolis, where the oathknight rituals were conducted, might be the closest he had ever seen to this, but everything here gave the sense of having always been in a way nothing man-made ever could have. The stones *grew* together, fused or joined so skillfully that the whole space seemed to consist of one giant rock, hollowed out in the middle. Whatever race or ancient god had built the room hadn't stopped there. Massive walls dripping with condensation rose into the unseen darkness, faces carved in their thousands—tens of thousands, maybe—onto those walls, looking down on him. The points and recesses of their features sent the pooling water pattering down all around him. Patterns and flowing script covered every inch between, reminding him of nothing quite so much as the inscriptions on his own skin and the gauntlet that lay beside where he slept. It wasn't the same, but it was close. A precursor, perhaps.

He stepped back, noticing the floor. The stairs were long gone, and with the ironclad logic of the dreamworld, he was in the center of the room. Where he had always been, of course. A swirling pattern beneath his feet spread out in all directions in dizzying complexity, an impossibility to comprehend without perspective. Lost in his investigation of this change to the dream he knew so well, Syl realized with a guilty start that he was alone. They were both gone. That was fitting, he supposed. Besides, it was just a dream. The guilt wouldn't be going anywhere, but he could be as curious or incurious as he pleased.

The change was unnerving though. He dreaded what usually came next. The scenes of rushing home from a victorious campaign after hearing of an uprising at home. Of finding his little growing family and the man he had been dead. With a start, he realized he wanted to see that again. See that and end this dream. Syl could almost dream that memory in this dream, but something held him here, as if against his will. He wanted to wake up, to struggle, to run, but he couldn't. Some dreams had to be seen through.

Instead, he strode forward, step by step, into the vast chamber in a direction chosen at random. If there was no leaving, it was better to face whatever this was. He looked up again, marveling at the clarity of the dream. The faces on the walls had a level of detail he couldn't even give the memory of his wife. It was so easy to forget the good in life, but never let a detail of tragedies escape. He recognized many of the faces and understood why they looked at him as they did.

Syl continued to walk across the never-ending hall until abruptly, he found himself in front of something new. An end, or at least the beginning of something different. A small door. He didn't hesitate, ducking through and immediately coming face to face with a stranger, an intruder in his dream. *It's my dream,* he corrected himself. *My stranger.* The solitary figure loomed in an appropriately menacing manner, hooded, cloaked, and impassive. The bit of his face he could see was obscured with some sort of bandage or wrapping that covered the skin.

"Who are you?" he asked. It seemed the polite thing to do.

"Wrong question."

Syl frowned. He didn't like feeling stupid, even if it was in a dream.

"What is the right question?"

"Not that."

Syl glared at him in irritation before turning to observe the rest of the chamber. Given who was dreaming, he had to admit it made sense that even mysterious strangers were impossible to deal with. The prehistoric dimensions of the earlier chamber had condensed to where he now stood, a grain of sand resting beside the mountain. It was a cramped, domed room, candles burning all around, and a large dais with a small pool of dark liquid in the middle. Behind the hooded, impolite man, door after door stood. No, not doors. Blank blocks of stone, where doors should have been.

"How do I leave?" he ventured. "To go back to my dream."

No answer.

"Which door?"

A glint of bright teeth beneath the overlarge hood.

"Better question. You're improving. But the answer to that is up to you."

"Well, then what is behind each?" Syl asked, frustrated.

"Oh, death and destruction and all sorts of dramatic nonsense. You've an interesting future, Syl. 'Futures,' I should say. But they all lead to the same place."

"Then does it matter which I choose?"

"Of course." The stranger laughed.

"But if they all end at the same place, why does it matter?"

"Doesn't every life end in the same place? Does that mean the choices made didn't matter?"

Syl chewed at his lip, thinking on that.

"Can I at least see what's behind each?"

The man shrugged, as if it were none of his business what Syl did or didn't do.

Annoyed, Syl started toward one of the doors on the left. He could feel the cool stone as he pressed on it and felt the patterns. It was real beyond real, and all the more dreamlike for it. He could feel every grain in the rock and the passage of air as the door—or maybe something in him—gave way to what seemed an infinite void, a thousand moments folding out before him, all seen at once and experienced simultaneously, endlessly overlapping. Future memories and possibilities entwined and whipped past faster than he could grab onto, let alone understand.

There were vast armies marching in the black and gold of the imperial legions, dominating everything in their path and raising the phoenix banner above all. Hundreds of young men and women, some who even looked like him, training on the fields of the Palatine under the harsh instruction of the Vigil cadre, and the towers of Upper Heliopolis behind them all. Another Riftgate conquered, and another and another and another, more than he had imagined possible. All captured and harnessed, controlled by

an empire resurgent and assured in its power, legions and titans marching forward, an unstoppable tide. The Vigil's dream realized: an empire
that could weather cataclysm after cataclysm. And still, an encroaching
darkness and a winter that battered against all that might and fury like the
sea against a lighthouse. A battle that hadn't been lost yet, but with only
one end in sight. A guttering candlelight, brighter for now, but soon to be
swallowed by the darkness.

With a breath, he closed the door. He looked to the man for explanation,
but all he received was a nod to the next door in line. Willingly, Syl followed.
Overwhelmed didn't mean incurious, and confusing and interesting often
came hand in hand. He was prepared this time as he placed his hand against
the slab, as his existence flipped to the far side of that stationary door.

He was drowning in another vortex of images and sensations. He knew
it was impossible, but he struggled to grab them anyway, see them one by
one, as a man who is drowning tries to pull in oxygen with his lungs, an
action beyond any conscious efforts or decision.

This time, hordes of horsemen and fur-clad tribesmen rampaged over
the boundaries of his world. Myriad upon myriad of ironspawn, awake
and boiling forth from the earth. That girl, Morana, that damn one-eyed
witchlet, up to her elbows in blood, staring at him with murder promised.
Beside her, a fiery figure crowned with a serpent of iron burned the land
about itself. Wyrms and monsters whose shape he could barely comprehend, but whose purpose was razor-clear. Entire penal colonies set
loose, and a new generation of ever-more-powerful Stained rising alongside
them, venting a generation's worth of revenge against any and all parts of
an empire that had promised safety and given them only shackles and slavery. Demons and Fallen, fire and blood, all flooding the land and washing it
clean of everything. But there was warmth there too. The crows circled in
clear skies, and the sun shone down on all that violence. Somehow, he knew
that there was a chance there. A chance for something beyond endlessly
advancing winters and skies of ash.

Another breath, as if surfacing from a deep dive, and he found himself
alone in the room again ... almost alone.

"What was that? Why did you show me that? Who are you?"

"I already answered that; because it's important; and we will meet soon
enough." He paused, amused. "These still aren't the right questions."

Syl thought for a moment. He knew what the right question was, but he hesitated.

"What was that...light? That way? How?"

"Excellent. Finally, a question worth answering, and you've answered it yourself: a way, Syl. And you'll know the how when it's time."

"A way to what?"

"Out of all of this. Do you think the world has to fall apart?"

"You're not making any sense," Syl decided, stepping back and shaking his head. "This is just a dream, and I'm done listening to you." He was a fool for listening this long. "Besides, what an inane question. Everything always falls apart. That's the one gods-damned truth I know, so fuck you, and fuck your riddles and nonsense questions. I'm done with you, and I'm done with this dream." He turned to walk away, willing himself to wake up, or at least slide into the oblivion of a dreamless sleep.

He was met with blank, featureless walls. The entry was gone, and the entire room had closed around him, smaller and darker than it had been before. The man hadn't moved and looked now at Syl in a way that somehow conveyed the deepest disappointment, even if his features were entirely hidden.

"You're not nearly as quick as I hoped you might be. Certainly not as clever as he claims. But if there's one 'gods-damned' truth I've learned, it's that you work with the tools you have, not the ones you need. If you don't find your way, Syl, there will be costs." He studied Syl again. "Maybe you need to see what you already know. I can understand that. But if you can't stop looking backwards, it's all you'll ever see." He flicked a dismissive hand.

With a gasp, Syl found himself beside the pit, kneeling in the days-old ash. How it always ended. Here, and only here, the details were perfect.

# LITTLE HISTORIES

S weating, struggling, Syl woke to a tangle of damp covers, hands aching from clenching at nothing. There was a moment of disorientation and panic where he could have sworn he heard bells. No. That already happened. With a sigh, he settled back, body relaxing as much as it could into the bed. Only a dream. Gods, what an odd dream though, even for him. Scattered images were seared into his vision, but disappearing fast, as if he had looked at the sun too long. Their afterimage left only impressions, but the sensation remained. He thought there might have been something hopeful there amid all that strangeness and confusion. Either way, it was all fading away, left behind in the dream world.

Slowly, he stripped away the covers and rose, orienting himself by the pale moonlight shining through the thin window. The stone walls of the room that had seemed so large in the daytime seemed to close around him. Yet another cramped stone room. This wasn't the prison, and these walls weren't the tunnels. He knew that. But the stifling, wet heat of the bed was too much right now; he needed to go outside, anywhere but here.

Bare feet padding across the cold floor, he left the room for the blessed openness and cool drafts of the hallway in the house that had been given over for their use. Some minor Getacian noble, hoping to curry favor. Undoubtedly hoping for a short stay, they hadn't bothered removing most of their belongings, and Syl could see little portraits lining the walls, even if it was too dark to see details. Closed windows into a family's life.

Turning his way through the unfamiliar rooms and halls made familiar over the last days, he found himself at the second-floor terrace. He pulled himself up short. She was there already. Syl hesitated at the cracked door, peering through that small sliver to where Liora stood, short hair and sharp nose silhouetted by the flare of a burner. She leaned against the railing, looking out on the silent city, a dark vista of suggested lines, but for the detail brought by the occasional arclamp moving along the nearest stretch of wall. Far behind and high above, the lanterns around the dam dwellings sparkled, stars against the mountain. Telling himself he didn't want to disturb her, he started to turn around.

"Who's there?"

A breath, two. *Coward.*

"It's Syl."

Another brief silence. "What are you doing? Come out here, it's nice."

An invitation. Maybe a peace offering.

Reluctantly, he stepped out onto the broad terrace, trying to focus on the crisp night air he had wanted so badly earlier. He tried to let it clear his mind. It was worthless. All he could focus on was Liora, her features flaring to life again as she took another drag from the burner before offering it to him. There was an electric thrill that ran through him as her fingers brushed his, before he drew deep, feeling the smoke flood his lungs in a warm rush. He drew again, trying to replace the hangover of the dream and the confusing sensations he felt being around her with the recollection of earlier, simpler times. Times sharing a rare luxury with laughing comrades around a fire.

"Slow down," she teased. "That's not all for you."

Handing it back, Syl held the swirling smoke for a breath more before blowing it out in a long stream, savoring the memories. "Where did you get that?"

"Our new friend, Colonel Gralinis. I've never seen a man so anxious to make friends. He's terrified," she admitted.

"Good."

Liora stared at him, eyes inscrutable in the dark. "Don't you get tired of it?"

"Tired of what?"

Sighing, she threw her arm in a broad circle. "This. All of this. The intimidating, the torturing, the killing. It feels...it feels...wrong?" Her voice trailed off.

"You still regret what we did at the farmhouse?"

"You mean what you made me do?"

"Answer the question." She was new to the team, so he understood her hesitation, but if she spoke to anyone else like this, there would be more issues. The Exarch's warning echoed in his memory.

Syl didn't need to see to know she was glaring at him. "Yes. I mean...no. Maybe. I think. But I don't know if I can bring myself to enjoy it like the rest of you."

A shiver passed down his spine, and Syl found himself almost outside of his body, a cold rage radiating through every fiber of his being. "You think I enjoy this?"

*Go on, lie to her. Tell her you don't.*

"How else can you do this for years?" She caught the tone in his voice, and her own hardened in turn. "And calm down. I'm trying to understand, to figure out if I made a mistake transferring from the legions to this."

"Why did you transfer, anyway? I saw the orders. You made quite the name for yourself there at the Gates. The Angel herself apparently signed off."

"Angel?" She snorted. "You've never actually seen one of the Chosen fight, have you?"

"No. Not personally."

"All the rest have names that fit. She doesn't. We liked to call her the Demon of the Pass. I think she liked that name. Absolutely terrifying. I mean, beautiful, holy, all that, of course. She's one of the Chosen, so, obviously. There's no doubting it when you see that light bleeding out of them. But by the gods, you did not want to be fighting near her. Would carve through a hundred riders like it was nothing. And then send another thousand of us to die without batting an eye."

"It's the nature of their role," Syl said, not sure why he felt the need to defend one of the Emperor's Chosen.

"I guess. Don't you ever wonder why they are the way they are?"

"They?"

"The Chosen. The Emperor Himself, for that matter."

"No."

"Really? Not at all?"

"No. Not my place. The prophecies of the *Vox Caelorum* tell you enough, and the fact that the Vigil they established has endured for a dozen cycles tells you the rest. It's enough that they're here. Can you imagine where we'd be without them? Our ancestors waited on a prophecy for, what—a thousand years? Two thousand? No one even really knows, there were so few that survived the Breaking and the first few cycles. And look at what's happening here. Another Riftgate, and the beginning of a new cycle, with Stained and separatists too short-sighted to see that we can't survive this unless we're united. It was nearly as bad in Heliopolis. Just barely clawing our way out of the last cataclysm when the gate opened. Stained running around with all that newfound power, and us all doing our best to kill one another off as fast as we could, same as we always do. We'd have destroyed ourselves, same as before, Vigil or not, without the Emperor and the Chosen coming back again. They are sent from the gods themselves. We aren't meant to understand everything."

"That's a lazy way to look at the world, Syl. Come off it, don't tell me you don't wonder what that means? The priests talk about the Breaking and the cataclysms and how the Emperor and them are meant to save us from ourselves...but what caused the Breaking in the first place? The cataclysms? Why does the world have to fall apart?"

Something echoed in his mind off what she said, but the source remained just beyond reach as he tried to remember why that was.

"That's the pattern of our world," he said, growing uncomfortable. He was intensely aware that he sounded like he was reading from a script, because that was exactly what was happening. These were not the sorts of questions he cared about. It was like asking why men had to die. "Why" didn't much matter, if the "what" was going to happen regardless. "No one knows what exactly caused the Breaking, only that we destroyed ourselves in centuries of conflict." Apparently, this was a night for Syl to feel stupid, whether that was in his dreams or not.

"Gods, you're boring. Talking in circles. The gods send saviors to stop the end of the world? And we caused the end of the world? Well, if the gods made us, then didn't they make the end of the world too? Who caused it to happen, if not the gods? Why didn't they stop us? Or better yet, change us?"

"I don't know," he said, frustrated with his own ignorance and her flippancy. He was desperate for a change of subject. "I don't have the answers. But at least I know why I do what I do. I control what I can. Speculation does nothing for anyone. The Vigil is still our best shield against what *is*. And you still haven't answered my question: why are you here?"

Liora threw up her hands. "Honestly? I don't know. Or I thought I did, I guess. They offered me two options: promotion at the Gates, or a knighthood. Oathknight. Bondknight, I've heard you all call it." She snorted. "Really captures the essence, doesn't it? Anyways... I knew I couldn't stay there. I know you and Leon spent years in the legions, so maybe you understand a little, but it is awful out there. I'd been at the Gates for three years, and it was the same every damn year. You freeze all winter, a new crop of recruits arrive, you try to get them up to speed, and then you spend the spring and summer fighting in the passes. See who survives, and start all over again. I mean it's...it's awful. There's no other word for it. Everything about it. It's not a real life." She paused. "You know they would give us junior officers poison, right? Tiny little bottle, neat. Easy to carry, and believe me, you made sure not to lose it. Because you did *not* want to get captured by those savages. Better to choose your own way out. Only the officers though—not because they were the only ones who'd get tortured, but because there wasn't enough to go around. The priests aren't great at the old alchemies. Not that they didn't seem to have plenty of time to make all those horrible miasmas and battle drugs of theirs." She took a deep breath, slowing down again. "My... Someone very important to me gave his away. Was selfless like that. They surrounded his whole company the month before I left."

"I'm sorry." Syl had never been good at this.

"It's fine." She took another, even longer drag. She coughed. "But yes. I figured anything was better than that. Anyone I cared about there was dead. I didn't have any other family left, so it seemed like the right choice. Hunting down traitors, keeping the peace, all that. But..."

"That's exactly what we are doing."

"Really? Torturing merchants and killing old women? That feels like keeping the peace to you? Is this really stopping anything?"

"Yes. And this place is the perfect example of what happens when we don't do our job. A light hand in the northern districts, and now we are going to have yet another campaign up here. A Riftgate opens, and every step toward the cataclysm is another thousand old women and merchants dead, at least. Even in this city, Stained pass through smuggling networks, and soldiers are murdered in the streets. Disorder is like a weed in a garden, Liora." He could hear himself repeating the Exarch—poorly. "You might have a flower sprout, and it might even be pretty, a little variety. But if you don't rip it out, roots and all, when you come back, it will have choked everything else."

"Terrible metaphor."

"Maybe."

"Definitely."

The burner had long ago been smoked to nothing, and Liora ground what was left under her boot, avoiding looking at Syl. He knew she was unconvinced, but he also remembered his own transition, from the straightforward fights of a defined front against a known enemy to the murky choices they had to make in this profession, parsing truth and loyalty from deception and betrayal. Those first few years, he was practically blind with rage, no room for doubts. Any he had now weren't worth sharing. And this felt like surer footing than any more theological and cosmological arguments. While he hated to bring up his past, same as any of them, he had to make Liora understand. Maybe she could learn from him. He could tell she wanted to ask.

"I was married before, you know. Before this."

Liora didn't look up at him, but she had gone very still.

"We had a daughter too. She was perfect." He stopped, expecting tears. But after all these years, there was nothing.

"What happened to them?"

"They died," he said flatly. Now that he had started, it was easier to keep going. "Killed. I was in the legions then. Up here, actually. We were finishing up the campaign, finally having some success, when we heard the news."

"The Mages' Revolt?"

"Yes. You have no idea what it's like to receive news like that. To be in danger, believing you are fighting to keep your family safe, for a better future for your child, only to find that the real danger is behind you. To not even be able to go to them." His voice broke now, as he remembered the feeling of utter powerlessness of that impossible situation. "It's not as if they could just let us go. We had to fight our war, while the legions by the capital dealt with that threat. Reasonable. Maddening."

Liora knew where this story would end. "I'm so, so sorry, Syl."

"I'm not done. This isn't a sob story, so don't fucking feel sorry for me. I'm telling you this for a reason. I want you to try and imagine that. Try. To know that the only people you've loved in this world are depending on you, the ones that you're supposed to protect. And there is *nothing* you can do about it. Just wait. Wait and let the guilt and worry eat you alive from the inside. When you're finally allowed home, you've been told they put down the rebellion, that they're pushing them back. You let a little hope spark inside of you, like the idiot you are. Maybe they're fine, they're waiting for you, and everything can go back to the way it was."

Syl gripped the railing until he could feel the metal grinding on his bones. He squeezed tighter.

"But of course they weren't. Those bastards may have lost their little revolution, but they made the empire pay in every way they could as they were beaten back. Scorched earth. Poisoned wells. Burnt villages. And killing anyone who seemed to be too loyal." Syl brushed away the hand she reached out to him. "You know, I think they killed them because of me." He laughed bitterly. "There was an old woman in the village we lived in. Sweet old lady. But she could draw from the Rift. Everyone knew it, but we never said anything, because she had a gift for soothing little aches, made life a little easier for everyone. But when the armies of the Mages' Revolt came through, apparently she was the one who pointed out anyone with families working for the local prefect or serving in the legions.

"When I got there, the place was abandoned. They had killed so many that they had needed to burn the bodies in a pit. I had to search for their bodies in a pit. A fucking pit. Couldn't even find them, there were so many. Impossible to tell bodies apart at that point anyway." He shook his head. "It's never a stranger, Liora. I never found that old woman, but death was too good for her. Domarik and his old team were conducting operations ahead of the front lines, and he was the one who found me there on their way back, told me what had happened. And that's why I'm here. That's why I know what we're doing is the right thing. You want to talk about ancient history and the Breaking, cataclysms and gods, magic and disunity pulling the world apart, but that's all bullshit. The Mages' Revolt. These northern districts. One and the same. You let one small thing slip, then another, and before you know it, you've got another province drowning in blood, and some other poor sap coming home to a butchered family."

"I'm sorry," she said again, so softly. "I think I understand."

Syl let out a shuddering breath, trying to let go of the hate that filled him every time he thought about those days. "Good."

There was a long pause. "Then why did you let the girl live?"

That caught him off guard. "I don't know. But it was a mistake."

"Maybe. And what about Gralinis? You were pretty heavy-handed with him, but I don't think he's guilty of anything. Maybe incompetence."

"I know," Syl agreed, grateful for the change of subject. Work he could do. "Probably a few traitors in his garrison though, and we've got people watching tonight. Hopefully the threat of the search tomorrow will spread and send a few scurrying for their holes. But as for him... He's just an idiot."

"Right?" she asked, with the forced light tone of someone equally happy to be changing topics. "That, or a great actor. But assuming he's not, if he is exactly as incompetent as he appears to be, then why is this whole city still under imperial control?"

"Well, probably because..." Syl trailed off as he thought about what she had said, starting to frown. "I don't know. We've found enough active cells here. There have been a few officials assassinated already, and it feels like half the garrison would run if you looked at them wrong."

"Exactly! Every one of the garrisons north of here was slaughtered or driven off, and their districts' prefects either switched sides or were assassinated. Why not here? Any group of soldiers we send out smaller than a squad gets murdered, so they clearly aren't afraid to act either."

"Too close to the provincial capital?"

"Crossing those mountains from Rasovus didn't feel like a short trip. At least the legions will start arriving tomorrow. I would hate to be stuck here on our own. Can you imagine how hard the passage will be in a month? Two?"

"Impossible." Syl drew in a sharp breath, struck by the implications. "Liora... What if they never wanted this city?"

She nodded slowly, climbing rung by rung toward the same conclusion. "They want them to come. It could work. Even if they couldn't destroy the legions, if they can contain the Twins here for the winter, it would be a disaster. They'd have a whole season to prepare the rest of the province and build their strength."

"And who would be necessary for any of this to work? Who would have to be protecting traitors in the imperial apparatus here, officers ready to turn within the garrison? It has to be either the prefect or the commander." Syl felt the warm, vicious glow of vindication for his disdain for Antinius as the man's arrogance and hesitation were painted in a new light.

"The commander can barely scheme his way into breathing between sentences. It's not him."

He stared across at her, grateful to be caught up in their work. "What do you say we explore the town a little?"

A mischievous grin showed itself. "I thought you'd never ask."

# APOLOGIES

Vali was on fire. It was unbearable. Tossing and turning, sleep was impossible for him to find. He kept thinking about the dinner. About Kass. He should call her that, not Kassara, shouldn't he?

Every time he closed his eyes, every time he tried to think of nothing and just let the day end, her face came up before him. Flashing teeth, a diamond-sharp little smile. That hair, so impractically, absurdly long for her line of work. Like she knew exactly how distracting it was. The slender neck that kept sweeping down to... She would be covered in the oathknight tattoos like Syl, wouldn't she? Now that image burned itself into his mind as his imagination kept going down the same paths.

Frustrated and knowing sleep was no closer than it had been when he returned from dinner, Vali threw away the covers with a disgusted grunt. He needed a walk. Anything but this. Maybe the balcony. Or maybe the courtyard. Anywhere where he could stand and let the bitter chill of the night clear away his thoughts, this unhealthy obsession. He didn't even know her, so what did she want with him?

With violent, furious movements, Vali dressed before barging into the corridor, knocking the doorframe with his shoulder and muttering curses under his breath. The woman was playing with him. She had seen his interest and was using it to toy with him, have him make a fool of himself.

Distracted, Vali didn't see the other shape in the narrow ground floor corridor until after they had bounced off him.

"Unghh."

It was Lucky, gasping on the ground.

"Shit. I'm sorry, I'm sorry! Are you alright?" He bent down to help him up, reflecting that he didn't need much help to make a fool of himself.

Lucky waved him away, wheezing. "Stop, stop. I'm fine."

Standing back, Vali watched awkwardly as Lucky pulled himself together and caught his breath. Lucky was about his age, a little younger, but had steadfastly resisted all attempts by Vali or his friends to engage in any meaningful sort of conversation. They had tried on the journey north, and again here in Seven Rivers. As far as his own efforts, Vali wasn't surprised. He had been busy learning from the Hunters and was aware of the limits of his conversational abilities at the best of times. Lucan, on the other hand, could make friends with anyone anywhere, and even his good-natured efforts had been rebuffed.

"What are you doing up?" Vali had meant it as an opener. Maybe this, of all times, would be when Lucky would let his guard down. It would be a good distraction.

"Mind your own business. And watch where you walk." Lucky brushed past him, more than a head shorter, but slightly terrifying in the way small dogs could be.

"Asshole," Vali muttered under his breath. Even with all he had heard about Lucky's skill, he couldn't believe the team tolerated his attitude. Not his problem. And what kind of name was Lucky, anyway? He'd be damned if he was going to ask.

Working his way up to the second floor, he barely noticed the finery of the furniture and the art on the walls, until he ran into a small shrine in the hall, a figurine surrounded by unlit candles. The details were lost in the dark, but Vali knew it was a shrine to one of the divine aspects. He remembered that his mother had set one up in their house for one of the aspects of the goddess embodying growth, renewal, and decay, a piece of that divinity meant for a plentiful harvest. Brushing his fingers along the smooth carved lines, he remembered his grandmother sitting next to their own, more than half blind and covered in blankets, but one hand on that little statue, as if it were her hold on life. Her own chance at renewal, maybe. She would tell him and Sorin stories about the gods and goddesses, their infinite aspects, their cycles of birth and rebirth, while they sat in rapt attention in front of the fireplace. The empire might have their five and five and the *Vox Caelorum*, but part of Vali missed the idea of the nine and their thousands watching over their world and all the others cut off since the Breaking.

Feeling like his mind was a little more his own again, he continued on his way, footfalls muffled on the rich carpet. Even when passing by the door he knew was Kassara's, he wasn't tempted by the idiot impulse he had been toying with of knocking. As he approached the far end of the house, he could hear voices ahead. He kept moving slowly, until he could see the balcony, where two figures stood sharing a burner. Their words were too quiet to hear, but he could tell it was Syl and Liora.

Did no one sleep here? The courtyard, then. Working his way back to the spiraling stairway, he even considered going back to his bed. He had just needed to take his mind off her. Perhaps he could sleep now. Then again, the courtyard had been beautiful in the daytime; it would be beyond peaceful right now, even if only for a few minutes. The cold had never bothered him much.

He almost didn't notice the open door, almost walked right past it. Almost wished he had. But there it was, and there was no ignoring it now. Kassara's door was wide open, a black rectangle within the near darkness of the hall. An invitation. He hesitated. She was playing with him, he told himself. Trying to make a fool out of him.

He walked in. Maybe he didn't mind.

A tentative step took him past the threshold. It hadn't been open before, he knew that. Straightening his back, he took another. He hadn't imagined what happened at the dinner, he was sure of it. Another, as the details of the room became a little clearer.

"What are you doing in here?"

Freezing, Vali could feel the heat rush back, in a panicked flood. How had he missed her? She sat outlined by the window now, that lounging form unmistakable.

"I..."

"You what?"

"I..."

She laughed then, a soft, husky sound. "Took you long enough. What's a girl got to do to drop a hint with you Getacians?"

Uncoiling from her perch by the window, she sauntered slowly toward him until she stood looking up at him where he stood, rooted to the spot. With a start, he realized she wasn't wearing anything. He couldn't move, couldn't speak.

"Come here." She grabbed his hand, pulling him closer, but Vali resisted, confused.

"Wait. No." Was this really what he wanted?

"No?" There was a biting tone now. "'No' now, after you walk in here? After I catch you staring at me, well, constantly?"

"Why, though?"

"Because I want to. And believe me, life's too short not to take what you want from it. You don't know that yet, but you will." She let go of his hand and traced her own gently, so slowly down his chin, and then dragged the nail down his chest, pushing in at the end. Vali flinched, feeling her pierce the skin through his shirt. "And besides, I know you want to. So, don't waste my time, and don't dare play coy now."

Leaning forward on her toes, she kissed him, soft lips parting around his own, melting any last bit of resistance there might have been. He pushed back against her again, but she brushed his hands away. He wanted to pull away, to ask her what she had meant earlier, about choices, but another part of him didn't want to take the chance of breaking whatever spell had put him here and her right in front of him. And what was he resisting, anyway? Inexplicably, he found his thoughts straying to Marika for the briefest of moments before giving in completely to the warmth he didn't think he could turn away from.

# WATCH AND WAIT

The peaceful quiet of the terrace became oppressive on the streets, as the rare foot traffic that might have existed at the late hour gave way to shuttered windows and locked doors. The curfew put out by the prefect was perfunctory at this point. Syl knew all too well what it was like to lose trust in your neighbors. When you saw the man who lived across from you—the one you bought bread from every day—snatched up in broad daylight as a traitor, all those things that seemed so secure and sure before revealed foundations of sand. Residents kept to themselves, and the city felt like one already under siege, but from within. Between the patrols, their team, separatist cells, and any Stained that might be about, Syl couldn't blame them. Not to mention the team that Domarik and Leon were leading tonight, capitalizing on any follows from the barracks, breaking down a few more doors and dragging a few more in for questioning. He would have locked his doors too. You only needed to learn that lesson once.

Stealing a glance at Liora as they worked their way silently along the street, he wondered if she had taken what he had hoped for from his story. That it had been a lesson, not just a depressing glimpse into his past. He hoped so. For now, they moved to their agreed-upon target, the prefect's quarters, a sprawling mansion that spread upward in tiers at the western edge of the dam, nestled between sheer walls, mountain and man-made. There was nothing to go on except for a vague feeling of pieces not fitting together as they should, not enough to wake Kass or go find Domarik and Leon. As they came to a stop at the last corner before the estate, Syl wasn't even exactly sure what they would do here.

"What now?"

Just because he didn't know didn't mean he was about to admit it. "Now we wait."

"For what?"

"Just wait."

"Hmmph."

Clearly, he wasn't the only one having second thoughts about their self-imposed surveillance mission. Nothing for it now. A short, whispered conversation later, they separated, each to their own vantage point. Syl's skin burned faintly as he pulled enough from his conduits to help him scale the crumbling concrete of one of the nearby buildings, finding a perch on the roof where he could almost make himself comfortable, crammed between the jutting timbers and shingles of the building.

Unfortunately, comfort was always a relative thing. A handful of minutes passed, and his joints started to stiffen. More time passed, and he could feel a maddening twitch in the base of his neck from where he craned it to peer methodically through the windows and along the streets leading to the house. Had it been an hour? Two? What the hell was he doing here? Perched on a roof in the middle of the night like an idiot, overlooking a target he wasn't even sure was a target. Still, he kept coming back to their conversation.

*Why not here?*

An excellent question. Their suspicions were sound, even if Syl felt half a fool for letting Liora talk him into this impromptu investigation without talking to Domarik. This was a major city, a regional hub, and the most obvious staging point for any army that crossed the punishing range of the ice-capped Severan Mountains behind them. This city would be instrumental in the upcoming campaign.

Syl had finally decided they had wasted enough time tonight, even if their theory was worth further investigation, when he saw movement. Or thought he did. Syl had sat freezing and motionless in enough overwatch positions to know that sometimes the mind saw what it wanted to see.

There it was again. A shape crossing from the shadows of one building, flitting across the moonlit squares, disappearing into another. There was only one possible destination, and the only question that remained was whether the prefect knew his would-be guest, or was tonight's target.

As he crept down from his vantage point to their agreed-upon meeting point, he could feel the familiar thrill course through him, chasing away the chill and any exhaustion. If he were honest with himself, this was the part of the job he lived for. The excitement of the hunt, the promise of conflict, and the possibility of death made him feel alive in a way that made the rest of the world seem gray and lifeless.

*And you pretend to everyone else that you do this for your family. Hypocrite.*

*He knows, he knows.*

There was a leaden pit of guilt that came with the thrill, but Syl knew both things could be true at once. Liora was already there, waiting for him, nodding at his approach.

"So?" she asked.

"We follow inside."

She hesitated. "We'd better be right."

"Well, either he's about to be killed, in which case he'll be happy to see us, or he's in on it, and then it really doesn't matter how he feels about it."

"Should we grab the others?"

"Too late." Syl grinned. "This was your idea. No time to back out now." He wasn't about to pass this opportunity up.

Low and fast, they made their way to the far side of the estate, climbing over the small outer wall and working their way along the edges, using what little cover the bushes and trees of the grounds provided. There was little enough, but there didn't seem to be a point. The periodic movement within the mansion Syl had noted earlier, the unmistakable patterns of bored guards, was nowhere to be seen. The interior, as far as he could see, was utterly dark, and whoever the unknown guest was had passed unobserved into that blackness. Or was welcomed.

Syl straightened from his crouch and gestured to Liora to follow him.

"What are you doing?" she hissed.

"They're all gone. Or dead." He thought dead more likely. "We need to get inside now."

Trading caution for speed, they advanced rapidly, climbing up to the balcony outside of the room they had all eaten together within only hours before. A locked door stood flanked by two windows, with the faint impression of the table and chairs within. Not enough time to find another entrance. Standing before one of the windows, Syl shrugged at Liora, before smashing the glass with the hilt of his sword, using the blade to rapidly clear the edges.

Liora flinched, grimacing at the gentle tinkling as the window fell apart inward onto the tiles within and the awful scraping of metal on glass as Syl cleared them a way in.

"Why?"

Syl vaulted in, doing his best not to catch anything on the jagged pieces that remained. "We need to get in."

Standing outside, Liora stared at him before making a sound somewhere between a sigh and a grunt before gently turning the knob of the door and joining him in the room.

*Ah.* Syl was glad she couldn't see his face in the dark room.

"I think you just like to break things," she muttered. "Let's go."

⸻⸻⸻◄O►⸻⸻⸻

Sometimes, uncovering the truth was something that happened layer by layer, until you could see to the core of things. Sometimes, bringing Stained or traitors in or putting them down was a savage, bloody affair. And sometimes, you surprised a flustered group of conspirators in their basement.

Three men were cuffed and kneeling on the rich carpet back at the house, little patters of blood dribbling down onto the woven designs. One, none other than Prefect Antinius, was adding his snot and a few dribbling tears to the mix. The fact that he was adding to the ruination of their host's house made Syl unreasonably angry. He cuffed the old man over the ear, causing him to fall forward, face nearly coming to rest on Domarik's boots. Of course, that only made things worse. Domarik looked up impassively toward Syl, who shrugged. This whole night had turned into a pathetic spectacle. At least one of the would-be traitors, a second-in-command to Gralinis and a local Getacian, had had the balls to fight. They had caught six of them in all in the mansion's basement. They had been holding a panicky conference of sorts, whispering in a circle by a carefully concealed entrance that led to the smuggling channel and several tunnels that stretched unbroken and undamaged into the distance. The very same tunnels that a sweating Colonel Gralinis, even now, swore were collapsed, entrances sealed.

"Ah, you must understand, Vigilus...there was no possible way of know-ing..." Gralinis trailed off as Domarik turned that impassive face his way, one that promised attention at a later point. The disheveled officer had just woken up, eyes bleary and uniform far from the polished ensemble of the dinner.

"What I understand," Domarik began, his deep timbre causing the prefect to cringe backward, "is that incompetence is not a victimless crime, Commander. We will discuss this later. As for you two, well done. This could have been a disaster."

Liora beamed a smile at Syl, tired, but full of life. Syl couldn't help but return it.

The moment fled as Domarik continued. "Question them. Now. We need to know of any other threats. Leon, arrange for a special shipment sent through your friends. To be delivered a few days after the legions arrive. I'll coordinate with the flamewardens for this particular cargo. Tell your friends they'll be paid handsomely."

"Should they be around afterward to enjoy those ill-gotten gains?"

"You know the answer to that."

Leon gave a salute so crisp as to be satiric.

Domarik continued. "Colonel, you will put yourself and your men entirely under our disposal as we search the city. Again. Oh, and arrest any and all Getacian officers in the local garrison. We aren't taking chances this time."

Gralinis stood there in shocked confusion as his world fell apart around him.

"That means now. Go now."

Gralinis bobbed his head hurriedly before all but running out of the room.

Domarik rolled his neck with a few loud, audible cracks. "Good work always means more work. Syl, Liora, Leon, start with these. Questions, answers, you know the drill. Kass and I will start in on the officers. It's going to be a long day."

Looking across the prisoners, Syl noticed Liora's pride fading into resignation, and he couldn't help but agree. It hadn't taken any time at all for the excitement of a successful investigation to turn into the same self-disgust as you watched your own sympathy morph into frustration.

Sometimes, when a man knew he was about to be questioned, he would beg and cry for mercy, soiling himself and leaving behind any shred of dignity he might have maintained up until then. The prefect was a blubbering, stinking mess, leaking excuses. Syl forced him to his feet, curling his nose at the smell. Sometimes, they held onto their silence or their anger, instinctively knowing that was all they had left. Liora looked as pained as if she were the one being dragged in for questioning, but the proud officer that she hauled up was stoic and grim-faced, steeling himself for what was to come. Not that it would matter soon. Syl looked to where Leon pushed along his own charge, chuckling at the man's distress. No, it wouldn't matter at all.

# WARMING UP

*The legions are here.*

The words on every tongue in the city. Some spoke them in hope, a long-awaited salvation, a bulwark against the chaos to the north and the uncertain times in their own streets. For some, a curse, the fulfillment of a prophecy they knew they couldn't escape.

*The legions are here.*

Tomorrow, they would be, Vali corrected himself, feet drifting slowly to newly learned positions, a thousand and one cues competing for his mental focus. It couldn't possibly be soon enough.

"Hands higher."

Vali shifted accordingly. A thousand and two cues.

Better to act before the next inevitable correction. He burst forward, uncoiling and feinting high, before twisting sideways with a brutal diagonal cut. Casually, lazily almost, Syl brushed it aside, only bothering to shift a little, his one concession to the strength behind that weighted wood. Vali pressed the attack, trying every trick he knew or could think of, and putting bone-cracking strength into every blow. If it connected, Syl would be fine. And if he wasn't, well, it wasn't as if it wouldn't have been fair. Unfortunately, that entire train of thought had remained firmly in the realm of the hypothetical, even after two weeks of this. Every blow found only air or was pushed aside in a way that left Vali struggling to adjust. He retreated now, sweating, and trying to find that inner calm that Syl always preached of, that flow state of seeing the pattern of what was to happen before it happened. All Vali found was sweat in his eyes and frustration.

Any chance for inner calm evaporated as Syl slipped forward in that eerie way he had. One moment, perfectly still; the next, limbs in liquid motion. He skimmed above the ground and thrust forward in a series of blows. Vali was able to push away the first couple, but one of those darting cuts found the inside of his leg, and he found it pulled away. And he was back in the dirt. Again.

He wanted to scream in frustration. On the side of the yard, his friends waited for their own turns in the dirt. Leon was there too. He had taken to helping Syl in these lessons that they still managed to find time for. Vali had no idea when the team actually slept, but Leon never looked quite as exhausted as the rest of them. There was an example of someone who found pleasure in their work, and apparently this was no exception. Lucan looked nervous, knowing he was next, but as usual, Marika looked like she was enjoying the show. Particularly the part where Vali ended the morning filthy and covered in bruises. She made a comment to Leon that brought a laugh.

"Good cut," Vali said past gritted teeth.

"It was alright."

The man was infuriating. "Well, it got me."

"That's because you defend like your legs don't exist," Syl continued, the list of Vali's inequities apparently endless. "And another thing. You are still far too obvious with your eyes. It's good that you're strong enough to pull some of those moves with that weight, but that only goes so far. Doesn't matter how strong you are if your opponent knows exactly where you're going to be. Speed, Vali. All of you. Strength is nice. Better than being weak, certainly. But nine times out of ten, a fast, weak man will cut a slow, strong man to pieces, as long as he stays outside his guard."

"I know. I've heard that plenty before," Vali said.

"Yes? Well, maybe you need to hear it again, because you're shit at it."

"What if one of them is armored?" Marika interjected from where she sat. "Or one of those Voraxians? Those giants?"

Syl shrugged. "First good rule of thumb is not to fight giants. I shouldn't have to teach you that. As for armored? Then make it seven times out of ten. I don't know, six? Unless you're talking about those drugged-up knightbreakers in all that heavy plate. Or a judiciar in chorusplate. Then run, obviously."

"Drugged up...knightbreakers?" Vali asked.

Leon took the opportunity to jump in. "That's what we call them. 'Linebreakers'? 'Berserkers'? No, not ringing a bell? You know, unsanctioned conduits, armored in heavy plate, half-insane with an overdose of battle drugs and set loose? Your side used them all the time up here last campaign."

Vali didn't bother correcting him. Syl shifted uncomfortably.

Leon caught the stony stares though. He waved them away. "Yeah, yeah, be offended if you like. You three are fine. But talk to your father sometime about that little piece of history, little lord Valerek." It had been a tragedy when Leon learned his full name. "Might be enlightening. And yes, the Getacian units used them. I would have too. It was smart. You use anything you can in war. I *did* hear some reports about the clans up here in the North trying to wake up the ironspawn. As if you could control those little monsters. That one struck even me as a bit stupid."

There was a long, awkward silence.

"My turn." Unfolding gangly legs, Lucan stepped forward. "Or are we going to talk all afternoon?"

Syl inclined his head in silent thanks and settled into a fighting crouch.

"Whoa, whoa. I need to get in there too. I'm getting cold." Leon sprung up from where he had been lounging.

Lucan's face lost all color. Syl might have been merciless on the training grounds, but Leon was almost as good and pulled absolutely nothing. Vali had a welt of opened skin on his thigh that hadn't healed after a week. He thought it was likely to scar. According to Leon, that was the best way to learn.

Looking like he was walking to his own funeral, Lucan dragged his feet to the far end of the circle. Syl had been replaced by Leon already, who was doing some sort of strange squat to warm up. He caught Vali's questioning look.

"What? It's key to be limber. Warming up will save your life, lad." He jumped up, a little too high, and a little too quickly. Vali had his suspicions about whether Leon cheated just a little during these bouts. "Fair" was not a word Leon put much stock in. "Well, Lucan, you ready or not?"

Swallowing, his friend gave a grim nod.

Before Leon could administer his own unique brand of instruction, the door on the balcony overlooking the yard slammed open. Domarik emerged to stare down at all of them. The spectacles he so rarely wore didn't soften the lines of that massive, angular head at all. If anything, he looked more brutish than ever, a bear that had found and eaten a scholar.

"Legions are here." Impassive eyes rested on each of them, weighing each in their turn. "You two, run them through unit drills. They are probably coming with."

Syl nodded, and Domarik went back inside, as abruptly as he had come out.

"Unit drills?" Vali asked. "And 'probably'?"

"Walls, houses, closers, escorts, and tunnels?" Syl asked Leon, ignoring Vali.

"Sure. We can get through a couple today. Though tunnels isn't our job. Not anymore."

"Still."

"All I'm saying is that it better not be."

"Different formations," Syl said, turning to Vali. "Commands for different situations. Shield walls and all that good stuff. You might know some already from your time with Askaris. Bit different when you're in a city or fighting Stained. Grab the shields."

Lucan looked sick with relief and fled to where the shields were placed against the courtyard wall, given license for few more minutes of uninjured and pain-free living. Syl started to walk back into the house.

"Where are you going?" Marika asked, tightening the straps of her shield on her arm and trading out the practice blade for a longer stave meant to emulate a spear. "I thought we were going to run through these drills?"

"You are. I'll be back, need to talk to Domarik. Leon?"

"You're good. I'll be here. I love teaching drills."

Vali and the others shuffled together in the middle of the yard as Leon picked through the staves against the wall. He selected one out and held it aloft admiringly. Vali could have sworn it was the one he himself had put back because it was a bit too heavily weighted. Leon grinned evilly at where the three of them huddled together. "It's my specialty."

# MOVING ON

L ong, thin banners rippled in the breeze, so many little serpents, writhing above the great one that slithered its way down the long, sloping switchbacks of the road down into Seven Rivers. Syl, the team, and the Getacians all stood on the walls, gazing southward. For once, the weather seemed to be cooperating, providing one of those beautiful cold and sunny days. The kind meant for sitting and watching. What felt like half the city was doing exactly that, from the walls or from upper-floor windows behind. Banners and streamers hung from the buildings and dripped, fluttering, down the side of the dam. Desperate signs of allegiance in the hope that the coming tide would pass them by.

It was an event not seen in half a generation. Two full legions—more than twenty thousand men and women—marched under those banners, along with all manner of enablers trailing behind. Those ranged from the mundane necessities of every army, like supply wagons, cooks, and whores, to the more esoteric, like nulls, flamewardens, and bloodhounds. Nulls were common enough in the armies, though not found nearly as often as conduits. Those two groups always went opposite directions whenever Hunter teams found them. Conduits to the capital, fuel for the fight, and nulls to the front, a human shield against whatever arcane fury an enemy might muster against them. Flamewardens though... They were as carefully kept as the relic animachina and secrets they maintained, and Syl had only ever seen them a few times. On one of the final days of the last campaign, as he was losing his mind with worry over his family, a few flamewardens had been escorted by judiciars through the tunnels where the likes of he and Leon fought "the little war," as they liked to call it. Masked, goggled, and with packs at their sides and backs loaded down, those all-too-intriguing souliron sidearms strapped to their chests or held at their sides, all but the very end of the handles wrapped and invisible to prying eyes like theirs. Rumor was that they were there to end the siege. Syl hadn't believed it until he watched half the fortress wall ahead of him rupture from within like a burst fruit, with a flash of light from the sunflare explosive that seared the eyes of any watching.

"Still nothing?" Syl asked Lucky. He knew the answer, but felt the need to check again.

Lucky didn't bother looking his way and kept watching the marching soldiers impassively. "I don't know why you keep asking. I'd tell you otherwise. They're gone, or they were never here."

Syl didn't respond. He tried to be patient with Lucky, he really did. Lucky was almost the same age as Vali, but with such a size difference that he seemed half a kid. The attitude did grate sometimes though. Leon had no such compunction. He cuffed Lucky on the side of the head. Not lightly.

"We will ask as many times as we gods-damned please. Politeness goes a long way, Lucky. Look at me. You think I'd be where I am without manners?" Leon stared at Lucky expectantly, as if waiting for an actual answer. All he got was a bit of noncommittal grumbling from the bondmage, who rubbed at the red side of his face and kept his eyes on the ground. Leon raised his hand again, eyebrow cocked in question.

"I'm sorry," Lucky finally muttered, in a way that confirmed he was, in fact, not sorry at all.

Some of the others on the wall were looking now, and Domarik glanced at them, curious at the disturbance. Syl couldn't help being a little embarrassed himself. He frowned at Leon. "Can't you be kind?"

Leon frowned right back, looking confused, as if Syl had suddenly sprouted horns. "Why? This little bastard probably got his last team killed with that sort of attitude. He can be an asshole on his own time. We need professionals. And be kind?" he scoffed. "You're getting soft, old man."

They'd known each other far too long. Syl sighed. "We're the same age. Fuck you."

"Fuck you."

Smiling faintly, Syl looked over to where the Getacians stood, enraptured by the scene. He had to admit, it did look good from a distance. Wasn't so glorious when you were in it though, eating dust and praying for a halt. They'd be coming down quick now though. Nothing like seeing the destination to lend you a bit of strength. Vali and the other two would find out soon enough. It had been a tense few days in the aftermath of the prefect's arrest, but Syl had no doubt they would be marching with the rest of them soon. Because for all the cavalry, infantry, and enablers the Emperor had committed to this, He had also committed something that implied a sense of urgency like nothing else.

The Twins.

He had never seen one of the Chosen up close, and he wasn't sure he wanted to. Stories from those like Liora, who had, were enough. Impossibly powerful, they were the seven reaching fingers of His hand. Even while serving with that moron Gralinis under the Leveler, Syl had only ever seen him from a distance, a massive glowing silhouette, armored and masked. But while the Leveler's legions were meant for systematic conquests, the Twins were only ever sent out from the capital with a single purpose: lightning warfare. Long-range strikes, retaliatory raids, and the sort of martial terror that would keep a territory in line for another generation. It had been them who had turned the Mages' Revolt.

"How long before we head out?" Liora asked.

"Within the week," Syl said.

"Sooner," Domarik said. "Especially after what we found here, they won't want to wait."

"A shame," Kass added, a sly twist to her face. "This place was starting to grow on me."

Syl shook his head slightly, catching Liora's disapproving look as well. The fact that Kass had found a new toy wasn't surprising to anyone on the team, but it disappointed Syl that it was Vali. For all his brashness, the lad was honest to a fault, and braver than most of the soldiers he had served with. He hated to see him being played with. The mouse that thinks it's made friends with the cat.

"Why do you torture him?"

"Torture him? Darling, if he didn't want to be tortured, he wouldn't keep coming back. Don't be jealous, Syl; doesn't suit you. It's just a bit of fun."

"He thinks it's more than fun."

"And why is that my problem?"

Syl stared at her, disgusted. She was competent, could always be depended on in a fight, but damn was she difficult to like.

He decided to go talk to the Getacians. They had grown on him, proving themselves loyal and eager to learn, both on the raids that had become nightly excursions, and with the techniques Syl shared during their practices. Seeing them there, awkwardly standing apart, made him feel like he owed them some kindness, even if only to make up for Kass and Leon, who enjoyed tormenting them in their own little ways. Domarik mostly ignored them, other than to account for a few more swords in a fight and a few more mouths to feed and bodies to billet when it came time to plan the logistics.

Liora came to walk beside him. "She's a snake."

"She's part of our team."

"Still."

"Still," he agreed. "But at that age, he's got to learn the lesson at some point."

"She's going to eat him up and spit him out. I swear, men are slow learners."

Syl coughed with the unexpected laugh. "We need more direct lessons, is all."

"Hmph." She considered him, eyebrow arched. "When did you learn?"

"I didn't." It was a bittersweet memory. "She just forgot to spit me out." There was an awkward silence. "Sorry."

"Don't be." She squinted upward, to where the sun shone warm and cheery, a rare cloudless day and the last gasp of summer sneaking through the fall. "It's so nice today. I've seen you down in the yard with those three every afternoon. And Leon, of course. Want some help?"

Syl was certain she had no idea how much he appreciated her optimism. Having her on the team was a breath of fresh air. He mostly succeeded in not showing how pleased he was with her offer. "Let's go, then."

<hr />

This is what Vali had been waiting for. Rank upon rank of armored soldiers marched out of the wooded foothills toward the town, glittering reflections making them a long stream working its way from the snows above. And with them, the type of war he understood. Or had heard about enough to look forward to, at least. The great battles of formations thrown against one another, like his father had told him and his brother about until those tales became part of their own childhood mythology. Now it was his turn. Opposite those mountains, locks and waterways spread northward and disappeared into the endless forested hills and farmland that swept away from them to the north. Out there, somewhere, among all those cities in revolt and escaped Stained, was a chance for him to prove himself, to make his own stories.

Lucan yawned broadly beside him, and despite his excitement, Vali did his best to suppress his own. The last few days had been a flurry of activity—multiple raids every night, interrogations into the mornings, with the garrison working triple shifts to sweep through the city again, checking for arms caches and tunnel entrances, along with any other surprises the prefect might have left for them. Vali looked over to where the team stood, apart as always. The schedule wasn't the only reason he was exhausted. Even with all of that, almost every night for the last week, he had found himself at her door, as if against his will. And yet, the one time he had tried speaking to her during the day, she had laughed him away. It was as if there were two different people there. One that wanted everything from him, pulled him close with a violent eagerness, and one that saw him as some street mongrel that for some reason wouldn't stop following them. It was infuriating. He glared at her, wishing she would notice and hoping she wouldn't. She didn't.

"Where do you think we're headed first?" Lucan asked, interrupting his brooding thoughts.

"What?"

"I mean, I assume we aren't going to stay here."

Vali hadn't even considered that possibility, and it horrified him now. The members of the team were no longer the mysterious and cold strangers of before, but really only Syl and Liora treated them with anything approaching respect. Leon too, if Vali thought about it. Any attention from Leon was going to be a little rough. It wasn't the team, but the work that grated now. If he had to return home, with his only accolades being pulling conspirators out of their beds, trussed and hooded...it wasn't worth considering.

"We'd better not."

"They'll head north, we'll secure the next set of towns, and then I imagine we'll be with whatever group is going toward the penal colony at

Bal Maru," Marika cut in. Her voice was flat, as uninterested as if she were talking about ancient history.

Vali knew there was something wrong between them, and he thought he knew what it was, even if he wasn't sure what to do about it. He missed the Marika that was always cheerfully needling him, a steady and kind presence. She seemed constantly disappointed now. In him, he was fairly sure. He had never been the best at understanding people, but he had thought he had understood her. One of his two real friends—family, really—and he felt like he couldn't speak to her anymore.

"Well, that'll be good," he said, trying to inject some enthusiasm for her sake. "Anything to get out of here."

"Agreed." Lucan grimaced. "Believe me, I've seen enough hangings for a lifetime. Not saying they didn't deserve it," he added hurriedly, looking around.

The image of the prefect and the other officials swinging there, to the jeers of half the crowd and the silence of the other half, sprang into his mind. Those robes had looked significantly less imposing as he swung from the gibbet, food for the crows. Domarik had insisted on it, apparently. Said that as the man had betrayed the empire in the capacity of his office, he should be hung in the same. Insisted that they and the team attend as well.

Marika gave a bitter laugh. "What do you think it's going to look like north of here? Less hangings? Please. Maybe no hangings, because no workmen in the world could build a gallows big enough."

Not knowing what to say to that, Vali decided to say nothing. Thankfully, he could see Syl and Liora working their way toward them. Rubbing his eyes, he tried to erase the weariness that had made a home there. The two Helians looked infuriatingly well rested, despite keeping the same schedule as them.

"There better not be three of them teaching us now," Lucan growled. He rubbed at his side. All of them were covered in bruises and welts. "Two is more than enough."

"I rather think I'll enjoy watching a woman beat the piss out of you two for a change," Marika said, cheering a little.

"You bitch," Lucan said. "It'll be you too."

"Worth it."

It would be worth it, Vali knew. Already, he had improved by leaps and bounds under the harsh but careful tutelage of Syl. Leon too. Maybe even

"Are they who they need to be?"

"They are a product of their place and time, as are we all. They made choices, and they still might have a few left. But life and the decisions we make send us along our own paths, and the branches often become narrower. You cannot possibly imagine how narrow they can get when your past stretches as far back as mine does. Your future is one of possibilities rather than unforeseeable predestination. Be grateful for that. There are still choices on your path."

"Well, I don't want to be a part of that. I want...I want anything else. I want..." She struggled, trying to place her thoughts in order and sift through them for what was true and what was temporary. "I want things to be the way they were."

As soon as she said it, she knew it for the truth, but that didn't make it less ridiculous.

"The most common and the most impossible of wishes." A small, sad smile stretched beneath the bandages. "A fool's wish, but I think we all might be fools. I wish that too." His voice hardened. "But Darya, dear, growing up is realizing that is impossible. All we can do is decide what we are willing to do to change what we can. There are so few *real* choices in a life, and you must be ready for them. Years can pass without such a choice. You must be prepared to do what is necessary when you decide what you truly want. Do you even know what you want?"

The men had successfully broken down the door and streamed into the building, the cries of those who had been hiding in some vain hope of being passed over by both fire and man echoing out into the dark.

"I...I want to not be part of this." *I don't want to have to kill Bohdan. I want to be brave enough to save Mikael. I want to not be weak, to not be me.*

"And yet you are. And you need them. This is not one of those choices, Darya. Do you really think you are alone in that? Do you really believe every member of the 'Thousand Tribes' is a Taharuk? A Janbek Crow-Eye? That none of them want what you want? They are in the same situation as you, bound to the greater whole, despite its faults, together for survival on a sinking raft."

"I *know*. I know!" Talking to him like this felt like trying to make sense of a dream, but Darya found herself caught up in the moment, too tired for her usual defenses. "And you were right. My..." She took a deep breath. "My brother wouldn't want me to die. I *decided*, for what that's worth.

But it's impossible. I'll die without these bastards. Alina too. But here..."
She trailed off. "I'll die here too. It's impossible."

"Then change them."

She barked a laugh, staring at him incredulously. "Change them? I
say 'impossible,' and you say 'change them'? Are you serious? You're the
Arkhan's prophet; have you changed them?"

"In ways, yes. No one diverts a river overnight. But do you really think
'the great and glorious Arkhan' decided for himself to unify the tribes?"
Vels was looking at the chaos around them with a faint sneer on his face.
"No, he was happy atop his little hill, plundering and raiding. Concerned
with nothing beyond gold, women, and horrible liquor. He needed a
prophecy to move him, to convince anyone." He laughed derisively. "And
'Arkhan'? Absurd. Of all things to be remembered... Hilarious, really." He
didn't elaborate.

Darya's skin prickled, even bathed in the fiery heat of the town's ongoing sack. Vels was no slave, certainly. The Arkhan's personal magus, a
prophet with powers of the arcane, if you believed the old stories. Which
someone did; otherwise they wouldn't be out here. But definitely not one
of the three great Sarkhanae, the warlords who ruled under the Arkhan. A
glorified, generally unsettling advisor. But here he spoke of the man who
had united the steppes into the most feared force in recent history as one
would a petulant child, one who needed a firm hand.

"Your mother was a leader too, Darya, was she not? On a smaller scale,
perhaps."

Surprised by the turn of direction, all she could do was nod.

"Great in her own way too, I'd wager. But even in the quiet place you
called home, do you really think she ruled with love and promises and
noble principles?"

Darya didn't bother answering. She was imagining a hissing pile of
snakes and her mother's words again.

Vels nodded, as if he could read her mind. "No, you're smarter than
that, aren't you? She ruled them with tricks, treachery, threats, and every
underhanded tactic every ruler from time before time has used. Why do
you pretend this should be any different? It's the same game, only larger.
And the stakes remain the same."

There was a heavy silence as they continued walking, the screams from
inside the building long since faded. The fire had almost caught up to them

anyway. She turned his words over in her mind, handling them carefully, then taking them apart.

"I don't care about power though," she said. This whole conversation was unreal, but she continued, most of what she said surprising even her. It was as if he had managed to ask the questions she hadn't even thought to ask herself. "Ruling. I just want... I want the way we win to be different. I want to live. I want Alina to live. Maybe even Kasym and Altan." She paused, fixated on the approaching wall of flames. "And I want Janbek dead." Darya didn't bother mentioning their names, but the faces of the other chiefs and advisors surrounding the warlord flashed across her mind as well.

"So, not too different."

"You know what I mean."

"I do. But do you think there is any way to change the course except from the front? If you want them to take a better path, you need to show them the way. And the only way they know now is blood and terror. That is how you must rise. What would you be willing to do for the power to shape your world as you see fit? Answer that question, and the rest will become clear."

It was her turn to mock him for once. "So, to bring them peace, I need to bring them war." Darya snorted. "Your riddles are getting worse, old man. And besides... You talk about choices. I don't have power. I'm not even much of a fighter," she admitted, fiddling self-consciously with the horsehair tassel on the pommel of her short sword. Distracting herself.

They had come to another house, where the demise of its neighbor even now threatened to spread onto its well-built surface. That wasn't stopping the merriment inside. Or the terror, depending on who you were.

"Leave the fighting itself for those stupid enough to think it the height of heroism to smash each other over the head with metal sticks. As for power, that comes in more forms than you know. Some are available to anyone with the ambition and guile to seize them. And some, as your little troop of riders is about to discover, are given out by a source beyond any of our understanding."

"The Riftgate? Where the Stained you want us to ally with are?"

"Fons Anima, actually. But yes."

"Well, good for them. Not really an option for me."

"What if it was?"

A pause. "It isn't though."

"We will see soon enough," he said. "In any case, gifts or no gifts, you must speak to them in the language they know. Or die a stranger among strangers in a foreign land. Time is running out."

He turned to go.

"Vels," she blurted. "Who are you? Why do you care about me?" He paused, and she gathered her courage. "Are you...are you one of the Fallen? A demon?" It felt absurd to ask it aloud, to give voice to the rumors that had always swirled about the camp.

As he turned to her, the contempt on his face was unmistakable. "I've always thought it so fascinating that those were the words they chose. 'The Fallen.' Such a ring to it, such implied depth. But fallen from what, exactly?" He reached out and tapped her temple before she could react—hard. "Nothing but a word. Breath without meaning. You cannot let the words they use dictate the way you see your world. Up or down is often all a matter of which way you're looking. Angels and demons, Chosen and Fallen... They are but names for two sides of the same wall, and Darya, I want you to ask yourself which side your life has found you on."

With that, he left her as he always did, passing between two burning houses and disappearing back into hell. There was no doubt that he was something different, maybe even one of the Fallen from their stories. Darya suspected as much. But past those stories, in the here and now, he was nothing more or less than an infuriating, condescending presence, and it seemed impossible that he was anything so *beyond* human as all that. Darya was ready to run after him, Fallen or not, demanding real answers, or maybe even help, if he was so gods-damned inexplicably interested in her problems. To wring an explanation out of him for what he had meant about walls and words and Stained ... and *her*?

Then she heard yet another cry from behind her. The plaintive, high-pitched sort. She knew exactly what kind. One didn't ride with men and monsters and not know that sound. Darya turned, meaning to block it from her mind, but it came again, insistent. Meant for her.

She tried to keep walking. Better to distract herself talking to Vels. Maybe find Alina. There was another cry before she had made it three steps. With a curse, she whirled on her heel and strode to the door, where she could hear a struggle from within. She was usually good at pretending to be anywhere but where she was. She was tired of turning away though, and it was all too much tonight. Their lost home, her brother's execution, the terror of just hours ago, and her inability to block out the horrors around her or even to stand up for herself. All of her insecurities and fears metastasized into an unreasonable compulsion, a *need* to stop this. This one senseless act of violence on a night already so full of them.

There before her, like some lurid depiction of a whorehouse, were three men and as many women in various states of violent undress, surrounded by furniture similarly broken and denuded. She was ignored, counted by the men as among them. The figures before her were hazy, and all she could feel was a mounting sense of revulsion and hate building up inside her, flowing through her veins. It was choking her, like some evil oil that couldn't find its way out. Even now though, she could still turn around.

And then she saw him. That rat. That scum. That piece of human filth. Erbol.

The anger roared into her like something blazing along those lines of oil within. She could barely see with it choking her awareness. Here was everything she despised. Here, distilled in a single human form, was the sickness of the warband. Maybe humanity itself. The reason Mikael was dead. The reason she had almost died tonight. The reason and the base animal justification for all the fucking awful, horrible things she had seen, had watched, had stood by and ignored over the years. The things she had done. Had had to do. The circumstances and selfish weakness that had her kill Bohdan to save herself. The reason that for all Vels's philosophical drivel, nothing would ever change. The same thing, the same tragedies, over and over and over and over until they all died to the ice, the ash, or one another.

Maybe not tonight though. Tonight it was too much. She might have frozen earlier in the mountains, but she would act now.

Darya was silent as she slipped forward, shashka out and cutting. Erbol and the second man screeched in pain and shock as her blade penetrated them, blood spilling out. The third man stumbled back, with a yelp of surprise as Darya leapt at him, bright blade flashing. The women fled.

Somehow, he had managed to draw his blade from pants that sagged to the midthigh, and he fought a desperate, stumbling retreat, manhood waving about as he tried to make his way to the door, but Darya pressed him. All the repressed frustration and rage of a decade bubbled to the surface, erupting without anything resembling control. She could barely see for the hate.

"You fucking coward!" she screamed, spit flying. "You piece of trash! Scum!" She shrieked at him, past words. Years' worth of hate trying to squeeze its way out in the span of seconds.

The man was too terrified to retort. A small crowd had gathered, alarm bringing them, and then curiosity and a natural desire for entertainment keeping them there, most laughing at the sight—Darya, half the man's size, spitting curses and chasing a half-naked, stumbling bear of a man around the floor. She didn't care. All she wanted was for him to die. No, not die—too quick. That would never teach anyone. She wanted him to suffer, to be burned away, to be cleansed. She needed to cleanse them all. She could feel the heat of the building around her as fire started to peek through one side, working its steady, hungry way up the side. And...it *was* hungry.

Suddenly, Darya hesitated, considering. There it was again. That warmth. That...presence at the edge of her awareness. The wall between, the one inside her, was nearly dust, and she tried reaching for that strange familiarity. She felt it reach back. The man started to pull his pants up, unsure of why he was receiving the reprieve, but not taking any chances. With his belt back around his waist and the immediate threat of death gone, the man's anger came flooding in to take the place of fear. Seeing the laughing and curious crowd, his face turned almost purple with rage.

With a wordless roar, he came at her, surprisingly fast for all his bulk.

Surprised in her own turn, the feeling of connection fled and Darya stumbled back as the man swung his heavy sword in great cleaving arcs through the air, trying to split her open. One whistled by her face as she ducked under and tried to cut at his legs. Not close enough. The terror flooded back in, leaving no room for any sort of righteous rage.

She was going to die here.

Tripping on a piece of broken furniture, Darya stumbled to the floor, catching herself painfully with her left arm and desperately trying to ward off the blows from her half-crouched position. The chance was gone. Contemptuously batting her sword so hard that it fell from nerveless fingers, the man stepped forward and plunged his boot into her side, like one might kick a disobedient dog.

Then he joined her on the ground, straddling her and wrapping huge, filthy hands around her neck. Snorting and feeling her own spittle spraying across her face, Darya struggled to do something—to throw him off, to reach a knife, anything. Her boots scrabbled for purchase on the wooden boards, and she bucked her hips frantically to throw him off. He didn't even notice. Massive rough hands squeezed, inexorable, and her own movements became slower and slower. Futile efforts to scratch at his hands, to pry them from around her neck. There was no noise anymore, barely even pain.

*See you soon, Mikael.*

The blackness was almost complete now. Feeling fled, and she could barely make out his face above her, a mask of rage and hate, eyes bulging. But the fire still burned around them, starting to lick up the sides of the walls. That, Darya could feel. It was so close. It wanted. It hungered. And suddenly, she knew if she called, it would come.

The hate returned, roiling inside, but it felt right. Useful. It brought strength with it, and the blackness receded, lucidity returning. But it needed an outlet. So, she called the fire, with all the hate inside her. She let them feed off each other, and in her mind, she held a perfect, beautiful, hungry flame. The man still squeezed, tighter than ever, but confusion grew on his face as he saw consciousness return to her, rather than continue to flee.

The breath never even made it past his hands, but she mouthed the word with cracked lips, staring up at him. Another prayer. It would be answered.

"Burn."

With a thought, the fire roared from her and the man before her was a man no more. Turned truly into a devil now, he howled wordlessly and mindlessly, a human torch. But those don't last long. In seconds, he was gone, collapsing on top of her. Consumed. She didn't even consider the possibility of being burned. The fire couldn't hurt her; it belonged to her.

Coughing, she pushed him to the side, rolling out from under the body to kneel beside it, her own clothes smoldering. The body became yet another shape lying on the floor, but this one slowly sent licking tendrils along the boards. The crowd was dumbstruck, silence reigning among the broken tables and fallen men. Only the crackling of fire was audible.

Darya wasn't done. Suffused with strength, she pulled herself to her feet and stalked back to where Erbol had pulled himself to a slouched sitting position against the wall, sweat beading down his long hooked nose and eyes wild with fear. She stared down at him. Pathetic. Take away his strength, his power over others for a minute, and he was reduced to this.

"Please," he breathed, scrabbling back into the wall as much as his ruined leg would allow. "Please. Have mercy. Mercy."

Mercy was for the weak. Pity for those too frightened to do what was necessary. She was strong, and he was weak. Why was he surprised now that this was how the world worked? It was his smile from before she saw, not his terror now. Darya felt the fire burning inside her, wondered at the lines of white that had started to snake their way along her hands, scouring away the weakness, the fear.

She was out of her body again, same as in the mountains. Darya watched herself step forward, crouching down to his level, cupping his chin in her hand. "Are you cold?" she heard herself croon to him sweetly.

There was time for a flicker of confusion to cross his face before Darya pulled her long knife from her belt and slammed it point-first through his groin, deep into the boards beneath. The shriek that came from Erbol was nothing human, but it only grew higher and more animal as Darya reached back to where the fire licked around the other man and fed it again. This time not all at once. She set Erbol's legs alight and watched as the monster in human skin started to cook. Her eyes sparkled triumphant with the reflected reds and oranges. It was beautiful.

Slowly, she turned to where the shocked and silent crowd watched. She looked at the blackened shape of the first man. Her awareness returned, and she found herself in a smoking, reeking room. Her own hair smoldered, adding to the stench. She listened to the keening screams that had turned into a long, high-pitched note, and she vomited. And with it went the anger and the rage and what was left was Darya. She looked back. The man—and she could see now, to her horror, that it wasn't even Erbol—was writhing in the flames.

What was wrong with her? Had she done that? They would kill her now for sure. Put her down. She didn't bother to wipe away the sick that clung around her mouth, but stared stupidly at the crowd as they stared back.

And then one of them roared with approval. It became a wave. Darya backed away in panic and confusion, initially taking the surge of people and voices for a death sentence. She wanted to scream, to flee, but was trapped. She was pulled and ushered out of the now truly burning building by a crowd of cheering and laughing riders. Mythology made manifest, a new champion, speaking in the immortal and universal language of violence. A new hero among devils.

# PART III

# A REAL BATTLE

In battle, a man had a chance to prove himself. To do away with all the distractions and half-measures and emotions of life and let his courage and strength lead the way. The best songs and stories weren't about lovers or kings or even gods. They were always about wars and the warriors and heroes who fought them. Of course, you could tell which were which because the heroes needed a steady supply of warriors to cut through.

With a breathless growl, Vali chopped down with a savage blow of his axe, burying it in the helm and head of the warrior before him. A powerful kick sent the tottering man flying off the wall where they fought onto the cobbled street below with a crash—but not before he bounced off a sloping roof of shingles. And took Vali's axe with him.

Fortunately, there were plenty of those lying about now. Unperturbed, Vali took the break to draw the short sword from his belt and let his breathing calm from the madcap combat of a moment ago, turning his face up to feel the gentle mist of the light rain. Gods! He felt alive! He had been first up the ladders, and it had been touch-and go for a minute, but he had come out on top. Like he had known he would. All along the length of the parapets, other soldiers of the legions continued securing their assault points, ever more flowing up the ladders, an unstoppable tide of men and metal. Despite the steady almost-drizzle of the day, it all seemed to take on a new layer of clarity. He could see every detail of the soldiers around him—grim faces, eager faces, and unfortunately, the occasional wounded man crying out. It was to be expected. There was no glory to be won in safety, and someone had to pay the price.

There were still a few pockets of fighting on the walls, but their portion was secure. Lucan and Marika were beside him, the comforting sound of their own rasping breaths close by. Syl, Liora, and Leon were with them as well. The platoon's lieutenant had taken an unlucky arrow to one of the gaps in his armor on their approach to the wall with those heavy ladders. Syl had taken over during that hectic charge. Now he directed the sergeants of the platoon as they prepared for the next stage, moving on from the walls to take the whole great stone-and-timber town, Towerfall. Closely fitted masonry made up the walls, and well-built houses all rose up in staggered intervals around the true heart of the town, its namesake. The base of an ancient watchtower, a sheer and mostly intact remnant circle, was unmistakable as it squatted atop the central rise.

At the gates, Vali could see a squad of those worrisomely large Voraxians covered in heavy plate from head to foot and standing half again as tall as the tallest men around them. They pounded at the doors in turn with massive hammers, great blows he could hear from half the town away, barely noticing the few missiles that were sent their way. The blows felt like they shook the air itself, they were so loud, iron on iron. All around them, other platoons, augmented here and there by oathknights from the legions, scaled the walls on ladders and grappling lines. Waves of metal-clad ants. Decorated officers directed it all, armor and short cloaks hung with scraps of cloth and ribbons, all reminders of victories won, honors gained. Some of the more decorated legionnaires looked like nothing so much as grim birds of prey as they gestured, sodden feathers flapping. A few of the very oldest proudly bared the Rift-powered prosthetics that replaced lost limbs and gleamed brighter than any medal might have. Any resistance was ruthlessly brushed aside. In all, despite the rain, the whole affair had a holiday atmosphere, veterans of half a dozen campaigns laughing to one another. For legions that had taken the great fortresses of the island warlords of the Medraki Sea, stormed entrenched defenders in the old southern kingdoms of the Margyr, and fought running engagements with the massive warbands of the East, this was like a rehearsal. Practice.

The Twins had split their forces for a massive simultaneous assault against the first set of towns that had fallen to separatist control, pushing the forward line of their troops in a lightning offensive meant to give the enemy no chance to organize. They would take this town and do their part, but Vali wished this battle, his first real battle, could have been in the East, defending the Gates against the Thousand. Not just an ambush in the forest. Or in the Far South, carving out a new imperial province among the inhospitable wilds of the Lakemen. Not here in Getacia, even if they were in the North. The clans were different up here, no doubt, but it felt a little too close to home.

"Gods be damned," Lucan breathed, looking at where the gate had been smashed open. "Look at them go. Should let them take the town."

"Tired already, Get?" Leon asked, coming out of nowhere. Before the battle, he had stripped almost everything away, leaving only a few seemingly random bits of plate and leather over a light shirt and trousers. And the gauntlet, of course. Leon always had a sinewy, gristly look about him, tendons and muscles seeming to strum beneath the skin of their own accord, but without a coat or cloak and drenched in rain and blood, he looked positively demonic.

"We're fine, Leon. Thank you so much for your concern. As always." Marika pointedly turned away. She looked sick, pale about the cheeks and her eyes restless, roving across the scenes of battle.

Vali lowered his voice, leaning close as Leon shrugged and went back to helping Syl organize their group. "You alright? Nothing hurt?"

"I'm fine," she snapped.

Taking a page from Leon's book—and gods, that was a depressing thought—Vali shrugged and descended from the wall, moving to the front of the formation, closer to Syl. No one ever made a name for themselves from the back, and he hadn't spent all that time convincing the Hunters to let them join the first wave for nothing. Besides, he was tired of Marika's constant foul mood, tired of making it his problem too. He had enough of those.

Syl had fallen silent, letting the sergeants reorganize the men after their assault. The whole company was over the walls now, and they joined back together to prepare for their final objective, a push to the ruins peeking out on top of the hill. That jagged silhouette would be a guide from down among all these timber buildings pressed close to the wall. Vali glanced at Syl, hopeful. Nothing. The Hunter was absorbed with what was ahead. Syl likely hadn't even noticed Vali's performance on the walls. Of course.

Lucan and Marika joined him at the front. They met his nod with their own versions of the same; a nervous grin from Lucan, and a resigned quirk of the lips from Marika. Sweat and rain slicked their armor and stained the leather another shade darker, releasing the scent of a thousand practice bouts before. Among the browned and helmeted faces of the Helian soldiers, Vali was glad to have his friends. There were three whole battalions of Getacian auxiliary attached to the Twins' expeditionary force, but not a one in the group that they would live or die next to today. The legions were always filled in and padded with all manner of soldiers, drawn from every corner of the ever-expanding empire. A dozen variations on a hundred regional specializations of the Middle Lands. Yet they were all leavening for the true iron core of the legions, the Helian veterans and new recruits, all possessed of that same fanatical devotion and utter, un-shakeable belief in the myth of their own invincibility and the direction of their people's story. Saviors of mankind from itself. The unifying force that would preserve their people through yet another cataclysm. What made them so infuriating, so infatuating, was that they hadn't yet been proven wrong. And it was hard to argue with the right to conquest of the people who had the messengers of the gods on their side, the flesh-and-blood manifestation of prophecy. Those around them were part of that core, all veteran Southerners, scarred and scornful, barely tolerating the presence of outsiders in the tight-knit circle of their unit.

With a final look, the unit's commander gave the go-ahead to continue, satisfied with the situation at the walls. Time to move again. Curt, shouted commands. They marched forward into the tight streets, splitting apart again, each into their own worlds. Vali's existence constricted to an earth of cobblestones, a forest of fitted timber and masonry, and a sky of steep roofs. His half-helm, his own raised shield, and the shields around him narrowed his perception even further, until all that was left was the next turn in the street ahead. With an intrusive, upsetting thought, Vali was reminded of the blinders they would have to put on the horses back at home to keep them calm and working. Pushing that down, he focused on fitting into his proper place. They had rehearsed with this platoon. One of the sergeants had even been impressed by how easily they had fit in; another point for Leon's method of instruction. They did their best not to ruin that impression now, marching in lockstep with the ranks as they moved uphill, formation flexing as they tried to accommodate the haphazard design of the town's streets. Minutes passed at a crawl.

"We need to hurry up," Vali gritted through his teeth, frustrated with the unnecessary caution. They were going to miss the fighting at this pace.

"Town's not going anywhere," Lucan whispered.

One of the veterans cut in. "Shut up, Gets. Shut up and fucking listen."

Grumbling, Vali did, trying to remind himself that the man was right. Slow and steady was better than getting caught in an ambush. He'd been on the right side of one of those, and it had still been rough. That said, trying to focus his hearing with the steady, dull clamor of a company's worth of soldiers in chain, steel, and leather was a fool's pursuit, so Vali searched the windows and doors as they slowly climbed upward. That seemed pointless too. Every wood-framed hole in every house was a possible hiding point. If anyone was there, first they'd know of it was an arrow or crossbow bolt thudding into armor or flesh. Still, the town itself grew more and more picturesque the farther up they climbed, the epitome of Getacian architecture. Which was to say, reclaimed stone from ruins, plaster, and sturdy wooden roofs. It was nostalgic. His father would have loved it, except perhaps for the little sodden flags that hung limp and defeated from half the roofs and doors. Poorly embroidered and hastily drawn gray wolves on whites, tans, and even burlap. The flags matched the coherence of that little dream of an independent Getacian kingdom. Ignoring them, Vali let himself admire the buildings. To watch for threats, of course, but also to take his mind off the maddening crick in his neck from constantly hoisting the shield.

His attention was pulled suddenly forward by a splitting crack of the very air itself. "Stained!" someone screamed. Unnecessarily. Vali could grasp that the flying shards of stone and exploding bits of wall around him weren't natural. Though the arrows slamming into the formation—and the one that slammed into his shield—decidedly were.

The calm evaporated. The sky itself grew dark as the soldiers around them lifted shields in practiced motions. Vali scrambled to get his into the proper position as well, the ricochet and dull thuds of the shrapnel around them lending urgency.

Another sound of cracking stone, closer. A scream to his left. For the first time that day, Vali felt his mouth go dry. He was shoved from behind. They were moving forward. *Shit*. Back in step. Focus on the steps. They advanced forward, with the inexorable, impossibly noisy machine of movement that could only be produced by a hundred armored soldiers set to grim purpose. The ordered steps and the calm to his left and right brought him back. This was the same as their rehearsals. Another blast, close this time. Vali felt something ping, bright and hot, off his armor. Two men to his left were down, screaming bloody murder. They were swallowed up in the all-encompassing existence of the formation moving forward, their places filled instantly, and only their cries behind proving they had ever been there.

Vali swallowed, feeling sweat trickling, burning, past his headband and into his eyes. Alright, not the same. The thought of pure chance determining whether he lived or died made him feel angry and sick all at once. He enjoyed fighting. He was good at it. Better now than he had ever been, thanks to Syl, Leon, and Liora. But the idea that some unknown assailant, unfairly and most certainly undeservedly given the ability to touch the Rift, might put him back in one of those gods-damned hospital beds without him even seeing them was intolerable. The very definition of unfair. No skill, no bravery, no matter of who deserved death or victory. Nothing but someone ahead who was born with power he could only dream of, given the ability to manipulate stone with a thought.

"Closers! Archers! On my call," an officer's voice roared among the grinding gears of men, shields, and armor.

The formation shifted, and positions were adjusted. The machine responded, and all Vali could think of doing was to keep his shield above him, making sure it interlocked with Lucan's and the others around them. He vaguely remembered this drill. His strength, Syl's lessons, the quality of his sword... It all seemed to matter very little right now.

There was another explosion to their right, a burst of sound and a confusion of dust and shrapnel, collapsing part of the wall of men. Someone screamed. Something sliced across his thigh, and he hissed more with surprise than pain. He knew he had been hit. Clearly not badly. He could still walk and didn't bother looking down, feeling the progress of the blood that had started to trickle down his thigh. Vali had the sudden, inexplicable worry that someone might think he had pissed himself.

"Ready..."

Ready for what? He didn't remember this in the rehearsals. How had the rest of the drill gone? He couldn't even see where the enemy was.

"Closers!" the officer roared.

Night became day as the shields all came down in a cavalcade so well-rehearsed that Vali and his friends struggled to match the speed. Archers popped up and sent arrows hissing forward into the windows and onto the roofs of the stone structures ahead. And in front of them, trusting their aim, were the closers, the oathknights. Syl, Leon, Liora, and two attached

legion oathknights burst forward, moving impossibly fast, strides pro-
pelling them further than they had any right to. Vali shrunk back, flinching,
at another unreal splitting of stone, the wall to the left coming apart from
inside and rocking the area of the narrow passage ahead, sending one of the
figures flying like a doll. The oathknight was on the ground now, already
picking himself back up and silent with shock. He was mostly in one piece.
Except for his left leg, which was a ruined mess that he held in confused
hands.

One wasn't enough. Vali could see the defenders now, the vague impression of faces, limbs, and dull metal milling about farther up the street. A
few more figures were on a low roof behind them. No way to tell who
the Stained was, or if there was more than one. It wouldn't matter. The
oathknights had closed the distance, and it was like tigers let loose among
children. Vali watched Syl vault up onto one of the roofs.

The fight was over. Any doubt Vali had, or any thought of joining in
vanished. The man was death incarnate. All the lessons, the close touches
Vali had gained? Syl had been playing with him. There was no wasted
movement, no superfluity. Just brutal, practiced economy, longsword cutting at a speed that was nearly impossible to see. He was easier to track by
how the bodies slumped and fell apart around him, the lucky armored ones
leaking their lifeblood out, the unarmored losing pieces of themselves. The
screams of struggle had ceased inside the building that Leon and another
oathknight had entered. It had been seconds.

"Bloody gods above," Lucan whispered.

Marika's face was grim, and Vali couldn't help but agree with both.
That...that was what it meant to be an oathknight. That power. To defend
the innocent, of course. To fight the enemies of the empire and delay
another cataclysm, of course. Here was the only way to bridge that gap
created when some in their world could rip walls and people apart at will.
This was how you made heroes. He tried to recall how it had felt when they
healed him, the rightness of it. Some people were meant to have that sort
of power, and Vali knew he was one of them. Had to be.

They kept moving forward, checking the bodies, preparing to move
through the rest of the town. He stared down at the mess they had left.
Only a few had arrows in them. It was impossible to tell which one had
been the Stained. All of them wore a mix of heavy cloth and armor, pale

faces that looked far too much like those he'd grown up with staring unblinking into the rain.

Syl jumped down from the roof, landing in front of them. He gave Vali a hard look.

"All good?"

Vali nudged one of the bodies with his foot, turning the man's face away from his own. "All good. Battle's going well," he said, for want of anything else to say.

Vali flushed as a scatter of harsh laughs sounded around him. Syl gave him an incredulous look. "'Battle'? This is barely a skirmish. Now get back in formation."

# AFTERMATH

There were three more points where the formation ran into resistance, separatists and another Stained chipping away at the soldiers, little instances of chaos in an otherwise endless, wet march. Vali could smell the iron-rich blood of the soldiers who had been torn apart by the last Stained, could hear the horrifying cries behind of the ones who had only been wounded, drowned out now by the squelch of boots and the endless chafing of his own wet equipment. The brief excitement of the fight on the walls had been knocked out of him.

*"Barely a skirmish."*

He had watched Syl tear through two more groups of defenders faster than they could flee, shrugging off wounds that would have incapacitated a normal soldier. The jealousy came fast as always, souring his gut.

Eventually, they emerged from the tangle of streets into a square at the crest of the hill, the brutal base of the tower looming malevolently above them. Up close, the scale became more apparent, and the picturesque became oppressive. It was enormous. A small castle, sheer black walls dotted with alcoves and bristling with defunct turret cannons. Growing out of it, as if in homage to the power there, was a temple. Or what had been a temple, repurposed at some point for imperial use and branded with an enormous gilded phoenix, the sigil of the empire. Except now, that bird was a broken and twisted mess at the foot of the temple, a fragile bird after all. At least a dozen men and women hung from the pillars of the building. Their faces were bloated, features marred by sun, rain, and carrion birds, but their clothing left little doubt as to their identity: members of the imperial garrison and those loyal to them. Yet even cracked and worn and covered in corpses, the temple retained some measure of beauty. Apparently, those left in the city had agreed. Vali could see them now, a mass of humanity overflowing onto the steps, with more pouring out of the city to its pillared walls, like ants fleeing a flood.

"They're trying to take shelter," Lucan observed, confused.

They watched as more and more legionnaires converged at the top of the hill, units rejoining and growing back into the massive formations that had charged the walls. They drove the citizens of the town before them. More soldiers flowed into the open area around the crest of the hill every second, standards limp in the rain. Bloodthirsty pilgrims.

"I don't think that will help," Marika said.

"The city's secure now. The fighting is done," Vali said. But even as he said it, he wasn't sure. Officers moved to the front, directing formations to surround the hill, as if preparing for a final assault on an enemy stronghold. "What are they doing?"

"Finishing the job," Marika murmured. "How did you think this would end?"

It wasn't only the legions surrounding the temple now. Sporting makeshift black banners and whatever imperial paraphernalia they could find, small, ragged groups of loyalists started to emerge from the city, hungry looks on their gaunt faces. Right beside them, one of the locals was pushed roughly away as he came too close to the formation, but he caught Vali's eye and gave him a nod.

"We have to stop them." Lucan was beside himself with agitation.

"Good luck," Marika said bitterly.

"How?" Vali was horrified. Even though the massed formations made no move toward the temple, he could sense the violence building, that pressure pushed before a storm. He kept his voice low though, noting the suspicious stares of the soldiers around them.

Syl had apparently heard him anyway. "Calm down. This is standard. We don't know who's in there. Ideally, we will separate any traitors, Stained, or anyone dumb enough to think there's still a chance of defending this place. The fighting's done. The rest of these morons can go back to their homes."

"And if we can't separate them?" Vali asked.

A startled cry went up from the whole hill as the downed golen phoenix screeched across the cobblestones, picking up speed, until it crashed into one of the packed formations, sending soldiers and parts of men flying, tearing a great bloody gash through the mass of men.

For a moment, there was utter silence, shock at the act of seemingly impossible violence, like the will of the gods made manifest ... or at least a particularly vengeful-minded Stained in the temple.

Then the orders came: advance.

With a collective roar, the legions and the loyalists alike surged forward. The legionnaires around them left them behind, eager to take their part. The first lines hit the mass of people, and the slaughter began. Syl looked disappointed, Liora horrified, but Leon only shrugged.

"Guess the fight's not done, then."

———————◄O►———————

Vali wandered back through the streets in a haze, the shouting behind growing faint as they found a measure of peace in the streets farther down from the temple. He couldn't look at Lucan. He especially couldn't look at Marika. That had been...

He put it out of his mind. A line of people were coming toward them. A squad of legionnaires was herding a group of prisoners from the chaos above into a central square behind them, where the legions were conducting the cleanup of bodies that followed any battle. The songs usually skipped over these parts.

A little boy was falling behind. A soldier tried to herd him back into line with the rest of the captives, but the encouragement of a spear butt proved a bit too much. He fell down, hard. Vali, Lucan, and Marika watched as he gathered himself up, quick as he could, staring far past anything here. The boy couldn't have been older than eight, nine, maybe a poorly fed ten winters. Old enough to know he wasn't supposed to show weakness, young enough that he couldn't hide the trembling of his thin little limbs, whether from fear, shock, or perhaps just the cold.

Wordless, Vali unwound the sodden cloak that he had slung, waist to shoulder, out of the way for the battle. He stepped forward to wrap it around the boy, but couldn't bring himself to look him in the eye. He squeezed that small, trembling arm. Maybe he could take some of his strength, his size. Vali would gladly give that too, if he could. This was not a kind world, and it was even more unkind for the small and the weak.

*Grow fast* was his prayer. Hopefully that and the cloak would be enough for now.

"We've got to keep moving." The soldier attached to that spear butt from earlier stared up at him. A plea and nervous request more than a command. His musical accent and dark bronze skin marked him a stranger here, and a young, overwhelmed one at that. At the front, the sergeant of their squad was already roaring for him to catch up. Vali nodded mutely, stepping out of the way. The column marched on, and they stood watching them. Another column was close behind.

"That was a massacre. *Is* a massacre," Marika said.

There was a group of legion medics ahead, hurrying along toward where the fighting had been, the white cloth of their uniforms long ago gone to red. Marika stared after them.

"What else could they have done?" Vali said. He closed his eyes, hating himself for that answer. He knew she was waiting for it.

"What else?" She rounded on him. "Did you see how many people were there?" she snarled. "*Our* people! Women? Children?"

"They attacked them!" Vali protested. He turned to Lucan for support, but found his friend shaking his head at him, disappointed. "A Stained in there attacked. What were they supposed to do? Sit there and take it? And they aren't our people."

"Hmmm..." Marika tapped her chin, pretending to consider. "Maybe, just maybe, there was an option somewhere between 'stand there and take it' and 'kill every last soul that tried to shelter there'? Maybe? And they're more our people than the ones we fought with today."

"They didn't have another option," Vali insisted. "They didn't."

"You can't even see it, can you?" She shook her head. "They slaughter us..."

"'Us'?"

"Yes, Vali, *us*. Or have you not seen the way they treat all of us?"

"Of course I fucking do!" he exploded. He brushed away Lucan, who tried to pull him back. "You think anything's going to change by complaining about it? Openly sympathizing with traitors? The independence they want will see us all fucking dead the next time there's a fortress city that tears itself to pieces."

He was close now, spittle flying, rain getting into his eyes, furious that she couldn't see what was obvious. Faced with her usual unimpressed look—the one that made him feel as if he was somehow incapable of stringing together a logical train of thought—he had the sudden, red-hot, almost overwhelming need to shake her, slap her, strike her down, do anything that might wake her up and let her see things clearly for once. To look at him, to think of him like he deserved.

The thought passed so quickly, it almost hadn't even been there. He was left with a growing frustration with friends who seemed bent on only seeing the downsides of their duty, as if they didn't stare him in the face every day as well. How could he help but be frustrated with her, with them?

"They hold the cataclysms over us like they give a single shit about any of us. We're the *buffer*, Vali. Us and every other frontier province. We're the stupid Gets they can have fight their battles for them and fill their stores, so they, the *real* people, can survive." She pushed him backward, features twisted with spite. "Is it because you're fucking one of them that you can't see what's in front of you? Is it that you think they like you?" she sneered. "Gods, you're blind. Blind and such a child sometimes."

"Really?" Vali was yelling now, and with an effort, he lowered his voice, worried others would hear what they were arguing about. "You want to pretend we'd be better off without them? This is how we win. This is how we show we're more than savages. And we wouldn't even be here without me," he managed to grit out between clenched teeth. "*I* asked them to bring both of you. You're welcome. This is what works: proving ourselves. Fuck what they think. And what business is it of yours who I sleep with? Are you jealous? Is that it?"

"Vali..." Lucan started.

"No. I'm tired of hearing you two complain. And yes, *both* of you. Though especially you, Mari. Yeah, it's not perfect, but it's better than the alternative."

"You talking about the empire, or the team? And I'm right about her."

"The empire. The team. Both! And it's the way things are now anyway. I swear, you both act as if this isn't the biggest—I mean, the *only* damned opportunity we are likely to get to become oathknights. To show that we are more than they think we are."

Vali had decided to give ground on Kass. If he were to be objective, to consider the situations that didn't involve him, he had rarely known Marika to be wrong about these things. Knowing the right answer didn't make following through on it any easier though, and he'd be damned if he admitted that right now. Right now, it gave him a vicious satisfaction to know how much it upset her, even if he was disgusted with himself for it.

"No, Vali. It's an opportunity for *you*. Lucan and I will never be considered for that. You know that, and don't try to feed me that shit about anyone being anointed if they're only fucking heroic enough. You have a chance, because of your name. And that is why we're both here. Not for us—for *you*. So, don't pretend you did us some massive favor by dragging us out here. We chose to come, and I want you to succeed. But don't forget where you came from."

He sighed, unclenching his fists, the rest of his body following. These were his friends. And Mari...Mari meant far more than she knew to him, and more than he remembered sometimes. "Look. I'm sorry. But you know I'm right." It was cold now, cold and wet, and he was exhausted. The anger that always surged in so hot and so fast was slipping away, as quick as it had come.

"I wish I did, Vali. Really. You have such a big heart. It's what I—what we both love about you. I just can't understand how you can't see what I see. We are on the wrong side of this."

With those impossible words planted behind her, she walked away, leaving Vali standing there, stunned. Before he could take a step to follow, Lucan grabbed his arm.

"Wait, Vali." Lucan pulled him away. Again. "That's not a battle for you to win. Not right now."

In a daze, Vali let himself be directed. Toward more fighting? Hopefully. That, he understood; those were the stories he loved. It was in battle, after all, that a man had a chance to prove himself.

<hr />

Syl, Leon, and Liora watched in silence as the day slipped into late afternoon. They were sitting in a public square immediately below the temple, a staging point for the ongoing work of moving the legion into the town and establishing their own—hopefully considerably more robust—defense plan for the city. One corner of the square had been dedicated for the triage and treatment of the soldiers wounded during the assault. There weren't many. Fewer than there should have been, given how many bodies were going the other direction, to the bonfires already burning on the outskirts. Most of the butchery had finished within the first hour in an outpouring of revenge killings and mass cathartic violence by the loyalists, and an old-fashioned bit of bloodlust on the part of the legions.

The temple above was the worst. The building might have been saved, but it looked like some awful ritual had taken place. It was drenched in blood and bodies, dedicated to a new god again, this one with an insatiable appetite for blood. The hanged men and women had been taken down, only to be replaced by others. The gods still needed their sacrifices.

Syl glanced at Liora. "That was... That shouldn't have happened." He didn't know what else to say, but felt he had to say something. Anything. The excitement and worry of the fight had long since faded, leaving only the tired hammering behind the eyes, even that muted, as if it too didn't entirely want to be there.

Liora shut her eyes tight at those words, as if she could shut off her senses and wish away the events of the day. She hadn't spoken a word since they had left the temple.

On his other side, Leon looked him up and down, unimpressed. "Oh, not you too. Come off it. They brought all of this on themselves. And don't pretend you didn't enjoy limbering up to kill some of those Stained."

"Just because it was necessary doesn't mean I enjoy it," Syl said, annoyed. This whole day was an exercise in frustration. Not enough fighting, and then far too much.

"That's your problem, Syl. You like to pretend you don't."

"Don't what?"

"Don't enjoy it."

"I don't," Syl protested. Leon was staring with the same amused incredulity. The same expression that he wore whenever they listened to prisoners giving the same repetitive, increasingly implausible and unconvincing answers. "I don't!" he insisted.

Liora wouldn't look at him. Instead, those hazel eyes were downcast and darkened, grieving for something or someone.

"I don't," Syl said, softer, to her this time. Maybe to himself.

There was another whisper though, one of those ever-present voices, the others that would pound through his temples, nothing but a scream sometimes. It was laughing quietly now, and it asked what it almost always did. Why *did* he still do this? Rooting out and destroying Stained, each instance its own imperfect, incomplete revenge for his family. And what then? *Then we find the next one, and the next one, and the one after that.* Well, Syl thought sourly, at least that was the good part of revenge against a concept: you would never run out of enemies.

"I don't," he said firmly, ignoring that voice. "Even if our charge means sacrifices have to be made, what happened up there was a disaster."

"Why?" Leon asked.

"*Why?* What the fuck is wrong with you? Because we slaughtered a few hundred people, half of which weren't even looking to fight. What do you mean, why?"

"They rebelled. We wouldn't even be up here if it wasn't for them, right? I mean, fuck, Syl. We were *here*, crisscrossing this gods-forsaken province ten years ago. And now we're up here again, bleeding and dying to take it back, right as the world gets ready to shit itself again. Thought I'd die before we had another cataclysm, but here I fucking am. You don't do things right the first time, this is where it leads you. Can't believe I have to explain this to you, of all people." Leon pointed down to where the smoke was billowing, black and bilious, from beyond the walls. "And I'll tell you another thing—I'd rather a dozen of them down there than another one of ours laid out here."

"Leon, we were soldiers. Soldiers are supposed to fight in battles against other soldiers, not murder civilians. Now, we do what's necessary with the Stained, but only what's necessary. Gods damn it, even you can't be this bloodthirsty."

"What a load of shit. Soldiers are supposed to win wars, and win the next one too, if they can. Maybe we weren't brutal enough the first time? I like being alive, thank you." He pointed to a neat row of bodies, where boots poked out from under stained black cloaks. "Pretty certain these poor saps up here did too. Which life weighs more? Which principle? It all gets a bit muddy around the edges. You like to think you're better than me—don't act like you don't—and that's fine, you're probably right. But be honest with yourself, man. Trying to pretend you know the scales is the definition of arrogance, Syl, and anyone who pretends like they know the exact answers is guaranteed to be the biggest bastard you'll ever meet. In my experience, you pick your side, you pick your people, and as for everyone else?" He made a rude gesture. "To the Rift."

"I can't do this."

Without another word, Liora got up and walked away from them, half stumbling in her hurry to be anywhere but there. Syl watched her go, feeling an inexplicable shame. Leon's vicious ramblings weren't his; couldn't she see that?

"She's soft," Leon said as she left the square.

"She's good." He didn't move from where he sat beside Leon.

"Same thing."

# KNIGHTHOOD

Syl stumbled toward the crumbling wall by the building where the team had set themselves up. His laughter was forced as he climbed what was left of the stairs to where two soldiers kept watch with a torch. Leon was right behind him, singing some tuneless and incredibly vile song that he claimed was a classic in "the right places" in Heliopolis.

"Move over, comrade!" Leon called out.

The two soldiers turned out to be none other than Vali and Lucan, who looked uncomfortable, and perhaps a little guilty, like they had expected to be caught out here by someone, if perhaps not by him and Leon. They shuffled a bit farther along the walkway. Gods, they were so young. Syl couldn't help but stare at them, swaying, still laughing a little in the distracted way of the very drunk. Had he ever been that young? Surely. Where were his friends, then?

*Dead. All fucking dead.*

*Like you should be.*

Syl's laughter died, and he glared at them in a furious, inconsolable, and unreasonable stupor. These ghosts from a better past. Vali and Lucan's surprise had become a profound discomfort. This was why he usually never drank.

"I think you're scaring them, Syl." Leon hiccupped. "I'm just happy to see you relax a little. Always so tightly wound. And you two! Celebrate! We won today."

Syl found it hard to believe this was the only friend he had left. A half-mad comrade from those days in the tunnels. It had been such a surprise to see him again when he joined the Vigil.

Lucan muttered something under his breath and went to pull Vali away.

"Speak up, lad," Leon said. "You bleat loud enough on the practice ground."

Hesitating, and clearly regretting having said anything, Lucan said, "Wasn't much of a victory is all. Sir."

Syl ignored them all and turned outward and upward. Away. Looking toward the skies, where a million stars wheeled overhead, untouchable and perfect in the clear night. It was beautiful, that crisp clearness of sky and air that sometimes came after rain. A perfect night to celebrate. His knuckles were white around the bottle he and Leon had been sharing.

"Don't 'sir' me. Save that for 'Sir Syl' here. I was born in the gutters of Heliopolis, in His shining light and all that. Unlike you little would-be lordlings. Speaking of, what is with all the self-flagellation today?"

Vali stepped forward now, brave idiot that he was. Syl tried to focus on the stars, the sky.

"Lucan's right. It wasn't a real fight. Maybe it had to be done, but we shouldn't be celebrating. I mean, it wasn't fair at all."

"Those are the best fights, you ogre. You ever been in a fair fight?"

"We..."

"And none of those pisspot little skirmishes on the borders either. I'm talking a real battle."

There was a pause.

"That's what I fucking thought. They're awful. People only *think* they want fair fights. You're still alive. So, relax, celebrate. We march north next! Into the savage hinterlands, to honor and glory." He took the bottle from Syl and raised it to the sky. "Any day now, we should be heading to the excavation site. We walk a little bit, explore some ruins, kill a few people, and we can all be home in time for the solstice. Sol Invictus and all that. Easy week."

Syl's mouth was already sour. It was probably the drink. He grabbed the bottle back and raised it in another toast. "To unfair fights!" He swigged down a bitter mouthful.

Leon patted his back drunkenly, too hard, and made Syl choke.

"To unfair fights! There's a prayer I can get behind."

Meanwhile, Vali looked like someone was kicking his favorite dog, face twisted in shame and some indefinable disappointment. The boy wore his emotions like an army carried banners. "You're both oathknights," he finally managed. "The Emperor's own." For him, that statement was question and accusation both.

Syl understood. But there was the irresistible urge to quash his youthful optimism and naivete, to drag him down to where he himself was stuck, so far from the stars, firmly in the mud and filth of the real world. He'd be doing him a favor.

"Bondknights," Syl corrected. "That's the better name for what we are. Impolite, but I wager you've heard it. And I promise you, Vali, that 'bondknight' is the right word. If Domarik listens to me, you'll never come close to being one."

Instead of looking pleased, as he should have, it was as if Syl had stuck a knife into the lad's back. "We've done everything you've asked. We fought well today, bravely." *Gods, this was pathetic to listen to.* "And now...damn it...you're supposed to be better. The best of us."

Syl looked away, too tired or jaded or drunk to care. He had tried.

Leon laughed, as if Vali had told the best joke he had ever heard. "Really?" His teeth were bared, only a smile by the loosest definition. "Are you a moron? Who do you think becomes oathknights? The noblest? The most virtuous? No, you overgrown child. The best fucking killers. I fought here in the nastiest, most unfair fights you can imagine, and then I became the best gods-damned knife in all of Heliopolis. Before they caught me, that is. Back into the black-and-golds for me. Now, Syl... Syl here was about as close to a war hero as you can get and still be alive. Which means that he's sent more men to the Rift than you've ever known."

"So, you're a rat bastard. We knew that." Vali's nostrils flared, and he stepped up to Leon, as if his size would intimidate the smaller man. It was good to see him standing up for himself to Leon for once, but that was a very, very bad idea. Leon liked close. "Doesn't mean every oathknight is like you. You just said it: Syl earned his place."

Syl really did like Vali, for all his faults. He had a good heart, same as Liora. This life would break him. He had to say something, to try again. "Vali..." He cleared his throat, the words catching in his dry throat. "Vali, you don't want this. I know you think you do, but you don't."

"Is this some sort of test? I do want it. It's all I want. It's what I've been training for the last ten years of my life. It's my chance to... It's my chance. My future."

"It's not a test," Syl sighed. "I'm trying to help you, so listen for one gods-damned minute, lad. If I've bought even an ounce of your respect, please shut up and listen." Syl waited until he could tell Vali was listening, really listening. Lucan too; this was good advice for anyone, and Syl was in a dispensatory mood. "Any Helian you see here isn't here because this is where we want to be. We're here because there's nowhere else for us. We are prisoners to our own poor decisions, or the cards that life has dealt us. Dead families, broken dreams, wasting diseases, or..." He grabbed roughly at Leon's shoulder here and shook him affectionately. Half-mad he might be, but he really was one of his only friends. "...or even psychotic tendencies. Point is, you still have everything you need to live a real life. Don't throw it away for something shiny."

Syl sent the words, sent the advice across the void between them and waited to see if it would land. Watched their faces closely, watched as Lucan's went from merely uncomfortable to pitying. Not ideal, but good enough. He was focused on Vali though. Here was the would-be hero, the one who would throw himself into the machinery of the empire if only they would name one of the gears after him. He watched as surprise became denial tinged with contempt. Not convincing enough, apparently.

"We need to go," Vali said stiffly. "Thanks for the advice." He pushed past, eyes far away already and fixed on some perfect future.

Syl leaned heavily on the wall, feeling himself on that teetering point of warm buzzing drunkenness falling into sour exhaustion, knowing that his words had landed on deaf ears. Hopefully he had planted at least a seed of doubt. Syl had seen too many oathknights chosen from the provinces not to understand the horrible, practical logic of the empire's criteria. You dangled enough power, enough prestige, and you could coopt any people's heroes as your own, to fight and die and kill for however long they lasted at the far ends of the empire. Even if the Vigil and the legions needed oathknights, Vali didn't deserve that.

"Eh, whatever." Leon examined the Getacians as they descended the stairs, taking their torch with them. "You tried. And you!"

"Me?"

"Yes. You've got to stop this."

"Stop what?" Syl asked.

"I can see it in you now. This endless back-and-forth. You'll tear yourself apart. We did what we had to do today. That's the all of it. And that ought to be the end of it. And if Vali wants part of this, then there's nothing you can do about it."

Liora's silent judgment from earlier in the day still weighed heavy on him, unspoken words echoing around in Syl's head, and he was drunk enough to voice them. To voice his own doubts. "What's the point, Leon?"

"What do you mean?"

Syl gestured back to the town, to Leon, to their uniforms. "All of this. It's never-ending. Another Stained. Another town. Hell. Another cataclysm. Over and over."

"You know the why, you don't need me to say it. Besides, you have better reasons to be here than any of us, Syl. I mean, look at me."

Syl snorted.

Leon chuckled. "Fair enough." He grew serious. "Maybe I'm a bad example, but I've got my code. I protect my own. That's. It." Leon squinted into the distance, drawing an imaginary line with his finger before him. "Consistent. Your problem is you think too much."

"Or you don't think enough?"

"Oh, for certain. Try it sometime."

They settled into a comfortable silence, both lost in memories. Syl tried to focus on the stars again, but looking up was making him a bit dizzy. He could pull from his conduits back at the Riftgate and burn the alcohol away, but if he didn't want to be drunk, he wouldn't have started drinking. So, he switched to the horizon, to the cold, refreshing hand of the northern wind on his face, that was even now sweeping the last leaves from the trees. Their destination lay somewhere out there, past wooded ridges and grassland valleys. The legions would be spreading out soon, reclaiming towns, but there was no doubt that eventually, their team would be moving to that faraway point, to half-excavated ruins, no doubt lousy with separatists and Stained.

He found his thoughts straying to that girl from the farmhouse. Morana. They would ask for her here, and they would search for her there. Maybe they would even find her and put her down. That would certainly be the best outcome. Now was not the time to be taking chances. Yet in the safety of his own head, Syl hoped Morana was somewhere far away, that she hadn't stopped running. Mind dragged along the inevitable chain of events that would no doubt come, Syl started to imagine the next steps in their mission, to plan and worry for it, but decided to take Leon's advice for once. He did have one more question.

"Do you think..."

Syl paused midsentence as the sky started to glow red. Sunrise? Already? Surely they hadn't been up that long. He pulled from his conduits, feeling the pleasant numbness burn away. The light was still there.

"By the fucking Fallen, what the hell is that?" Leon braced himself, eyes wide.

At least he knew it wasn't just him. Syl wanted to yell something, a warning, but wasn't even sure what he would be warning anyone of. There was a hissing and rumbling so faint that it was almost imagined, until it continued to grow louder, a wave of sound that came from the earth itself. Now Syl grasped what was happening, and he stood there with Leon, looking to the west. To the Old Empires and the epicenter of the Breaking. The chasm that split the land, where echoes of old cataclysms would still sometimes belch ash that could cover the skies for weeks.

It had been years since the last eruption. No wonder they hadn't understood at first. They weren't the only ones. There were panicked shouts throughout the moonlit town, confusion as a regiment's worth of soldiers attempted to come to grips with an invisible enemy in the dark. Many of them would never have seen this before, too young or having grown up too far from the western border of the empire.

Now the rest of the team, along with the Getacians, emerged piecemeal from the building in various states of undress to join them. Domarik was furious at being woken, brows furrowed and half of his hair sticking up from his balding pate at an odd angle, lending him a decidedly unhinged air.

The light pulsed brighter, the glow of sunrise. Blood red and shining orange. But sunrise was hours away, and no sun Syl had ever seen rose in the west. Pulsing like an evil heart, the crimson light made the stories they told about the Breaking and the past and coming cataclysms a little easier to believe. Still, there had been eruptions in his lifetime, and a score of cycles before this one. It was comforting, in a way, to think that each generation before had been just as overwhelmed, just as surprised by what, in the grand scheme of things, were commonplace disasters. The world fell apart, and the universe spun on.

"Gods damn it all," Kass said. "Of course."

"It's...it's starting again, isn't it?" Marika asked quietly. "This is bigger than any I've ever seen."

The Getacians were looking west with a sense of horror that Syl couldn't help but sympathize with. It was one thing to stare at the possibility of another cataclysm every day in the Vigil, and quite another to know the life you thought you would have was about to become very different. They still couldn't go around yelling it from the walls. They needed all the time they could get to consolidate, to crush rebellions and build up supplies in the capital. Delay and preserve. But Vali, Marika, and Lucan deserved the truth.

"Yes," Syl said. There really wasn't anything else that needed to be said.

Domarik glared at him, another breach of protocol marked against him. "That does not get spread, if that was unclear. It has been years since the last, and the seals of the Veil are failing; it makes sense it would be larger," he said, as if that changed anything.

"I've never actually seen it," Liora whispered.

"Enjoy," Leon said. "Syl and I were up here the last time it had a little hiccup. Looks pretty now, but if you thought things were bad in Heliopolis after one of these, you're in for a treat. You can look forward to breathing, drinking, eating, and shitting ash for the next month, at least."

Domarik sighed, scrubbing at his face with both hands in a vain attempt to wake himself up. "It's as good a time as any, I suppose. You won't be needing to worry about the ash for a while."

"Why not?" Vali asked. He and Lucan were back now too, pointedly avoiding eye contact with Syl. Still, he looked more excited than anything after hearing that they were at the beginning of another cycle.

"Because there's been a delay, and we won't be pushing to the excavation site yet. The Twins' generals are nervous about the lack of resistance so far with this offensive. Bal Maru is still a ways yet, but those tunnels crisscross the entire North. They aren't willing to overcommit and extend their lines, with so much unknown and unsecured terrain between us and the objectives farther north. Not to mention, we still haven't determined where the bulk of the escaped Stained have gone. Lucky, tell them what you told me."

Lucky cleared his throat and managed to not look anyone in the face, while still scowling at all of them. "It's true. We don't know for sure."

"Lucky."

A deeper scowl. "Well, of course these things are never exact"—Leon snorted at that, which Lucky ignored—"but we are at least a few days away from the locus of this new Riftgate at Bal Maru, though of course, if we assume it follows the same pattern as the one at Heliopolis, its properties will extend for at least—"

"Enough. Keep it on topic, Lucky. Signatures, the like."

Lucky was warming to his subject, some excitement creeping in despite his best efforts. "Loads of them! The North is a mess of signals and flashes, but—"

"To the point, Lucky," Domarik interrupted again.

"Ah... Well, that is to say, I wouldn't want to have to find them by my senses alone. It would be like wandering in a field during a storm, waiting to catch the lightning. You're as likely to be caught yourself. Safer to see from a distance. Oh, and one other thing." The scowl was gone, and Lucky looked genuinely worried for once. "There was...something out east. Not too close, but close enough to sense last night. A very strong, very distinct pull. I could be mistaken, but I suspect an extremely powerful emergence. Thought I should mention it now."

Domarik looked thoughtful, but kept his counsel to himself.

"So?" Syl asked, not liking where this was going.

"So, considering the uncertainty, the Twins have prioritized a steady advance across the board," Domarik said. "Too many unknown factors in play. We will march on the excavation site whenever they make their final push toward the separatist headquarters at Nordea Kerest. It means no quick strike forward for us. It does, however, mean those passages under our feet. The separatists know them too well, and we can only move forward at the pace we can secure those routes." He gave a rare, tight smile. "Thankfully, we have a couple of experts here."

Apparently, even Syl hadn't heard all the curses Leon knew.

# OMEN

It had been a bad dream—one of those horrible, awful nightmares that left you waking into a tangle of your bedroll and soaked in your own sweat, freezing the rest of the night away. Her mother's death, leaving their home, the last few years on horseback, the town, the fire... Her... All a nightmare. Surely. Yet every time Darya opened her eyes, blinking slowly as if to give the world a chance to right itself, it all seemed very determined not to change.

They were a few days' ride from the town they had sacked, in rolling countryside, following the old roads through grasslands and forest. There had been another village. A farmstead or two. All destroyed in passing as the warband worked its way westward like a cloud of mounted locusts. Now they had settled in a low valley, more of an extended dip in the earth than anything, the few small tents and the many large campfires springing up among the scattered trees and tall grass almost before they had stopped moving. The riders sat illuminated before their fires, the great beast of the warband slowly fading off into sleep. The soft murmur of conversations disappeared with the gentle wind through the tall grasses, drifting up with the smoke to darken the night sky. Darya had stopped with them, but only after Alina had pulled at her reins. It was hard to notice much anymore. The days since that first town had passed in a haze, a hangover from that nightmare.

Alina hadn't believed her when she had told her. Darya hadn't believed it herself. She felt a rush of bile again as she heard the inhuman sound that not-Erbol had made as he died. No, not died. Was consumed. She tried not to reflect on how certain, how sure she had been that it had been Erbol in there. In the grand scheme of what had happened, she told herself it was a minor point.

Darya rubbed at her forearm nervously, as if she could scrub something invisible away. She watched the riders around them from under hooded lids. There was a space between where they had stopped and where the rest of the warband settled for the night, as always. Only now there was something new in that gap, where there had been only disdain before. No one had approached her like in the mountains, though, so maybe that was an improvement.

Not only that, but there were interlopers in the no-man's-land between the fire she, Alina, Altan, and Kasym shared, and the others. Other outcasts, lonely little islands in the sea of the Thousand, remnants of scattered peoples, dead tribes, and broken petty kingdoms. They were drawn toward her, but all they did was add to her fear. What did they want? She had nothing to offer them. Yet they set up a little closer each night with the gravity of genesis. They watched her, and Darya knew what they wanted to see. She suspected there would be consequences if they had to wait too long.

"Are you trying?" Kasym asked.

"Shut up," Alina said from where she stood. "Of course she is. And keep your voice down, for all our sakes."

Darya tried to drown out the sound of their voices, staring into the small fire they had built on the hard ground, little weeds shriveling and blackening where the fire licked out. Stared, and stared, and stared until tears poured. The wind shifted, and she got a face full of smoke in reward for her concentration. Coughing, she spared a fire-blind look around her, to where she knew the others were watching, waiting. They would probably slit her throat in her sleep if she failed to live up to their self-told prophecies. They would kill her, kill Alina, and probably even poor Kasym and Altan, still stuck with them.

She focused back on the flames, willing them to...do anything. Darya would have settled for an ambiguous flare, an excessive spark, a loud crackle...anything. And yet this fire seemed to insist on continuing as the most ordinary fire that had ever existed in the history of men putting spark to tinder. In the town, it had been so easy. She hadn't even really tried. It had come to her, wanted, *needed* to be used. It had been hungry. She searched in her mind for that feeling, but it was like a fish in her clumsy fingers. Always just around the corner in her mind, but impossible to grasp.

In the center of the camp, she could see three circles of camped riders, more defined and cohesive than the scattering around her. Kursagai, Taharuk, and Serik. Bad, worse, and perhaps the most dangerous of all. Last night, Altan had told her Kursagai was joking about how Darya had used all of her luck and would certainly get herself killed during the next fight. She had no doubt he wouldn't mind helping her along. Taharuk, according to Kasym's acquaintances, was for a more direct approach, killing her along with the other handful of individuals who had manifested differing levels of connection to the still-distant Riftgate. She really had to appreciate his forthrightness. Taharuk was not a man who enjoyed unknown variables. Most of those other unfortunate individuals cursed with the touch found themselves among the dispossessed around her, for lack of better options.

And the one she was truly worried about: Serik. He had sought her out, almost immediately following the...the incident. Darya didn't like to dwell on it. On that first night after looting the town, he had managed to catch her on her own. She thought he was there to kill her; the men she had burned had been his. Instead, he had come with honeyed words and grand ideas. There was a man who saw opportunities, not obstacles. She suspected her mother rather would have liked him. Yet if Darya had to pick her fastest way to the grave, she thought it would be listening to him. They all saw threats, tools, or symbols when all she wanted to do was shrink into nothing, be nothing. Maybe she could have revenge for her brother one day, but he would want her to live first, wouldn't he? And if she had to choose? Better to not be noticed and fade back into the peripheries of the Thousand Tribes. Surely there was room enough for one more.

A roar of laughter from within one of the circles of camped riders made her start. Alina and Altan looked nearly as nervous as she, while Kasym looked resigned. Guilty by association.

"They want you dead," Kasym said, idly poking at the fire that was keeping them warm as the cool, clear skies promised an even colder night.

"Thank you, Kasym. What a revelation." Alina shot him a frustrated glance. "You're always such a help." She turned to Darya, who sat with her back against her saddlebags, absently playing with the weeds between her crossed legs. "Darya. Listen to me. You turned down Serik. Fine. But then you need to show them why they shouldn't want you dead. Either too useful to them, or too dangerous. How did you do it? Can you do it now?"

"Stop asking her," Altan spat. "She couldn't do it last night, or the one before that. I doubt she can suddenly do it now. You should have listened to Serik. We would have at least had a chance."

"Keep your voice down," Kasym said without looking up from the fire.

"Or what? So sorry if I'm a bit anxious about all this. I didn't do a gods-damned thing but follow orders, and now I'm stuck here with you three, who couldn't find their way out of a bush. The one fucking chance we had, what does she do? Throws it away." Altan sneered. "Now I'm dead, same as you idiots." Standing, he threw the pieces of grass he had been tearing apart into the fire with a violence of motion that was betrayed by their lazy float down to their doom. "I can't just sit here. We have guard tonight, unless you three forgot that too."

Darya watched as he stomped off toward the edge of the camp, where the firelight gave way to the gentler moonlight that painted the rolling hills in silver. She would have to join him out there soon and would be captive to his endless diatribes and complaints. At least it would be easier to ignore him with the full moon providing a view of something beyond his pinched, always scowling face.

"He is going to be a problem," Kasym said.

Alina watched his receding form. "I agree. We need to lose him, push him away. Or—"

"No! No." Darya reached up to grab Alina's hand. "Please. He's just scared." Too many people had died because of her already, and Altan, skinny, lazy, malcontent that he was, didn't deserve that. She was scared too.

Alina paused, thinking. "Fine. We can talk about that later anyway. We have enough problems as it is." She grasped Darya's hand back, squeezing fiercely before letting go. "Darya, Altan wasn't completely wrong. You need to talk to Serik. Are you paying attention to me, Darya?"

"Yes."

"And?"

"And it's a bad idea. They'll kill us if we get involved."

"They'll kill us if we don't," Alina protested. "What am I saying? You." Her voice became a desperate whisper. "Darya. This is a chance for you to help us. To help *me*. Why not go talk to Serik, tell him you changed your mind?"

Darya didn't bother repeating herself. She was hardly ever sure of anything, but she was sure that it was bad idea to be involved in the vicious politicking of the Thousand.

Alina exhaled her frustration. "And here I thought you were finally willing to do what was necessary. Do you know how happy I was to hear you had killed those bastards? That you lit them on fucking fire? Darya, this is a blessing. And you are going to let them throw you away. You need to use it!"

"I know."

"So, what's the problem?"

Her voice was barely above a whisper. "Altan is right. I can't. I...I tried."

That caught both of their attention. Kasym leaned forward while Alina squatted down, coming close.

"What do you mean, 'can't'?" Alina asked.

Darya shrugged, finally looking up at Alina, not bothering to hide her fear. Her voice cracked. "I don't know. I've tried. I just...I just can't now."

"Bullshit," Alina said. "Try harder."

"You think I haven't been?"

"Oh, so you try for one gods-damned day, and now you 'can't'? You are apparently blessed with the power to...hold on...*manipulate* fire, and you give up because you can't figure it out in a day?"

"You don't understand what it's like."

"No, you're right. I don't. If I had that sort of power, I would be running this place. Stop feeling sorry for yourself."

That wasn't what Darya had meant. She closed her eyes, but even closed, all she could see was the man she had turned into an inferno. All she could hear was the man's screams as he was slowly eaten by the flames. And her smile, like a stranger wearing her face. She had enjoyed it.

*No! I did what was necessary. He would have hurt me, killed me. I gave him what he deserved.*

Alina forcibly calmed herself again, looking around them and fidgeting unconsciously with the end of her braid. The other little circles all carried on with their own conversations, but there was a brittle air around them, the conversations forced and the attention clearly on them. On Darya. A new factor in the delicate ecosystem of the warband.

Lowering her voice, Alina tried again, voice as gentle as she could make it. "Darya. I try to protect you. I think you can count Kasym as having protected you, even if he would rather be anywhere else." Kasym nodded in polite agreement to both statements. "And even Altan might not be completely useless one day. But we need your help now. Difficult, painful, whatever. I don't care. We need to survive. And right now—I can't believe I'm saying this—our best bet is you. You don't want to take Serik up on his offer? Fine. Then win these bastards over." She gestured toward the curious and desperate souls that surrounded them. "They are all watching you. If you give them a reason, they will follow you. But no matter what, we have to do *something*. Do you understand?"

Darya looked into those brown eyes and saw...love? Desperation? No matter what she saw, she knew Alina was right. She pulled herself, at least for now, out of the hopelessness she had so often found herself in since Mikael's death. Maybe since they had left their home. She would try again, as long as it took. They deserved that.

"Good. Then..."

Alina trailed off as a rumble of alarm passed through the camp. Darya realized that she could suddenly see everything more clearly than before. The western horizon was glowing a pulsing red. The rumble of alarm turned into a full-blown panic, as men and horses cried out and moved about, trying to understand why the sky itself seemed to be ablaze. There was an unearthly hissing and rumbling like the world itself was preparing to split apart, and Darya stopped, halfway to her feet. What could she even do? Run? Run where?

Then, just as suddenly, the noise receded to a distant, almost imagined echo. The panic died slowly, as riders wrestled with animals that didn't realize the danger had passed. Slowly, note by note, the camp fell silent. Then, as if by prearranged signal, all started to drift toward the western edge of camp where Darya and her group were, all staring silently into the distance. To the west. To the point where the night sky flickered red with the colors of blood and fire. To the west, and back toward her. More circumspect, more considering, and even less certain of what they saw. They looked down to where Darya still knelt, not yet standing, fire reflecting off of a face that looked west like they did. In fascination. Toward the doom of the West, the ruined lands of the Breaking, and the origin of the ash that choked their skies every few years. Toward Zavayoth's Folly. The ending to that story she had always hated. None of them had ever been this close to its source. And seeing it now, seeing the scale, there could be no doubt. They were running out of time.

"A good omen," Kasym said, after a moment of consideration.

"Or a warning," Darya whispered, conscious of the eyes on her.

"A very good omen." Alina smiled, watching the reactions of those around them to the glow in the West. "A very good one."

Darya listened to the cries of wonder around her. Watched with a shiver as faces turned, not as one, but inevitably toward her. Away from where the flashes started to slow, the fading pulse of a dying god. Those faces were hungry. Hungry for nothing she could offer. But those who noticed those looks too were the ones Darya watched. Calculating and waiting, like vultures. Serik's offer echoed again in her mind as she threw another cloak on to join Altan on watch, trying to ignore the superstitious muttering. If anything, this was proof that she was right. Surviving was tough enough without meddling in the petty politics of the Thousand. And if anyone had asked her, which they hadn't, the world tearing itself apart in preparation for another cataclysm hardly seemed a good omen.

# DEAD MISTAKES

I t had certainly not been a good omen, Darya decided.

"Unnngh."

There was another fist in her gut, doubling her over before she was pulled roughly back up. It would have hurt either way, but not seeing it coming was infinitely worse. The wet bag over her head was claustrophobia itself. She thought she would suffocate. Falling again, she jerked frantically, helplessly, wrists firmly bound behind her, struggling to breathe and feeling the darkness closing in on her, gag filling her mouth. The strange collar they had slipped on her neck felt as if it was closing in on her throat, inch by inexorable inch. Her chest heaved, feeling every bruise, and she tried to scream again. It only made it worse.

"Find your feet, you stupid bitch," one of them hissed in her ear, "or I swear I'll hit you again."

"And then she'll fall again," the other said, amused by the whole situation.

There was no mistaking that first voice. Altan. Why was he doing this?

The answer came at once. *It's obvious. He wants to save himself. And I'm his chance out of the mess he's in.* It made a horrible, inevitable sort of sense. She should never have gone to her watch shift without Alina. Shouldn't have been so distracted by Altan's casual conversation, or the periodic flashes still lighting the western sky. Shouldn't have made and not made any of the countless decisions that had brought her here to this present moment.

Altan pulled her back to her feet and got back to dragging her to...well, nowhere good, that was clear. She had been conscious for several minutes now, after the utter surprise at the edge of the camp. Now he must have had his hand wrapped around the back of the bag, twisting it tight to her face and pushing her forward in a miserable, shuffling half-crouch. The bag pressed tight to her nose, the only point she had to breathe from. Darya's panic came with hate hot behind it. Why couldn't they leave her alone? That's all she wanted. She had watched her tribe fall away one by one, had watched them condemn her brother to die, had never even spoken against any of the scheming, brutal, sly-eyed chieftains, and yet here she was. She stumbled over something beneath her and fell on her face, hard, stunned momentarily with the impact. If only she could call the fire, like she had before, but where earlier it had felt as if what had answered lay behind a thick wall, now there was nothing. The absence of a presence she hadn't noticed until it was gone.

As if he could read her mind, she could feel the warm, moist breath of a mouth against her ear. Altan again. "If you're thinking of pulling your little trick, witch, think again. Don't know where they found it, but that trinket around your neck will put a stop to any of that. Some fancy Sunlander relic. Now it's just you and me."

*Who is they?* she wanted to ask. Someone had promised him safety, or maybe even a position for this little betrayal. Even now, bag over her head and being marched to her death, she wanted to know.

Altan drew back, and Darya lay there in the dirt, trying to catch her breath and feeling that if the bag didn't suffocate her, she would drown in her own sweat, or be choked by the tangled, wet mess of what was left of her hair. Mistakes made or not, this was it. Her only chance lay with someone back at the camp noticing she was gone and caring or being curious enough to investigate. Bound, gagged, and blind, she didn't have a chance of escaping on her own.

"Bitch."

She gasped as a boot thudded into her side, all the breath gone out of her. Any thought of hope fled, and she writhed on the ground, trying and failing to protect herself as Altan kept kicking.

"You...and...your...fucking....brother." He punctuated each word with a kick, growing more incoherent with each one. She felt him stumble and fall heavily on her. It was better than the kicks. Her whole body felt like it was on fire, the pain everywhere, but somehow far away as breathing became an all-consuming effort. She was going to suffocate.

Altan pushed himself away with a grunt. "We're far enough. They'll already be moving. Let's get this over with."

Absently, she could feel hands pulling her up, placing her against a tree. Darya felt a surge of misplaced relief as one of them removed the hood, and she sucked in the cool night air through her nose greedily. Before her were two shapes. The taller one must have been Altan. She didn't recognize the other man. It was dark, but the gray-black of the early morning hours, when the cold really set in. Not that she felt that right now.

"Do you think we have time for some fun?" the other man asked.

Altan looked at him in disgust. "By the dead, you're revolting. We're not monsters. Slit her throat and be done with it."

"Fine," he said, sulky as a child whose toy has been taken away. "Was just asking." Muttering, he drew a wicked-looking knife and advanced toward her, businesslike. "Sorry about this," he said, a lopsided smile on his face. "Nothing personal."

Darya squirmed backward against the tree, eyes huge. She was sorry too, and it felt more than a little personal, at least to her. There was nowhere to go. What a stupid, ridiculous way to die. She had heard people say that your life would flash before you as you were about to die, a comforting bridge of memories to the afterlife. All she could think about was her mistakes. So many of them, over and over. And the most important, most recent two. She should have said yes to Serik's offer. And she should have killed Altan.

Too late. At least Alina and Kasym might have a chance now.

He leaned forward to pull her head back, almost gentle now. She could barely move, but still struggled frantically, air hissing though nostrils, trying to pull away from the blade that kissed, cold and full of promise, right above the collar. Pain forgotten, even mistakes forgotten now, only a noiseless scream as she was ushered politely but inexorably through that last door.

There was a spray of warmth, and Darya knew she was dead. She hardly felt any pain. That was nice, but she looked back at the man above her in confusion. He looked just as perplexed, throat spattered with a bit of her blood. Then he slumped forward, and the pain came. She could see the arrow jutting out of the back of his neck now, gasped around the gag as she felt its front tip tear at her chest as he fell onto and then off her.

Altan flinched in surprise. "Fuck."

"Fuck is right, you little rat," Alina snarled, coming out from behind a tree, sword drawn. On her left, barely ten paces away, Kasym lowered

Darya's bow and absurdly chose to give her a lazy wave. He nocked another arrow and pointed it at Altan.

Even in her pained, confused state, Darya could feel relief rush in hot and fast, the swing from death to life almost too much to believe. No, she was in far too much pain for this to be her imagination. Tears leaked from her eyes, and Darya knew she had never been happier to see anyone in all her life than those two at this moment.

"Put it down, Altan. It's over," Kasym said. His voice was even, reasonable.

"What? So I can be butchered even easier?"

"Fair point." Kasym let the arrow fly.

At that range, there was no moving, or even reacting. It sunk up to the fletching in Altan's chest, and he gave a surprised cough, like someone had punched him in the stomach.

"Oh." He looked down. "Oh."

Kasym kept watch over Altan while Alina hurried over to where Darya sat, ripping away her gag and then pulling at the dead man half in her lap.

"I'm so, so sorry." Alina's voice cracked. "I woke up and I saw you gone, and I knew. I should have known. I'm sorry, Darya, I can't believe... I'm sorry. I should've guessed."

Coughing, Darya leaned forward for Alina to cut the bonds and then stood up, rubbing at her wrists and testing the strength of her legs. Nothing broken, but Sun above, everything hurt. Alina grabbed her shoulders, bending down to inspect her, cataloguing the last hour of cuts and bruises, growing angrier with each one.

Alina had come back for her. Had saved her, again. Darya had no idea what she had done to deserve a friend like her. Looking at Kasym, a sob stuck in her throat. Even he had come. The sob escaped, and she almost bowled Alina off her feet as she pulled herself into her friend's arms, holding on like she would drown otherwise. Tears streamed freely. Alina caught herself and then wrapped her strong arms around Darya, gently stroking the back of her head.

"It's alright. It's over. I'm here now."

The words were a cold splash, and Darya stiffened. Her brother's words, from what felt like years ago. Her protector, risking everything for her again. She wouldn't live through that again.

Alina leaned back to look at her. "What's wrong?"

"Nothing." Darya tried to smile for Alina, looking up at her and seeing the concern in her eyes. "I think I just realized something." And she had.

"If you're both done with your little moment, what should we do about him?"

Giving Alina one more squeeze, Darya walked on unsteady legs over to where Altan was rasping his life away, somehow still on his knees. His turn to want to breathe. Darya almost sympathized, but the memory of all that pain and desperation just made her know she never wanted to feel it again. People like Altan took advantage of your sympathy. Sympathy and all those other nice things they had back when they had a home belonged back there. Not here, among the Thousand. Here, they were nothing but a weight and a softness that would get you killed. Darya tugged at the collar. Almost had gotten her killed. Still, better to learn too late than not at all.

"Who put you up to this?"

"Why..." Altan gave a phlegmy cough. "... why would I tell you anything? Fuck you. Only thing I regret was not killing you sooner."

Darya had been absently fingering the collar, staring down at him, but his casual cruelty, even as he died, acted as a spark.

"I stood up for you!" she screeched, lashing out with her boot. It sunk into his ribs, and he made a horrible wheezing sound as he fell backwards. It wasn't enough. She kicked again, as hard as she could, aiming and wanting to hurt, as he had hurt her. This hurt her too, tired and beaten as she was. "I tried to protect you, I tried to do the right thing!" She kept going, teeth bared, leftover tears running down her face, stinging against the cuts and bruises. Darya only stopped when it had become a struggle to breathe again, and she had to put out a hand to steady herself against Alina. It still wasn't enough.

Altan made a mangled coughing sound and tried to roll away. Alina and Kasym watched as Darya let him. Finally recovering enough breath, Altan spat out blood, adding more to the gory mess that coated half his face.

"You can't even protect yourself," he croaked. "Your brother got most of us killed. And then I'm stuck. With you. The last person, the last person who deserved it... You had power, touched, a chance with Serik, and you..." Another cough wracked him, his face spasming in pain. "... you threw it away." He somehow managed to pull himself back to a tree, slouching against it and coughing weakly. The arrow had hit a lung. He was wincing more with every wheezing breath, and there was a film of pink bubbles around one corner of his mouth. He wiped it away and looked down at the blood, reflective, eyes sad and angry and far away already. "I just wanted to live."

Darya could understand that. Could even understand why he'd tried to kill her. But understanding only counted for so much. She wanted to live too. At least he had helped teach her a lesson, one even her brother had failed to teach her. If you wanted to survive in this world, you couldn't wait for the threats to come to you.

Calming herself, she tried again. "Will you at least tell us who it was?"

"Really? Even now? They're gone. You're dead out here, same as me." A weak laugh, tinged with bloody froth. He winced. "So, does it matter?"

She would learn from their mistakes. No speeches or wasting time. She leaned down, face blank, eyes dry, and cut his throat. She watched as he fell back. *Thank you*, she thought, and meant it. Because he was right, and she finally was starting to understand why. Did it matter which of the three ruthless, scheming, power-hungry chieftains had asked him to kill her?

No, it really didn't.

# DOWNWARD AND BACKWARD

T ry as he might, sometimes there was no escaping the past. Syl looked down the long corridor, where their arclamps threw slivers of light into the never-ending black. The smooth stone of the walls was interrupted by the occasional rusting steel support beam, and the eerily straight lines ahead were broken by the occasional side passage, branching off into the impossibly complex warren of tunnels, halls, depots, and transit passages. The ones that were still intact, that was. They had spent the last few days exploring them, poking through dusty rooms and listening to the whispers echo through the bones of the faraway fortress city. Removing rubble where it was practical, and finding ways around where it wasn't. Catacombs were what they really were. Already, they had found multiple spots littered with the dry, crumbling remains of those who had fought the last iteration of this little war.

Syl poked his foot at the shape huddled in the small dip where the wall met the floor and watched part of it crumble with a puff of dust. Couldn't tell what he had been wearing. Nothing but bleached bones and a grinning maw. Could have been someone he fought with, could have been someone he killed.

"Un-fucking-believable." Leon stomped past. "Fighting in these bloody tunnels once should excuse someone from doing it again, not guarantee you live the rest of your life as a rat." He kept marching forward, grumbling curses under his breath.

Behind him, the rest of the team and the Getacians, along with a platoon of soldiers, trailed along. There was another platoon ahead. The unit behind was one of the Twins' own, a veteran cadre of legionnaires, half of whom had also seen action up here the last time. And the other... The other was made up of the sort of Getacians that Syl couldn't stand. Vali, Lucan, and Marika had each proven themselves worthy of respect, and he had even grown to like them, in his way. Unfortunately, their compatriots were the worst sorts. Gregariously loud when they should be quiet, sullenly quiet when you needed an answer, and motivated by a more mercenary and conditional loyalty than Syl had thought possible. He wished they had given him even a squad of the short, compact Ilkyani. They might be the most ill-tempered people Syl had ever worked with, but they were each worth their weight in gold in the tight spaces of the tunnels, so like the extensive networks of their mountain homes. Unfortunately, like so many things in life, you worked with what you had. Syl might not have liked Domarik's decision to use the Getacians' element as their probing force every time, but he understood the logic. If one group was going to suffer casualties, and if you were going to depend on another group to hit hard, hit fast, and without hesitation...Syl knew who he would have picked for each role too.

They had been at the clearing operation for a week already. Checking passages. Securing exits. Spreading their slow way underneath and outward from Towerfall. Now clearing the way to one of the neighboring towns, Breakstone, taken by a sister regiment, the Fifth. They were to rendezvous along this main passage with another team of oathknights leading their own two platoons halfway. As if anyone knew where halfway was.

"Was it really that bad down here?"

Syl had hoped it was Liora who asked. He knew it wasn't. Instead, Vali stood there, a peace offering in the form of a question. The awkwardness since that night on the wall hadn't completely dissipated, but he couldn't quite keep the eagerness out of his voice, as if he was on a grand adventure. Some people were slow learners.

"Yes."

Clearly not satisfied, Vali continued to trail after him. "What about the ironspawn? You run into them?"

There was a bedtime story to frighten little children. All the better because it was true.

"The ones up here were in piles. We burned them when we found them."

"And in Heliopolis?"

"Had to take the city back from them. That was far before my time though." Syl slowed in his step, almost making Vali run into him. It wasn't Vali's fault, but Syl resented that it wasn't Liora he was having this conversation with. "Why are you so talkative all of a sudden?"

The lad—it was hard to keep thinking that with the great lout looming over him—just shrugged. "It's a bit of a trip, right? To the rendezvous point."

"Do you know how far it is between Towerfall and Breakstone?"

"Two days?"

"Good rule to double that under here. So, at least another day until we run into them, if they're moving at the same pace."

"Damn it."

"Agreed. We'll probably have to spend two more nights down here."

"And...and the cataclysm?" Vali whispered. He was tentative for once, like he wasn't sure how to ask. Or if he should. "That's why the team is really up here, isn't it? But how do we delay it? What happens next?"

"You know as much as me, Vali. I know I seem old to you, but I wasn't there for the last one. Slowing the use of the Rift reduces the strain on the seals, but there's no telling what point is too much. So, we do our job, simple as that."

He tried to cut the conversation off there by walking a bit ahead. He hadn't lied. That was how the Vigil had always put off the end: with the frantic harvesting of humanity's evil crop. But Syl didn't have the heart to tell him about the other half, the brutal, unspoken arithmetic of the Vigil's method of preserving the empire through each cataclysm. Conquer as much land as possible, consolidate resources, and let the fringe provinces starve in darkness to preserve the core. Bleed from the edges. At least Vali and his friends would be on the right side when the time came.

Anyway, Syl thought their current task was an improvement on the last few days. Sweeps and searches were mind-numbing, and with the number of side passages, floors, and the general impossibility of guarding it all afterward, it felt like nothing so much as make-work. At least now there was a definite goal, the next step in the preparations for the final stage of the campaign. They would be marching to the Bal Maru excavation site within days, along with whatever forces the Twins were willing to carve off their main assault on the northern districts' capital of Nordea Kerest. The legions would kill the pretender, and they would kill any Stained they found. And the girl, if they found her. Syl still wasn't sure if he hoped they would or wouldn't. He packed that away. Then they would be back in Heliopolis to await another assignment. Events were almost approaching their normal cadence again, and he was grateful for it. For all the second

Riftgate, rebellious cities, rogue prefects, and looming cataclysm, his life hadn't really changed. Find Stained, and then kill or collar them. Simple.

Looking back, he could see the rest of the team. Domarik was speaking with the Helian platoon's officer, Lieutenant Pallas, in a quiet, serious tone. Kass looked bored and was ignoring glares from Marika and Vali's clumsy attention, who had given up on conversation with Syl. Lucan chatted amiably with one of the Helian sergeants. Lucky stood apart, attention far away, endlessly worrying away at the amulet under his coat. And Liora. They hadn't spoken since that argument in the square. Syl desperately wanted to reach out to her, to bridge the gulf that seemed to be opening between them, but wasn't sure how.

Leon jogged back, interrupting his reverie. The scowl was gone, and Syl wondered who had died.

"You've got to see this. Bring the Gets."

"What is it?"

"Come on."

With a grunt of exasperation, Syl grabbed a nearby soldier, passing word to let Domarik know, and then motioned for the Getacians to follow. They all hurried after Leon, who had almost immediately turned off the main passage, the white-blue light of his arclamp bobbing ahead.

Syl caught up. "Where are you going? How far is this?"

"Stop asking so many damn questions."

"You shouldn't be wandering off. Damn it, Leon, you know better."

Leon rolled his eyes. "Alright, alright. Noted. But come anyway."

Liora had broken off to come with them, clearly curious. They all trailed Leon, taking tight turn after tight turn as the passage became smaller and narrower, until they were crouched, working their way under a fallen and darkly dripping portion of wall. Their footfalls echoed wetly as they sloshed through the watery grit that had gathered on one side. Eventually, they emerged in a storeroom of some sort, roughly rectangular in shape. The arclamp Syl carried and the lanterns of the others illuminated the debris that littered the area—far more than usual. Syl could hear the barely-there skittering of the ubiquitous rats, the real lords and masters of this underground domain. Something about the debris on the far end of the room caught Syl's attention. Taking a hesitant step forward, he pushed the light before him to better paint the details.

"Gods..." he heard Vali breathe from behind.

Curses, gasps, and at least one hiss greeted what they saw before them. Stacked haphazardly, limbs splayed out, like a heap of broken dolls, were at least a dozen relics of a bygone age. Ironspawn.

Leon looked like he might die from self-satisfaction. "Worth it, right?"

It had been years since Syl had seen one, and it was just as disconcerting as the first time. There was something atavistic in the revulsion they inspired. It was as if a creator, bored and more than a bit drunk, had taken the clay of man and mashed into and onto it a variety of machinery, rust and flesh all melding together in a way that seemed to lack any sort of plan or design, ending in an organometallic creature about half the size of a man. Relics from ages past, certainly, but somehow Syl doubted they were made by the same ancients who had built the relic he wore now. The clean lines of ossanite and delicate runework of his gauntlet came from another world than these.

Crouching down, Syl put the arclamp closer to examine the creatures, a sick sort of compulsion preventing him from looking away. The priests and academics of Heliopolis dissected the pieces that were left from the butchery of taking back the fortress city so many cycles ago, and even still experimented on a few live ones, if you believed the rumors of what could be found in the Sanctum Numinary, but he had only ever seen ones like this. Never alone, but piled together like the forgotten toys of some twisted god. Inert, lifeless, and falling apart. Yet rats and decay alike wouldn't touch them. A man down here would be dust in a year, but these creatures seemed to be only sleeping, dull glass eyes closed and mouths agape, row upon row of tiny, razor-sharp teeth as bright as the day they were born. Or made. When you were down here long enough, and you stared at them for a bit too long, it was easy to imagine you saw a twitch, maybe something not quite right in the corner of your vision. He could see it now, the movements that stopped as soon as he looked, another before him rearing up to slash at him with the claws stretching out of too-long arms. Still and inert when he checked. There was a reason they always burned them.

Leon was watching the expressions of disgust and horror on the faces of the Getacians with delight. "Never seen one of these before, have you?"

"I've never seen one either," Liora said, moving closer.

Syl felt absurdly grateful to the little creatures. It was good to see her any other way than brooding over what had happened in Towerfall, even if disgusted curiosity was only a small step up.

"Gods above. What are they?" Lucan asked.

"Do I look like I know?" Leon snorted. "We call them ironspawn. If you listen to the priests, they fought in the Breaking, and to be honest, that seems pretty believable. Tunnels this far out, they aren't that common. But I guarantee if you were in Bal Maru itself, the place is probably littered with these little fuckers."

"They're dead though," Syl said, trying to reassure them. "Only live ones were in Heliopolis. Relics of the Breaking, but I don't think anyone knows who made them or why."

"I think I can guess why," Liora said. She was worrisomely close now, face inches away from a particularly large specimen, a black machine eye staring back at her, unblinking, from the ochre rusting side of a drooping, gray-skinned skull. Its lower jaw hung open unnaturally wide, like a scream stuck in place. Reaching out, her hand drifted closer and closer, as if to feel the sharpness of those dozens of fangs that jutted in silver and white rows marching around the interior of its mouth.

"Don't!" Syl hissed. With the scenarios he saw playing out before him, he knew he was letting his imagination run away with him, but he'd be happier by far once they had set oil and fire to the pile.

Liora stopped in place, but Leon only laughed. "It doesn't matter. They're trash at this point." He kicked one squarely in the side, careful to aim for one of its fleshy parts. "See?" He kicked another with a dull thump, as if to prove his point.

Frowning, Syl stepped up from his crouch, feeling the creeping tension across his temples worsen. "Idiot."

"Yeah, yeah. Anyway, we'll need some oil. They don't catch right away, but it should do the trick. And believe me, you don't want to be anywhere nearby when they start burning." With a creak, he turned around to go fetch some.

*A creak.* Syl froze, staring back to where the pile of ironspawn lay, all as motionless as they had been for years. Liora looked toward him, concern blooming on her face as she registered his alarm. And behind her, all was the same. All except for one little detail. One little eye, which now, in its very center, glowed the deepest sort of red, a window into the fires of hell.

"Liora—"

It was all he had time for. Before either could react, the creature sprang forward in a jerking motion, upper body twisting out of the pile. Liora shoved herself backward with a surprised shriek, holding up her gauntlet and reaching for her knife as she fell backwards. Faster yet, Syl dropped the arclamp and lunged forward, sword drawn and swinging in a tight downward cut. The ironspawn's rusty squeal grated the ears as its twisted arm separated, dropping to the floor with a fleshy clang.

They were both too slow. As she scrambled to her feet, Syl could see Liora holding her left arm close to her side, tufts and dark patches marking where the talons had shredded through her coat sleeve above the armor of the relic.

"Kill it!" Vali roared, even as Syl hacked downward again with a snarl, burying his blade halfway into its head and cutting off the keening screech. Syl half expected the other arm to come swinging around as he struggled in a frenzy to pull the sword from where it had stuck in the inner workings of the ironspawn. Instead, he watched as that red, glowing light faded back into nothing, the creature sagging back into the pile as the green-black fluid that served as its blood leaked out.

"Haven't seen that before," Leon said, clearly as shocked as the rest of them. "I'll get that oil now, I think."

"Hurry," Liora hissed, sword drawn now, but cradling her left arm. It would be healing already, but the cut had been deep.

"Wait," Vali whispered, pointing with his lantern. "Look."

What Syl saw was impossible. Or he would have said it was impossible, would have known it to be the half-imagined hallucinations of only a few seconds ago. Those few seconds seemed far in the past as here and there in that mess of limbs, Syl saw more twitches. It wasn't their lanterns they saw reflected in some of those glassy eyes.

No one said a word. As one, they stepped forward, lanterns placed on the ground. Shadows leapt on the wall as swords and axes rose and fell in a frenzy, the small chamber echoing with the soft sounds of metal on flesh.

# THREE IS COMPANY

"'Three will be fine'? Are you serious?"

Alina was furious, and Darya could hardly blame her. Three was a holy number. Father Sky, Mother Earth, and the blessed Sun. Three was an auspicious number. The three great warbands of the Thousand Tribes, and the three fiery deliverers of humanity from the ice. Three was a perfectly acceptable number—unless that was how many of you had to cross a broken, unknown, and most likely hostile land. Especially when you were one of those three.

Alina had not appreciated Darya's attempt at optimism when considering the path in front of them. The other member of their tribe of three poked dejectedly at the ground with the spear he was using as a walking stick. The horses were behind them. They'd refused to come this close. Even then, they had needed to tie them, watching the animals snort and pull back, hooves stamping a warning pattern.

Darya thought that her horse might be a bit smarter than her, if she was being honest. He hadn't been kidnapped and almost killed at the hands of someone she thought she could trust. She tugged at the cold weight around her neck, as she had done at least a hundred times already that day as they tried to catch the traveling warband. There was another thing; the horse also didn't have a heavy, smooth, black metal collar around his neck. They had tried everything they could think of to remove the collar, but it was stuck there, an uncomfortable reminder of that night, heavy and too smooth. Darya had kept complaining about it until Kasym mentioned he knew of one foolproof way to remove the collar, but thought that she might not like it. She had stopped complaining.

Another gust of wind brought another overwhelming, almost physically tangible smell of decay. Some smells took a minute or two before they settled into the background. This wasn't one of those. There was her horse's most astute bit of wisdom. Because, despite all entreaties to the contrary, he was smart enough not to consider crossing the no-man's-land that stretched in front of them now.

It looked as if the earth had taken a city, chewed it to bits, and then spat it back out. And had itself died in the process. Dirt, sky, old stone—it all looked like it was sinking into a putrefying sludge that stretched for miles in all directions. A few portions were blurred with the haze of fumes or maybe steam. Even the green scum floating on top of the water looked wrong. It reminded Darya of the swamps they had fled through, so long ago. *Back when he was alive.* Every so often, that desperate loneliness and grief would grab her like a hand trying to pull her beneath the earth. Those memories seemed a bit further away as she swallowed, surveying the land below. This was worse than the swamps. Far away, there was the hint of something that broke the natural lines of the horizon for more space than anything man-made should have ever stretched. One of the fortress cities. There was no doubting it. Darya had never seen one before and felt an unaccountable pull towards those soaring towers and massive walls that cracked the sky, its highest structures rising from earth through the ash-filled heavens. *A bridge,* she couldn't help but think, for no reason she could put a finger on.

Now she needed the daylight to see those towers, but even with the collar's smothering field, she could remember what it had felt like the day before. How had she not known it for what it was? It was obvious now in its absence, and she suspected that yesterday, even with her eyes closed, she could have turned to that city, a guiding star for her and her alone. She felt no such pull, visible or invisible, from the blighted outskirts that lay before them. But that was their path.

She heard Alina spit, and she didn't know if it was from frustration, or if the ash that still fell from the sky had made it through her headwrap. Darya wondered if it really had come from so far west, from the land of the Old Empires and the center of the Breaking. Little snowflakes of the past.

"'Three will be fine,'" Alina muttered again, glaring down at the swampy mess before them, as if she could make it disappear if she could only disapprove of it with enough conviction. Maybe it would have worked if she didn't have to glare through the tiny fringe left to see through after wrapping a cloth around her head. They all looked like those raiders from the farthest and most frozen fringes of the utmost East, man-eaters savage even by the standards of the Thousand Tribes.

Kasym stood on her opposite side, surveying their path with his own detached disappointment. There was a muffled sigh. He started to walk back to the horses.

"I'll start a fire."

Half an hour later, they were clustered around the fire, a cloak stretched above them against the ash, and Alina was trying to change Darya's mind.

"It's madness."

"It's our only choice. The rest of them will be taking the long way round."

"Yes! Because they aren't insane! Did you see what I saw, Darya? That makes the swamps with your brother look like a lark. The fumes alone are likely to kill us, if you believe the stories about some of the weapons from the Breaking." She was growing louder and more agitated. "And if not, I guarantee that place is absolutely riddled with creatures like the ones that tore us apart before. There's a reason no one is left in the old cities that were hit with the blight. Or lives there now."

Kasym perked up, curious. "What do you think the creatures eat, then?"

"I don't know!" Alina exploded. "Each other? Us, if we are that stupid."

The memory of being thrown from her horse into that oily-slick water made Darya shiver, but she knew what they had to do. Didn't matter if she feared it. She was finally learning that fear would get her killed if she let it.

"It's the only option. We *have* to beat them there. If we can get to the Stained before the others, if we can show them this..." She fingered the collar they had tried and failed to remove. "... then maybe we can have a chance. Vels said they would want allies they know they can trust. Who else better than someone who's like them?"

"Darya," Alina started slowly, as if explaining something to a particularly simple child, "if we take this path, the last thing we will be worrying about is who gets there first. I didn't save you just for us all to die the next day. We need to circle around too, follow their tracks."

"They'll try again," Darya insisted. Her path was clear now, for the first time in maybe her whole life. This is what Alina wanted, had asked Darya for; couldn't she see that? "And this time, they can say we deserted. Or maybe they'll all just agree they're all safer without me." She didn't have to say that would include Alina and Kasym. If her mother had taught her anything, if yesterday had imparted any lesson, it was that as a leader, it was better safe than sorry. Better to cut away too much than too little.

Unfortunately, there was nothing worse than agreeing with someone who was trying to talk you out of something. Well, plenty of worse things, but it was certainly up there. Alina's increasingly frustrated arguments were the same doubts that gnawed away at the resolve that had seemed so ironclad in the adrenaline-charged aftermath of Darya's close call with death. A feverish sort of energy had animated her then. Now, with all her bruises and cuts aching, the exhaustion of a sleepless night weighing down her eyelids, and the dying light illuminating a drowned ruin that still smoked centuries after the end of the Breaking...it was easy to have second thoughts.

"Alina," she said, as much to herself as Alina, "if we can get to the Stained first, if I can show them this collar, if I can show them what I can do...then maybe we could have some better allies. Well, allies at all. A chance."

Her friend gritted her teeth and stared off into the distance, as if running the odds in her head.

Kasym laughed, startling them both. "That's a lot of ifs and maybes, Darya. But why not? No one ever did anything worthwhile on a sure thing. And anyway, we're probably dead either way." He gave a rare smile. "I'd rather go our way than their way."

"Even through that swamp?" Alina asked incredulously.

"Oh?" Kasym frowned. "Didn't I mention? The fortress city over there, the one Vels has been telling us to meet the Stained at? I've been near one before in the Far East. They're like trees. Roots for miles. There's sure to be tunnels, even this far away."

Alina snorted. "Oh, much better. I've always hoped to die in the dark."

Finding herself in the rare position of being the one to encourage Alina, Darya stood up, brushing away the layer of ash that had settled on her like light snow. It only smeared it everywhere. "Look on the bright side, Alina. We won't have to deal with this demon snow down there." Darya perked up. "And we definitely won't have to worry about those things from the swamp."

— ◄◆► —

It didn't take them long to find an entrance to the tunnels. Part of Darya hadn't believed Kasym. It had seemed too good to be true and far too convenient of a solution to their predicament. Life didn't work that way, at least not for her. But all they had to do was look for the only structures that had maintained a semblance of their old shape. Everything in this place, this once-a-city, this sinking mausoleum, was old. But the ancients had used special care in the construction of these parts of their city. The roots of the fortress city were strong and had kept their form far longer than any building had a right to, even if their function had long since passed into myth. Darya had always loved the stories of the great battles of the Breaking, between the gods, their armies and heroes battering away against one another beneath the walls of these cities. Her mother had always told her it was nothing but overimaginative storytellers making another awful war into something interesting, because it was far enough in the past for people to have forgotten. Being here, it was easier to imagine where they had come up with the stories.

It had taken the rest of the afternoon to wrestle the horses down the slope, picking their way into the city, from dry patch to dry patch, until there was nothing dry left, and they squelched their way through filthy, calf-deep water made into a gray-green slurry by the ash, which had mostly stopped falling. On the hill, there had been a stiff breeze, but down here it was utterly still, and their trespassing echoed loudly in the silence. There were a few walls standing, a few twisted metal remnants of old machines of war, everything only the suggestion of a shape rotted away and absorbed back into the earth. A titanic limb with a barrel still pointed straight up, a last volley against the heavens. More than anything, though, there was the stink. Every step stirred up something vile, and soon they were all coughing, eyes red and weeping, wrapping the cloths around their faces as tight as they could. Fortunately, they had been able to pick out their target even before they set foot in the ruined city. A short, flat block of a building, the closest of the few mostly intact structures they could see. It was covered with moss, streaked with rust, and crumbling at the edges. Yet it looked haughtily sturdy, as if to say it had stood before their grandparent's grandparents, and knew that despite their judgment, it would far outlast any of them, rust or no.

And it looked hungry. Darya knew she was letting her imagination run away with her on the outskirts of her childhood stories, but the yawning black mouth of the single door seemed to be waiting for them. Horizontal slits to its sides had widened over the years, crumbling downward, like tears. Reaching it, Darya placed a hand on the door to steady herself. Then with a hiss, she pulled back. Blood welled from a small cut on the inside of a finger. She sucked at the blood, staring with reproach at the door, while Alina and Kasym cursed in the background, dragging their own animals toward the entrance.

"Is this it?" Alina asked in a hoarse whisper. They all felt the oppressive atmosphere of the place. It felt wrong to break the silence, even if anything that had lived here had died long ago.

Darya nodded. As if she had any better idea than Alina. She pulled her horse in, careful to make sure he didn't catch himself on the leftover pieces of whatever rusting iron was left, like she had. He came through unscathed and miserable-looking.

Soon, they were all clustered inside of the crumbling space, contemplating the stairs before them. If the door had been a mouth—and Darya's cut finger could attest to at least a couple of teeth left—then surely this was the beast's throat. The stairs were wide enough, a gentle enough angle, that she thought they would be able to bring the horses. Not that they were happy about that. The hardy little ponies had quit straining quite so fiercely, but they were clustered together and pulling half-heartedly toward the door. Alina and Kasym looked at least as skeptical as the animals. The miasma of the swamps around them was bad enough, but what if the tunnels were flooded? Or collapsed on them? A thousand equally horrible ways to die ran through her mind, but she pushed them into the corner where she had decided to keep those worries for now.

"Are you sure about this?" Alina looked uncharacteristically nervous.

Kasym seemed calmer, but his white-knuckled grip on his spear spoke louder than any question. They were both looking to her, a sight more terrifying than any swamp or tunnel.

Darya nodded again, not trusting herself to speak. She was most certainly not sure. She tried to pretend she was her brother. Mikael had always looked so confident when he had chosen a path. And if being a leader was anything, it was making a choice and sticking to it. She tried not to think about where that had led. With Kasym's help, she started lighting their torches and pulling her reluctant horse toward the stairs.

To no one's amazement more than her own, they followed.

# CLEANING UP

"**W**hy are we still down here?"

Vali's hackles raised. It was the third time Lucan had asked, the brittle edge on that rhetorical question a little more fragile each time. Marika grumbled a bitter agreement. It was getting harder and harder to ignore them. Mostly because Vali was starting to ask the same thing.

Those ironspawn—and there really wasn't a better name, in Vali's increasingly expert opinion—had set the entire group on edge, members of Lieutenant Pallas's Helian platoon and the Getacian auxiliaries alike. The discontent had been rising among the Getacians long before that, but now the snatches of whispered conversations he heard from some of them were downright poisonous.

After the massacre at Towerfall, the eruptions from the chasm in the ruined wasteland to the west seemed to be a denunciation from the earth itself that affirmed everything Vali had felt as he watched the massed companies of soldiers and giants wade into that crowd. It only made it worse that the long-suffering loyalists of the town surged ahead of them, their hate so much more personal. Made it harder to ignore the fact that Marika had been right, even if he hated her for saying it out loud. It had been a massacre. There was no other word for it.

Kass had laughed at him when he tried to talk to her about it, shameful and sweaty after one of the visits he couldn't seem to stop himself from making. He gritted his teeth with the memory, trying to put her out of his mind. But he couldn't. The more he tried, the more the little barbs of her tore at his attention. The feel of her hair between his fingers. That harsh, mocking laugh and bright, sharp teeth. He rubbed at his lip where a cut was still healing. They really were quite sharp.

And then there was Syl. That haughty, self-centered, morose, taciturn...Vali couldn't think of enough descriptors to capture his frustration there. He had even tried swallowing his pride and starting up a conversation with the bastard, trying to break the ice that had formed since that conversation on the wall. In return, Syl by turns ignored and talked down to him, as if he wasn't even there, or if he was, was beneath notice. Vali had heard the term *bondknights* before—who hadn't? Not everyone saw service in the empire as a path to advancement. Vali pushed those rumors and now Syl's words from the wall into the puzzle he was piecing together of the man. Where he had seen someone worthy of respect, the very image of an imperial oathknight who could have and should have been a mentor, a clearer picture was emerging. A broken man too wrapped up in his own worries to care about anyone else. Of course, for Syl, being an oathknight was a burden and a prison. Vali knew he would be different. Because for all Syl's self-righteousness, how could someone born into duty and loyalty to a cause understand their value and costs in the same way as someone who chose them? The fact that he could spread doubt even now, on the eve of another cataclysm, was yet another indictment.

A call from the front brought him back into the cold drafts of the endless tunnels. Vali had seen the tunnels before, of course. Had explored a small piece of them when his father took him and Sorin on a visit to an ally in these northern districts. They had seemed wonderful and terrifying all at once, a world of possibilities and reeking of history. Now, it was mostly terror left, and the endless strain on the senses of reaching for anything, anything that might let them know if more of those little monstrosities were close. The separatists seemed a distant worry in comparison.

They jogged up, along with one of the Getacian squads, and immediately began to spread out, the actions routine at this point. When those in the front thought they heard something, it was the Getacians they sent forward.

"Why is it always us?" Lucan asked under his breath.

"Because we're expendable, Lucan, didn't you know? At least they've stopped pretending otherwise," Marika said.

There was a chorus of grumbled agreements around them, dull resentment building. They had already lost two in this squad to one of those piles, too slow to disable or burn them all before they started that eerie puppet show. It seemed that their presence was waking them up, which, in Vali's opinion, was another excellent argument behind turning around immediately. Leave the ironspawn and the separatists the privilege of fighting each other for these musty old tunnels, half of which were collapsed, flooded, or filled with rubble anyway.

That was part of him. Most of him had had enough of her endless complaints. He might not agree with Domarik's decision and might resent the obvious disregard for the auxiliaries, but this was his chance, and he wasn't about to complain or bring up his father's station. And he could hardly blame them for not trusting the auxiliary soldiers among them. Vali had learned that lesson once back in Rasovus and had no desire to repeat any part of it.

"Stop complaining and just do the job," Vali muttered as they cleared another side room. "I swear, you haven't stopped complaining since we crossed the mountains."

"I'll stop complaining when they stop treating us like dogs. 'Looks dangerous? Send the Gets, we've got too many anyway. Dirty work? Send the Gets, they don't mind.'"

One of the squad, a mean-looking woman with a shaved head and a leathery face, gave a bitter laugh. "Aye. Not sure why we're taking orders from those shit-eating black-and-golds anyway." She spoke in the heavy accent of the northernmost districts, vowels disappearing before they made their way out. She made no attempt to be quiet, and it would be a wonder if the soldiers behind them hadn't heard her.

"Shut your mouth," Vali said, looking back toward the main group. "Your oaths mean nothing to you?"

She stopped now, squaring up to him. The effect was only slightly spoiled by her having to crane her neck to glare at him. "Oath? You got mush for brains, boy? None of us here had a word to say in the matter, not no oaths nor otherwise. As I see it, we'd be well within our rights to leave these Southerners not so high and not so fucking dry down here. You'd never catch one of our own stupid enough to be wandering this death trap by choice."

Vali thought his teeth would crack for clenching, listening to her in frustration. His hand ground into the grip of his axe, all of his will concentrated on not hacking her down where she stood. He thought about it, and thought about it seriously, for longer than he knew he should have—how to strike that ugly, complaining head from its shoulders. It would be so easy. She deserved it, and Domarik would probably not even take much of an issue. It was people like this that confirmed everything the Helians believed about Getacians. Untrustworthy, disloyal, and good for nothing but sending in headlong to the dirtiest tasks. He didn't trust himself to speak and felt his weapon arm inching upward, almost against his will. Almost.

Of all people, it was Marika who came to his rescue, pushing down gently with her hand on his. The moment passed.

"Calm yourself, and mush-for-brains yourself. We have enough people and things trying to kill us without either of you two speeding things along. And it's not his fault he's got more brawn than brains."

Vali wasn't sure what to make of that, but the woman held her glare for a bit longer before giving a bark of a laugh and spitting a long stream expertly between a gap in her teeth. "More brawn than brains. I like it." She turned to the squad's sergeant, a taciturn and compact man named Albar. "We done here?"

Albar, unmoved by the confrontation, and apparently their whole situation, stared impassively ahead, to where several more rooms branched off, unsearched. He shrugged. "Why not?"

As one, the members of the squad started making their way back to where the main force and the safety of those numbers awaited. Vali wanted to say something. He could feel things falling apart, almost able to see it as it happened.

If they wouldn't do it, he would. "We need to check those rooms." He had the metal tin full of oil in case they ran into one of those piles. If they were quick, and if the creatures were asleep or at least sluggish, it would be more than enough. A few too many "ifs," but still.

"'We'?" Marika asked. "Lucan and I—"

"Come off it," Lucan snapped, surprising them both. He snatched the oil from Vali and started walking toward one of the rooms, lantern outstretched. "You've been giving him shit for nearly a month now. Let it lie." He whirled back around, to where Marika and Vali stood uncomfortably, looking anywhere but at one another. "Oh, is it awkward now? Hmmm? Is it? Think how awkward it's been for me. I'm sick of it. *Sick* of it. Mari, he's a grown man. If he wants to sleep with that snake of a woman, that's on him. Vali, you're an idiot. If you stick your dick in a fire, don't be surprised if it gets burned. Now, please, enough of whatever"—he waved his hand at them in a vague, encompassing gesture—"*this* is. Either make up, or keep quiet. Either way, leave me out of it." He started stomping toward the far end of the hall. "And come on. These little monsters won't burn themselves."

Vali stared at Marika, shame and amusement fighting for the front.

"I'm sorry," he said.

"I'm sorry," she said over him.

They both laughed, and with that embarrassed laugh, it felt like some of the weight on Vali's back fell away.

On an impulse, Vali crossed the distance between them and wrapped her in a firm embrace, feeling her stiffen and then slowly reach her own arms around him. He wasn't sure what there had been between them, or what could be. This hadn't solved anything, and part of him wanted the simple friendship of their childhood back. But they weren't children anymore, and this was better than before, and better was always good.

They followed Lucan.

# BROKEN RENDEZVOUS

The tunnels closed in on Syl in a way they hadn't since his first month in Getacia, those long years ago when he had volunteered to join the second, bloodier fight below the surface. Creeping through the dark next to Leon and the others, most long dead, in their blackened uniforms with soot-painted faces. Everything padded, secured, and torches and arclamps only ever used as a trap. The overwhelming fear that threatened to choke you and left some hyperventilating. Hours and days under the earth turned into weeks, an eternity in the dark, and tried even the bravest men. That was before you ran into the enemy, just as quiet, just as camouflaged. A fight of knives and hatchets in the dark, hoping one of your mates wouldn't stab you by accident. Patrols, and dead ends, and traps. A thousand ways to die, rubble, flooding, and knives all paling in comparison to the unspeakable horror of simply being lost or trapped down here, wandering in circles until you found the corner you wanted to die in. The one thing they didn't have to worry about then was the piles of freakish animals they would occasionally find. Disturbing curiosities, nothing more.

Now that was taken away. Not only for Syl, who had more excuse than the others to feel as close to at ease as one could in these passages, but for the rest. The mild chatter and relatively relaxed posture of the soldiers were gone. When the main tunnel turned into a series of branching options, they no longer walked blithely past, trusting in the size of their element. Squads leapfrogged from passage to passage now, the team split up to support each, all moving in grim silence. With a distracted sense of shame, Syl noted that Domarik had assigned the Getacians, to include their own, to clearing the side tunnels. The most likely to come across any danger first.

They found four more spots where the dead ironspawn had been laid out in their dozens and had been ready to burn them this time, moving on only after they were sure the fire would consume everything. No, not dead. Sleeping. Also, he couldn't say for certain, but Syl could have sworn the layer of dust that lay heavy on everything here was disturbed in a few spots around the pile. Yesterday, he would have blamed an overactive imagination. More than a day down here had you seeing all manner of ghosts. It was harder to discount them after reality showed its own more imaginative side.

It didn't help that they should have met the party from Breakstone yesterday, if their estimate on the distance was correct. They might be ahead, farther than they supposed, but every hour that passed in their endless march forward told Syl the lie in that hope.

*They're dead. Exactly like you should be.*

Syl shivered. He tapped the hilts of his weapons, one, two, three times, breath coming more evenly with the ritual and thoughts clearing until it was just him again.

"You alright?" Liora whispered from his side. They were paired together, part of the squad currently in the rear, preparing for the word to leapfrog to secure the next point ahead.

"Fine." He made an effort to soften his voice. "Surprised we haven't run into the other platoon." He continued, unusually talkative, seizing the chance to talk about anything but what they should. "What about your arm?"

Lifting it, she poked the holes in her coat with a wince. "It healed...I think. Still hurts somehow." Her uniform was shredded between the plates overlapping on her shoulder and the iron encasing her forearm, but the skin underneath was smooth again, not a trace of the claws that had torn in nearly to the bone. "Caught me off guard is all."

"Caught us all off guard. Damn it all, I should have thought about it."

"Thought about what?"

"They cleared them out in Heliopolis all that time ago, but they still occasionally find some in the deeper tunnels, right?"

"Right..."

"So, if this Riftgate is open now..." He left the rest unfinished.

"Shit."

"Yes, exactly. Obvious, I guess, but I thought it wouldn't extend quite this far."

She chewed at a fingernail, eyes reflecting some light from far ahead as she stared forward, to where the other squads held their positions in the branching mess before them. "The team we're supposed to meet... You don't think..."

"I don't know."

Waiting there, no sounds but the breathing of the soldiers around them, Syl felt the irresistible urge to say something, anything. To keep her talking, to reestablish a sense of normalcy between them. He didn't know where to begin. For all the weapons he kept razor-sharp, the equipment he kept perfectly repaired, and the fighting instincts he drilled incessantly, this part of him was rusted almost beyond use.

He creaked forward anyway. "About the town. Towerfall..."

"What about it?" Liora asked.

Syl could sense the subtle turning away, the downward turn of the features. He'd dealt with enough people who didn't want to answer questions to recognize when the walls came up.

"Look," he said, voice low. "I wanted to say I'm sorry for how it all happened. It feels like you've only seen the worst of the job since you've joined the team."

"Oh, really? It gets better? Lucky me."

"I'm serious," Syl said, growing frustrated. "What happened in the town was wrong. But look what they've woken up down here. The chaos in this province right as we enter another cycle. We help make sure events like this don't happen."

"Well, it is happening. Right now, right here, in fact. So, great job on our part, I guess."

"Why are you... Why can't you just believe me?"

Liora considered him for a long moment, studying his face for something there. Syl would have done anything for her to find it, whatever it was she was looking for, but she shook her head eventually and turned back to watch ahead.

"Syl, I believe that you believe what you're saying. When we caught the prefect, I was even proud for a minute there. We saved lives. And honestly, I don't disagree with half of what you or even Leon say. Some of it makes a brutal sort of sense, or is just how our world works."

"Then what's the problem?"

"It's the other half, Syl." She was so quiet as to be barely audible. "It's the things you and Leon and the rest have convinced yourselves are necessary, because it's also what you want to do. And it's me. I don't care how necessary it is, I should never have joined the Vigil. It was a dramatic, romantic, foolish decision, and I made it at the lowest point of my life, when it felt like everything worth living for was gone. It was a mistake, but now I'm stuck, sure as if I'd killed myself. Can you understand that?"

Those rusted parts within him ground and turned and stuck and pushed, all to no effect. Syl didn't know what to say. He certainly didn't want to tell her the truth. He wanted to reach out to help, but knew he'd only drag her down with him.

There was a flash ahead of them, impossible to miss in the darkness. Twice more, and then a third separated by a space. "Time to move," the squad's sergeant rumbled, a massive man, more beard than face.

Liora hesitated before suddenly reaching across the gulf herself, squeezing Syl's hand. "Look. We'll talk more once we're out of here. Let's focus on finding the other patrol and keeping each other alive for now."

Syl nodded numbly. He wished he had thought to squeeze back. Together they kept to the core of the squad as they passed the first group of soldiers ahead of them, kneeling and standing in a scattered knot, crossbows pointed down the paths that veered away from their nexus point. Before long, they found themselves passing the final squad, another group of nervous soldiers wordlessly moving apart for them as they flashed their signal. Hopefully, this would be the last major branching section of this particular stretch, and they could give the signal for the standard march again. Whether the platoon ahead was alive, lost, or dead, it was the not knowing that wormed into the heart of everyone today, eroding the foundations of courage that took a lifetime to build.

The tunnel ahead stretched without break, save for one opening on the right Syl thought he could see. "Let's push another two hundred yards," he whispered to the sergeant, distracted, mind still on he and Liora's conversation. "Might be the last one up there."

There was the vague impression of a curt nod in the dark.

They continued, slower now, blades drawn, crossbows at the ready, eyes and ears peeled. Their heavy boots were unconscionably loud, echoing from every direction, so it sounded like a dozen squads were all converging on their location, silent when they were silent and hurrying forward as they did. Twice, the lead man held up a fist, calling a halt, and they all stood rooted in place, sweating and trying to hear something in that eerie quiet besides the constant, distant dripping of water. It was impossible not to hear something when you tried hard enough, even if it wasn't real.

A hundred yards down.

Ahead, Syl saw their destination. That hint of an opening, a patch blacker than black, betraying another set of tunnels branching off. It wouldn't have surprised him if the other platoon was having to do this too. They wouldn't see each other for a week at this rate.

Almost at the intersection now, the sergeant deployed his soldiers, pairs forming of their own accord as they ran through the practiced drill. Syl tried to pierce the blackness ahead. If he could see a little farther, perhaps he might see the other platoon's lights, maybe leapfrogging their own slow way toward them. Yet...something closer pulled at his attention. The air was different here. There was a heavy quality to it, a metallic tang and an acrid foulness.

His confusion was interrupted by a muffled grunt and then a clatter as one of the soldiers hurrying to his position slipped and fell to the ground, equipment making a racket. *Fucking amateurs.* Syl glared at the offending man, who was cursing as he tried to gather himself.

The curses died and the man went stock-still.

"No, no, no, no..." the downed soldier started to whisper, almost a prayer.

Something was wrong. "Lamp. Now," Syl hissed, moving in a crouch toward him. He could hear the sergeant coming from behind, could see their surroundings start to take on color as they let some of the arclamp's light through.

The light painted their section of the tunnel in broad swaths of cold blue that slowly lost the fight to the encroaching blackness of the branching tunnels. But here, where the soldier knelt, frantically wiping his hands on his uniform, the walls were painted in gore. Blood congealed on the floor where the soldiers' boot prints had cut through the thick layer, and the smell hit Syl like a blow now that he could see it. In the light of the arclamp, it seemed wrong. It didn't look red so much as black, splatters of it painting the walls a darker shade than they were already and spackling the recesses of the ceiling, as if a great tide of oil had swept through here. They could see where it had gone. Catching the edge of the light, packs and bedrolls lay strewn haphazardly, flotsam from that tide.

"Come with me," Syl said, voice dead.

Stepping forward, he could feel the slickness now. It only got thicker the closer they came. Slowly, the shape of a bivouac site, much the same as they had set up on the way here, emerged and took shape. Except this one was painted in the same awful shades as the walls, equipment crusty to his testing fingers.

They had found the other patrol.

# AGAIN

Syl had been wrong. Knowing what happened to the other patrol wasn't better than not knowing. Beside him, he could smell the panic coming off the soldiers assigned to the detail Liora, Leon, Lucky, and he led at the front. He had been the one to drag an almost fainting Lucky to the front, the poor bondmage gripping his own lucky charm in a skinny fist. Not that he thought the bloodhound would be able to sense the ironspawn any more than he or any of the others could hear them coming, but any chance of an advantage was worth seizing. Any thought of leapfrogging squads, or worry about separatists, or even Stained was long gone. Domarik had taken one look at the charnel house where the other patrol had been dragged and eaten, prints scattered throughout and heading off in a half dozen directions, before calling for an immediate double-time march to Breakstone, or any exit between.

Despite the cool drafts that persisted, even this far from any known exit, Syl could feel the sweat trickling down his back. Sleeve already damp, he wiped his forehead as they moved as quickly as they dared, feeling their way forward with the arclamps and lanterns dark by their sides. It wasn't fear, he told himself. Well, perhaps a little fear. The ironspawn were a horror story from another age. Trapped underneath the earth with only the breathing of those around you for company was enough to drive a man mad without the images of what he had seen stuttering through his head.

The main group had the use of a couple of dimmed arclamps, but Leon and he had insisted on absolute darkness now for their forward element. They could see enough with the light thrown from behind. Even the smallest beam could split the darkness. And better to be a bit blind yourself than to be seen from too far. Old instincts resurfaced, and any comfort of knowing there was a regiment's worth of legionnaires less than a day's march ahead did little for them down here. Quite a lot could happen in a day.

At the front, Leon raised a hand, and their little column halted immediately, breaths held. Syl strained his eyes to look forward and find what had spooked Leon, but there was nothing.

He crept forward to lean toward Leon, barely more than mouthing the words. "What do you see?"

Instead of him responding, Syl could make out Leon lifting his arm to point a little off to their right. There, in one of the small side passages they had been ignoring in their haste, was a variation. It became clearer second by second until there was no mistaking it. There was a light source, somewhere far away. It was impossible to tell, but it looked like it might be getting brighter.

There were a few shifts as the rest of the group saw it, but they were nervous enough and well-trained enough not to say anything. Their sergeant was a silent shape in the middle, unmoving and waiting for orders.

"Imperial?" he whispered to Leon.

"Probably." A pause. "Maybe."

With a murmured order, Syl got the sergeant moving. It might be one of theirs, but they would be sure, either way. He sent a runner back to let the group behind know and moved forward with the rest of the squad, slowly rounding the corner. The light was still so far away, only visible because of the utter darkness of the tunnels. It was coming from at least one level below them, but such distinctions were hard to draw down here. The stairs stretched ahead of them, more visible than they might have been otherwise.

There was only the barest hesitation before Syl and Leon started their way down, followed by the rest of the squad. Liora was with Lucky in the back, and Syl had a stab of panic, wishing he had thought of sending her back as the messenger. Not that she would have gone, and he'd be glad of her help if things went bad.

Before long, the stairs leveled out into a wide space, the impression of a circular room, with passages leading off in all directions. The soldiers filtered in, skittish and eyeing the dozen passageways, large and small, that branched off like the spokes of a wheel. Syl couldn't help but agree.

He pulled Leon close. "Awful position. Back up the stairs?"

"Yes."

Liora had come up beside them now from the rear and grabbed Syl's arm. "Wait. Look."

The light ahead clearly came from one of the larger tunnels, growing brighter by degrees. Brighter, and bluer.

"Fuck me sideways," Leon breathed. "Lucky break for once."

"Probably," Syl agreed. He straightened a bit, some of the stress falling away. None but imperial soldiers had access to the arclamps that gave off that unique shade. Right then, he couldn't think of a more beautiful color. Maybe there was another patrol coming from one of the other recaptured cities. It was a perfectly reasonable and believable explanation for why someone might be coming from this angle. *"It was reasonable and believable"* would also make for an exceptionally poor explanation for getting this squad killed, to say nothing of himself. "Crossbows on me. I'll flash the recognition signal."

There was a flurry of activity as the soldiers formed up at the choke point where the tunnel met the larger chamber, a kneeling wall of shuffling men to his left and right as Syl prepared to remove the cover of their own arclamp. There was nothing like a dozen loaded crossbows beside you to lend a sense of confidence. Some even had the new repeating models that could fill you with a half dozen quarrels before you realized the first had hit you. He just hoped no sweaty hand slipped and sent a bolt flying toward what were likely their allies. It was all too common of an occurrence down here, he remembered. Trigger fingers got itchy, and most men would rather live with a guilty conscience than take the chance of not living with one.

The other arclamp was in sight now, bobbing its way toward them, with only a vague impression of a disembodied hand visible. The color was unmistakable at this distance. Holding his breath, Syl gave a final check behind him before opening his lantern to its full capacity, its sudden brightness almost blinding after so long in the dark. Not too blind to see the other lantern stop though.

For a heartbeat, it did nothing but hang there, suspended. Then it began moving toward them, a bit more rapidly now. There was a hazy outline of a person behind it now.

"Sixth regiment here," Syl called out. "Are you with the Fifth?"

There was no answer. The arclamp kept bobbing forward, the shape behind taking ever more shape, light glinting off a helmet now. The hint of metal pauldrons. Behind him, he could hear a second squad filing into the room, more crossbows no doubt pointing down the tunnel. Domarik and Kassara would be with this one. The rest would be coming any minute.

"It's not them. Syl, it's not them. We need to shoot." Leon's whisper was urgent, and Syl could sense the hair's breadth that balanced the triggers around them.

"We need to be sure," Liora hissed.

Syl frowned, trying to ignore them both and his own internal voice, screaming at him not to take the chance and to *shoot them, shoot them, kill them!* Maybe they hadn't heard him. "Which unit are you from?" he yelled, doubt creeping into his voice. "Announce yourself!"

The footfalls behind the lantern were heavy now, fast and harsh. More than one, with the clatter of metal on metal behind them. They had heard him; it was impossible they hadn't.

"Shoot!" roared Leon, right as Syl opened his mouth to call for them to fire. "Shoot, damn you!"

There was a chorus of heavy thwacking reports as the soldiers discharged their crossbows into the dark, aiming at the source of the light and those shapes that started to loom out of the darkness behind them.

Too slow.

There was a shriek from behind them, and the walls flared to life with brilliant and fiery illumination. One of the men stumbled back from the line, his fellows yelling in panic as they tried to avoid the flames that licked outward from him.

Syl only had time for one last look back down the tunnel before their line disintegrated. The other arclamp lay abandoned somewhere farther back, but their own and the burning, screaming man provided more than enough light. Silently charging out of the darkness with inhuman speed were four massive shapes—hunched, primeval monsters of metal. Hooks and spikes covered their armor, and in their gauntleted hands, they held enormous maces and bearded axes. Armor to smash lines and weapons meant to crush and cut more brutally and completely than any channeled strength could heal.

Knightbreakers.

He didn't have time to yell. Didn't have time for anything but a panicked push backwards, as fast as he could. He drew as quickly as he could through his bonds, feeling the rightness of that strength flow into him. Still not fast enough. The armored men crashed into their line with the awful sound of metal hitting more metal and flesh, and one of their gauntleted hands caught Syl in the side as he tried to sidestep, sending pain lancing through him. The spikes took flesh with them, and he barely managed to throw himself out of the way, counting on the energy flowing through him to heal the wounds.

"Close ranks!"

The sergeant? Probably. But there was no chance of that. Those heavies had broken any semblance of a line, and behind them flowed a score of indistinct shapes. The air was already chokingly thick with smoke. Another man burst into flames, screaming mindlessly. Syl froze, indecisive, trying to force a sense of order and understanding onto the chaos. Four knightbreakers and at least one Stained. The flames and arclamp fought against the milling figures in the room, throwing a hundred shadows and providing fleeting flashes of clarity where they intersected. A separatist pushed forward to die screaming on a snarling soldier's sword. The massive overhead blow from a knightbreaker's mace crumpled a soldier into a boneless pile. Another soldier in the corner of his vision stabbed at one of the smaller figures in front of him and was snatched backward with a cry, slamming into another man behind him before tumbling into the wall. At least two Stained, then.

It had taken a breath, a precious handful of seconds when there were hardly any to spare down here, but now Syl had the shape of it. He could see the pattern before him and where he needed to pull to tear it apart. The carapace monsters weren't going anywhere. Those were not the threads he needed to pull.

"Kill the Stained!" he heard Domarik roar over the din a heartbeat later.

Syl was already dodging around one of the berserkers, who was barely being held at bay by six soldiers like a great boar. One of the soldiers strayed too close and was pulled in by a spiked gauntlet and cut nearly in two in a spray of gore. Another thrust in with a cry, stabbing the joint behind the knee, and getting clubbed backward for his efforts. Dodging around the melee there, Syl cut the legs out from underneath a man trying to get around them. Ahead of him, one of the Getacians was charging toward the main body of the enemy. One minute, he was there, lungs bellowing a war cry, shield held high before him, and the next, he was bloody mist, another victim of one of the Stained. He burst apart ahead of Syl, the bones of his own body turned against him. Pieces of bone and flesh spattered against

Syl, piercing a few unprotected points. Keeping his head low, Syl ignored the lines of pain traced by the human shrapnel and pushed forward, fast as he could, gauntlet at the ready. Three Stained, then.

There. The enemy had heard Domarik too, and the few not engaged had huddled protectively around three figures where they had made entry into the room. An understandable mistake. Finally, here was an enemy that wasn't hidden behind lies or with any sort of guilt attached. Not some freakish, murderous relic of a bygone age beyond understanding. They had even done him the courtesy of organizing themselves. Syl had hesitated before, shrunk back from what was necessary. He would make up for that now.

Sprinting toward them, he pivoted at the waist at the last second, scooping up a fallen shield and spinning to hurl into their front rank. It hit two of them, nearly decapitating the closest. Syl leapt snarling into the gap, using the shock to punch through their lines and trusting that he could heal any minor damage they might inflict. He was already pulling as much as he dared right now, and it felt as if his whole body was aflame, limbs singing with energy. Everything stood out in vibrant detail, while his actions seemed to take on a life of their own, inevitable outcomes of obvious choices.

Whipping about him with the heavy longsword, Syl made a shield for himself of the scything steel. Now he could see the real targets—the ones he was really here for. The Stained were steps ahead, and now it was their turn to be shocked, stumbling backwards from broken lines. One fell over with a cry, and the other two called out for help as they raised their arms, trying to call some devilry they thought might stop him. *Too late, you bastards.* Their magic wouldn't be quick enough, and the armor on those lumbering line breakers was now a liability. High on a cocktail of battle drugs, they were faster and stronger than any man had a right to be in that weight of armor, at least for a time, but they wouldn't be fast enough.

Syl thought he could probably close the last few feet quickly enough, but the enemy was already rushing to fill the gap. No reason to take chances. With a twist, he whipped the longsword forward, one half-turn sending it plunging into one of the two on their feet. The Stained flew backwards with a gurgle, and Syl threw himself back, using the squad of Getacians that had charged forward to support him as cover, darting low, letting them take the attention. He heard screams as two of them burst into flames as suddenly as if they had been struck by lightning, beating at their own heads as they fell to the ground, senseless and frantic with pain. Had that been Lucan? No time to tell.

There was the absurd, unexpected sound of hysterical laughter cutting through the clamor as Leon smashed into them from the other side. Half of his face was covered in blood, and a maniacal smile was plastered on his face as he started cutting through them. Syl felt his own lips twitch up involuntarily as he drew the heavy knife at his belt, joining him as the circle around them started to dissolve. Syl lashed out, fast as he could, aiming for fatal strikes with the knife when he could, disabling blows with his gauntlet when he couldn't. Trying to inflict as much damage as possible. Leon was another whirlwind of arcing metal and spurting blood to his right. Syl could hear Vali roaring like a madman somewhere behind him.

It was too much for the lightly armored separatists, and it was certainly too much for their remaining Stained allies. They had given up trying to direct any attacks against him. There had been a moment, when he had thrown the sword, that he thought he might have pushed too far, too quickly. When he had started to feel that distant pressure on his eyeballs and in his ears, like being underwater for a bit too long. But that chance had passed, and the tide here was changing. A few had started to flee like rats down the endless tunnels, and Syl could sense the melee dissolving, that crystalline moment before it all shattered and it turned from a fight into a slaughter. The knightbreakers were still an issue, but he could see one down behind him already, and Syl trusted the rest of the team and the soldiers behind to take care of the other three. He closed in for the kill.

In that half-lit, smoking room, Syl could see the panic written plain across those thin, pale faces. He grinned. He had no idea where they had come from, but they had nowhere to go. He knocked another man aside, sending him screaming to the floor with a blow from his left, sending grasping fingers for the nearest Stained. The man darted backwards toward the imagined safety of the dark, but Syl caught the edge of his coat, ready to rip him back toward the fight.

His fingers lost their grip, nerveless for a second, and the Stained in front of him whimpered with fear as he ripped himself out of the coat and fled down the tunnel behind the other. There was a shaft growing out of the meat of his arm, unreal as a dream. The enemy didn't have crossbows. *Amateurs. Morons.* One of the soldiers in the room had hit him. Was it too much to ask them to check who they shot at? It could have deflected off something else, a wild shot into the confused melee he could hear behind him. It hardly mattered. He was burning, veins on fire from pulling from those bonded to him for so long. Odds were high that they were unconscious at this point, breathing shallow. They would be fine. He just needed them for a little longer. Syl ripped the bolt out and flowed into another who had stepped between him and the fleeing Stained, ramming it into a better target.

Now for the part he loved.

Syl knew it was impolite to bring up. Beneath his position as an oathknight, as a member of the Vigil. But there was nothing quite so animalistically satisfying as when the enemy broke. The feeling of teetering on a knife's edge, the constant struggling not to drown in the contest of the battlefield was suddenly reversed. The superiority you had always known, but that had been called into question during the terror was suddenly vindicated. And those who had tried to kill you, make you so much dirt and worms, were suddenly running, backs turned. Syl regretted that he never had enough time. A few always escaped.

He sprang forward, wringing a smaller man's neck and tossing him aside, like some horrible predator let loose among lesser creatures. These people—and for him right now, they *were* the same as those who had killed his wife and daughter, never mind delaying any cycle—were so happy to kill and maim when they were in control. He relished the ecstasy of that point, when he proved them wrong and started to show them they were just as much sacks of blood and bone as those whose lives they stole.

"Syl!" someone called.

An insistent voice, from the fog of the fight and his own mind. He ignored it, sprinting after the two Stained and another man who were fleeing back the way they had come.

"Syl!"

Softer now. A problem for later. He was steps behind. With a lunge, he caught another, slamming his blade through a skull. Knife ruined. He pulled another free. Never enough time.

The other two had run headlong around a corner, thinking that they might have a chance in the darkness away from the main room. He was barely a step behind them.

One of the stumbling Stained turned to face him, getting a dagger in the chest for her efforts. She slumped to the ground, a small gasp all that marked her passage into the Rift.

The last Stained had sunk back against the wall, and there was enough light thrown by the lantern behind them for Syl to see. Eyes rolling with terror. Pockmarked cheeks and a smashed-flat nose. It was a man. Young. Scars still raw around his neck where the collar belonged. He stretched out his hands, as if he could forestall what was coming, or maybe trying to will his concentration to produce one more act of devilry to save him.

No need to wait and see.

"Wait! You need to listen—"

"I don't think so."

Syl pounced on the smaller man, headbutting him and smashing his fingers between his hands. They broke apart like twigs, and he screamed. His face was a picture of disbelief. Syl took his head between his hands and started to squeeze, bringing himself forehead-to-forehead with the Stained. Staring into his eyes as the light started to fade. Never enough time.

"Hard to believe, isn't it?" he breathed. "One minute you're all-powerful, pulling from the Rift. Pulling it for your filth. Killing..." He started to push his hands together, fingers burrowing into the crevices and contours of the skull, finding purchase. "... mine."

He started to press in earnest now, watching as the spark left. The Stained couldn't scream anymore. Only a choking sound and a mindless struggle to remove Syl's hands. Easier to stop the roots of a tree. Syl couldn't deny taking a sick satisfaction in the animal squirming and noises the man was making. He could feel the skull cracking, shifting under his relentless hands. *Kill* my *friends?* My *family? Try to kill* me?

The Stained was mouthing something, trying to form his dying brain around a last word as the blood started to cloud the irises.

"The...the..."

"Something to say, bastard? Speak up." Syl pulled the pressure back a bit. Maybe he really had wanted to talk.

The eyes were almost completely bloodshot now, and sense seemed to have fled the man's mind. He mumbled, trying to work his way through some next word.

"Spit it out!"

The man was too far gone. He was on his knees, staying there through some immense force of will as his broken skull slowly killed him. His mouth twitched, and air hissed out, but there was no more sense to it. Another gasp for air.

Feeling the heat creeping up his face now, not from the conduits this time, the hate rising like black bile, not for the Stained this time, Syl smashed the man's head into the wall, ending his misery. He pitched forward, another corpse for a land full of them.

———— ◦◉◦ ————

Returning toward the main room at a jog, Syl rounded a corner, only to almost run into Lucky.

"Lucky?"

Lucky looked disoriented and more than a bit battered, half of his face already an enormous bruise. In his right hand, he held his short sword with the awkwardness of unfamiliarity. In his left was a null collar. He stared in terror at Syl.

With a twist in his guts, Syl realized how much blood was spattered across him. He still held a long knife in one sticky hand, and the gauntlet was clenched in a fist. He tried to relax.

"It's alright, Lucky. Won't be needing a collar. They're gone."

"Gone?"

"Dead."

Lucky continued to stare, clearly ill at ease. Syl didn't know why he of all people had thought he could have helped with those two. He appreciated the gesture though. Lucky was turning out to be an asset for the team under all those scowls and dull resentment. Syl grabbed the collar from Lucky's nerveless fingers.

"Thanks anyway. I'll take that. Let's get back and check on the others."

Together they made their way to the entrance to the main room. Syl was utterly drained. Such long bouts of pulling from the bonded conduits might be hardest on them, but it drained him as well. Syl slowed as he approached; there were no more sounds of fighting.

Soldiers were pouring up and down the stairs at the far end of the room. The floor was littered with men, weapons, and nearly as much blood as where they had found the other patrol. It always felt wrong somehow, creating such chaos in the eerily quiet tunnels. Like desecrating a tomb.

The exhaustion gave ground to wariness as he heard the sergeants ordering their men to different points around the room, securing ingress points and preparing to move back to the main tunnel. There was a note of panic there, not the tired but self-satisfied tone of a victorious force. There were bodies scattered everywhere, but now that Syl took stock, he realized with a start that he could only see two of the knightbreakers. They looked more like piles of plate and weapons than men, with the number of blades stuck into those heaped masses. Did they drive the other two off? Not that they wouldn't be dead soon too. Hardly anyone survived the cocktail of drugs they fed those mad bastards that lent them the strength to tear through formations like that.

He picked his way as best he could through the mess. It was always messy after a fight, and Syl distractedly promised himself he would punch the next storyteller he met who waxed poetic on the shining armor and spotless livery of battle. You picked your way through the mess, counted your living, counted your dead, and prayed you weren't among the wounded. Here was no different. There was still smoke in the room, along with the smell of viscera, burning flesh, and terror. Medics triaged the wounded, and a self-appointed priest was giving last rites where the medics knew better than to bother. A last weighing of worth before they joined their ancestors in the Rift. Soldiers moved among the fallen, transporting the bodies that were once friends back up the stairs. Maybe they could recover them eventually, to bury them when they finally left these gods-forsaken tunnels. The long frontiers of the empire were always marked with the graves of its soldiers.

"Finally. Where the fuck have you been? Both of you." Striding towards Syl, heedless of the scuttling activity around him, was Domarik. He grabbed the Helian lieutenant in passing, spinning him around roughly. "Two minutes, and we're gone. If they're dead, leave them."

"Taking care of some stragglers. Couple Stained made a run for it." Syl frowned as Domarik's expression grew darker. "Where are the other two knightbreakers? Haven't seen those used in years."

Domarik ignored him. "They took Liora."

The sound left the room. Gone was the smoke, the smells, everything. "What?"

"You heard me. Liora is gone."

"How?"

"They hit us from the other side. Those four heavies had us occupied, and they hit us from another tunnel before our reinforcements could get here."

"Impossible," Syl breathed. He could barely think straight. *They have Liora. They have Liora.*

*And you weren't there to protect her*, another voice tittered from the deepest, darkest part of his shocked mind. *Again.*

"Very possible. Very much just happened. All while you were running off who knows where."

"Maybe she went down another tunnel?" *Yes, that had to be it.* "Maybe..."

"No. I saw it." That shut Syl up. "We were doing fine, turning the tide, and then you run off."

Syl could feel his stomach in his feet at the accusation, the truth, horror, and anger warring for supremacy.

"Before we know it"—Domarik snapped his fingers in Syl's face—"another score of them, at least. Hit us hard, hit us fast, and beat down and collared Liora before we knew what had happened. Almost got Leon. And then gone. And I mean *gone*. Like disappear gone. Like *riftwalker* gone, Syl. Along with Liora."

"That's impossible," Syl breathed.

"Don't make me say it again."

Syl could see now, a space on the far side of the room where there weren't any bodies. A clean spot where there should have been the corpses and debris that littered the rest of the space, leaking out into the side tunnels. A couple of the corpses nearest were starting to claim that untouched spot, reclaiming it with blood seeping from torsos neatly severed in half. The other half being gone. Transported.

*Possible, and just happened.* Syl tried to order his thoughts and reached for that cold detachment that sometimes he suspected was the real him. Why was it so difficult now?

*Doesn't this feel familiar?*

*It certainly does, it certainly does.*

Leon and Kass were approaching, both disheveled and covered in blood.

"There hasn't been a riftwalker since the Mages' Revolt," Syl said, fixing on that detail of Domarik's story. A safe detail. "It's been years. It's not like they send them to the penal colonies. Where did they find one?"

Domarik continued, his glare not deviating from Syl an inch. "Funny you should ask. I didn't get a good look, but I saw something odd in the group that hit us from behind. Someone small. Slight. Long black hair. Black eye."

"Come off it, Domarik," Leon cut in. "It was that damned girl. It had to be. And I'll tell you what, she knows how to say thank you for sparing her life." He spat blood, wiping the residue from his chin. "Emperor's balls, they fucked us up."

"We need to follow them," Syl said suddenly.

Domarik shook his head in disgust. "Really? They're gone."

Syl looked to Lucky, pleading. "Lucky?"

The bloodhound looked miserable, battered and bloody like the rest of them. He could, of course, pull from the Rift to repair injuries like the rest of them, but only like any other Stained. It was enough to nudge along the healing process, rather than provide the unnatural acceleration produced by bonding six conduits to one knight. The rest of them watched as he pulled himself together a bit, eyes rolling back into his head and going pale as he searched that alien plane. Focus returned, and Lucky looked thoughtful.

"Well?" Kass asked.

"A trail like a bonfire." He pointed off into the darkness. North. Toward the fortress city.

Hope surged in Syl. They could fix this. *He* could fix this.

*She's dead already.*

*Shut up! Shut up! Shut up!*

His face twitched a little, but he grabbed Domarik by his arm. "Let's go. With these tunnels, we can make fast time anywhere. If we move fast, we can—"

"No."

Leon looked rueful, and even Kass had the grace to look embarrassed. Lucky was back to unreadable and watchful.

"What do you mean, 'no'?"

Domarik shrugged him off. "Syl, we can't."

"We can't just leave her!" *Dead, torn apart, sacrificed.* A thousand images flashed through his mind, each fate worse than the last. *The pit, the pit, the pit...* "We have to find her." His mind was racing. "What about us? The team. Move fast, leave the platoon to head to Breakstone?"

"Even if we could track them, it would almost certainly be a trap."

"But..."

"No." Domarik spoke with finality. "We will go there, but we aren't rushing off to be slaughtered. I know you two were close, but use your head, Syl. You can't help her if you're dead. If we follow through these tunnels, that's what you'll be. It'll be either them or those damn ironspawn that kill us, and I'm not sure which would be worse."

"Dead is dead," Leon added.

"Thank you, Leon. Now shut the fuck up."

"You coward," Syl spat.

Domarik gave him a hard look. "Careful."

"You are going to leave her with them?"

"She's dead already, Syl. Whether she died here or dies there. The sooner you accept that, the better."

It was infuriating to hear him say it, and all the more infuriating because Syl knew at some level that it was probably the truth. The cowardly part of him wanted to accept that. Not to throw his life away, to take the safe route, the easy route. He didn't care.

"So, that's it? We give up on her?"

"That's it. You know the game we play."

"Bullshit. As long as we move fast, it'll work. A strike team to hit at their heart while the rest of the legions secure the local strongholds. We hurt them today."

"Look around you, Syl," Domarik said. He leaned in. "We hurt them? Really?"

Syl ignored him, refusing to look back to the dead and dying. That was done. Instead, he looked him in the eyes, willing him to say it again. To give up on her.

One of the voices returned as he tried to keep his stare steady, amused. *You couldn't save your wife either. Your daughter neither. And now Liora makes three.* A cackle.

"You think she's the first Hunter I've lost on my team? That she will be the last? My job is to help put down this revolt. Seize those ruins, the mission the Exarch himself gave us. To kill that brat we should have put out of her misery a month ago." Domarik paused, true disdain working its way into his expression. "You know, if you and Liora hadn't... No, no. That was my fault too. For listening. We are still the Vigil, Syl. We *delay*. This isn't a storybook. There's nothing to win. No happy ending for any of us here. We watch, we delay, and we preserve. Liora gave her life for that, and that weighs against any earlier failures. *Nothing* has changed."

Syl had to convince him now, before changes were made, plans agreed upon. But it was too late. Already, Domarik had turned, mind made up.

"Sorry," Leon said, before leaving to help the rest.

There was an awful sense of weight crashing down, and Syl threw out an arm to lean against the wall, bent over. His head felt like it would split with the noise inside. He wanted to vomit. The sense of helplessness, of crushing worry, was so familiar that he felt as if he were back in time, and all the grief and long years since then were just a premonition of what his life would be. Year after forgettable year, fading into one another, faster and faster. Again.

They were finished here, and the sergeants were yelling at the soldiers, hurrying them back out to the main passage. Syl started toward them numbly, everything around him taking on an unreal, dreamlike quality. Before long, he was at the foot of the stairs. He was the only one left in the room, and the small noises and lights of the soldiers above were growing more distant.

There was nowhere else to go but to follow.

# DEAD WEIGHT

L eft foot. Right foot. Left again, right again. Turn the mind off. The endless pattern, head down, watching the ground fall behind him, one foot at a time. Shoulders burning and hands sweating, constantly slipping on the spear shafts that made handles for the improvised litter. There were two injured on each litter now, and the rotating bearers tried to block out the cries and whimpers of the wounded as every little jostle brought them a little closer to death. And maybe, just maybe, to a surgeon in the next city, Breakstone. That was the hope, the only one they had left. No one dared to mention what they might find when they got there ... or whether they might get there at all.

"You'll be alright," Vali whispered. "We're almost there. You'll be alright." It was a mantra he had repeated half a hundred times, and Lucan gave the same rasping non-answer he gave every time, every breath a labor. His left side was a red ruin, dirt and rubble ground into the sticky mess. Blood and something clear was oozing through the field dressing. Opposite him, sweat matting her hair to her head and helmet long since abandoned, Marika poured out her own soothing words for Lucan.

*I'm sorry.*

It's what he wanted to say. Had tried to say. It wouldn't come out. He promised himself he would say it later, say it a dozen times. When they made it to Breakstone, and Lucan could tell him he forgave him from a hospital cot. Maybe he could tell Marika that too then. They could all laugh at each other and...

"Pick it up," Leon rasped, voice hoarse. "Faster, you fuckers, or we're all dead."

Vali did his best, but the others couldn't keep up when he pulled forward on his side. The whole precarious load started to tip over. Lucan gave a shriek, and the other injured man piled beside him gasped with pain.

"Stop, stop. Set them down. Down, you cockless wonders. I've met smarter donkeys than you Gets. Gently, damn you! Going to finish what the enemy started for them."

The words washed over unnoticed. Vali was too numb to care and bent down with Leon to help readjust the wounded. *The wounded.* It was easier to think of them that way. Not Lucan. Not the best friend that might die.

Vali thought back to when he had been wounded. Twice. And really, those had been quick recoveries, thanks to the Exarch's healer. There wouldn't be one of those here. He thought back to how a poisonous, traitorous side of him had wished he could trade places with one of them, the friends who were all kind words and sympathy, but loomed over him with their unbroken bodies. What a lie. He would do anything to take this from Lucan. Would trade places with him in an instant if he could.

"Alright. Up, up, up! Now go."

They picked the litter up at Leon's command and started the death march again. He barely felt the squeeze on his shoulder as Leon passed by. He watched him walk up to Syl, words distant. Syl had barely acknowledged them in the aftermath. His eyes were strangely vacant in that scarred face. He had taken a look at Lucan on the stretcher and walked on, helping to lead the group out. Behind them, he could hear another team of litter bearers being berated by one of the Helian sergeants and Kass. Another time—yesterday, even—he wouldn't have been able to stop himself from staring her way, drinking in what he could. He couldn't care less now.

"You were right."

Marika didn't bother turning from beside him. Left, right, left, right. "About what?" she managed.

"They don't care. About us. Any of us."

"Shut your mouth," one of the bearers hissed from behind him.

"Vali," she said, breath ragged. "Now is not the time."

She was right. Of course, and as always. He kept going anyway. "I know, I know. But when..." He didn't want to say "if"; none of them did. "...when we get out of here, and *when* Lucan is healed up, I'm done. You were right. About everything."

"We can talk more then. Once..."

"I just...I just wanted us to succeed. Wanted *me* to succeed. To be more. And I led us here."

"Vali," she said, "stop. This isn't your fault. He could have just as easily been cut or trampled on the borders by a rider, like you. None of this is safe. Now more than ever."

Lucan had been injured here though. Burnt alive here, not on the borders where the fighting could be fierce, but infrequent. Here, with the separatists and Stained, the knightbreakers and ironspawn. With a team that used them like pawns on a board and legions that could count on a steady supply of local fodder on the front lines of the battle against the next cycle. It was a wonder that none of them had been hurt before, and Vali resolved to find a way clear of this. Not for himself; he had done too much for himself already. For Lucan and for Marika, who had followed him without question in his selfish quest. There were worse things than being a second son.

The unnaturally level gray-black walls continued endlessly, fading into nothingness. There was no light yet at the end of the tunnel, but there had to be one somewhere ahead. They trudged on. Left foot. Right foot. Left again, right again. Turn the mind off.

# IN THE PAST

*S*he's dead already.

"Dead already," Syl whispered. Was he trying to convince himself?

They were camped outside Breakstone, with too many from the legions already crowded into that city. The open skies were a blessing after that eternity in the darkness, but one he could hardly appreciate. Standing on a rise past the neat rows of tents, Syl stared to the north, where the narrow valley ended and rank after rank of trees marched up the hill. The towers of Bal Maru peeked out behind them. They were barely visible in the cloudy, ash-filled sky, but those spires pulled at him, nearly irresistible. He knew, *knew* she was there. And here he was, stuck. Again.

It was all white now—the trees, the roads leading out of the city, and the little roofs within all pointing to the sky. A cold day too, but Syl knew that the fine powder that covered everything wasn't snow. Too fine. Too dry. The ash no longer fell from the sky, but it still coated everything, paths appearing where people and the wind wore it away. Those heavy clouds of raining ash from a week ago had only ever made their way as far as Heliopolis once, as far as he could remember, but the gray, overcast days would last for weeks even there. He squinted upward, vainly searching for the sun. At least they didn't have to wear the masks and goggles any longer.

*You trying to distract yourself? She's dead already.*

*Or maybe they have their own questions? We know all about those, don't we?*

His head felt as if it would burst, and he let it fall between his arms where they rested on the scabbarded longsword, point planted in the earth. Leon, for all his faults, was the only one beside him now. There were no wry smiles or jokes from him for once.

"You alright?"

"Am I alright?" Syl coughed, disbelieving.

"You know he's right."

"That we should forget about her? Let them imprison her? Torture her? Kill her? Pretend that none of that is happening right now?" Syl could feel the burning at the edges of his vision and turned back to the hills, blinking and clenching his jaw. It had only been a day, and already he and Domarik had rehashed the argument at least twice more since the tunnels. Each time, Syl hated himself a little more for letting Domarik win.

"We don't have a choice."

*You didn't have a choice last time. You never do.*

*Don't worry. You'll find her, same as you found them last time.*

*Too late, too late, too late.*

Syl's face twitched as he rounded on Leon, teeth bared and vision blurry. "I...I can't do this again." He could feel himself slipping.

Leon let out a long breath. With his face this serious, it was almost a different man who stood before Syl, a stranger. "I know, Syl, I know. I remember. But you've got to. Find a way to put it in the past. We'll bury those bastards. Make them pay for what they did."

*We know that path, don't we?*

*Round and round we go.*

"When does it end?"

"End?" Leon seemed confused. "Ah, I forgot you weren't at the briefing. We should be marching north tomorrow. The commanders have all gotten their courage up, apparently. Or lost their patience, maybe. We're heading to the ruins, along with two cohorts of the Fifth Regiment. I hear the Twins themselves will be leading the assault on Nordea Kerest." He snorted. "You remember that place? What a shithole. Can't believe the separatists want that as their capital."

"Royal seat," Syl corrected distractedly.

"Excuse me, royal seat. Not that they've even decided on who would be their king, as far as we can tell. At least Seven Rivers is big enough to be a real city. Anyway, we've got the numbers, and thankfully, the powers that be seem to have given up on the idea of securing all these damn tunnels. They've got the flamewardens filling up the entrances they can find. We'll head out in force, secure the ruins, find their leadership, and kill them all," he finished on a cheery note.

As if to illustrate Leon's point about the tunnels, there was a massive, muted *thwump* somewhere behind them in the city. Syl felt that one in his chest. It had been a big one. He could see the fine layer of ash beneath him shift, that debris taking another small step toward the inescapable patterns of its existence, dictated long before and irresistible.

It had all gone to shit. They would take the province and put down this rebellion, buy back a measure of order, he was sure of it—but he couldn't bring himself to care. Liora would be dead. They would be marching to seize the excavation site at the foot of Bal Maru, barely a day's march north, the same direction as they had taken Liora, but without a thought to saving her. She had been written off, another unfortunate casualty in the retaking of Northern Getacia. And not just her. There was the cold realization of his own self-absorption as he realized he hadn't even checked on the Getacians. On Vali, Marika, Lucan, who had all borne every undignified and dangerous task without a word of protest or complaint. Now Lucan was burned half to death, and he hadn't even bothered to pull himself enough out of his own misery to check on any of them.

They were both drawn from their respective thoughts by a noise from behind them. Puffing like a bellows, Lucky was scrambling up the hill, forehead covered in sweat even in the cold. He reached the crest and finally looked up to see them staring down at him.

"Oof." Lucky tried to catch his breath. "There you are."

Syl frowned, pulled out of his own misery and self-flagellation. He had never seen Lucky this agitated. Apparently, Leon was of the same opinion.

"Slow down, freak. What's the issue?"

Lucky staggered to a tree next to Syl, leaning his back against it, head tipped back and trying to catch his breath. "It's fine, it's fine." He gave a long exhale, steadying his breathing. "I was looking for you."

"Syl? Why?"

Lucky avoided making eye contact with them, trying to recover. "Eh, well..."

"Spit it out," Syl said.

"Maybe he thought you would leave anyway? When we couldn't find you in the house or even at the hospital with the Getacians, he thought..." Lucky spread his hands apologetically. "But I found you. I guess you knew it was a bad idea anyway."

"Yes. You can tell him you found me." There was no doubt as to who "he" was. "And what do you mean that it's a bad idea anyway?"

"Oh, about tracking down the riftwalker and Liora."

Syl could feel the bitterness threatening to choke him again. "Well, it's too late for that now, isn't it? The trail's cold."

"Hmmm..."

"Lucky. What?"

"I mean, well, that's why I came. I told Domarik it might still be possible."

"Lucky, that was yesterday. How can you still tell exactly where they might be?"

As always, Lucky warmed to his subject, the one thing that seemed to inspire enthusiasm on those narrow, bored features. "It's very interesting, actually. Usually, you'd be completely right. A little bone or blood magic, setting something on fire, something small? Yes, a flash in the dark, the less pulled, the more difficult to see..." Lucky trailed off. "I really shouldn't say more."

Syl grabbed Lucky's arm. "Tell me. Now."

"There's a sort of...parallel plane I can see, right? The Rift. That's how I usually sense things. Ah, well, that...that thing yesterday? The girl? What she did yesterday? Not something small." He brought his hands up, miming a pulling-apart motion. "As far as I can tell, she ripped a hole in that plane. The hole doesn't close right away. I guess."

"You can still sense it then? Track it? Her?" There was a flash of hope, and Syl tried to push it back down. Failed. "Yesterday you said it was like a bonfire," he said probingly, trying to lead Lucky on.

"Oh, yes. And there's plenty of smoke."

Lucky's grin faded as Syl pulled him along toward the town.

Syl could see the way forward now. He could feel the towers pulling at him, the solution obvious with Lucky's information. Liora would no doubt be close to wherever they were keeping that damned riftwalker. Save Liora, and kill a Stained too dangerous to let live. A life for a life—what was more natural?

"Guess you're coming with me, then."

"You can't, Syl."

"Okay."

"No. Stop, damn you."

Syl didn't stop, and Leon hurried after him. Lucky was held firmly in Syl's grip and trying not to stumble, still sweating and looking more anxious than ever. Syl was half carrying the bloodhound at this point. The cramped walls of the houses on the street flew by as Syl worked his way toward the middle of the town. There were a few scattered soldiers patrolling the streets, and Leon lowered his voice.

"Syl. Syl, stop. I'm supposed to be the impulsive one. What do you think you're doing?"

"What I should have done yesterday. What I should have done last time."

Now that he had made up his mind, it felt as if a weight had been lifted from him. The ash-covered streets seemed to take on new color, and it felt like he was truly present for the first time in a long time. Living. Seeing and hearing and smelling the world around him. Not trapped behind bars hammered into place over the years.

"Lucky, tell him."

"Tell him what?"

"You know what, you freak. Tell him he's an idiot."

Lucky squirmed a bit, and Syl released him, suddenly aware of how much his fingers had been digging into those thin arms.

"It does seem unwise to leave after Domarik told us specifically not to." Lucky rubbed at his arm with a grimace. "And not...entirely safe."

"You're right." Syl started walking again. He would make sure to check on Lucan, but after that, he was gone. Lucky was coming with him, whether he liked it or not, but he wouldn't endanger anyone else with his newfound conscience.

They *were* right. There was a small voice inside him, screaming at him to listen, to do the smart thing, the safe thing. Not run off like some idiot hero in an idiot storybook. That always worked out in the stories because they were stories. In the real world, that got you and your friends killed. Or maybe hung as a traitor if you were lucky. He didn't care. It was the right thing to do. There were a thousand doubts and second guesses in his head, but he could feel the rightness of this decision in his bones. It's what he should have done last time. Maybe he couldn't change the past, but he could at least learn from it.

"Syl. Stop. Talk to me, you moron." Leon grabbed him, spinning him roughly to look at him. "This is suicide. We will find her, but we need to do it with a legion behind us. They have an army of separatists, a penal colony worth of escaped Stained, not to mention a gods-damned riftwalker. The legions will be heading there tomorrow!"

"They are going to take the ruins, not look for her. We have to beat them there. They will move her or kill her the minute we show up. You know she won't live that long."

"She might not even be alive now!"

But there was part of him that *knew* she was still alive. Knew without a shadow of a doubt that if he went to find her, he would. The power of wishful thinking, maybe.

"Look, Leon. You're right. But I have to try. You can't convince me to stay, and I'm not arguing. I'm leaving. I am going to go see Lucan first. They deserve that much, at least. So, please just let me do this."

Leon stared at him, those often-cruel eyes thoughtful and searching. "Alright," he said finally. "I guess we're doing this. Idiot."

"We?"

"Yes, *we*, shit-for-brains. You, me, and Lucky. I'm not letting you go off and die on your own."

"Absolutely not."

"Me?" Lucky squeaked at the same time.

"Absolutely, yes. To both. You don't get to go gallivanting off on your own and then have the nerve to tell me what I can and can't do. And Lucky?" Leon shrugged. "Sorry. Should've kept your mouth shut, I guess."

Syl hesitated. He knew he could use him. Was touched. But Leon never did anything for anyone else. "Why?"

"Because you're my friend, asshole. Maybe my only one." He pointed an accusatory finger at Syl. "And don't look at me like that, or I'll change my mind. I might not be in love with Liora like you..."

"I'm not in love with her."

"Yeah, whatever. Anyway, I'm not doing this for her. But if you're going...." He drew an imaginary line out in front of him, squinting his eye to aim along it. "Then I'm going. Consistent." Leon laughed at the expression on Syl's face. "Oh, don't go getting all sappy on me now. I like the grumpy Syl better. Save the tears and thank yous for when we get back. If we don't..."

"We will."

Leon bared his teeth in that devil's grin Syl knew so well. "Good. Because I really am getting tired of saying 'I told you so.' Enough talk. Let's go."

# BEDSIDE MANNER

The only worse place to be than in a hospital bed had to be beside one. Vali stared down, bleary-eyed, to where Lucan rasped his way, breath by labored breath, toward an uncertain tomorrow. His friend's face was a ruin, red pits and black crust oozing, unrecognizable past the cheekbone. Inhuman. Lucan's shoulder and arm were bare as well, and he couldn't look away. It was like seeing a perversion of what he *knew* to be true. His friend was healthy, happy. Strong. Not maybe dying. Not passed out from a mixture of painkilling herbs and exhaustion from screaming during the last cleaning. At least if he looked at Lucan from the other side, he could pretend that he was sleeping. Face sallow and pale, breath wheezing and weak, but sleeping.

Vali wanted to be reminded though. Lucan was here because of him. His selfish wish from so long ago had come true, and now he was the one standing by his friend's bedside. Praying to the gods, to anyone, that he might be alright. Not back to what he was—the past was gone, eaten by the insatiable present—but maybe...alright. There was no illusion of a grateful Exarch swooping in with a personal healer to set things right. He would have given anything for their places to be switched now, but that miracle had been used up.

There was a hand placed softly on his shoulder. Marika passed him a canteen she had brought in.

"Drink."

Numb, Vali went through the motions, only realizing how thirsty he had been as the cool liquid ran down his dry throat. He coughed, sputtering as he tipped it back too far.

"Slow down."

Shoving the canteen back toward her, Vali barked a low laugh. "Look at us. I think we spend more time in hospitals than anywhere else."

"This isn't your fault."

"Really? Then whose is it, Mari? He wouldn't have been up here if not for me."

"Don't do this."

Vali couldn't understand it. She had been harping on this same message for weeks now, and here was the proof, the culmination of all her warnings. He massaged his temples with the heels of his hands. "You were right. You were fucking right all along. Is that what you want to hear?"

"Vali," she whispered, crouching down next to him, hand on his knee, "I didn't want to be right. Don't do this to yourself. He wanted to follow you. And you couldn't have known."

"I can't even pretend they'll heal him, like they did me," he said, forcing himself to stare again at the burns. "None of them give a single shit about any of us."

"The medicus said he'll live. And I can't believe I'm saying this..." she sighed, "but some of them do. That's not fair. You can't tell me Captain Askaris, Liora, and Syl haven't looked out for us. Maybe even Leon." She hesitated.

"What?" he demanded.

"A few good ones don't make you wrong either."

"So, I'm right."

She gave a sad, lopsided smile. "Half-right, as always, Vali."

Vali was ashamed that it took Lucan at death's door for them to be able to speak like this again. He wanted to tell her so much. Not just that she was right, but how much he had missed her. They'd been side by side for weeks now, barely a moment spent separately, but there was something uncrossable between them. Or maybe not. He wanted to tell her that he'd messed up—with Kass, with the team, with so much. To tell her that more than anything, he wanted to be able to talk with her like they used to. That he was an idiot who acted before thinking half of the time, letting his emotions lead the way. And that he was a coward for shying away from the feelings that had been building between them for years, pushing her away over and over, but still asking her to follow him wherever he wanted to go, knowing she would.

He could tell her. What better time than now? And why not? She deserved it. And how many times did he have to be in one of these rooms before he learned how short life could be?

"Mari, I..."

There was a wave of muttering and noise through the low hum of conversation and intermittent cries of pain in the tent. Vali and Marika turned to look, seeing Syl, Leon, and Lucky striding toward them, the conversations sparking back with renewed volume in their wake.

"Vali, Marika," Syl acknowledged with a nod. "How is he?"

"How is he?" Vali asked. "Look at him, damn it."

Syl obliged, impassionate as always as he surveyed Lucan's injuries. "Will he make it?"

Vali stood, finding a focal point for the anger which seemed to always be right beneath the surface these days. Syl might be one of the better ones, but right now he represented the people Vali had watched use him and his friends like tools as they cut their bloody way through the province.

Squeezing his arm in warning, Marika cut in. "They say so. But it will take time."

Vali shook her off. "Don't pretend like you care about him now." He took a step toward Syl. He could see how tired the Hunter was, but Vali wanted nothing more than to beat his face in, even if he knew it wasn't his fault. Not really. "Lucan wouldn't be here if it wasn't for you."

"I know." Syl didn't look away from Lucan. "You're right."

Caught off guard by the confession, Vali was unsure of what to do. Syl solved that for him.

"That's why I came here. I wanted to tell you—him too—that I'm sorry. You deserved better. I wish I could change what happened, but I can't."

"Why?" Marika asked, as wrong-footed as he was.

"Why what?"

"Why now?"

Leon snorted. "You really can't take a nice gesture, can you?"

"No, no," Syl said slowly. "It's a fair question. Because I should have earlier, and I don't know if I will be able to later."

"You're going after her, aren't you?" Marika asked softly.

"Always with the questions from you, eh? And no idea what you're on about." Leon circled the cot, looking more curious than disgusted as he inspected the burns. He reached out a finger as if to press a point on Lucan's side before Syl made a disapproving noise. Leon straightened. "But we should be leaving anyway. Unrelated."

Vali could see it now. In Lucky's nervous hunch. The calm decision in Syl's bearing. And the inexplicable excitement from Leon. With a flash of guilt, he realized in his worry over Lucan that he had done exactly what he had hated these three for: completely forgotten about Liora. Assumed she was dead.

"Do you think she's alive?" Marika asked.

"She is," Syl said, with a level of certainty that bordered on madness. "And Lucky knows where she is."

Lucky was sweating, and his eyes darted about the room, nervous as Vali had ever seen him. "I, uh, *might* know." A patrol marched past outside, and Lucky jumped, only calming when the noise of their shouts passed beyond hearing.

Syl didn't seem to have heard him. He gave one last solemn look at Vali and Marika before turning away. Vali knew if anyone had a chance of finding Liora, alive or not, it was Syl. Small chance, high risks, but with the only sort of reward worth it. With a glance back at Lucan, Vali had a flash of inspiration. There might not be a healer here, might not be another one in the whole province, but Vali knew where the better medicine, the better medicus, and the better chances of living were. Down the street in the hospital for the Helian legionnaires. Or in the private houses where the nobles and oathknights who needed care were kept. New Riftgate, new war, it didn't matter. Status, real status, meant more than money and respect. It meant a better life and a longer one. It meant his family and his friends having a better chance of surviving whatever this cataclysm might bring. Vali couldn't help Lucan right now, but he had come far enough on his own ambitious, selfish journey that maybe he could finish it for someone else.

"I'm coming with you."

Syl kept walking down the rows of cots, not acknowledging Vali, until he caught Syl by his coat, stopping him. "I can help. Take me with you."

"Absolutely not. Your friend needs you here."

"Lucan needs more than I can give. He needs what they gave me back in Rasovus, but I don't see that happening anytime soon. Let me help."

Leon forestalled another protest from Syl. "I'm starting to like the big one. Let him come. Don't tell me we couldn't use all the help we can get."

Sighing in frustration, Syl rubbed at his temples. "Vali. There is no healer here. Or coming here. I can't do anything for Lucan. And at the end of the day, this is desertion. Means the noose. Only chance of living is if we come back with Liora and that riftwalker's head. There's no failing here. Success, or death."

"I know," Vali insisted. "But I can do something for Liora. She deserves more than being forgotten out there. Isn't that why you're going?" He shifted under Syl's glare. "I'm going."

Eventually, Syl nodded. "Fine. But don't expect to be thanked by anyone for this one. Now, we've wasted enough time already. We're leaving."

Vali was surprised to see Marika grabbing her own gear behind him. "What are you doing?"

"Don't start. I'm coming too."

"But..."

"What did you say earlier?"

"About Lucan?"

"No, about me."

"That...that you were right?"

She reached up to pat his cheek. "Look at you. Learning."

# BAD CROSSING

Useless. She was worse than useless. Darya could feel the cold sweat prickling her back as she held out the torch and considered the intersection before her for perhaps the hundredth time. One day with her trying to make decisions, and they were already lost. Turned out calling yourself a leader would only get you so far.

Trying to stuff down the panic, she indicated the passage to the right. Not that it had anything to recommend it over the other two.

"Are you sure?" Alina asked.

"Yes." Darya splashed forward. "Mostly."

"Mostly?"

"Do you know?" Kasym asked, cutting Alina off. She didn't need to answer. "Then mostly is good enough." He started to follow Darya, leading his own horse. They had needed to blindfold all of them. "That said, Darya, I would really love not dying down here. Let's find the main passage again."

Too many parts of the tunnels were damp and leaking for her not to constantly imagine what would happen if the walls collapsed suddenly. They had seen what that looked like earlier. When the tunnel they had started on—one that was clearly a main passage, the path they had hoped would lead them to the heart of the fortress city—ended in a pile of stone and metal rubble before them, the rusted iron rails on the ground continuing into a wall of debris. A few detours, changes in floor, and blocked passageways later, and here they were.

Darya wished they had more time to look at the place. It was fascinating. Even in ruins, it was a better-preserved piece of the past than she had ever seen before. But between fascinating and terrifying, the threat of death had a way of coming first. A small part of her found time to wonder at the endless side rooms, the smooth, endless lines of the passages, the countless details that were so obviously functional, and just as obviously beyond any frame of reference she had for the specifics. More than anything though, the scale. Incredible, unbelievable scale. If the fortress city were a tree, its roots would have choked the forest. It was another world. Which, of course, was part of why they were...she didn't want to say lost yet. Disoriented, maybe.

*If we stay disoriented much longer, I'm going to die in another world. What a privilege.* Darya swallowed nervously, turning away from the dead end in front of her to face the blinding torches of her friends. It was probably better not to see their faces. She wasn't sure which would have been more painful; disappointment or resignation.

"It's alright, we'll try..." Alina started.

"Shhh!" Kasym was perfectly still, and they both followed suit. They watched him with the primed readiness of prey. And if there was anything else down here, that was exactly what they were.

After a long silence, Kasym relaxed, shoulders dropping. He breathed out. "Sorry. Thought I heard something."

"Whatever." Alina yanked at the reins, turning around. "Let's try again. It's got to be..."

She cut herself off this time. They looked at one another, eyes wide. Darya's stomach dropped. They had all heard that time. Far away, quiet enough that it would have been easy to think it was imagined, there was a splashing sound. And...there had been something else, but she chose to believe she had only heard the splash. That was bad enough. Darya had thought there could be nothing worse than the three of them being trapped alone under the earth, slowly dying as they wandered in circles, knowing she was to blame.

No. Knowing they weren't alone was far worse.

---

"This way," Darya gasped. They were in a maze now, and whatever was behind them knew it better than they did.

They sprinted around another corner, dragging the horses as fast as they could. Darya wished they had left them outside of the city. Not everyone should have to die for her poor choices. And they were probably going to die. It didn't matter how fast they moved; the splashing sounds from behind were louder again. Louder every time, so that now they could all hear it over their own ragged breathing and the blood pounding in their ears. Splashing, and the sound that she had heard earlier. Little screeches so high-pitched that they could have been imagined. But there wasn't any point in denying she had heard them any longer, no wishing them away.

"We need to leave the horses," Kasym rasped out. He was stumbling now, still dragging at the poor, panicked horse behind him with his lanky arms.

"No," Darya groaned, pulling with all her weight against the reins. "Please, please, please." She was pleading with the loyal little bastard to stop trying to tug away. He knew it had been death to come down here. She couldn't leave him now. But he would get her killed if she didn't, she knew that.

"Do it!" Alina ripped the reins out of Darya's hands and pushed her forward. Darya was absurdly grateful to her. Knowing something was the right choice was easier than taking it. Sometimes it took a push. It was a blessing, having the privilege to resent a friend instead of yourself for once.

They surged ahead now, abandoning the animals. Darya spared a glance over her shoulder, straining to see whatever the skittering, shuffling horror was behind them. In the utter blackness, she could see little swirling pinpricks of red light, like a hundred evil stars. And the horses—blind, terrified, and alone. A sob stuck in her throat. Somehow this felt worse than anything she had ever done. Worse than Bohdan. Worse than the man in the town. It was like throwing a babe to the wolves.

Alina grabbed her arm and dragged her along, making her drop her torch. She wanted to cry. But she was too scared for herself to have room for any more grief. There were horrible, horrible sounds behind them now. Screams of pain and fear that sounded more than human. The sick squelch of sharp fangs and claws into soft flesh and sucking sounds. A feast of the damned. And above it all, a single long screech, a predator glorying in its gory kill.

All of that for a few more minutes of life. Maybe.

They sprinted headlong now, any thought of keeping to a direction long ago fled. The only direction that mattered now was away. Whatever could put more distance between them and whatever was tearing apart the poor animals. It hadn't bought them long. She could hear the screeches again, closing in. Whatever those creatures were, they weren't stupid. They weren't about to let another meal escape them.

Their boots pounded on the hard stone, and the torches didn't seem to shed light fast enough to keep up with their headlong rush. Darya dodged a piece of metal jutting from fallen masonry at the last second. Alina hit it and went stumbling with a cry, skidding to a stop on the slippery floor. Darya wanted nothing more than to keep running, but she turned around to drag Alina up, feeling the years of accumulated filth from the ground as her hands pulled at her coat. Alina slipped, letting out another cry. She had twisted or broken something. Darya could barely see her, another one of their torches dropped and sputtering to nothing on the floor beside them. Darya snatched it back up. *Get up, get up, get up...* She made a sound, not quite a whimper, grabbing at Alina again, willing her to get up, but too frightened to scream the things she wanted to.

Why didn't Kasym help? Had he made the same calculation she had? Sure enough, she saw his torch ahead, slowly leaving them in the dark. *Bastard.* Darya hated him at that moment. Hated herself more. Because even as she pulled Alina up, dragged her along, shoulder under the heavy woman's arm and her gritted breath in her ear, the thought that hammered at her was the same. *Leave. Leave! I need to leave her, or I'm dead. It's what she would want. What Mikael would have wanted.*

But she couldn't. Alina was all she had left. And Alina had come for Darya, had been there for her again and again, every time she had needed her. Darya couldn't protect her, not earlier, and sure as the screams behind them, not now. The least she could do was die with her.

Darya shuffled with Alina as best they could. Their half-drenched torch barely gave enough light to move by as they splashed through stagnant water. She focused on the ground right before her, trying not to trip. An itch built in her back as she imagined what it would feel like. Without warning, those teeth sinking into her, tearing great chunks away. It would be soon. Her legs started to feel like lead, nothing that could help her, only two heavy burdens she had to drag forward, one at a time, fast as she could. The sounds behind them were so close now.

"Here! Hurry!"

Out of nowhere, she realized she had been placing her feet by the light of Kasym's torch, not her own. The one in her own hands was useless, nothing more than a dripping stick now. She dropped it. To their left, she could see what Kasym meant. A corroded, moss-covered, jagged door. But a door. Rusting, but thick iron.

Darya dragged Alina inside, not bothering to check the room. Couldn't be worse than on their side. Together, she and Kasym started pushing at the door. There was a circular wheel that was apparently the handle, and Darya placed her hands on either side of it, Kasym beside her, and pushed with everything she had. Her heart sank. It wouldn't move. Didn't even make a sound, just stood there, as still and stolid as it had for centuries, slowly melting into the crumbling concrete beneath it. Kasym was straining, tendons standing out on his neck as he snarled, feet struggling for purchase on the slick ground. Alina was beside them now too, back to the door, pushing against it, face slick with sweat and grunting with the pain. It wouldn't move.

Kasym started throwing himself against the door, heedless of the sharp edges. Darya joined him, frantic now, hurling herself against the iron. She couldn't feel the pain. Still, nothing.

No... There it was! A creak. Darya could swear she had heard it over the sounds of pursuit, the scrabbling claws and otherworldly screeches. Then a great groan as they all threw their bodies against the door, desperately fighting centuries of momentum. Slowly, so slowly, it was closing. It could work.

The small gap between wall and door was shrinking to nothing. Darya felt herself slip, exhausted, as she tried to hurl herself against the door again. A final effort. They could make this work. Buy another few minutes of life, claw their way to another, and another, until they got out of these gods-damned tunnels and back into the light.

The scrabbling little creatures were almost outside of the door now. She could hear them like they were in the room with them. There was a heavy thump against the door from the other side. A frustrated screech. Darya drew her sword, nearly cutting Kasym, and kicked again at the hunk of metal, almost slipping and falling.

"Push, damn you!" Alina snarled. But she couldn't see the still-open sliver, the gap where questing, too-long, metal and flesh arms and talons were worming their way in against the pressure they were placing on the door.

Too tired to scream, Darya started hacking, half-blind in the dark, praying she didn't hit herself or Kasym by mistake. The blade alternated between deep bites and sparking, glancing blows against whatever armor the creatures were wearing. There were more screeches, and one by one, the arms were drawn back, except for a final one, a hissing sound coming from the other side of where a long, gray-green arm clawed in a futile effort to find purchase in flesh. Darya could barely feel her limbs at this point. She was beyond tired and out the other side. Grunting, she chopped down with everything she had. There was a final screech, and her blade cut through, slamming into the floor and bouncing out of her hand.

It was enough. Cleared of obstacles, Kasym and Alina's final push worked. With a peal of finality, the door slammed closed. The torch leaning against the wall inside was down to almost nothing. Outside, hungry claws scratched, and bodies slammed against the door they leaned against. They were lost, out of food, without horses, and without an apparent way out of the room. But they had bought another few minutes.

Good enough for now.

---

Turned out, good enough for now wasn't all that good. It had to be a truth of life that removing a bigger problem just gave more room for all the smaller ones. There was another slam against the door, and Darya felt it vibrate through her, jarring her head from where she had been resting it. None of them even remarked on it. They scooted back against the door again, the ritual long established. Too tired for fear. Well, almost. Even with the awful creatures just outside, the panic was gone, the fear down to a steady hum. Darya wondered if you could burn out your ability to feel fear. Was there only so much a person could feel over a lifetime before it started to wash over them? She hoped so. She had to be close.

"Well." Kasym's voice was a sigh.

Alina joined him. "Yup."

"It isn't fair." Darya knew she sounded like a child, but couldn't be bothered to care. "None of it." She stared into the darkness. There was nothing there. No way out. They had checked. Another impact shook the door, but only a little. Maybe their pursuers, whatever they were, would leave. Darya doubted it.

Kasym gave a humorless chuckle. "This is as fair as it gets, Darya. It's your fault for being born on the wrong side of the Gates, didn't you know?"

Alina snorted, amused. "And don't get me started on being born a woman. That was a major fuck-up on your part, Darya. You really ought to think these things through."

They both started giggling like children, hysteria creeping in.

"But what can we do?" Darya didn't understand how they could laugh at a time like this, how they weren't spending their last moments cursing her stupidity for leading them here.

"Hmmm..." Kasym pondered the question. "I think next time, I'll choose to be born a nobleman in Heliopolis. Or if not one of them, maybe the Emperor Himself. I'm a simple man."

Alina sputtered with laughter.

"What about you, Alina? Going to be my lady?"

"Not in a hundred lifetimes, you oaf," she shot back, catching her breath. "No, no, if I get to choose, I'm choosing well. A lord, but not too important. Too much trouble when you've got stuff other people want. Some out-of-the-way holdfast by a lake, and a few miserable peasants that would bow and scrape whenever I would haul my fat ass out of the keep. And a library."

"A library? You can't even read!"

"And ladies can't be lords, what of it? This is my world, so I get to choose. In my world, I can read. I can read, and maybe you're one of those filthy peasants. Definitely."

"Not sure I like your world. I offered to make you an empress, and now I'm a peasant."

"What about you, Darya?" Alina asked, ignoring Kasym.

"What would I be?"

"Yes."

Darya thought about it. More than she meant to. It was nice to think of anything other than the here and now. A life not started in the cold and spent in the saddle. One where her brother was still alive. Where she wasn't trapped down here with those hungry red eyes. It was hard to imagine another life, even if she didn't particularly like the one she had, hard as she fought for it.

"A sailor." There was another half-hearted slash at the door. They didn't even acknowledge it this time.

"Darya, you've never even seen the sea."

"Doesn't mean I don't want to," Darya protested. "I want to see...more than this. There's so much out there, but all we do when we get anywhere is kill everyone we find and burn anything that's left." The image of that first town after the mountains was fixed in her mind, and by the silence of the other two, she knew it was what they were thinking of too. It hadn't been the first, or even the largest they had seen pillaged and burned in their time with the Thousand, but there was no avoiding the sense of responsibility for that one. Their survival had cost those townspeople their lives.

"So, yes," she finished. "A sailor. Or anything where I can see the world. Whatever's to the south, and then past that."

"It's a good wish, Darya," Alina said.

It was just a wish, after all. The only thing she would be exploring soon was the digestive processes of the creatures outside.

"I want to be a carpenter," Kasym confessed suddenly. "I want to be able to make something with my hands." He fell silent just as quickly, embarrassed by the honesty of the admission.

"I'd like to see that," Darya said, smiling at him in the dark. She had never liked him more than right then. Except maybe when he had saved her. That would be hard to top. "Alina?"

"Oh, don't look at me to start getting emotional. I meant what I said. Small holdings, bowing peasants, warm weather." She paused, before continuing in a quieter voice. "But it'd be nice if you both visited."

"Ha!" Kasym exclaimed. "She has a heart." There was a thump. "Ow!"

They fell into a companionable silence, trying to keep their minds on these other selves. Warm, and happy, and not trapped behind a rusting door in a labyrinth of leaky tunnels. There was another screech. Unfortunately, reality had a way of overwhelming even the most compelling fantasy, real discomforts trumping imaginary pleasures.

The silence slowly became more oppressive as each settled into their own respective hells. Darya was soaked, bruised, and every time she shifted, she could feel scabs stretching and splitting where her body did its best to keep all the important bits inside. And the collar. The gods-damned, filthy fucking collar. She silently cursed Altan again, feeling for a catch, an irregularity, anything, on the collar for the thousandth time. For all Darya's self-recrimination and second-guessing, Alina had been right. The fire she had called was a gift. A weapon and a shield. And now, when she needed it most, it had been stripped from her because a few petty, would-be warlords had been afraid of someone else having a bit of power. Fingers traced the smooth almost-metal, circling and circling. Finding nothing.

"One of us could make it."

"What?" Darya asked, startled by Kasym.

"One of us could make it. We just have to do what we did before."

"With the horses?" Alina asked.

Kasym's silence was answer enough.

Darya flushed as the thought flashed unbidden into her mind. *It should be me. I have the power, the collar.* She tried to push it away. They had risked their own lives to save hers. She couldn't let them do it again.

"If we wait long enough, maybe they'll leave," Darya said instead.

"Maybe," Kasym agreed, in a way that made it clear he didn't.

"We've been here for hours, Darya. They're doing what we're doing." Alina was her usual self again, all thoughts of holdings and visits in the imaginary past where they belonged. "Don't know how smart those little buggers are, but I can't see them just leaving. Not when they have a nice meal stewing in here. Kasym is right. And it needs to be you."

"No," Darya protested. In her heart though, a guilty hope soared, and she hated herself for it. A coward. That's what she was, what she had always been. Didn't matter if it made sense, or it was practical. A practical coward was still a coward, and what coward's logic didn't make sense in their own head? "It should be you, Alina," she tried.

Alina gave the answer Darya knew she would. "No. It needs to be you, Darya." Kasym didn't disagree. "You were right about getting to the Stained first. Maybe even finding that devil, Vels. He seems to like you, gods know why. No point in all this being a waste."

"Aye." Kasym started to stand, unfolding those long limbs and still leaning against the door. "I would appreciate you killing Serik though. Taharuk and Kursagai, too, if you can manage. Might as well. Don't know if it will matter when I'm gone, but I like to think I'll know."

Things were taking on the inevitable momentum that seemed to characterize all the events around Darya, and she struggled to react as Alina dragged herself up with a groan, testing out her bad ankle. Darya stood up, numb, watching it all happen. Again. As soon as she started to care for someone, they died. For her. For another few moments of a life she hated.

"No point in dragging this out." Alina drew her sword, a dull rasp in the dark. Kasym handed Darya their last, failing torch.

"Wait," Darya whispered. It was all happening too fast. It felt like the air itself was closing in around her.

"Be ready," Kasym warned, grabbing the handle of the door. He paused, considering. "What if it won't open?"

Alina laughed. "Then I vote we eat you first." She spun her sword in her hand, readying herself, balanced as best she could for one last effort. "Don't waste this, Darya. Get that collar off and then burn them all."

*I'm staying.* It's what she wanted to say. What she should have said. But her throat was dry, and she couldn't find the air. Palms sweaty, she drew her own sword. To fight with them? To cut a way out and leave them behind?

There was a knock at the door, and her heart stopped. A knock. Not the scratching, or the slamming, or the screeching from earlier. It came again.

"Hello?" A muffled voice from far away.

"What the hell?" Kasym was rooted in place.

The weight fell away, and Darya found her voice. "Open it. I know who that is." And she did. No one else would be down here. No one else could have found them. And no one else, not a single other soul in all the circles of the worlds, would have sounded amused.

Creaking inward on squealing hinges, the great rusting door slowly gave way. And there, face half-hidden under a hood, a furious-looking black-haired girl to his right, one bandaged hand resting lightly on one of the creatures to his left, and smiling his death's-head grin, was Vels.

"Hello there."

# PART IV

*Military victory is not the end. It is but one option in the pursuit of compliance and integration. If conventional means do not produce the intended effect, the commander must consider the unconventional. Famine, disease, and population displacement must all be weighed in the implementation of any strategy.*

—*The Art of Conquest*, The Leveler, Imperial War College, Heliopolis

# REUNITED AT LAST

*D*on't waste it.

Across from Darya sat the three chieftains, stiff and ill at ease in those fine chairs. If looks could burn, she would have turned to ash long ago. Taharuk and Kursagai glowered with suspicious hostility. No doubt she was the last person they had expected to see here when they arrived. Serik did a passable job of mimicking them. *Good. Unless...*

Darya tried to put the alternatives out of her head. She had done everything she could have. She had finally learned there was no sitting out of this game. Keep crawling to the top, or see yourself crushed beneath. When Darya had rejected Serik's proposal, she had made that mistake. Mistaken what should be for what was. Alina and Kasym had saved her from that stupidity. Vels and that worrisome girl with the black eye had provided her with yet another chance. She didn't appreciate his constant meddling, his infuriating questions, or his turning her brother's coin into something with which he could track her across the circle of the world, but she didn't resent any of it so much that she'd thrown it away. Darya had only the one wise man, and she wasn't quite ready to give him up. Guardian spirit Vels was not, but he *had* saved her twice now, and that counted for quite a lot in Darya's estimation. He had been right about the sides of the wall too; what were the Fallen and demons of old to her when the Chosen of today would butcher her without a second thought? Now his words echoed in her mind again. *Don't waste it.* This was her chance to help her friends. And herself, of course.

It had been an eerie journey, too similar and yet so different from that exodus from the swamps so long ago. At least the ironspawn had left to scurry back to whatever warrens and crevices they had crawled out of. When pressed on why they listened to him, why they didn't try to eat *him*, all he would provide was a cryptic comment about creators and children. He would explain no more, no matter how she asked. There were enough stories about the Fallen and tools of war for her to make her own guesses though.

Darya had heard a story once where the creature had killed its creator, but apparently these vicious little monsters were a bit more charitably minded. Or perhaps simply less intelligent. There was a lesson in there somewhere. Maybe it was best to have allies who were incapable of seeing the big picture and who could be trusted to focus only on the bounds of their own little world, driven by natural, predictable impulses.

If only she had some of those. But who ever got everything they needed? It was enough that the places were set and every player in their position, including her. All there was to be done was to see whose story was about to be told. Nervous as Darya was, silence was her best bet for now. The chieftains could glare all they liked.

They were all seated around a beautiful table, dark polished wood mirror-bright and reflecting the white-blue arcane lights that dotted sconces along the wall, too new to Darya not to be a marvel. The walls were hung with rich tapestries and bright paintings depicting a people's history and its heroes, all unknown to her. They looked important. Or at least, they looked like they were important to someone. There was a cabinet and shelves, all of the same wood, richly decorated by some skilled carpenter. Kasym would swoon when he saw them. All in all, it was a beautiful room. The sort of place she had always imagined—no, she hadn't had the frame of reference—but what she now suspected was the sort of place the wealthy of the empire lived in.

Which was all the more jarring, because through those windows, from this beautiful estate on the escarpment, she could see a mining penal colony nestled within the bones of the fortress city. The great towers rose, indomitable and imperious, to the immediate north. However, where they were, the centuries had seen the lower half of Bal Maru become subterranean. Further south, the land broadened into a wide, sloping valley, hills rising gently on either side. The estate, the colony, the converted barracks where Darya had tossed and turned for a sleepless hour or two last night, even the valley and hills, no doubt—all of it was built on solid dirt that had fallen on the even more solid foundations of pre-Breaking ruins. Years of human toil had unearthed more and more patches of land. Now, the general effect was one that tricked the eye into wondering whether the earth was swallowing the city, or the city was growing out of the ground, bit by bit reclaiming its historical place. Walls reared up at the steep, sloping entrances of each of the excavation sites, with gates meant to be manned from the outside. In the nearest pit, one wall of the mine was man-made, little passageways and rooms of the ruin jutting out of the loose rock and dirt and given an ordered shape by the scaffolding that rose precariously along its sheer length. It reminded her of the inside of an anthill. There was no mad scurrying there though, or among the shacks down below. It was all perfectly still, a sense of expectation heavy.

The estate was still in its own way too. The motley group around the table stared across at one another, none willing to be the first to speak. One of the windows was smashed, a cold draft seeping in. It was welcome in that tense room. It felt like clarity. One of the sets of shelves was smashed apart. On the far end of the table, the carpet and the tapestry behind were splashed with something dark. It didn't take a lot of imagination to guess that the man who sat there now wasn't the one meant to sit there. *"Meant to." There's yet another lesson.*

The man at the head of the table finally broke the silence. "Well, this is profoundly uncomfortable. Should we start anyway?"

"It would be more comfortable if you gave us back our weapons," Taharuk spat. "And what is she doing here?" he asked with an accusatory finger.

The apparent leader of the freed Stained, Duras, was more patient than Darya would have dared believe. He was tall, graying, and possessed of warm, patient amber eyes that seemed to be extraordinarily unimpressed by the world, but most especially by Taharuk's posturing. He had been just as calm, even kindly, when Vels had brought her here. Amused, but supportive when she had explained why Kasym and Alina needed to slip away in the early morning.

Duras adjusted the polished spectacles that framed his seamed face. "First of all, I'm not sure why you think you need weapons to talk. Especially to those you profess to want as allies. None of us are armed."

Leaning against the wall behind him, a grizzled, middle-aged man was twisting long fingers with surprising dexterity. A little spark, barely more than an ember, danced between them. He saw Darya watching and winked. Taharuk watched this interaction as well with mounting frustration. No one would have ever accused Taharuk of being handsome, but the red flush that crept now to the tips of his one good ear and to the ragged stump on its opposite side made him positively hideous.

"And second of all, she is our guest. We found her wandering alone." Not quite true, but Darya appreciated the lie. "And with a collar around her neck."

No lie there. They had shown Darya the trick of unlocking them using a key that relied on producing a certain resonance.

Duras leaned forward now, hands splayed on the table. They were oddly delicate, for all his ragged appearance. Except for the fact that two fingers of the left were missing, as well as a digit of the right. He tapped them now in a broken staccato and craned his neck upward, as if examining the ceiling beams. "You know, I'm really not sure you can appreciate how poorly we consider the use of those collars."

Darya thought that no one could miss that. Taharuk and the other two chieftains looked unsure of what to say for once, shifting uncomfortably in their chairs or examining the others in the room. Because almost every other person around the table shared something in common—something that Duras's stretched neck made all too obvious. A thick layer of pale, scarred skin around their necks. Darya's own neck wasn't unmarked, though it was more red and raw than pale and would likely heal without a mark. Days compared to years. Now that it had been removed, she could feel the strength flowing through her, little pinpricks of light in her veins. Every color, every sound around her seemed more vibrant, more *real*. She couldn't imagine being cut off from it for years. For a lifetime. Would you forget what it felt like? Darya didn't think so. People never forgot what they had lost.

Taharuk wasn't quite ready to back down. "It's the same as taking our weapons. A precaution. And she is—"

"Our guest," Duras interrupted, more forcefully this time. "And forget about the weapons. You'll have them when you step out that door. For now, you are our guests too. You are safe here. After all, we're not savages," he put in pointedly. "Now, if we are quite done with all of that, I understand you have an offer to make. Oh, and before I forget, this is Colonel Ardelan."

"Just Ardelan, please."

Darya had never seen a colonel, but she thought the man sitting beside Duras looked the very picture of one. His appearance practically matched one of the portraits on the walls—the angular face, short hair, and stiff bearing of a lifetime officer. There was no uniform though, and he was dressed in simple warm fur and worn mail draped with a wolf pelt.

"As you say. Former colonel though, now leader of those fighting for an independent kingdom here. Despite the Riftgate emerging here, our little prison riot would have failed without them. None of us can do this alone. Which brings us back to you."

"Yes," Kursagai cut in, clearly uncomfortable having Taharuk trying to take the lead here. "Vels says you need allies."

"Funny, he told us the very same thing. But it's true," Duras admitted, "we need allies. The empire is relentless, and gods know there are enough of them. Better equipped and organized than any of us. But I know I'd rather no friends than friends I can't trust. Friends that treat their own like her."

He pointed toward Darya. She remained silent. The play was made; she could only pray that Kasym had reached Serik. And that Serik hadn't killed him.

"So, tell me why I should trust any of you."

"I've always found that necessity builds the strongest bonds," Serik said thoughtfully. The words were said to the room, but Darya knew who they were meant for. It had worked. This could work.

"Well put. I, however, would like to add something to that. Necessity is nice, but there really is no substitute for demonstrating one's commitment by putting one's life on the line. Call me old-fashioned, but nothing brings people closer together than suffering and death, and there is likely to be a lot of that before we are through. We ask for a gesture."

"What gesture?" Taharuk asked.

"A proof of loyalty to the cause. Or at least one of competence. Our scouts inform us that a contingent of the enemy will be here within a day. Help us fight them."

There was a stretch of silence as the three tribal leaders shared a conversation of glances.

"We are only here to convey the Arkhan's wish to—" began Kursagai.

"Then convey away. We need warriors, not glorified messengers. Prove yourselves to be our allies, or take back the message of your failure. Oh, and if you choose to fight with us, I refuse to continue this sort of roundtable discussion with all of you. It's unseemly and counterproductive. We were slaves a month ago, and as far as I can tell, we were and are more organized than your lot. There needs to be a single representative. A liaison, if you will. Is one of you in charge?"

"I am," Taharuk said at once.

Kursagai flushed. "He is not."

"See," Duras said, leaning over to Ardelan, "this is what I mean."

Ardelan stared, unimpressed, to where the three had pulled themselves aside to whisper furiously at one another.

"Gentlemen." Duras raised his voice. "Gentlemen, do you have a decision? What about this one right here?" he asked, indicating Darya, who did her best to keep her face blank. "She seems a bright girl."

"Not her," Taharuk snarled. "She is a deserter and a coward."

*Only half right, you miserable bastard.* But she kept her peace.

"Well, if not her, then which of you?"

Silence again.

"She...could work," Serik said eventually. The other two rounded on him, but he addressed Kursagai. "It's her or him. You know that." She couldn't believe what a good actor he was. He sounded regretful, disgusted by even having had to suggest her. No trace on those clever features of the proposal Kasym had conveyed to him sometime in the night.

Kursagai stared at her, while Taharuk looked seconds away from drawing on Serik, face nearly purple with rage. But it was working. They didn't have a way out. After all, power was a jealous thing. None of them could afford one of their rivals being designated as the sole leader, even if only to a bunch of foreigners. Roles had a momentum to them, and appearances often became reality. Their fragile little rule by committee would fall apart. Better a non-threat, a non-entity, take the role than a competitor. Darya did her best to look like such. It wasn't hard. Even as everything finally went her way for once, the last thing she felt was threatening. Anxious? Yes. Terrified? Certainly.

There was a curt nod from Kursagai, a disgusted grunt from Taharuk, and it was done. Darya was, for lack of a better option, the warband's designated representative, as far as the Stained and separatists were concerned. Not that anyone would have any illusions as to her actual role. A glorified messenger, that each chief would do their best to bully and control. One that Serik already counted as in his pocket.

"Excellent. Then, assuming you don't wish to return to your Arkhan a failure, I suggest you ready your fighters. Ardelan will have a few of his officers accompany you to address finding a place for your group, supplies, and all those pesky details. In the meantime, we will start planning a warm welcome for the imperials."

"We will consider whatever you come up with, Stained," Taharuk said, biting off each word.

"As you say." A couple of younger men stood up from around Ardelan and headed toward the door. "Oh, and do try to stay warm. It's going to be cold tonight."

Grumbles and glares as the three chieftains filed out, followed by the two officers.

Darya stood to follow.

"A moment."

The door closed, but not without another suspicious glare from Taharuk. Let him be suspicious. He should be. It shut, and Darya found herself alone again with the freed Stained and former imperial auxiliaries turned freedom fighters. The separatists looked to her exactly like what she imagined the soldiers of the legions looked like, but she kept that to herself.

"Can we trust them?"

"They will fight," Darya said after a pause. It would take more than a bit of kindness to fool her. These people were not necessarily any different from the tribes. That remained to be seen.

"A fair answer. I suspect we can trust them as long as their own interests align with ours. Like most men at most times. This Arkhan of yours is not a forgiving man, is he?"

"He's a leader."

"You're smarter than you look, you know that?" Darya frowned, unsure what to make of that.

"What about that...the tall one, missing ear—what was his name?"

"Taharuk?"

"Yes. Are we going to have to kill him?"

The boldness of the question stunned her. For all her hate of him, her fear, he still felt more like one of her own than these people, these strangers. She opened her mouth to protest and then thought better of it, returning his thoughtful look.

Duras nodded. "I see. You're new at this, but you're learning. We can discuss him later though. In the meantime, what about you?"

"You can trust me."

"As a person? Or as a leader?"

"Both?"

"Oh, Darya. They are hardly ever the same thing. You ought to know that by now."

Duras's condescending tone was starting to grate on her. She needed them. If she failed here, she was done. Again. Vels had spoken for her, but he didn't seem to control these people any more than he did the Arkhan and the tribes. Influence only got you so far, and Darya needed allies.

"You want me because I'm not like them. I can be different. And because of Vels." There it was, the unspoken connection between them. When Vels had brought the three of them here, hobbling and bleeding, he had passed them over to the care of Duras. Passed them over in the safety of the tunnels. Darya was safe because of him. She still couldn't shake the image from her head of him standing there, hand on the head of the creature, like an indulgent father with a wayward child. It was a bit too familiar of a picture.

"Good points. I agree that one day, we might learn to trust one another. Certainly more than any of those three. But why on earth would any one of them follow you?"

So, it came back to the same thing it always did. "Because I can do this," Darya said, reaching out and pulling the grizzled Stained's spark to her own hands from across the room. She wanted to show them she was one of them. That she had strength, the only thing people seemed to recognize in this world. What she hadn't realized was the level of control needed for that little trick. The flickering flame she had meant to show was suddenly a blazing inferno in her hand. Panicking, she tried to stop it, but it grew like it had a mind of its own. There were cries of alarm, and a few in the room drew their weapons or cringed back from the heat. The sounds around her faded, and she could feel that hunger again. There was a power to it, all out of proportion to what she had felt before. She was close, so close to whatever allowed her to pull that power out of nothing. She was fascinated, terrified, staring into the flames. It felt good, right. Overwhelming. And it was suddenly so easy, she could...

A hand found her arm, cool in all that heat. Another. Darya looked up and saw that the Stained she had taken the fire from had closed the distance. His hands were clasped gently around Darya's forearms, both of their coat sleeves burning away, skin untouched. He was forming words that were inaudible among the louder roar in her ears. Something about keeping herself? Maybe she couldn't hear him, but the touch brought her back and let her see the terror in the room behind him as the flames rose. They died to nothing as Darya reined herself in and pushed the roaring hunger back from where it had come, feeling sick and sweating and cold all at once. The hands on her arms relaxed, and then he met her confused look with one of understanding.

"I like her," was all he said.

Duras had fallen over backwards, and the smell of burning hair filled the small room, some of it hers. There went a bit more of the little she had left. The tapestry nearest her was smoldering, and a woman was beating at it frantically with a cloak. Someone's history was going up in smoke.

Duras picked himself up carefully from the floor, wary eyes never leaving her. Weighing. "Well, don't be upset with me if I withhold judgment for now. But I think we can work together. That sort of strength can always be an asset, especially if guided by someone who could teach you to control it." He waited for a nod from Ardelan before giving a weary smile. "Just don't burn the house down in the meantime."

# NEW HABITS

Syl had always wondered. Now he knew. This was what it felt like to be an idiot. Jogging through the lightly wooded hills, snow drifting down steadily and getting caught and melting in hair already wet from too many miles of the same. The snow covered the ash on the ground and turned every step into a gray-white muddy mess. They moved as fast as they could anyway, because they hadn't brought enough food, enough water, or enough clothing to do anything else. Every step toward those towers in the distance reverberated from the strike of his boot all the way to the pain behind his eyes, in what felt like an impossibly direct line. As the sun rose again, the towers were a perfect compass, but they wavered in the early morning air, lines blurring in time with the pounding in his head.

Syl stopped to look behind him. Leon was already there, face flushed and arms bare, swirling runes not yet covered in sweat. They'd been moving at a trot or jog for almost a full day now, the only way they would make it to Bal Maru before the legions on this longer, circuitous route. The map Syl had taken showed the wonderfully direct, easy march between Breakstone and the penal colony. An old road with wide-open spaces, where the legions wouldn't have to worry about getting bogged down in forest ambushes. A commander's dream, and the answer to any infantryman's prayers...and not an option for them.

Lucky had done his best to guess where on the map he could sense the riftwalker's signature. The bloodhound had a gift for maps and spatial awareness. Based on the direction he could provide, he had narrowed their destination down to an area where they might be able to find a side entrance to infiltrate the mass of ruins. Syl had wanted to object, to point out that there was no possible way they could know if there was an entrance there—or if there was, whether it was closed, blocked by rubble, or simply overgrown with nature. He hadn't, simply because he didn't have a better option, and he would have taken any chance, however slim, that Lucky offered. The consequences of that idealistic fervor were creeping in now.

The three shapes a couple hundred yards behind looked like coals on the patchy white of the forest floor. Dark blots of cloth and pale skin, clouds of steam rising from figures that took a little longer to catch up each time he stopped. By now, they were all but bare from the waist up, as much removed as could be removed.

"We're too slow," Syl muttered.

"What do you want to do? Carry them? They can't go any faster."

Leon was right. So was he. Being right wasn't enough; they were still too slow. Syl was keeping a brutal pace, but he knew that if they didn't find their way in before the legions, Liora could be moved. There was another, more likely alternative, but he tried not to think of it. Syl tried to remember what it had been like before he had conduits he could pull from at will, when all he had was his own strength. Lucky at least could draw a little, as all those connected to the Rift could. Marika and Vali had grown up running in woods like these. As the three of them drew closer, hunched over and winded, it looked like it all evened out in the end. Syl waited for one of them to suggest a break. They stooped there, heaving, sweat dripping from noses and pattering, steaming, onto the cold earth. Vali stood straight with an effort, pride burning in those eyes. He nodded to Syl, who couldn't help but turn away in shame. He should have made them stay.

There was no turning back now though. And to his surprise, he found he didn't want to. Ahead, he could see the crest of the hill, where the trees started to give way to the gray sky. They were getting close now. Together, they worked their way forward, until they crouched among the rocks and trunks at the top, surveying the valley.

Before them stretched the works of a decade of human ingenuity and suffering, all scattered atop the relics of millennia of mythology, primordial in scale. Labor camps and excavation pits dotted a portion of the land between the valley beneath them and the towers of Bal Maru itself. The clean, enduring lines of the bones of that beast that peeked out of the ground put all the newer buildings to shame, rust and cracks or not. Undoubtedly, some of those roots were beneath their feet now. Around the pits, small shapes scuttled about, little ants in the carcass of a fallen giant. They knew the legions were coming. There would probably be scouts crawling these hills already. It was a wonder they hadn't run into any yet. Syl motioned for Lucky to come closer.

"Can you tell exactly where she is?"

Lucky was flushed and dripping with sweat. Too tired to be surly, he looked more nervous than usual. Another one he should have left if he could have.

"Liora? No. I don't think so. I…"

"Not Liora," Syl cut in. "Unless…? I know you can tell when we pull on our conduits."

Lucky winced and tapped his finger to the side of his neck. "Probably."

"Ah." Syl hated the idea of Liora in one of those collars. That control used on one of his own. "And the riftwalker?" he asked. "That's still our best chance to find Liora."

*And fix your mistakes, and tell Liora what she means to you, and fix your life, and, and…*

*A fantasy.*

Syl shivered, the fever-bright quickness of his mind difficult to ignore now.

"Yes. I can sense her. A little farther ahead. I think she jumped again. Punched a hole in the Veil. As recently as last night."

"Syl, we can start circling from here," Leon said, "cut in every four hundred paces or so to check, and then…"

"I think that point on the map will work," Lucky interrupted. "We should head there soon. Now," he added, voice cracking.

Leon stopped to stare in amazement at Lucky. "How dumb are you, boy? That was a general point to aim for, not some magical point that you can tell from a piss-poor map is going to have an entrance."

Lucky looked out over the valley and studiously avoided Leon's glare. "I think there's a door," he whispered, barely audible.

They were all staring at him now, Marika and Vali looking even more skeptical than Leon.

"Why?" Syl asked, doing his best not to take his frustration and the pain from his pounding headache out on Lucky. The poor bondmage was nervous enough, dragged out here against his will. "It's much farther than the nearest possible entrances. What makes you think we will find one there?"

"I'm lucky?" suggested Lucky.

Syl sighed. That was a terrible reason. However, today he was more than a little willing to rely on the intervention of the gods, fate, fortune, or even a lucky bloodhound, when it came down to it. They needed the time and any advantage they could grab. He shrugged, exchanging a look with Leon. "Why not? We can start there. Can always search with that as a starting point."

"Fine," Leon muttered. "But there's not just going to be some door."

# ALMOST THERE

There was a door. Tall and wide and as undeniably there as the clouds above. It was also closed. The iron door was set in the middle of a low, wide wall that faced south and rose slowly in a mostly unbroken, sloping line all the way to the central towers. Those towers were close now, and Vali felt that they loomed over him, temples to some ancient god. One of the gods of war, no doubt. The priests said there were uncountable gods for every fragmented aspect of the five and five of the heavens, but if any one of them had the most gods, it had to be war. Too few, and they would have been overwhelmed by all the offerings, prayers, and followers.

The edifice before them was stained black with moss and weathering, crumbling at the edges. That made sense too. The Breaking would have sated any number of gods, to hear the priests tell it. That, the cycles of cataclysms, years of arcane warlords, the Mages' Revolt, and now this... Maybe they were tired of it all.

Vali had no idea how Lucky had done it, but they had moved in an almost direct line to this entrance. He had only the loosest grasp of how the bloodhound's skills worked, but it was little wonder they were so in demand for every Hunter team. The entrance looked like it had been used, and used recently and often, with little trinkets nailed to some of the trees around it, and symbols painted fresh about the door. Syl had stopped them short and had them watch in silence for at least half an hour. No one came or went though, and the buildings, huts, and tents of the Stained and separatists were behind and below them. Now Vali and Marika were at the edge of the hill, keeping watch over the valley below while the others tried to open the door.

The headlong rush through forest and over hills had kept them sweating and too busy to think of much. Now, Vali found himself wet and cold and suddenly not so sure he hadn't done the same thing he always seemed to do.

That tendency he could see more and more in himself of leaping without looking. Hopefully, it would be done soon. They could get in the ruins, kill the riftwalker, save Liora, return to the legions, help Lucan, and he could ascend to knighthood. Vali tried not to think of the hundred ways that any one of those events could go wrong. The only thing that kept him optimistic was the fact that Marika was shivering in the dirt beside him. If he could see a hundred ways things could go wrong, she would have already seen a thousand. She usually didn't agree to things unless she thought they were a good idea. Usually. Unfortunately, even if this was the halfway point for their little adventure, and not a dead end for all of them, that meant making their way back across all those hills again. Vali's empty stomach grumbled in protest against that idea. Maybe dying here wouldn't be so terrible. At least he wouldn't have to keep running.

"Tired already?" Marika asked.

"Just...just trying to make you feel better."

"Uh-huh. I see that." She gave a little smile.

Despite the fatigue, the danger, and all those other weights, Vali melted a little inside. He straightened, focus returning. They wouldn't die here. Couldn't.

They were pressed close, side by side, slowly adding back layers as the chill turned their sweat against them. Out of sight of where Lucky was fiddling with the door, they could hear his soft curses of frustration drifting their way. Apparently, finding a door didn't mean you had found a way in. Vali tried not to be distracted and resisted the impulse to go and watch whatever Lucky was doing behind them. Not that it did much good looking to the front. The cloudy afternoon and sprinkle of snow had turned the valley below into a painting of suggestions—and it suggested that there were a lot of people moving there.

Next to him, Marika stiffened. "Vali, do you see—"

Anything else she was about to say was cut off as there was a screeching, clunking sound from the direction of the door. It continued for an agonizing second, two. It wasn't possible no one had heard that.

Silence. Holding his breath, Vali counted out the beats of his heart, waiting for something to happen.

"It's open." Lucky's voice, a loud, embarrassed whisper.

More of the vilest sort of curses drifted over to their lookout point, from Leon this time. Vali started to stand.

"Wait." Marika hadn't moved, and she pulled Vali back down. "Look. Tell me what you see."

"Snow?"

"No, damn it. Look, *really* look. I mean it."

Settling back onto the cold earth, Vali looked again at the valley below and the dotted excavation points past it. He scanned from pit to pit, as best he could, the details getting harder to see with every minute. "I mean...there's definitely people moving around down there." Marika hadn't moved an inch, so he kept looking. "I see some buildings, like...barracks, maybe? And on the far side of that..." Vali squinted, willing the vague colors and shapes to coalesce into definable parts. "Horses?"

Marika nodded grimly, suspicion confirmed. "A lot of them. I wasn't sure."

"Well, neither am I," Vali protested. Horses were just his best guess. Could have been cattle, with all he could make out from this distance.

"Two people not sure is as sure as we're going to get. The Thousand are here. We need to tell them." She was up now, moving quickly to the door.

Vali hesitated, eyes burning as he forced definition on the faraway milling shapes. They did look an awful lot like horses. A worryingly large number of horses. The Stained or the local auxiliary garrisons wouldn't have had so many. On the far side of the valley, he thought he could make out flashes of metal and movement too. The legions? What a clash that was going to be. A little pit of jealousy settled sour and heavy in his gut as he thought about the battle they would be missing. Down there was where names were going to be made and heroes born. Unless...unless he could help kill the leadership here. Or that riftwalker witch they kept talking about. Knighthood and glory guaranteed there, no doubt. Maybe here was better. Oh, and save Liora. And help for Lucan. Of course. That didn't need saying. That was why he was here, after all. He hurried after Marika.

"...that's too far for them," Leon was saying. "They've never come this far in numbers like that. The passes are too difficult. Might be a cavalry wing of one of the auxiliaries. Gods know enough of them went over to their side."

They were gathered around the cracked-open door in a semicircle that even Vali found a bit bold, considering the fact that they weren't the only ones who used this door. Syl looked troubled and paid only the barest attention to Marika and Leon's argument.

"It's too many to be some auxiliary unit. Come see for yourself."

"No time. We need to keep moving. The legions can handle it either way."

"Maybe they should go. Warn them," Lucky offered.

Leon rounded on him. "Since when have you been so gods-damned opinionated? I swear, usually we can't get you to talk, and now you won't shut up."

A full day of frayed nerves and accumulated fatigue had taken its toll on Lucky. The surly bondmage who had rebuffed every friendly overture and practically sneered at Vali every time he had seen him had been replaced by a scared-looking boy who looked too young, drained, and colorless. He swayed there under Leon's glare.

"No, he's right." Syl looked thoughtfully at Lucky. "You should go, Marika. Both of you."

"After we've come all this way?" Vali asked. "Let us help finish this. We can help." Plus, he wasn't Lucky. Knowing his own luck, he would miss the chance to help here just to make it in time to the legions and warn them away from the battle brewing in the valley below. His resolutions to do the right thing and to fight for his friends rather than himself would all count for nothing. No knighthood, no chance to help Lucan. And it really was a lot of running.

"It would be good to have a couple more blades down there," Leon said.

Vali's heart soared with gratitude. Leon had come to respect them.

"A bit of a distraction when they get killed."

*Ah.*

"No." Syl shook his head. "You both need to go. If there's a chance to warn them, then it's worth the risk. Good looking out. Now go."

"But what about Liora? The riftwalker?" Vali asked. He could feel yet another chance to prove himself slipping through his fingers.

Syl seemed to be looking for the right words, eyes searching his. "Vali...in life, you need to decide what you're really loyal to. You're a good lad, brave and loyal beyond sense, but too *hungry*. You want to be a hero? Get to the legions down there. Warn them, and save hundreds of lives." He paused. "And remember what I said about oathknights. I promise you, there are worse things than settling for being a good man. I know you think there isn't, that another cycle is here and there's no other chance, but it doesn't change anything, not really. Life doesn't stop. People..." He stopped and looked away, voice suddenly thick. "People don't stop needing you."

Syl looked guilty, like something he had said shamed him. But instead of saying anything else, he simply nodded one more time, a goodbye. He pushed Lucky ahead of him over the threshold of the ruins. Fist on his heart in a mock salute, Leon shrugged before closing the door after them. Metal dragged along rough concrete with a teeth-grinding scraping and ground to a heavy, dull thump as it settled into its frame. The door was shut. Tall and wide and as undeniably closed as his way to knighthood.

Marika pulled him away.

# GOOD FORTUNE

The path was cleared enough for them to pass. Massive, rusting hulks, reminiscent of the railcars of the capital, had been levered all to the same side, with rubble piled atop, leaving the right side of the wide passage open and practically clean. Their footsteps disturbed a thin layer of dust, and as far as Syl could tell, there had been time enough for the faint footprints he saw ahead of them to be mostly covered. A good sign. They would need time and space for this next part. Syl knew any chance they had was in turning the tables on the Stained and surprising them in their own den.

"This way," Lucky said, pointing. "Pretty sure."

They followed after the bloodhound, their path turning off the main passage and sloping downward now. The concrete here was giving way on one side to solid stone, a passage bored an age ago through the bones of the earth. Lucky kept looking from side to side, even when no turns presented themselves, looking for all the world like his namesake, as if he really could smell the burning hole the riftwalker had punched through the fabric of the Rift.

Catching up to Syl, Leon picked his way around a pile of crushed stone that had been pushed to the side, careful not to send any of the little pieces of debris skittering ahead. "Syl, I know he can sense where that riftwalker is, but we need to be moving slower. Going like this, we'll be on top of them before we know it. Or they'll hear us and be waiting. I know we're good, but good only gets you so far. We can't help Liora if we're dead."

"We need speed," Syl said, not slowing a step. His head was pounding, and the hundred different ways this could play out were assaulting him. It was an effort to focus, and Leon was distracting him. "And Lucky's led us well so far. Trust that he'll take us the rest of the way."

The bloodhound spared a nervous glance backwards at the compliment. Leon grumbled, but kept in step.

"Don't stop," Syl pressed. "Keep moving, Lucky." He pushed the bloodhound ahead of him until he resumed his swivel-headed way forward. "Speaking of, why 'Lucky'?"

"Hmm?"

"Why do they call you Lucky? I always meant to ask."

Lucky didn't bother looking back. "Because I'm lucky. I always find the target. And I always live."

"Lucky enough to be born a bondmage?" Leon asked. "Not my idea of luck."

Waving for Leon to leave it, Syl watched Lucky consider another forking branch, nose out before him and eyes rolled back as he searched. Distractions would be counterproductive at this point. It would have to be soon; there was no doubt they were getting close. Lucky returned, another nod, another point. Another little bit of fortune.

Syl nodded back, moving up to join Lucky. He laid a gauntleted hand in brotherly fashion on Lucky's back. Syl could feel the discomfort there at the heavy weight, but he wanted the bloodhound to pay attention. "Good work. You know, I've got a confession, Lucky." Syl could sense Lucky's confusion, knew Leon would be wondering too. But it was too late not to say what he meant. How many times would he have to learn that lesson? "I've been guilty of taking you for granted, Lucky. We all have. We ask a lot of you. This is a lonely job for all of us, but for none more so than you, I'd wager. I don't even know your real name. You never told us, but I also never asked."

Lucky had stopped, and Syl felt a tremor pass through the bloodhound. Maybe too little, too late, but Syl was glad he had gotten it all off his chest before the uncertainty of the violence that was coming, soon and sure. He gave another friendly squeeze. "So, I'm sorry, I guess."

And Syl meant it. Nicknames didn't come from nothing. Lucky had earned his moniker a hundred times over since Syl had known him. Maybe the members of the team who had died before he saw his transfer to theirs would have disagreed, but Lucky had been lucky then too. He was a bloodhound. He had found the threat. He had even survived, which wasn't a requirement. Hardly his fault the rest of the team had let themselves be torn apart by a few Stained. They were lucky to have Lucky. Syl knew that.

There was such a thing as too lucky though.

Syl tightened ironclad fingers around the bondmage's neck until he could feel the vertebrae creak under the pressure. Lucky gasped in pain and surprise.

"But I'm not the only guilty one, am I?" Syl hissed, dragging the blood-hound close. "You were clever, I'll give you that, you traitorous fuck."

Lucky twisted in his grasp until he felt Syl squeeze tighter yet.

"No, no, no, none of that."

Leon was confused, but catching up quickly, and he moved forward with the null collar from his belt. Syl twisted Lucky's face toward his own, needing to see. And there it was. Underneath the animal responses of fear and pain, there it was. A soul-deep eddy of resentment that would have happily walked them all to their deaths. Had no doubt seen Liora captured. The riftwalker freed from the prison in Rasovus, like as not. How long and how deep did the treachery run? Had he worked against them, even from the first day he joined the team? Or had they found him after, and poisoned him by degrees? Twisted his service into indignity in his mind until every day served only to distill that discontent into murderous intent?

"Have you heard what the Tribes do to our wounded soldiers? Make another noise, and I'll crush your spine and leave you here for them. You can see if they or the ironspawn find you first. I know where my money would be."

Another whimper escaped Lucky, who was squirming involuntarily despite the warning. Syl thought about closing his grip. It wouldn't take much. He could see it. A few more pounds of pressure would be enough. Lucky was already starting to faint from the lack of blood. With an effort, Syl removed his fingers long enough for Leon to place the collar there.

"You going to catch me up?"

Syl ripped the amulet from Lucky's neck and dangled the offending talisman before Leon. "I didn't connect it right away. But he got sloppy at the end. Or maybe just scared. A little bit too lucky, a little too often. Gods, it was right in front of us the whole time." Syl stared intently at the bronze medallion that spun dull and unornamented before him. There was nothing he could see to distinguish it from the most basic of coins. It was beaten into a smoother shape, and any details or imperfections had been rubbed away with the bondmage's worrying hands. There *was* something about it that pounded in time with the pain behind his eyes.

The talismans scattered at the gate had unsettled him. They had kicked loose a pebble of doubt, bouncing down the mountain of past events that had seemed so solid, revealing the true surface underneath as more and more actions took on alternate explanations. Lucky's gift to Morana in the prison. The bloodhound's desperation to find them at Breakstone, and his manipulation of Syl's desire to find Liora. The door itself. Now, the metal flashed the light of the arclamp back at him, its true nature reflected in the light of a thousand clues that Syl cursed himself for missing.

"It was this. A beacon. Someone marking these, no doubt. Or maybe just nabbing some Vigil trackers." He tossed the medallion to Leon, who caught it like it was liable to bite him. "He betrayed us, Leon. This little moron let someone convince him to try and kill us all."

"No!" Lucky protested, "I..."

Syl took hold of the collar and yanked down, slamming Lucky to his knees. He stared down, searching the bloodhound's expression. "At least tell me why."

"I...I didn't have a choice." Lucky looked beyond miserable, and so, so young right then. Collapsed in the pile of spindly limbs where Syl had thrown him, all the fight and resentment had fled and left behind nothing that would make this easier. "I'm sorry."

"You're *sorry*?" Syl barely resisted the urge to shake him and force something more venomous to fall out. "It's too late for that. Liora's probably dead because of you. They're waiting for us, aren't they? Set a beacon at the door and walk us in. Gods, I'm an idiot for not seeing it sooner. At least I saw it in time to send Vali and Marika away. Is the rest of the team even still alive?"

"Yes! Though I had to kill a guard," Lucky said miserably. "I had to. All of it. And they didn't kill Liora! Wouldn't have," he added, less sure. "It was supposed to be you."

"What?" Leon asked.

The relief was palpable on Lucky's face as the façade fell away, any need for pretense long gone. "It was you they wanted, Syl! Can't you feel it? You're one of us. They grabbed Liora in the tunnel by dumb accident. Wrong place, wrong time."

It had been so long ago. Two days and a lifetime ago. Lucky's form seemed to double, to triple in front of Syl as he stared down at him. *"Can't you feel it?"* Lucky had asked. *"One of us."*

No. Syl rejected that. Madness would be preferable; at least he knew the borders of that land.

In front and not in front of him, Lucky was standing before him, collar off his neck, ready to collar Syl. Lucky, and then the stranger from his dream, and then Lucky again. *No! No, no, no! That was then. In the tunnels. Not now.* Syl was rooted in place. He could only stare down motionless as his mind tried to rip itself apart to make room for what Lucky was saying.

"Syl, please. They want to talk. Liora is still alive. You were right. And you *knew*, didn't you? You knew. That's why they want you."

At his side, Leon squatted down, knife out. He placed the tip under Lucky's chin, forcing him to raise his head and cutting off anything else he might have said. "Before you say another word, boy, keep your voice down. Nod if you understand." Lucky moved his head not an inch. "Ah, fair enough." Leon removed the knife, and Lucky nodded vigorously, a slow black stream running down his thin, pale neck, glowing in the dim blue light.

"Syl, please. Listen," Lucky whispered. "You need to talk to them. They're expecting us, but this will all be a lot easier if I can go ahead and tell them you are willing to listen to what they have to say."

Syl stared down at Lucky, expressionless, and the bloodhound fidgeted nervously, eyeing the knife only inches away from his throat. "A better way, Syl. That's all they want. A better way. The world doesn't have to fall apart."

*We know better than that,* the voice in his head whispered, dark and familiar. *Don't we?*

*Everything always falls apart.*

"Do you really want to keep listening to this?" Leon asked. "I say we kill him here and take our chances. Maybe he's telling the truth and we can still find Liora, but we're in a death trap sitting here. And what is he on about with you? They wanted *you*? One of them? Is he saying..."

"Wait," Syl said, tearing his way back to the solidity of the present and definite shapes of the world around him with an effort. He swallowed, feeling the dryness and building mental anchors to the physical sensations of his body. Syl pulled from those faraway conduits, feeling a measure of surety in that strength. *Feel* it? He *knew* this. This was strength. He ran through his little rituals. The weapon hilts, the collar at his belt, the straps holding his armor to him, the mental checklists, all the accumulated habits that meant survival and sanity. Here was order. Here was the fight against the end. A measure of self returned. Every life might spin upon its prescribed wheel, but how else could anything, from the universe to the individual, impose a sense of structure and sanity on the chaos that awaited beyond? The axiom of entropy could only be fought with the choice of effort.

"No," Syl said. "No. I *am* sorry, Lucky. But you're right, there is a better way. And you are going to help us there." He forced out Lucky's words, pushed them back with a hundred other things he had learned to forget. It was easy when he focused on what he knew.

"What about the beacon?" Leon asked. "They're tracking us right now."

"I don't doubt it. But hold onto it." Syl squatted down to Lucky's level and watched the hope die in the mage's eyes. "I have an idea for how our loyal bloodhound can help us one last time."

# ONLY TWO

Darya decided that perhaps, upon second reflection, sacking defenseless towns was not so terrible. It certainly seemed more practical, more attractive right then. She was on her belly, the snow- and ash-covered ground soaking her thoroughly and covering everything in a filthy, ghostly gray. She tried to shift, to scratch that itch right above her hip, where the constant wear of leather belts on wet cloth had created enough chafing to drive her mad. She also tried to remain perfectly motionless while doing so. Impossible.

Better to not be seen and to live with the itch, all things considered. In the valley before them was the flower of the imperial legions, bright steel and standards clear even through the falling snow and clouded afternoon light. Their lead elements were working their way onto the broad, snow-whitened field, churning it to a mess they left behind them. Light cavalry scouts were spreading out and clearing a wide swath before them as the whole glittering machinery worked its way forward—forward to where the front lines of the separatist forces waited, arrayed for battle at the high end of the valley, nestled between arms of the fortress city and with the excavation pits behind them. Darya couldn't believe she had ever thought it possible to confuse the ragtag band of Getacian freedom fighters with these polished machine-men before her. And there were so *many* of them. Yes, the towns held a certain appeal at the moment.

Keeping her face as impassive as she could, she looked at Serik, who was taking his time to survey the enemy as well, making a count. "They said it was only two cohorts," Darya said, trying to sound more confident than she felt.

Serik's voice dripped with cynicism. "So it would seem. But I'm not about to tell Taharuk and Kursagai that we are trusting our lives to strangers. Or you."

*Ah, so it's still like that.* She had done everything he asked. Was working with Serik and had promised to be his eyes and ears, to back him when it came time. It didn't seem to make a difference, and he was far from enthusiastic about their fragile little alliance.

*It's because they're scared of me.* Which was ridiculous, really. Darya wished she could explain that she was far more afraid of them. Anything she had done, she had done in self-defense. Every long step from her home had been a series of choices between bad and worse, most of them made for her. Even now, she was only playing their little game because she had to. That was likely to fall on deaf ears.

She turned back to observe the infantry as they spread out in practiced order across the field where it widened. It was clear that they would try to close their jaws around the ragged formation at the far end. Darya had to stifle a gasp as her mind registered the gigantic shapes that strode among the soldiers, the same height as the standards. Hearing stories about the empire's giant soldiers was one thing; seeing them was quite another. A few of their mounted outriders galloped close enough that Darya could see hints of faces under helms and wraps against the cold. She pressed her own as deeply as she could into the dirt, ash, and snow, those scents competing with the smell of her own clothing, which she hardly noticed at this point. Nothing but a sour echo, a reminder of how long it had been since they had rested or bathed.

"We've seen enough," Serik said.

"It's only the two cohorts."

"It's only two," Serik agreed grudgingly. "Of imperial regulars," he insisted on adding over his shoulder. They crept back to where the warband was gathered in a forested bowl over the far rise. "Those were Helians. More than a thousand of the best-equipped, best-trained soliders you can imagine. You haven't fought them before, have you?"

"There was the ambush," she said.

"Nah, those weren't regulars. Nothing but some locals they have guarding their borders. I fought in a couple of pitched battles with the real legions around the Gates." He stopped, regarding Darya with suspicion. "If those Stained don't help us, those 'only two cohorts' will tear us to pieces."

"I told you, they said they would help us. We just have to help them. The Getacians will hold their front, and we will each hit them from the sides. It's a good plan."

"I believe you," he said, in a voice that very much suggested he, in fact, did not believe her. "Nothing for it now, anyhow."

Darya couldn't help but agree there. It always seemed like there was never a choice anymore. Only a series of increasingly distasteful tasks undertaken to stay alive.

"Next time, you find a way for me to be at that meeting too."

"What about Taharuk? Kursagai?"

"Hopefully, they fall in the battle. If not, make sure they do. You've got enough trash that listens to you, Sun above knows why. Have one of those filth do it. Otherwise, there'll be more opportunities. Perhaps right after the battle. Yes, that could work. With your rabble and my men, their own riders won't feel strong enough to do anything about it." He grabbed her arm, fingers digging in painfully. "Then it's just us. But you can't turn away when it's time. Can you do that?"

Darya looked into his eyes, saw the hunger there. They looked through her, nothing but another branch on the long arc of his story, the one where he was the hero reaching for his destiny. She was less than nothing to him. She had no doubt that he would still try to kill her the minute he thought he could get away with it, no matter how much she helped him.

She gave a tight smile.

Predictable.

"Yes."

# FAMILIAR TERRAIN

The easy part about following your own footsteps was that you knew the way. The tracks were easy to follow backwards. It didn't make the distance pass any faster though. Vali spared a look for Marika, making sure she was keeping up. He was setting a fast pace, half to forget about the fact that he had been dragged all the way out here, had seen a chance to help Liora, Lucan, and himself all with one heroic, long-shot effort, only to be turned away at the literal and figurative gate. The other half was that, having been given this mission to warn the legions, he'd be damned before he failed in that too. Syl... Syl was a bastard. An infuriating, arrogant bastard, but he was right. Here was a chance to save hundreds of lives.

"Good?"

A sweaty, terse nod was Marika's only reply.

They kept moving.

Vali fell into the rhythm of letting his feet carry him forward. They were making good time. If they made it to the legions within the hour, it should be plenty of time to have them turn around, wait for reinforcements from the rest of the legions, which were even now marching on the pretender's seat at Nordea Kerest. If all went well, they could...

Any other thoughts were cut brutally short.

An arm swung out from behind a tree, throwing Vali to the ground with a tremendous amount of force. The air left his lungs. Adrenaline and alertness rushed in hot and fast though, any thoughts of the cold, weariness, hunger, or the future long gone. Rolling with the blow, Vali used the momentum to push himself up, snarling and pulling his axe and short sword from his belt in a smooth movement. He was very much in the present now, and very, very angry.

The object of his anger emerged from behind the tree. A huge frame holding a long, heavy-looking sword.

"Domarik? Sir?" Vali coughed. He started to lower his weapons. Domarik did not, instead moving closer. Vali had never noticed quite how large the Hunter Primary was before now. About the same size as Vali, and that was not something he usually had to worry about. He took an unsure step backward and raised his weapons again. "Sir, it's us!"

Vali looked around and saw he was surrounded. Marika was struggling in the implacable grip of one of the others, efforts not even noticed by her captor. More oathknights, few that Vali recognized. Perhaps a dozen altogether, along with a score of legionnaires. And Kass.

"What are you doing here?"

Domarik stopped in his advance. "We ask the questions, boy. Speak out of turn again, and we cut her throat. Understood?"

There were a hundred things Vali wanted to say, to explain. But he saw no pity there. Domarik meant every word. Behind him, Kass didn't bother looking their way, instead focused on watching their rear. Vali kept his mouth shut, feeling sick.

"First, where is Syl?"

Vali pointed back up the hill, not trusting himself to speak.

"Was Lucky with him?"

"Yes."

"And where are you going now?"

"We were going to warn the legions!" Marika blurted. "We aren't betraying anyone."

With a lurch, Vali realized what this must look like to Domarik. "It's true! We saw the horses, then they went in, so we are going to—"

"Slow down. Horses?"

Vali rushed to tell the whole story, short as it was. He couldn't stop looking to where Marika was held fast.

Domarik exchanged a look with one of the other oathknights. "Alright, let her go. We're moving again."

Marika stumbled to the ground, cursing under her breath at the man behind her. He paid as much attention to those as the earlier struggles. They were all consolidating and starting to move up the hill.

"You're up front, boy. Bring us there. We might already be too late."

"Wait, what about warning the legions? They're walking into a trap."

"They can handle it. They have two cohorts and plenty of nulls to counter any Stained." Domarik looked unconcerned either way.

Kass walked up beside Domarik, staring up the hill with as hateful an expression as Vali had ever seen on her. "We have bigger problems, darling. Oh, and I knew, I *knew* that little shit couldn't be trusted. How many times have I said it?"

Domarik ignored her.

"What is going on?" Vali asked. Anything between the two of them was long gone, but seeing how much spite could be concentrated into a single form, Vali wondered how he hadn't seen it before—how there had ever been anything there at all.

"And why are we being punished for it?" Marika muttered, working her way closer to Vali.

Domarik rounded on them. "I will explain this once, and then we move. You will not ask questions after that. You will follow and do exactly as you are told. A principle you seem to struggle with. Lucky is a traitor. Killed a guard back at Breakstone. The judiciars had a team closing in on a supposed leak, and that little eel slipped through the cracks. Syl and Leon are either collaborators, or guilty of gross incompetence and disobeying multiple direct orders. Not to mention violating a host of imperial and Vigil statutes. I made the mistake of trusting Lucky's loyalty and assuming common sense on the part of Syl. We are going to rectify my mistakes. Satisfied?"

Vali was not sure how that bewildering array of accusations and revelations was supposed to satisfy anyone or anything. Most importantly, he couldn't believe that after all they had sacrificed, after all they had gone through together, Domarik could still doubt their loyalty.

"We can still warn the legions," Marika insisted. "You don't need us."

Kass snorted in agreement at that.

"You are correct that I don't need you," Domarik said. "What I also don't need are any unknown pieces in play. Perhaps you are loyal. I suspect so, in fact. That's the only reason you're alive right now. For the time being, you will bring us to wherever Syl and the others made entry to the fortress city and will wait there along with one of these knights."

"Let's go, let's go, let's go." Kass was stalking back and forth in furious impatience. "We are going to lose them."

Domarik gestured to the front. "Lead the way, Vali."

Once again out of options, Vali started back up the hill with Marika at his side. He didn't bother following the footprints. He knew the way by now.

# A NEW DREAM

It was a plan. It wasn't a good plan, but any plan was better than what they had only half an hour ago, following Lucky like lambs into the slaughterhouse. Leon would distract them with Lucky, buy a few moments as Syl paralleled them and ambushed the welcome party from the rear. Their only hope lay in surprise, in Syl hitting them hard and fast from behind and then Leon joining the fray. Maybe they could grab one to question. Or kill them and keep moving. Opportunities would present themselves, or they wouldn't. At least now they had a chance. Liora had a chance. Vali and Marika could warn the legions, and they could kill the riftwalker. There was a chance to salvage this disaster.

*And you can all live happily ever after.*

No, there was probably no salvaging this. They were well and truly fucked. But he could at least try and save Liora. If he died, he died. Overdue, probably.

Creeping forward, Syl could hear the beating of his heart. It pounded in time with the hammering in his head, with the flex of the walls around him, with the voices that pressed in close now—too close to block out any longer. Syl focused on his surroundings to drown them out, but that brought its own issues. He could see it now. Every passage was an artery, and he worked his way to where a heart beat. Syl knew it with the same unexplainable certainty he knew which turns to take, which half-collapsed gaps to crawl through to stay parallel to Lucky and Leon. Another uncomfortable fact he pushed away with Lucky's words. He knew the way to go. That was it. Why concern himself with the theoretical when the practical demanded all his attention? He had spent half a lifetime in these tunnels at this point; of course he had absorbed a near-instinctual ability to navigate this labyrinth. Any other explanation was fantasy and conjecture. Unprofessional.

So, Syl tried not to think too much about how confidently he moved down side passages, between levels, around debris, and through the heavy stillness that pervaded the whole place. The concrete and rusting iron lines of earlier had long ago given way on all sides to solid rock, strata pointing the way forward and down. Lines of black veined through the layers, vines reaching outward and questing for the faraway light. Or perhaps for the light below. With a start, Syl realized that for some time, there had been an ambient glow, and he twisted the cover to switch his arclamp from near nothing to nothing. He hooked it to his belt. There was no doubting it. The same direction he *knew* he had to go. The walls ahead were bathed in a faint glow of the darkest blue, a primordial echo of the light trapped in his own arclamp.

He continued down, and the glow intensified until there was no mistaking its source. Glittering lines of a cobalt blue now threaded their way among the stone walls. These were the true veins of that beating heart, Syl knew suddenly with a certainty that alarmed him. Here was *the* path. To Lucky and Leon and maybe Liora, but past them as well.

Tentatively, Syl reached out to touch one of the lines. He paused. Was it...moving? He hardly trusted his own senses at this point, but it had looked like a branch of one of the larger lines moved, imperceptibly encroaching on one of its darker, more inanimate neighbors. The hint of whispers called to him, overlapping voices indistinct. Syl looked farther down the passage. It must be from there. The whispers sounded like they were right next to him though, from those snaking lines. Or maybe inside his mind. A trick of the tunnels. There had to be a group ahead. Syl turned back to the wall, where his hand still hovered, fingers inches away from touching the pulsing lines. He looked again for any sort of movement. Nothing. He had imagined it. He was tired, that was it. Understandable. He withdrew his hand and picked up his pace forward. If that was the group heading to meet Leon and Lucky, then he was running out of time.

Hardly a minute later, and Syl could see an opening ahead. More light, and the suggestion of open space beyond. The pulsing, glowing veins, whatever they were, were thick here, almost displacing the walls themselves. Everything, from the walls to his own arms and uniform, was bathed in a cold blue light, dark, as if he were far, far under the surface of some unimaginably vast ocean. There was no sound anymore, beyond the pounding of blood in his ears. The time for caution was rapidly passing though. He strode through the opening into the vast, blue-washed space beyond.

Syl froze in place. He had been here before. In a dream, but that only made it all the stranger. It was different, true, but there was no doubting it. The vast chamber from that eerie dream, the scale of something built by and meant for more than something as temporary as humanity. He took a step backward, overwhelmed with the dream memories. The details that had faded upon waking came rushing back, slamming into him, relentless.

It wasn't all the same though. The lines were there, sure enough, snaking under his feet and up the walls, everywhere, in patterns beyond comprehension. But here they pulsed with that living light, the heartbeat of something. And the scale... His dream hadn't the imagination for the scale of reality. The space was larger than he could see across, stretching into blue, into black as the chamber extended away from him, dotted on all sides with entrances as small as his and large enough to march a battalion through. And the center—in the center stood a...a tree. It was stone and iron and ossanite, and it throbbed with that same light, but there was no doubting it was a tree. A tree that had grown impossibly tall and spread its petrified, undead branches into the unseen ceiling, where the moisture gathered and dripped rain-like onto the floor, only to eventually find its way back up again.

There were whispers again. Footsteps too. Syl could see their source this time. He pressed himself back into the relative darkness of the entrance and watched, forcing his mind to focus and trying to put blinders on to everything else. The room, the tree, the lines—all of it could wait. They were too far away to see clearly in the half-light, but there were at least a dozen of them, moving along the rounded edge of the room purposefully to one of the many side entrances. They passed within. Syl waited for a breath, then followed, keeping close to the wall with blade drawn and ready to sprint. He was already pulling energy through his bonds and took comfort in the familiarity of that strength, in the ritual of the hunt. This he knew. Those Stained ahead were ready for an oathknight, a Hunter. They were not ready to be surprised themselves, and most importantly, they were not ready for him. Let Lucky keep his luck, Leon his brutality, and Domarik his strength. He was the best when it mattered, and if these Stained didn't know that, they would soon.

Syl reached the entrance and heard the liquid murmur of a conversation beyond. Cautious, he crept forward. There would be no second chances down here. He had to survive to find and save Liora, and that meant he would have to fight like he had never fought before. Syl crept further up, started to see the suggestion of shapes silhouetted in the light where the tunnel widened into a landing for intersecting paths. There were raised voices, the notes of alarm clear. They must have run into Lucky and Leon. Any second now. Syl pushed forward at a light-footed jog. Their confusion wouldn't last long.

Their backs were to him. Perhaps a score of Stained, all unprepared and facing away, an opportunity that would have made the Exarch slaver with anticipation. Elementals and telekines, no doubt, Rift-users of a dozen different unsanctioned abilities, rogue threads ready to be snipped before they could snarl the pattern. And one more. A weapon of supreme potential, the ultimate affront to imperial authority. A riftwalker. Her. There was no mistaking her.

Riftwalker. Stained. *Monster.*

*Morana*, a little voice inside of him insisted.

Syl knew better than to pay attention to that voice. Or usually he did. Listening to it had spared her in the first place, contributed to all this mess, and gotten Liora captured, maybe killed. The failure in his charge had accelerated yet another cataclysm, when the fuse of one of their world's remaining fortress cities was already burning. Time to listen to sense. To do his duty. Kill her. Kill as many of these monsters as he could. He knew he could do more good here in two minutes than the Vigil had done in the province for years. He could buy the world time.

So, why couldn't he move? He had done this before, followed out his orders to the letter. Sometimes the children had to die; it was the way of it. People died every day—children died every day—and the world went on. And these weren't people, not really, in the same way she wasn't a child. Only future threats, would-be warlords, seeds of chaos that would grow to blot out the sun and choke the world, like their predecessors had before them. The world would be better for their deaths. For every single one that lived a quiet life, there would be another that sought to use that power to remake the world as they saw fit and hastened its end instead. Men and women couldn't be trusted with that sort of power. So, why did he hesitate, even now?

That quiet voice inside him had fallen silent. Or maybe was overwhelmed by the others that screamed at him now—screamed for him to step forward and take the leap with broad strokes of his sword, blows with his gauntlet to soft, unprotected heads. It was always such a relief once the decision was made.

There was still time to decide. The Stained were shouting now, spreading out, and he could hear Leon yelling something back from farther up the tunnel. Skin flushed, Syl stepped forward on the balls of his feet. He felt feverish, heat radiating off his skin. His eyes felt like someone had their thumbs pressed in on them. For all the chaos, the world constricted in his vision until all he could see was the riftwalker. His target. He was steps away now. They hadn't noticed his presence.

It was time. He would never have an easier chance. He couldn't see individual details, but there were sixteen figures ahead. He had counted. It would be important for afterward. Syl didn't have Lucky's gift, couldn't possibly determine the strength of any of the users ahead. There was really only one that mattered. Kill the riftwalker, then kill the rest. He was within striking range now. Pulling the blade backward, Syl blocked his other thoughts. The weakness of sympathy and the cowardice that was his doubt. There was a cacophony in his head now, threatening to split it apart, and his vision wavered, walls and bodies becoming, two, three, ten, a hundred shimmering shapes. Then there was nothing there at all but the dark.

He blinked, bringing them back into being and trying to focus on the next three moves. Blade through her skull—he wanted it to be quick—heavy iron of the gauntlet into the gangly youth beside her, loop the blade into the three to their right. Motion into more motion. There wasn't any more time. The decision had to be made. Had been made. Cut his bloody way through here and rescue Liora. Do what he had failed to do the first time.

Syl pulled the blade back, body coiling for the final strike.

She looked back.

Right then, Syl felt as if she had taken all that arcane energy that swam around them here and rooted him in the stones beneath him. It wasn't true, but it made it easier to explain why he stilled his hand.

*She's right there! You can save a thousand lives! Right now! You can save Liora, you can finally, finally do the right thing. Do something that matters!*

He killed her. Thrust his blade forward, into that confused face, the beginning of that hate he knew so well mirrored on her face. Crushed the seed. Syl killed her and moved on to the next.

He did his duty.

# INTO BATTLE

"A battle is not a place for intelligent people, Darya," Alina said as they mounted their horses, surrounded by nearly five hundred half-frozen and starving riders. Less the ones who had actually frozen or starved. "Let's not get in the habit of being in the front."

Darya could smell the fear and excitement around her, the sour scent of unwashed clothes and the earth-stink of hundreds of horses crammed close together. Even with most of them at least making a nominal effort at preparing quietly, it seemed impossible that the Helians couldn't hear them.

Taharuk rode his horse through the press toward the front, exhorting them in a roaring whisper as he went. "Quicky, quickly. You good-for-nothing, cock-rotted, stinking excuses for warriors, hurry!" He glanced through the snow up at the sky, where the vague notion of a sun was starting to set. "We are going to lose the light. Hurry, you bastards. We need to catch them in the open."

Darya was staring at him, so when he turned toward her, there was no mistaking the naked hostility in that stare.

"And you! At the front. Your plan, your risks."

Darya gritted her teeth, pulling savagely at the saddle's straps. She immediately regretted the action, and stopped to soothe the horse. A new one. Hopefully he would fare better than the last two. She had stopped naming them.

Kursagai and Serik were with the other flanks. Here at the center, Taharuk's men and her own motley assortment were forcing themselves into an approximation of a formation. Darya could barely bring herself to make flinching eye contact with the ones who had gathered around her, closer than ever after her return from being left behind. Might as well have returned from the dead, for the excitement that had caused. She couldn't bring herself to think of them as hers, for all the idiotic prophecy they whispered amongst themselves. Not followers. Maybe fellow survivors.

Alina was glaring at Taharuk as he rode away. "That jealous little shit. He doesn't want you stealing any of the credit if this goes well."

"You think it will go well?"

Kasym started. "Why would it not go well? You said you made a plan with those Stained. And the Getacians."

"I did... I mean...I did! But..." She wanted to tell them about those clean lines, the sparkling armor, fluttering banners, and...and the hell-spawned *giants*, but she didn't want to appear more frightened than she already was. "But you never know for sure. The plan is solid," she said, a bit louder, with something resembling confidence finding its way into her voice. "Time to go."

There were scattered nods from around her, faces a mix of anxious fear and curious appraisal. More riders than ever had worked their way into the periphery of her circle, and not only the outcasts and rejects.

Alina examined the point of her hastily made spear with a critical eye. "He's trying to get you killed, you know that, right?"

"Of course I know that," Darya snapped. "Help me survive?"

"Always, Darya." Alina grinned. "After we escaped that underground hellhole, once you had us sneak in to make that agreement with Serik... This is what I've been wanting to see. I'm your fucking *shadow*."

Darya had time for an uncertain smile back before turning to her other side.

"Kasym?"

A shrug and a nod from the gangly man, too-long arms raised as if in prayer. "Why not? I'll promise anything before a battle."

Not a ringing endorsement, but life was all about taking what you could get. And if leadership was anything, it was seeing if people would risk their lives for you. All the cunning plans in the world wouldn't matter if she couldn't survive this battle.

With a kick, Taharuk started his horse forward, setting off a chain reaction of boots into flanks. They moved forward slowly, not all at once, the hundreds of little pushes necessary to overcome the momentum of a great boulder, ready to tip over its perch and begin its heedless downhill sprint. Taharuk may have put her at the front with thoughts of removing an unwelcome variable, but Darya couldn't fault his courage. Any warband leader led through connections and cunning, of course, but by strength above all. And that meant the front. Part of Darya wondered if that was just another way the great Arkhan and his three Sarkhanae kept their factions from getting too restive. A steady turnover of leadership never hurt their control.

The trees started to thin, and they were able to bring the horses closer, breaking into a trot. No more time for thoughts on politics or plots. Darya readjusted her grip on the short lance that Kasym had found for her. More of a glorified sharpened tree branch than anything deserving the name of a lance. But better than her bow for this charge she'd been assigned to.

The trees faded away as the forest gave way to the broad grassland, and the first ranks picked up their speed and tightened into a wedge. The flanks led by Kursagai and Serik spread out to circle wide and harry and harass the enemy. Darya wanted nothing more than to follow them. She was good with a bow. Great, even. Not to mention the fact that, albeit inconsistently, she could apparently call fire now. The lance felt like a poor choice. The warriors around her started to spin sabers and axes, but most held tight to their own lances, faces presumably grim under the rags. There were no war cries yet, and in that thundering silence of hoofbeats and snorting animals, the snow lent the whole scene a surreal air. Reality, dampened.

*Survive the first clash. That's all I have to do.*

Darya's hands were clumsy all of a sudden. Strength from the nearby Riftgate or not, she thought she might drop the lance as Taharuk roared them into a gallop. The cries came now. Whoops and roars and calls to the honor of ancestors long dead, or the aid of gods yet living. Calls for courage and for strength, for hate and for savagery. Ahead, there were commands yelled, faint in the snowfall, but their urgency unmistakable. There was nothing hidden now, no secret gambits. Kill or be killed.

The thundering hooves had become overwhelming, the snow blinding, and her vision constricted, the rest of the world falling away and leaving only a narrow tunnel of perception. It was as if she was outside of her body again and could only watch, horrified, as actions long ago preordained played out along their rutted paths.

Forward, only forward. The legionnaires in front of them were milling around, scrambling to reorient themselves to this new threat. Darya thought she could already hear screams to her right, could feel the world holding its breath as its elements were brought to bear by the Stained on the far side, burning and flashing against these men so far from home. The plan. They had said they would stop them. Now they would hit them. Were hitting them. She could barely think.

They were close now, so close. Close enough that she could make out the individual faces from her perch above them, terrified, furious, and every emotion in between. She saw one right in front of her, her own fear reflected on his face. That one. She lined up the lance, preparing for the impact. She dug her heels into the horse's flanks one last time, and with a cry of her own that was echoed all across the wedge, she plunged into the maelstrom of flesh and metal.

# EVERY TIME

S yl killed her.

Or ... he would in a moment. It would be a mercy, he knew. That girl would be a tool if she lived, driven and manipulated by her need for vengeance. No one deserved that.

And yet, he couldn't move. Couldn't put the blade down, couldn't thrust forward. He wanted it to make sense. Maybe if he saw a flash of his daughter's face on hers, a clear connection to that fading past, he could understand. But all he saw were those familiar unfamiliar features twisting with hate and resentment. She had not forgotten his face either. If anything, he saw himself, and that made it even harder to understand his hesitation.

One thing was clear, however: the time for any decision was quickly disappearing. Other heads were starting to turn. Hesitation or no, they would rip him apart if Morana didn't. So, he ran from the choice. A decision in itself.

Syl dropped the long blade and struck out with one hand, quick as a whip, and pulled her to him. With the other, he pulled the collar from his belt and snapped it around her neck. Syl didn't want to kill her, but had no pressing desire for half his body to be transported elsewhere either. He danced back, dragging her with him, and drawing the long knife from the back of his belt. It had all gone smoother than he had dared hope. That in no way changed the fact that this was also probably the stupidest thing he had ever done, on a day with intense competition.

The youth that had been at Morana's side and a gaunt, patchy-haired skeleton of a woman took a step toward him, furious. Morana, for her part, was squirming like an eel and screaming bloody murder, cursing and thrashing in his grip. He ignored her.

"Stay back!" he yelled, feeling more than half a moron. "Stay back, or I cut the little witch's throat." He would too. Or, he told himself to look like he would. This could still work. He could still save Liora, but only if they believed him to be everything he thought he knew himself to be. Ruthless, professional. Not given to impractical kidnappings followed by trite demands. The others turned, and those closest two took another half-step forward, not convinced either, apparently. "Gods damn it, don't fucking move!" he roared, pulling the knife even tighter at that line where her jaw met her throat. Her piteous whine stabbed at him.

They stopped, but at this point, the rest had turned to face him. Stained all, he had no doubt. The faces of most lost in the murky light, but the ridges of scars were clear on most of their necks. Their intent was clear too. Lucky's words forced their way in. *They want to talk... A better way.* All well and good, but Syl knew exactly what would happen to him if he moved the knife a fraction from Morana's throat. Exactly what he should have done a minute ago. Time to improvise.

Syl forced the calm detachment, the lucidity that usually came in a fight. He stared levelly at the group, who waited, expectant. "You will take us to wherever you're keeping a captured Hunter. You will do it now. If you try anything on the way, she dies."

None of them moved. At least he had been right about how important she was.

"If you harm my friend ahead, she dies. If I find that you killed that Hunter..."

"Syl!" one of them cut in.

Syl stumbled on his list of ultimatums. He tried to continue. His sense of hearing was past trusting. "If I find that—"

"Syl!"

The group ahead moved finally, reluctantly, as one of the indistinct shapes pushed themselves forward. "Syl, it's me," said Liora. She flashed a nervous smile. And it was her. Syl tried to find the illusion, the lie, but it was her in every way. That absurd, unruly short hair, those playful, judging hazel eyes, all the little scars and imperfections. That little bend in her nose from a break badly set. The eyes a bit too large, a bit too wide apart. Too trusting. Too naïve. Too much of a reminder. It was her. She wore a collar to match Morana's, but she was unbound.

"Liora?"

"Yes, Syl." She smiled again, tentatively. A little light that flickered, unsure of itself. But in the chaos of his own mind and the blue-black pressure of this subterranean, otherworldly city, it shone brighter than any beacon fire. "You came for me."

"I did," Syl said. He swallowed, gripping tight on Morana's collar, an anchor to the present moment. He glanced behind him. There was a shuffling whisper of movement somewhere far behind. Syl turned back to Liora. "I did. Is it really you? Are you... Is this real?"

Liora stepped forward and motioned to her side at the Stained, as if worried that her new friends might spook him. "It's me, Syl. I'm real, and I'm right here."

"Why are you with them?"

She nodded at that, maddeningly agreeable, and took another step forward. Syl took a step backward and dragged the girl with him. He hardly heard her cry of pain this time as the knife nicked her. "Liora. Why are you with them?" A note of accusation crept into his voice. "Leon?" he called.

"Up here!" He heard Leon's voice echo across the chamber to him. Barely a stone's throw ahead. "Alive, though can't say things are going to plan. I've got Lucky."

"Syl, no one has to die today."

Syl barked a laugh. "A lie." He dragged Morana another step back out of the chamber. There was another noise, he was certain of it. He whirled his head from the tunnel stretching behind, to the shadows in the small chamber, to the Stained ahead, who watched him silently.

One of them darted forward. Syl cut the girl's throat. Liora died.

*No, no, no!* None of these things happened, and yet Syl saw the echoes of them playing out before him. He shook his head violently. "It never works like that, Liora," he said finally, plaintively.

"Syl. It *can*. It's up to you right now, though. You came here to save me, not to kill."

He wanted to protest, to tell her that it wasn't true. Deep down, Syl knew who he was. He could have, would have killed all those standing around her, and would have enjoyed every second of that red work. He always did. Still, he listened greedily.

"Syl, you spared her before. Domarik didn't care what I had to say; it was you. You're the reason she's alive at all." Liora took another careful step forward. Syl didn't move. "I know we've disagreed—gods know I don't know what I'm doing—but I do know you're a good man. Or you could be. You want to be."

Syl let the knife drift away from the girl's neck, and the roaring in his head, the echoes, all faded as he clung to this fantasy, this imaginary version of himself in her head.

"All you have to do is choose to try. Every time. Right now. Let Morana go, Syl. I know you don't want to kill her."

And she was right: Syl didn't.

He let her go.

Watching her push away from him and run back to where the rest of the Stained received her with worried checks and pats and held breaths released, Syl knew he had made a mistake. This was a failure in his duty, in every oath he had ever taken. He would probably die now. It was a mistake, there was no doubt, but the right mistake, maybe. Syl knew his life was made of mistakes. What was one more? At least this one he might even be proud of for the time he had left.

The men and women before him looked ready to tear him apart, and he could hear screeching and shuffling from far down the corridor behind him, but that all faded into the background. Inside, it was blessedly silent for once.

Liora closed the distance between them and threw herself at him, arms folding him in an embrace. Syl collapsed into her, the forces holding him there falling away. She held him up. He felt tears against his face.

# DEVIL'S TRUTH

S yl pulled himself together again. He half expected to be somewhere else when he opened his eyes. Maybe it had all been another dream. But there she was, in his arms. The world reemerged, the dangers and the concerns taking on shape and immediacy again. The Stained were still there, with Morana glaring at him, green eye and black alike radiating a malevolence he hadn't thought possible for one so young. Leon was still somewhere ahead, likely more confused than ever, with a no doubt miserable Lucky. And behind him... Syl turned, holding onto Liora's hand, not ready to let go.

If this had been a dream, it would have been the worst sort of nightmare. Scuttling along the floor and over one another was a roiling mass of iron-spawn. In their middle was a cleared space where an invisible force repelled anything that came too close. A figure strode there among the creatures, closing the distance rapidly, hood thrown back this time. Syl didn't bother running, didn't ready himself. He knew for certain now, this wasn't real. For despite the differences, there could be no doubt: the stranger here was the stranger from his dream.

"It's alright," Liora said, though the way she squeezed his hand betrayed her nervousness. "They won't attack you."

"Syl!" Leon called from ahead, alarm clear. "You alive?"

"Yes. Yes," he yelled back, distracted. "It's alright. Hold on."

"Liora," Syl asked, ignoring the shouted questions from Leon, "why won't they attack? Why are you with them? And who is he?" There was no accusation this time, only calm curiosity. He had made his peace with whatever happened next. He traced his finger along the collar on her neck, another question.

"His name is Vels. And they don't entirely trust me yet. Which is understandable."

Syl didn't take his eyes from hers and waited for the ironspawn to tear him apart as they surged around him.

"...But they didn't kill me."

The ironspawn didn't kill them now either, though Syl could feel Liora's discomfort as the masses of locomoted flesh and iron boiled past them into the room, hissing and eyes glowing red.

She raised her voice. "I thought they would, but they just threw me in a cell until he,"—she gestured to where the dream-stranger, Vels, had leaned against the nearby wall—"came to talk to me. It was you they wanted, you know. In the tunnels."

Syl nodded, not accepting that explanation, but not wanting her to stop either. He squeezed her arm, as if to reassure himself she was real. She smiled at him then, and he couldn't quite keep one of his own from stretching the dirt and sweat on his face, despite everything.

"This is all very lovely, but you really ought to get on with the explaining, dear. Sooner rather than later," the stranger named Vels said. "I have reason to believe we will have company soon, and I didn't come here for my own health or out of boredom. A few too many irons in the fire today."

Liora gripped Syl's hand. "Listen to me." He opened his mouth to speak, but she cut him off. "No, just listen this time. The empire has been lying to us, to you. What we've been doing... Syl, there's a reason it feels wrong. They've had us hunting Stained for the wrong reasons, and more than that..." She seemed on the edge of saying something, but even now, was unable to voice it.

"Girl, spit it out! We don't have all the time in the worlds." The stranger sighed. "Gods before, must I do everything myself?" Pushing away from the wall, he strode toward Syl and Liora. The creatures parted for him, a sea of flesh that opened before him and closed after.

"Syl, don't tell me you've never questioned why your so-called Emperor-savior has you hunting down any who can touch the Rift? You strike me as a bit slow, but not without some capacity for self-reflection." He laughed at Syl's expression. "See! Even now, I can see those cogs turning furiously up there." Vels reached out to affectionately pet the head of one of the creatures, looking down paternally. "Not so different from them. An animal trying to understand its place in the events of a world too big for it. Lashing out furiously at what it is incapable of understanding."

"We hunt them because of what they are capable of. People can't be trusted with that sort of power. Every time they're free, they accelerate another cataclysm. There is a reason—the only reason that matters. Do us a bit more credit." This was an argument Syl knew. He could feel the heat rising again, the resignation and peace of just seconds ago burning away a bit. He might hate himself for how easily he fell into his old pattern, but it did feel good. It felt...focused. "And I've seen you before."

The man's smile said he saw exactly how Syl felt. "That you have. One of those forms of power you're so skeptical of. And bear with me, Syl. I want you to entertain the possibility that your beloved Emperor has lied to you. That you and all your oathknights don't protect the realm, the innocent, or even order, unless you count the false order imposed by that fragment of a dead god, serving the interests of his own masters. That your savior is no savior, and your Stained only pieces on the board like yourself. Can you imagine that version of the world?"

"You have no idea what you're talking about," Syl spat, but his heart wasn't in it. He was past confused.

"And you have no idea how funny that is." The man snorted. "So much is lost every time. It makes it easier for them. Understand, at least, that these 'Stained' are the best of your people, persecuted for no other reason than their ability to wield the power of the Rift. A soul, or a splinter of something greater reaches out to touch them, and you damn them for it. The most dangerous you cull like some population of wild animals, and the rest you send to work and die in mines and lumberyards in far-flung provinces, as far from the active Riftgate as possible. The ones that can merely channel its power harvested like so many stalks of wheat for the grindstone. Their window is closing though, and they'll pull them all close soon. They gather them in Heliopolis, breeding them like cattle, but only for now. Empires are ravenous gravity given form. They always pull to their center when they can, and Syl, you stand but upon the furthest edge of empires."

"I can claim anything I like too, doesn't make it true!" None of this made sense to Syl, and he could feel himself flailing for the old justifications, the reasonings he had repeated to himself countless times, prayers against his doubts. "Even if it were, can you imagine those with such powers let loose on our world without control? No limits to what destruction they could wreak? Each cataclysm coming faster and faster. The Vigil exists because people are greedy, power-hungry, and violent by nature. Control is the price for peace. Pretending that isn't true is a fool's errand, and has been for hundreds of years."

"Such has been the price of freedom," Vels responded equitably, "and for far longer than that. So many great wars and cataclysms visited upon more worlds than yours in the name of fighting the inevitable. Besides that, even within the tiny scope of your existence, there will be more every year. More to kill, more to imprison. Gods forbid you let them choose their own futures. Because we know what they would choose now, after how you've treated them." He gestured around him, encompassing Morana, Lucky, the Stained in the room, and even the whole empire beyond the walls. "The only choice you've given them. Such is the horrible arithmetic of power, from here to the Halls of Caelorum. So, you continue as you have, as they do, the momentum of oppression gaining its own reasons and its own ends, an endless wheel. Fighting against your turn in the mud." He bared his teeth. "And such a pronouncement is so easy without context, Syl. Be careful not to project what you find within onto those around you. Not all must choose between harsh order and violent chaos."

Leon had pushed his way into the room, and Syl could see him through the Stained and the ironspawn, all waiting, but ready for violence. For his part, Leon looked more rattled than Syl had ever seen him. He held Lucky like the bloodhound was the only thing keeping him from death. Not an unreasonable conclusion.

"Syl, what the fuck is going on?"

Syl didn't think he could tell him if he tried. He gripped Liora's hand tight, his only lifeline in this new world he had been thrust into.

"Ah, and here we have a perfect example," Vels crowed. "Yes, you hunt down and imprison those you can, but that's not it, is it? Power is practical, above all else. Why throw away that which you can safely use?" He gestured to Lucky. "Your friend here, forced to help hunt his own. They do their best to indoctrinate, but how hard do you really think it was to turn him?" He laughed, and Syl tried not to meet Lucky's eyes. "And we haven't even touched on the real matter! Look at your arms! Your bodies! You take those more blessed than you, you harvest them and chain them in a slavery of not only their bodies, but their minds and spirits as well! Tell me, do you even think about them when you use them?"

"We are bound together," Syl protested. "They make a sacrifice, but so do we." Having the questions he knew but dared not ask himself thrown in his face, damning him for his part in all of it, made him sick. "It burns us up, being the focal point for all that energy. And that's if you live long enough for it to matter. Most of the time, you are ripped apart by these 'innocents' you keep going on about long before you have to worry about that, or you die to some leftover beast from the Breaking. I mean, look at her." He pointed to Morana. "You can't tell me she wouldn't tear me to pieces, given half a chance."

"Nothing less than you deserve, murderer," Morana snarled. "I made a promise. I'm going to kill you, Syl. This will be the last face you see."

"For the sake of the gods, quiet, child! Calm yourself. And Syl, she might be in the right, but she hasn't killed you yet, and perhaps more importantly, *you* haven't. You didn't kill her when you had the chance. Twice now. Still time, I suppose. And you know so little, it would be hilarious if it weren't so sad. Look at that gauntlet on your hand! This room! Look!" he demanded, sweeping his hands and spinning about. "These creatures, half the peoples of your world, the Voraxians, your precious relics and an-imachina, *everything*," he hissed. "Like children playing with their elders' things, understanding neither origin nor purpose. But sometimes...some-times! These oathknights..." His laugh was brittle, more than the edge of madness there. "Binding others to a single human vessel and yoking their strength together. Absolutely ingenious advancement. Profoundly diabolical. Quintessentially human. I can guarantee the Emperor and His Chosen were surprised when you showed them that this time. An earthly echo of the divine." He cackled, or maybe cried. "Your kind always did have knack for the clever and the practical."

"Just tell me what you want to tell me, old man, and stop rambling." Syl had a thousand questions, and every word brought more, but he could tell this stranger was driving at something.

The laugh was easy again, the madness gone, or maybe imagined. "You're right, you're right. Besides, we are running out of time. Let me cut straight to the matter, then, my oh-so-serious friend. You follow your orders, you seek your revenge, but would it be so easy to pronounce such judgments for this greater good if the accused was one of your own?"

Syl thought back to all the families he had separated, their tearful pleas falling on deaf ears. He had hardened his heart then, and he hardened it again now. He hardened his mind, the beating heart of that tree echoing in his mind dismissed with those other dream memories, Lucky's words, Liora's confession.

"That's the price of order," he said stiffly. "We all make sacrifices."

He thought Liora would look angry at that, or maybe frustrated, but she only looked at him with such sadness.

"Oh, that last bit is more true than you know. And listen to yourself. The price of order, really? So easy to say when you are the one enforcing it. A noble principle. Rolls off the tongue, and you can even say it with a serious face. But what if it were you? Killing one of your own to delay an uncertain cataclysm? A wife? A daughter?"

Syl looked to Liora, enraged. "What did you tell them?"

"Syl," she whispered, "they told me."

"You're full of shit. They died during the Mages' Revolt. Those fanatics killed my family. Burned the ground they couldn't hold. Killed..." He had to pause, even now. "Killed my family. Killed hundreds, lashing out, because they could. Punishment for anyone they thought too loyal."

A choked cough from the man before him. "Too loyal? Is that what they told you?" Syl felt Liora squeeze his hand even tighter as Vels stared at him in disbelief. "You're smarter than that, or you'd better be. We have so little time left now, and the empire will do its best to take that away too. The legions pushed fast back then too, but you know who was ahead of them, deep behind our lines? You, or those like you. Your precious oathknights, hunting down enemy Stained. Not that they discriminated too finely on that point. Like you said, either an enemy today or one tomorrow, eh? Better safe than sorry?"

An awful dry, chalky feeling in Syl's mouth. "What do you mean, 'our'? How do you know so much?"

"Because I was in charge, boy!" Vels shook his head. "Gods, I don't know if you'll suit, if I'm being honest. Liora here picked it up twice as quick, and with less than half the posturing. I didn't burn through everyone I've ever known just to fail again because some bloodthirsty bastard can't face what he is, or who his masters are." He laughed at the expression on Syl's face. "Really? So surprised? I've been trying to get to that Riftgate ever since they opened it back up, but your Emperor and His Chosen have well and truly dug themselves in there. What I've managed here is nothing short of a miracle, and even now, they march to take it away." There was true hate for the first time on the man's face, and Syl could understand that, at least, even if the rest of the world seemed to have been tipped on its head.

"In charge?" The room was losing its sharp edges, and all Syl could see was Vels before him.

"Yes, yes. Focus!" he snapped, staring farther up the tunnel. "We are out of time. Your family? The one you've grieved and butchered for? My point is, I was there. I was there, and I was in charge of that rebellion, before it fell apart. It wasn't us visiting the villages in the dead of night." He pointed an accusatory finger. "It was you. Or those like you, at least. And your wife—or more likely your daughter, given your own gifts—clearly caught their attention. Someone like Lucky here noticed them, and then"—he snapped his fingers—"threat eliminated, am I right? Order preserved? Cataclysm delayed?"

No, it couldn't be true. This was just one of those awful dreams. The Vigil...because of him? It was his fault, and more his fault than he could have ever imagined. *Can't you feel it?* And Syl could, there was no denying it... He had spent the last ten years hunting down those stained by the Rift and... *You're one of us...*

*You knew, didn't you? Always suspected, deep down.*

*We cannot choose what to believe.*

"No. No! Domarik said they caught the group of rebels there. The ones that killed my family. You're wrong. They caught them. That's why I joined." He choked out the last desperate argument. A man lost, drowning at sea, the waves over his head now. It was hard to breathe.

Vels looked at him with contempt. Beside him, Liora's voice was soft—so soft, it was hard to hear—but it still fell like a hammer blow.

"Syl, how do you think Domarik knew what to tell you?"

# IN THE MUD

Darya's world was chaos. An assault on all the senses, every muscle pulled tight, lungs bursting, and adrenaline leaving her viewing everything through the tiniest crack in the fog of the present. All she could focus on was what was right in front of her. In this case, not dying.

With a gasp, she rolled again in the mush of mud, ash, snow, and blood that coated everything. She was filthy; clothes, face, everything covered in that mix of nature and man's violence. The legionnaire's axe smashed down where she had been a moment before, and Darya came to a halt against another body, too panicked to do anything but try to scrabble to her feet. Grunting, the man pulled his axe squelching from the mud, cursing her with words she barely understood. Darya knew that language, spoke the same one, but between the heavy accent and her own panic, she couldn't understand a word right now. Only the intent. The deadly, murderous intent.

Reaching behind her with slick hands for support, she came across something solid. A shield. Salvation. Limbs leaden, she threw herself backwards as best she could again, pulling the shield with her this time. Where was her sword?

*Call the fire!*

But she could barely think, much less muster the concentration to summon fire, even as she could feel it tugging at her, this close to the Riftgate. Instead, she raised the shield above her. Just in time. The impact of the blow smashed her backward into the mud, nearly onto her back again. The only thing that stopped her was an angled spear shaft, propping her up. It felt like he had broken her arm. Why would no one intervene? Where was Alina? Kasym? Anyone? All around her, little pockets of fighting swirled, devolved into that oldest form of warfare, all fighting for their lives in the freezing mud. Little worlds unto themselves, and she was stuck in her own. She would have to fight her way out of this world or see it be her grave.

Darya threw what was left of the shield into his face, earning a curse for her efforts. She stumbled backwards over the spear and rolled over the dead horse behind it. There. This was what she needed.

She had only bought a breath. The legionnaire's helmet had been lost somewhere in the fray, and blood was pouring from his nose. Had she done that? He rushed at her, teeth locked in a snarl, chest heaving with exhaustion. His axe swept upward for another blow to split her open ... and he tripped. Simple mistake, overlooking that spear, a filthy piece of the flotsam of battle among all the rest, but sometimes that was all it took. And it was what Darya was waiting for. A big man, he was strong enough that he almost righted himself from his stumble in time.

Almost. Too tired for any sort of cry of triumph, Darya lunged forward with the sword she had found half-buried in the muck.

They were so close, it was almost like an embrace. Intimate. Darya thought at first that she had failed. His face was contorted in rage, spittle flying as he struggled with her. And then she saw the blade through his other side. Cleaner now, truth be told. His face started to relax, confusion replacing anger. Trying to pull the sword free, Darya was dragged back down into the mud with him. He looked at her with such accusation then, such disappointment, that she wanted to apologize. She hadn't meant it; it had all happened so fast. Then she remembered the grunts as he swung that brutal axe, the curses. Her expression hardened. Nothing but another bastard in this cold world that was constantly trying to kill her. Spitting in his face and trembling with the effort, Darya stood, putting a boot on his chest to draw out the sword. She pushed him back into the mud.

She was back in her own small world, a bubble of calm now in the midst of all that chaos. The snow was falling harder as evening fell and stripped the scene of some of its awful specificity. Men fighting, all voices lost in the symphony, but above it all, the rush of fires she could see blooming along the periphery, and the occasional crackling of lightning as it impacted and spread, harmless, across the invisible fields of safety woven overhead by the mage-priests of the empire.

Their net wasn't perfect. Darya saw one of the crows screaming, running from the front and clutching at his head, blood running from sightless eyes, something broken inside. A masked and cloaked legionnaire stood calm and alone against a charge, arm extended with one of the soulirons Darya had only ever heard of held parallel to the ground and roaring out a blinding fire, the firearm tearing man after man apart with horrifying precision. A heartbeat later, he was swallowed by the tide, and after another, the relic fell silent. Another six soldiers disappeared into chunks and bloody mist on the flank nearest her. Roaring, fur-clad Getacian fighters flowed into the gap they left. A bit farther, she could see some sort of armored monster of a man laying about with a massive hammer, bodies flying away. One of those giant imperial soldiers was advancing on it, a sword the size of Darya held before it.

Chaos.

Stumbling a little, Darya looked about for Alina, worry gnawing at her gut, but faces were impossible to find in that mess, and they had been separated from the start. She would have settled for finding Kasym, at least, but she had no such luck. She was alone.

The battle had mostly moved on from where she stood, swaying slightly, another leftover of the violence. It was too much to take in at once, hundreds of smaller engagements, not some grand battle, much less anything like tactics, but she thought she could sense a shift. The legionnaires' discipline was being overcome in the face of numbers and the elements being thrown at them. They were starting to break, fault points showing. One good push, and it would fall apart. She could see it now.

There was movement and the squelching of someone, or multiple people, coming from her right. She whirled, panic lending a bit of energy to tired limbs. But it was only Taharuk. Taharuk and a few men, some mounted, a few dismounted.

"Still alive," he yelled over the clashing beyond, more statement than question.

Based on his expression, Darya couldn't tell if that spoke of being impressed or disappointed. Maybe a bit of both.

"Still alive," she muttered under her breath. She pointed with her borrowed blade toward the milling group, louder now, to make herself heard. "We need to hit them there."

She looked back to the cluster of robes in the middle, where even in the dying light, she could distinguish the mage-priests who were protecting the soldiers from the brunt of arcane violence directed against them. One of the riders next to Taharuk spurred his horse close to her, forcing her to stumble backwards. Her foot slipped sideways in the mess, but she managed to stay upright.

"One battle, and the bitch thinks she's a commander," the rider snarled.

Darya examined the man in front of her, memorizing his features. A lean, cruel face with a long cut bleeding into the matted furs he wore. She wouldn't forget him. She couldn't blame him for doubting her though—gods knew she doubted herself. But she was right this time, and she knew it. Darya turned her attention back to Taharuk. He looked troubled, looking up at the sky, at the arcane and natural fury raining down, as if judging the likelihood of a storm. He grimaced.

"No, she's right. We hit them now."

The man before her spat on the ground again in disgust, but wheeled his horse back toward Taharuk.

"And you," Taharuk said. "You're coming with. Can you call that witch-fire of yours, girl?"

Darya hesitated.

"Yes or no?" he demanded.

"Yes," she said finally. "I can." And she could. Or she told herself she could. Darya could feel it pulsing beneath her skin even now, begging to be let out, yearning for something to feed on, consume. It was always hungry. Like something alive. And according to Duras, the closer one was to the Riftgate, the easier it was to use. She could do this.

"Good. Then follow right behind us. When we break their line, I want you to unleash hell. Yes?" Darya nodded. "Alright. The rest of you, on me!"

With that, Taharuk whirled his small horse around, and with a cry, spurred it forward. Despite her hate for the man, Darya thought he looked almost heroic there. She couldn't help but be reminded of her brother, charging forward on his horse with his blade raised overhead, leading his men into danger.

*And depending on you, fool! Move!* She shook off the stupor and tried to shake the utter exhaustion that permeated her very bones. She did her best to sprint after the riders through the mud, accompanied by the others without mounts. The horsemen closed the distance in a few seconds, unnoticed in the failing light. They cleaved through scattered groups without slowing, slashing at their sides in a frenzy. Following as close as she could behind, Darya saw more than one tribesman laid open in their passing, gurgling their last. A necessary sacrifice, she was sure Taharuk would say. She didn't have time to disagree.

Ahead of her, one of the horses reared back, screaming, impaled on a soldier's spear. She watched another rider split apart by one of the enemy's giant soldiers, a massive blade cleaving through horse and man in a shower of gore. And from behind that rider, another, suicidally brave, charging forward and skewering the brute through the narrow slit in its helmet, his whoop of triumph cut short by another spear thrown from somewhere in the milling mass of men. Through it all, Darya stayed as close as she dared to where the horses pushed their way forward, men and beasts screaming and dying around her. The adrenaline had long since faded, and she struggled forward a lungful of cold air at a time, breath coming in gasps, face plastered with her own ragged brown hair and sticky with blood.

Another rider fell in front of her, and Darya threw herself to the side to avoid a thrashing horse. They had to almost be there. It had seemed such a good idea. Another instance of her speaking before thinking. There would be no luck to save her this time. She pushed after, one step at a time, trying to keep behind the force that was rapidly falling apart. Their momentum stopped suddenly, and Darya almost ran into the back of one of the horses in her surprise.

There was a shouted command from the front. Was that Taharuk? Stumbling around the pockets of combat, she worked her way forward to where the melee had grown the thickest, watching Taharuk and a dozen of his best fighting against two men and a giant who stood between them and the imperial mage-priests, who chanted quietly, eyes closed and mouths moving in gentle, practiced motions. They had made it. And yet...those three were laying waste to those in front. The giant was predictable, but deadly. The other two were death incarnate. She had heard of these. Oathknights. They moved with a preternatural grace and speed and delivered half of their blows with gauntleted hands, tearing apart their lightly armored opponents. And with nearly a score against these three, they were going to win.

If she could bring down one of them, maybe they would have a chance. Hands shaking, she tried to remember how she had called it earlier. She felt the fire coursing through her and let it lead the way. And there it was, a roaring flame in her hand. She couldn't have been more pleased. At least, she would have been, if she had been allowed to appreciate her little victory. The consequences were immediate.

"Stained!" the nearest of those killers bellowed, even as he staved in a rider's skull. He rushed at her. Darya reached for the fire, but she could barely think for the terror. A surging leap through the muck toward her. Still nothing. A rider split nearly in two as he came between the two of them, his halves thrown sideways. Another span closed. She could see the furious, slitted eyes behind the helmet now, that face screwed up in hate and sprayed red. Her blood soon.

All thoughts fled, and something inside her reacted on instinct, made room, pouring everything she had into the fire, into him. Screaming, the oathknight transformed into an inferno, features blurring and disappearing in the fire. But still he came on, only a step or two away now. He held an armored arm up, as if to ward away the flames, but he was slowing now, fighting against the current. Darya screamed out her terror, reaching for more, more, as much as she could. The enemy oathknight fell to his knees in front of her. Too close. With a last effort, he struck at her. He lashed out with one armored hand, smashing into her left arm and then into her side past that. The force was incredible. Clothes smoking, she flew sideways, bounced, rolled in the mud, and slammed into something on the ground. She felt the air leave her lungs. Panicked, she tried to push herself up. She screamed again in agony and fell back down. If her arm hadn't been broken before, it was now, there was no doubt. And her side... Every gasp for air sent spasms of agony through her whole body.

She could feel consciousness slipping away and fought to claw her way back to the light, to stay awake. Around her, the tide had shifted. Killing the oathknight had been enough. The other enemy oathknight and giant went down like great beasts in a massive hunt, circles of hacking and stabbing riders taking their revenge, while the first few screams started to come from the huddle of imperial mages. It was over then. Darya could see the seams she had seen start to tear apart as the battle turned in favor of the warband, the Getacians, and the Stained that could now pour their unbridled fury into the unprotected ranks. The ranks of separatists that had started to fracture while trying to hold back the legionnaires surged forward with a cry now, venting their own hate on the enemy.

Turning away from what was quickly turning into a slaughter, Darya looked about. Immediately around her were none but the dead and dying.

The fight had moved past her. Gritting her teeth against the pain, she crawled forward with her one good arm, feeling her way back to where the fiercest fighting had taken place. Every move forward was agony, but she knew what she had to do. Protect Alina. Kasym. And find a better way forward. A better path. But to do any of that, she had to stay alive.

The rest of the riders were pushing forward further into the enemy's line, trying to meet their new allies in the middle. Darya kept crawling toward the center of the churned mess, where the dead were piled thickest. The knight hadn't thrown her all that far, but it felt like an eternity to crawl back to where she had stood.

Around the giant, she found Taharuk. He was wounded too, but alive, spitting blood from his knees and watching their victory unfold with a grim smile on that weathered face. He took in her state with a glance.

"Still alive?"

Darya pulled herself to his side.

"You surprise me, Darya." He winced in pain. "I'll admit I didn't expect for you to live this long. Tough as your brother."

"Don't talk about him," she managed to croak.

"He was a good man," Taharuk said, ignoring her. "Didn't want for him to die, but you don't stay a leader by disagreeing with Janbek." He wiped at his face, as if trying to remove the memory, or maybe just the dirt. All it left was more blood. "It was nothing personal, you know."

"I know."

He turned back to watch the battle. "Good, because I think...I think..."

Coughing, he looked at Darya, shock written across his features. Another shuddering cough, and he collapsed. No final flash of rage, no pithy last words. Nothing but another corpse among the rest.

Darya wiped her knife on his body. It was his blood anyway.

"It wasn't personal," she whispered, trying not to look into those sightless eyes that watched her with reproach.

To find revenge, to find a home, to show them a better way, she had to stay alive. And for her to stay alive, he had to die. Simple as that.

# CONSEQUENCES

I t was impossible. A trick. They were using Liora against him. Little details of his life, of his condition, twisted into a convincing fiction. Somehow, they had convinced her of this...this absurdity. Syl felt like the world was crashing down around him.

No, there was crashing, but maybe not the whole world. Screeches, sounds of steel on steel, and sharp impacts into flesh came from farther up. There was another thud, this time of a body impacting a wall. Ahead, covered in mud and gore, Domarik strode into view, dark shaven head glistening with sweat and expression furious. Behind him flowed Kass, a core of legion oathknights, and a few veteran legionnaires, all filthy and looking like they meant murder.

Vels bowed. "Ah, the man himself. Liora here told me about you."

"You."

Syl couldn't understand. "You know him? How?"

Domarik ignored him, staring to where Liora stood, unbound. "So, you let him worm his way into your head with his lies, did you?" They flowed into a protective formation around an uncertain Leon, who held Lucky by the collar. They had cut their way through the ironspawn to get here, but the monsters held back now, snarling and testing the reach of their outstretched blades. "At least you two morons figured out you were being led by your noses. Not until it was too fucking late though."

"Liora, you spineless little bitch, I cannot believe we came here for you." Kass's voice was all venom, but Syl could see the panic beneath as she fought to keep aware of all the threats around them. "And you." She gave a humorless laugh as she looked to the team's erstwhile bloodhound. "Oh, Lucky. Luck's run out, has it? You should hear the plans Domarik has for you. And that's before we hand you over to the judiciars."

"This is exactly why I knew he was telling the truth," Liora spat. "Fucking monsters."

"Monsters, dear?" Kass was incredulous. She darted back and cut at a probing claw. "Curious choice of words from where we're standing. Kill her, Syl. It's time to go."

"Remember your oaths, Syl," Domarik said, raising his voice over the noise of so many packed into the small space. "We can..."

Domarik interrupted himself to spin and loop the point of his sword into one of the creatures that had darted forward. It was hurled backwards in a choking mess, spraying its green-black blood across the faces of the others. The snarling and movement among the entire agitated mess of them seemed only to intensify. They buzzed like a hive of insects as they clawed over one another. They were closing in.

Syl looked over to the robed stranger. For all his words earlier, all he offered now was a raised eyebrow, as if to say, *Well?*

Another of the ironspawn ventured too close and went down with a gurgle as Leon neatly cut its throat with an efficient thrust. "Syl..."

Syl felt like he was looking at the scene from above, falling backwards out of himself. Everything he saw, everything he *knew*, conflicting with what the woman he cared for...no, loved, or maybe wanted to love—it was too late now for half-measures—was telling him. The figures before him were blurring again, and he could see the branches of the future spreading outward, innumerable, from this knife-edge of the present.

"Remember your duty, Syl. There is still—"

"Answer me, Domarik." Syl felt cold now, all the oathknights, Stained, soldiers, ironspawn...everything in the room forgotten. "Do you know him?"

"I know of him. He's one of the Fallen, Syl. He's half the reason we're here. The other is the riftwalker. Speaking of, good work, you found her. Kill her. Now."

Syl didn't move, but the killers around the room started to fan out, systematically taking space back from the ironspawn, who kept just out of reach. They were picking their targets, moving deliberately to the inevitable confrontation. The Stained spread out in turn, slipping behind clumps of the ironspawn and finding cover in the shadows of the room. Events were taking on a momentum of their own.

"Domarik. How do you know him? And one of the Fallen?" Syl wanted to ask the real question, the only question that really mattered, but couldn't quite bring himself to voice it yet.

"What did they tell you?"

"Answer the question, Domarik," Liora cut in viciously. "Or do you only ask them?"

Domarik didn't bother looking at her. "You'll be taken care of presently. I took a chance on you. Soon to be rectified." He sighed. "Syl, yes. I know this...'man' here. Or know of him. I'm sure he's told you, but he's been a thorn in the empire's side for decades. Before any of us were born. It's creatures like him, left from the Breaking, that doom us to this endless cycle. We've tried to kill him more times than I can count. I was on a team with Gregoris that got close, back in the Mages' Revolt. He and I were the only ones who survived. Trust me when I say you should kill him now. If you let him, he'll fill your head with enough lies to blind you. Don't let him—"

"My family," Syl interrupted again, almost choking on the question as it clawed its way out of him. "Why were you there when I found them? Is...is it true?"

Domarik looked annoyed. "Is what true?"

"Is. It. Fucking. *True?*" Syl roared, vision swimming. He threw Liora's grip off and advanced on Domarik, white knuckles around the blade he had picked back up. The Stained between them separated even more, giving him a clear path. The oathknights around Domarik took a protective step forward.

The ironspawn stopped moving, or at least slowed their ceaseless movement, holding their collective breath with those in the room. The echo of Syl's words slowly died, and Domarik stood there considering him, disdaining to acknowledge the drawn blade.

"Yes."

"Why?" It came out as a groan.

"Because we do what has to be done," Domarik said calmly. "Same as we've always done. As you've done. Your child, Syl, was a monster. Incredible potential to pull from the Rift, as far as we could tell. She could have been anything—another gods-damned riftwalker, maybe. A disaster in the making. And you know as well as I do there is no order in a world with people like that. No chance for peace. You don't get to pick and choose when that is true."

"She hadn't done anything. She was innocent," he snarled. "She was perfect." He could barely see now, between the tears and the blood that was pounding through his head, a drumbeat of murderous rage. There were no more possibilities ahead. This was a path he knew already.

"She would have, Syl. People aren't meant to have that kind of power."

"And my wife?"

Domarik shrugged. "Syl, you know how these things work. The only reason you weren't killed is because you weren't there." He tried to soften the blow. "What does this change? You've still been doing the right thing, fighting to preserve the empire, to preserve this delicate order we've built after the chaos that came before! Delaying yet another cataclysm. Buying our people *time*. That's all it's ever been. Nothing has to change. If you were to kill him right now"—he pointed accusingly with his sword—"along with that riftwalker we should never have spared, you'd be doing more good in an afternoon than I've managed my whole life."

"You lied to me. You lied to me from the start."

"A mercy. I could have had you killed too. Probably should have. You should be thanking me. Where you saw only grief, I saw a weapon that could be forged to protect our people. Purpose, Syl."

"That's all we are to him, Syl," said Liora quietly, coming up behind him. "I know you're more than that."

"But what a weapon, Syl! Think of all the horrors we've prevented! Years fighting the spread of this corruption, decades of peace bought each time. And now these...these Fallen and demons would tear that away, have you pretend that they want anything other than power? Do you think he wants anything but to use you and all these others?"

"We don't want power, dear Domarik," Vels cut in. "That's the thing. You only see the world one way, so you can't imagine anyone else seeing it differently."

He was about to say more, but Syl didn't care. It felt like his head was going to explode.

"You killed them!" he screamed. The man who had found him and pulled him from his grief. He tightened his grip on the sword and took another step forward. "You killed them and lied to me." The mentor who had been at his side for years. Another step. The oathknights around

Domarik started to edge closer. Syl looked at the blade, at the gauntlet on his arm, shaking with anger. His friend. "You made me do the same fucking thing!"

"Wait!" pleaded Liora, pulling at his arm. "Let them leave. This doesn't have to end in a bloodbath. Domarik, leave. Please. No one wins here. This doesn't have to end with half of us dead."

Syl could see in Domarik's eyes he knew the lie there too. *Yes, it does. It always ends in violence. The one indisputable truth of the worlds. The inescapable reason the world has to fall apart.* Perhaps there was another path here, but not for him. The silence stretched, heavy and oppressive. Fingers twitched and limbs tensed.

Syl moved first. The room exploded into violence.

Leaping forward, Syl hacked savagely at one of the oathknights that had rushed to cut him down from the side. The blade caught on something inside. *Move!* Syl grabbed the dying man and threw him into Domarik's path. Domarik didn't bother dodging, instead smashing the body aside with a brutal blow from his armored left arm, barely stumbling in his rush. He did stumble though, and Syl found that gap faster than any snake had ever struck, tackling the bigger man, too furious to even think of pausing. He thought he glimpsed Kass surging toward Morana as he grappled with Domarik. He didn't care. Syl ignored the heat and the motion all around him. There was only one thought hammering into his skull like a great nail, deeper with every blow.

*He killed them, he killed them, he killed them. HE KILLED THEM!*

The voice was shrieking, all-encompassing, echoing, driving away any other thoughts. He had Domarik's arm pinned to his side with one hand and scrabbled at his thigh for another knife with his other, but Domarik was built like a bull and just dropped his own blade, falling with him and rolling over to straddle Syl, ramming a knee into his stomach.

"Should have listened," Domarik said, calmer than could be believed within the fury of noise around them. "This is my mistake."

Syl was spitting fury, raining blows at weak spots, anywhere he could reach. It was like hitting a boulder. Ignoring the blows, Domarik wrapped his gauntlet around Syl's throat and started to squeeze with all the power granted him, traces of runes on the iron swimming in Syl's vision as the world became a bit hazier. The other hand rose and then slammed forward. The force of a mountain into his face. A flash of white. Syl's head bounced against the stone, and the world vanished for a moment. Again. Domarik took a half-second with each blow, a craftsman with an unruly piece of metal between hammer and anvil. Again. Again. Again.

Struggle. Squeeze. Suffocate. Syl bucked, snapped, and struck like an animal in a trap, with all the fury of a decade of betrayal. His awareness stuttered with every blow. Domarik deserved to die. He had lied to Syl from the beginning, taken away everything that ever meant anything to him and given him a hollow purpose instead. Syl deserved to overcome this monster in the form of a man. For once in his cursed life, he had made the right choice; he knew it with every fiber of his being.

And it seemed not to matter. Syl could feel the black creeping in at the edges. This couldn't be how it ended. Not now. He had survived creatures and Stained of every stripe, not to mention years in the legions. And now he was to die, strangled and beaten like a child after he found the truth?

He tried to capture that feeling of utter rage, of the strength that came with it, but it was gone. All that was left was the creeping, nauseating feeling that he was about to die. That his whole life had been worse than a waste. Punctuated by the blows knocking him out of his own body. Syl pulled everything he could, more than he ever had before. Among the rest of the blood spattering and leaking across his face, he could feel a warm trickle deep inside his nostrils, more inside his ears, and it felt as if his bones themselves were creaking with the strain. It wasn't enough. The strength of those bound to him leaked away, leaving his limbs a bit more deadened, a bit heavier every second. They were probably dead. He had killed them, same as half a hundred Stained before. He thought he might see flashes of his life at the end, glimpses of his daughter or wife, but all he could see was a vague, dark, bearded shape above him, crushing the life from him.

Syl's scrabbling hand hit something. A hilt. Domarik's sword. It was so close... If only he could...

It was too far, too late. He could feel the dark swallowing him, finally losing the last of his strength.

Blackness.

A gasp, and the pain of the light. Syl lurched back to consciousness, feeling the horrible-sweet sensation of dragging air into his lungs through his tortured windpipe. His eyes were almost swollen shut.

Above him, he felt as much as heard a roar. Domarik whirled, some of the weight coming off him. He could see the knife sticking out of Domarik's back. Whoever his savior was had missed the spine by an inch. Syl didn't question the source of the reprieve. With a final effort, he twisted, reaching for the blade. Fingers scrabbled at the hilt. Domarik turned back and pulled another knife, knee still on Syl's chest. He reached to stab it into the man he had grabbed.

Syl felt his hand close around the grip. He swept the borrowed edge up with every ounce of strength he had left, cleaving through Domarik's right arm, right below the elbow. Domarik continued the blow forward. Syl was dumbstruck, not understanding how he could have missed. But there was the forearm, hand wrapped around the dagger, and the rest of the arm swinging wildly into nothing.

It was Domarik's turn to be shocked, but it didn't last long. He threw the other figure to the floor and ran.

It was only then that Syl had the chance to see the rest of the chamber. He understood why Domarik had fled. The dead Stained and ironspawn were stretched out alongside oathknights and legionnaires, all in imperial black. His own, dead because of him. *What have you done?* The foreshadowing of an existential hangover wasted no time in robbing the moment of its victory. The chamber was smoking and splattered with the aftereffects of the Stained's contributions. He thought he could hear the remaining ironspawn pursuing the survivors farther up the passage.

Hunting. What he should be doing. Domarik was getting away. Syl surged to his feet, almost falling back down again. Every breath was a choking effort, and the edges of his vision were black.

The someone who had saved him now steadied him.

"Leon?"

Hesitation. A grim nod.

Syl grabbed at him for support, beyond grateful. He straightened, blood dripping from his face. He spat. A worrying amount of blood and more than a few flecks of teeth splashed out onto the floor. "Come on," he choked. "Help me finish this."

Leon looked uncomfortable in a way Syl had almost never seen him. Not since those dark days so many years ago, as he watched Syl lose his mind after the news came from the core of the empire. "Syl..."

"What? I'm fine."

"Just wait. Liora..."

His heart stopped. *No, no, no, no...* Syl pushed Leon aside, searching the chamber frantically for her. He searched the standing, the limping, the blood-spattered and bruised survivors of the fight. "Where is she?"

"Syl, I..."

He ignored Leon. There. There was a cluster of the surviving Stained, Vels kneeling in their midst. Morana on the ground. And beside her, Liora. Syl tottered over, blade gripped tight. There was nothing left to fight.

They parted for him. Vels withdrew, collar removed and in hand. It was too late. Liora almost looked like she was sleeping, eyes closed and face peaceful. The black uniform she wore was a little darker, a little wetter than it should have been. Morana was holding her hand, examining it as if it were something almost familiar, but just beyond the edge of comprehension.

"She...she saved me," Morana managed, spitting the sour words out. She looked up at Syl as if she was about to say something, mouth working her way around some new accusation or threat. In the end, she decided against it and moved aside to give him room.

Syl sank to his knees beside her. He took Liora's head in his hands, cradled it. There were no tears now. No pounding headaches. He wanted to remember every detail of that face before decay and the years stole that away from him. Again. A few drops of his blood fell from him onto her. He ran a shaking, battered hand over her face, tried to wipe away those bloody tears. He tried to see her smile too, the way her eyes could never hide what she was thinking, the blessed strangeness of that openness. Gone. Every chance for something different—it was all gone.

If only she hadn't joined the Vigil, she might never have been here. If only she hadn't had that gods-damned collar on, she might have shrugged off the wound. If he had listened to Lucky... If he had listened to her! Listened to her, when all she tried to do was tell him the truth. If he...if he wasn't who he was, she might never have been captured. If she wasn't herself, she wouldn't have had to throw her life away defending a girl that the worlds seemed so desperately to want dead. If only they had had more time, if he could have been honest with how he felt, if he had just...

Syl collapsed over her, rocking back and forth. He held her as tight as he could. Tried to take her into himself. Take away the hurt, and maybe, if he held her tight enough, take a piece of her with him forever.

If only this wasn't how it always ended.

*If only you could have loved her.*

*If only you weren't you.*

# WEAKNESS OF DOUBT

"**M**ove. Now."

Domarik, Kass, and three others barreled toward them out of the iron door and into the dark woods, where Vali and Marika had been keeping watch with a silent and sullen legion oathknight who watched them in turn. Every passing second had felt like the hangman's axe above their head.

Vali saw Domarik cradling the stump of his right arm. It was grotesque, like he had forgotten the rest of it somewhere. It had already started to coagulate, a raw red circle that started where the middle of his forearm had once begun.

"Your arm!" Marika exclaimed.

"What about Syl? Leon? Liora?" Vali asked.

They were shoved aside. "Move now if you want to live." Domarik didn't bother to see if they followed.

Vali exchanged glances with Marika. Were they dead, then? He tried to imagine any of those three dead. He had seen the way they fought; it seemed impossible. And yet, here was Domarik, a bit less than he had been when he had told them to guard this entryway with their lives.

They sprinted after Domarik and the other surviving oathknights, slipping and skidding in the snow-slick darkness. Not a single legionnaire had returned. More oathknights than he had ever seen together at once and a score of the most hardened veterans he could have imagined had gone into the ruins. Five had come back, and every single one bleeding or limping. The side of Kass's head was a matted, bloody mess, and she looked around them glassy-eyed and far more eager to leave than she had ever been to go in. She twisted suddenly, back toward the door, fear plain on her face. Vali and Marika looked with her. Had he heard...? Perhaps not; he was letting his imagination run away with him, most likely.

It came again, a faint screeching sound. Suddenly Vali was shamefully glad they hadn't gone down with Domarik. He and Marika started running after them.

That didn't mean Vali wouldn't have gone, wouldn't have tried to save them. "We can't just leave them," he protested, half to himself. Every reason that had brought him out here was falling apart. "Syl was..."

Kass heard him. "That fucking traitor is dead," she managed between breaths. She didn't stop moving down the hill. "They all are. That fucking bloodhound and that uppity bitch too. Maybe not yet, but they will be. I almost got that riftwalker myself. And you want to join them? Go! Otherwise, shut your mouth and hurry. We still might not make it out of this alive." She picked up her pace.

Vali jerked at her arm, pulling her to a stop. "Traitor? Why though? Are you saying that Syl—"

Kass turned and slammed her fist into his stomach. Vali found himself breathless and gasping on his back in the mud and snow for the second time that day.

"Don't. Touch me," she hissed. Then she straightened and gave a bitter laugh, eyes wild. "Still so, so stupid, aren't you? Because you two played at swords and Syl loved to play the gruff mentor, you think you know him? That man is addicted to tragic causes. Causes and power. They offered him a sweeter drug, that's all. Better than those boring old oaths to the empire. Go see for yourself, if you like."

Vali lay there, stunned. It was an impossibility given voice. Why... How could they even consider that? It didn't make sense. Liora had always been a bit of an unknown, Leon an unpredictable bastard, but Syl... He thought he had known Syl. Why would he take up with Stained, especially right as another Riftgate had opened?

*"Never underestimate what a man will do for power."*

His father's words made him sick. Vali knew the lengths he had already gone to for a cause, for his own chance at power. Could it really be that simple? For all his talk and superiority, was Syl just as hungry as he accused Vali of being? It fit, and fit better than he wanted it to. That was why he had pushed against their inclusion from the beginning, had turned them away at every turn, at the very doors of the fortress city, where he had gone over to join his new friends, Liora among them. Vali felt the shame and embarrassment erasing the weariness that gripped his bones. It pushed out those doubts—the ones that Syl had introduced with all his moralizing and talk of living a quiet life. It felt good. It felt vindicating.

"What do we do?" whispered Marika, uncharacteristically unsure of herself. She helped him up.

"We do what they could not," snarled Vali. "All their talk about earning the right to wield the Rift. All they ever wanted was more power. Who knows what they promised them?"

Marika looked less certain, placing a hand on Vali's shoulder. "Exactly! Who knows? Maybe it was something else? Think about it! Syl wouldn't betray them without a reason. Or Liora. Lucky and Leon, I don't know, but Leon follows Syl everywhere. This doesn't make any sense."

He shook her off savagely. "It makes perfect sense, Mari," Vali said emphatically. "And if we leave now, we prove Domarik and the rest of them right. Getacians can't be trusted. Barely citizens. We need to show them we're loyal when even their own betray their oaths. Now more than ever. Besides, Lucan needs us. We have to go back."

With that, he started after Domarik and the others. Marika could disagree; that was fine. She would follow. Vali could already hear her behind him, and those footsteps did weigh heavy on him, for all his dismissals of her concerns. He had his own doubts. It was human to doubt. But being a man meant laying aside those doubts and doing the right thing.

———◆———

They had followed him here, all the way to the end of the world. Vali knew it was ridiculous, that they were certainly not the same riders, and likely not even from the same warband, but that changed nothing. It felt like long-delayed revenge being meted out for the ambush weeks ago, watching the riders circle and harass the tattered formations as they struggled to retreat to the relative safety of the woods. This time, the sky was darker, and the swirling eddies of flakes whipped across the valley, blinding all.

Flashes of brilliant color marked the advance of Stained with the horsemen, those not satisfied with the slaughter on the plain, the pent-up vengeance and daydreams of every prisoner breaking their way out into reality. He could see the legions retreating as best they could, holding together, fighting their way backwards and making them pay for every step. Vali couldn't help but find it beautiful.

And hopeless.

They were crouched, hidden by the twilight, where the woods met in a narrow strip on the ridge that ran along the far end of the valley. Domarik was starting to shiver, but seemed not to notice, his body not as immune as his mind from the pain of his missing arm and the blood loss. He had brought them this far and now studied the situation before them. He reached a verdict.

"We can't help them," he said. "We go west, make contact with the Twins at Nordea Kerest. They are two days out, at most. Breakstone is too close, and that will be the first direction any pursuit will sweep."

Vali couldn't believe his ears. There were at least three hundred men left alive out there, loyal soldiers, fighting, bleeding, and dying because they had marched here, following orders. Even closer, and moving toward them, there was a pocket of a dozen or so that had been split from the main element. They were fighting their way to the trees on the high ground, harried by a small group of riders. They were close enough that Vali could hear the shouted orders, the gurgle as another man went down with an arrow jutting from his neck.

"We can't leave them," Vali pressed. "They're getting slaughtered out there."

"And what are you going to do? Add your corpse to the pile? We can't help them, boy. Best we can do is avenge them."

"No," Marika said. "Look, there's hardly a dozen of the riders here. We could save this squad. They're close, no Stained. If we can take them by surprise—"

"No," one of the oathknights Domarik had brought cut her off. "All you'll do is get the attention of the rest. We can't do it quickly enough." His eyes were black pits in the dark. "They're done."

Vali saw another rider dart in, spinning a net and throwing it around one of the retreating soldiers. The others continued their desperate backwards scramble, leaving the man thrashing on the ground. The tribesman vaulted off his horse with a whoop and closed in for the kill, spinning a hatchet. The rest of them were being cut to pieces.

Vali started to object again, but Domarik spoke over him, calmly, as if speaking to a child.

"If you go, you go alone. I wish you were right, boy, I really do, but sometimes the heroic choice is the stupid choice. This whole venture is done. You shouldn't have listened to Syl, but you couldn't have known. You've done your part. Both of you. Help us get back to the legions, and I'll recommend you be chosen as an oathknight to the Twins myself. But the intelligence we have is more important than those men out there, than any of us. We need to go now. Understood?"

The screams and the clash of metal were so close, Vali was sure that if they just pushed through, they could make the difference, change the tide of this little portion of the slaughter. But he couldn't do it alone, and if Marika followed him, he would be leading her to her death without Domarik and the others' help. Not to mention any hope for Lucan dying with him. There was more he could do for his friend alive, and even more alive and as an oathknight. He could make up for this a hundred times over then. He knew he would. Which made it all the harder to understand the inescapable sensation of something unspeakable burrowing its way inside him.

He found he couldn't look at Domarik. "Understood."

# ALIVE AGAIN

Whether it had been minutes or hours, Darya wasn't sure, but it was dark then. Dark and cold, the wind whipping the snow that fell into little flurries, stinging her face. She had moved away as far as she could from the fighting, but she was still surrounded by the dead and dying. Propped up against a dead horse, slipping in and out of consciousness, she thought she might be dying too. What a joke that would be. All that effort for nothing. But she held on. There was still so much she had left to do.

Snorting through the pain, she saw torches moving in the field, little stars in the blackness. One loomed out of the dark, blinding her, and voices shouted. Suddenly, she was surrounded. There was a struggle, and someone shouldered their way into the center. Alina. Thank the Sun above. She was alive. Darya gave a weak smile and tried to sit up, but sat back, groaning.

"Kasym?"

"He's fine. Better than you. By the dead, look at you. Hold still, hold still. Let me see." Alina worried over her, surprisingly tender, before looking back and holding her eyes for what seemed like forever. "I thought I'd lost you," she said, pressing her forehead to Darya's and breathing deep.

Darya swallowed and tried to compose herself. "Almost got lost," she managed. "But you came for me. Again."

Alina gave a laugh that was half a sob and held her head between her hands, gently kissing her forehead. "Always." She seemed to remember the torches around them and regained some of her composure, gruff voice returning. "Now let's get you up. Enough lying about."

Together with a few of the others, she hauled Darya to her feet. Her blood rushed to her head, and she almost fell right back down, sagging into Alina. She felt frozen through, like a wet coat left outside, liable to break before bending. She breathed through the pain, trying not to scream.

Standing with her good arm around Alina hurt, but it was better than the alternative.

Kasym arrived, concern across his face.

"Are they gone?" Darya asked.

"Mostly. We have riders harassing their retreat."

"But Taharuk is dead," Alina added.

"I know," Darya said. "I saw."

"Kursagai too," Kasym added, face flickering in the torchlight.

Darya felt like that should have been satisfying, but it just felt like a waste. Surely there was room enough for them south of those mountains?

Maybe not.

Maybe there wasn't, and for these soldiers, it was a choice between killing her people, or seeing their own go hungry when the Tribes came south like a swarm of locusts.

Really, no choice at all.

# ROCK IN A RIVER

They looked at her differently now. All of them. With wariness, certainly. Fear too, maybe, but perhaps that was her own nervousness reflected. Except for Serik. She'd have thought they had named him Arkhan, considering how pleased he was with himself. Strutting about the edge of the battlefield where they had set up camp in uneasy proximity to their new allies. Giving orders to the confused remnants of Taharuk and Kursagai's men. The sun itself did homage, piercing through the clouds to set the fringes of his clothing afire and lend him a golden halo.

Now Darya stood in the middle of the camp, that place where the three chieftains used to argue and joke and jockey for position. It felt a little emptier, a little quieter, truth be told, without Taharuk's booming voice berating someone or other, and Kursagai's furious scowling at any and all who came too close. Now it was only Serik across from her, pleased as could be, and a few friends that he had made among the remnants of the other tribes. Maybe he had made them the same offers he had made her? Darya wouldn't have put it past him.

At least she wasn't alone. Alina and Kasym were at her sides, not completely immune from enjoying this reversal. From outcasts to leaders. Close enough to the top to stand here, at least. And part of being a leader surely had to be being grateful for any progress, however small. She wished Mikael could have seen it.

And yet, Darya felt less safe than ever. Close enough wasn't all that close, after all. Serik and the others talked as if she weren't there, already making plans, dispatching some of Serik's men to send news to Janbek and the Arkhan. Others to scout the surrounding lands, the first soft step toward the inevitable divvying up of this province among the Tribes. The Getacians and Stained were mentioned only in passing, a storm far on the horizon. She wondered if their new allies could see that storm too.

Darya looked down to watch the small flame dance from finger to finger on her free hand. She was getting better. But not better enough, and not nearly fast enough. Her arm in a sling and the widespread, throbbing, and generally inescapable bodily pain were both reminders of the costs of not learning fast enough. Darya wanted to meet that old Stained from earlier. Maybe he could teach her something, some measure of how to harness that power, to control when and how it came. Hell, if he knew anything at all, he could teach her something. She realized she was distracted again, seconds passing into minutes staring into the flame. When she looked back up, some of those around Serik were considerably more reserved, with a definite pale shade to some.

Not Serik though.

"News?" he asked.

One of them spoke up. "Our men chased them as far as they could. There are still some pursuing them. No word back yet."

"Darya? What do our new friends say?"

"Their scouts report a much larger force marching toward us," she reported, passing along what Ardelan, the Getacian officer, had told her earlier. "At least two full legions." Far less safe than ever.

"How far away?"

"They said it depends. The majority of them were at some big city nearby, apparently. They may stop in some of the towns on the way. Less than a week if they keep on."

Serik chuckled. "They are going to be furious. And what do our friends want to do?"

"They said we should push farther back into the fortress city. They have supplies cached. But the Getacians want to fight here."

"Of course they do." Serik shared a look with one of his own new friends. Apparently, Darya wasn't part of this new inner circle. Plans were already being made. "What about Vels? What does he say?"

*"How should I know?"* was what she wanted to say. But she knew what he meant, even if he, along with everyone else, overstated the extent of their relationship. "I don't know. Probably whatever the Stained do, he's either suggested or agreed with already. They seem to listen to him." "That sounds familiar."

She nodded. What did he want her to say?

Enjoying her discomfort, Serik waved for the others to be about their tasks. Once they left, he clapped a hand to Darya's bad shoulder, making her wince. She was healing faster now, there was no doubt about it. But she still felt as if she had been chewed up and spat out, and maybe stomped on a bit for good measure. "Cheer up, you. This couldn't have gone better. Both of them gone, and all it cost us was half their men." He grimaced. "And mine. But I told you it was smart to take my side, didn't I?"

Darya nodded again. She was better now at understanding what people like him really meant. All this "conversation" required was acknowledgement on her side. She wanted to ask if it had been him that convinced Altan to try to kill her. But it hadn't mattered then, and it mattered even less now.

"As for Vels, and the Stained, and all those locals, they trust us now."

"As they should?"

"Of course, of course. And you'll make sure it stays that way, won't you?" Another nod. "Good girl. I think we'll get along well." He slapped her shoulder again, harder this time, and squeezed, fingers digging deep. "We'd better."

Striding jauntily away, he started to make a beeline for the point where Duras and the other leaders had convened, confident enough in his position to dispense with any illusion of Darya's role. She had no illusions either. Serik never meant to share power. Just a place closer to the top. A bit safer, in return for support. No one ever gave something for nothing.

Alina and Kasym came closer now, eyeing him with contempt.

"Snake," Kasym said, as idly as if he were naming something he saw under the leaves.

"Yes."

"We should kill him now. Right fucking now, Darya," Alina pressed. "That bastard wants a leash around your neck, and he'll hang you by it when he gets the chance. Don't wait."

"We can't," Darya said. And they couldn't. Did Alina not see that? Kill Serik now, and one of his inner circle took his place, and they were right where they had been before. Too powerful to be unnoticed, and too dangerous to be left alone.

"Darya," Kasym said, staring after Serik, "Alina's right."

She was too tired for this. "Trust me, please. It won't work."

Her friends—and they were her friends, the only ones she had left—stared at her for a long moment. Finally, they relaxed.

"Fine," Alina said. "Doesn't mean we have to do this the stupid way." She gestured to the little groups of outcasts that had started to gather wherever Darya happened to be, a following that both she and they seemed reluctant to acknowledge. "I'll get this bunch organized, or at least as much as I can. And you should talk to the ones who can do...well, whatever it is that you can do. There are more than we know, I think."

"And we should gather what we can from the dead," Kasym added. "I'll get a group on it." He surveyed the ruin of the battlefield to their south, and then the barricaded entrances to the tunnels of the fortress city. He shivered. "Can't say I'm looking forward to being back underground. Between Vels, those ironspawn, and our allies, this ought to be interesting." He seemed in good spirits. Unwounded, he was enjoying his new position immensely and was taking to it quickly. "And as for Serik?" He made a rude gesture. "Get him scared again. We'll think of something. It's not over, but we aren't dead yet either."

"I'll go talk to Duras."

"Do that. Don't let Serik be the only one there. I'll help organize this rabble out here. And don't leave without me!" Kasym called behind him as he started toward the churned field.

In the light of the morning, the whole ordeal seemed a distant memory, the frozen carcasses a macabre monument to a shared nightmare.

"He's right, you know," Alina put in.

"About what?"

"That it's not over. Serik, those puppets he's found among the other tribes? None of them are keen on having to listen to a newcomer, especially a woman." She grinned proudly at Darya. "Even if that woman could turn them into ash."

Darya grinned back, but it felt forced. It faded.

"You're right, but I don't know what to do."

"Well, that's the whole thing, isn't it?"

"Hmmm?"

"Being a leader? It's not knowing, but pretending that you do. That way, everyone else can feel like they are heading in a direction. Doesn't even have to be the right direction. Besides, if someone tells you they've got it all figured out, they are either full of it or have no imagination. None of us know. We figure it out, choice by shitty choice. And that's fine."

"That seems...pessimistic?"

Alina shrugged. "Well, then *you* figure it out. Just try to make the right choices for the right reasons." Her eyebrows suddenly came together as she glanced over Darya's shoulder. "Maybe ask him. If he'll give you a straight answer. I'm off."

And suddenly, Darya was alone. Alone with Vels, but that was essentially the same thing. He was all smiles today, face crinkled with pride. Uncovered now, the skin was graying, scarred, and nearly dead-looking, but those green eyes were lively as ever.

"Darya, my dear Darya! It warms my heart to see you so ascended. Truly."

"Vels."

"I don't mind the cold reception, really, I don't. But I want to say I knew you had it in you."

"Then why didn't you help?"

"No, Darya. There are some things you have to do yourself. Besides, I feel like I've saved you often enough for a while. It's not as if I have nothing else to do. So many moving parts right now. Even if they are all heading in the right direction, sometimes they do need a bit of a nudge. And if you're too concerned with the details, you can never pull your head up to see the big picture. Would you like another piece of advice?"

Darya stared at him.

"Well, I'll give it anyway. A privilege that comes with age. Know your strengths. I wasn't made for battlefields. That's not where my gifts lie. I tie people together. I provide a nudge here, a whisper there, and the right word when it is needed. You can accomplish so much more in the grand scheme of things if you can provide people with a vision of the future than you ever could with brute force. Violence is the first and last resort of the unimaginative. Not to say it isn't quite useful occasionally."

Darya knew then with an exhausted certainty that nothing that had happened on that mud-churned battlefield with Taharuk was a secret to him—that it was as clear to him as the flashes of memory that ran through her head now, twisting her gut. There was a hint of teeth flashing under a lip drawn back in amusement. It was all the more disconcerting now that she could actually see the face under all those bandages.

"Do you know your strengths, Darya? Surely you are coming to understand them a bit more."

"I can call fire?"

"Pfah. Not what I mean. You have incredible potential there, I'll grant you that. But an ox is strong too, and yet it is not the one with the whip."

"What do you want from me, then? Or is that it? A yoke?" Darya was too tired to be nervous around him, to dance around her questions any longer.

"No! I want nothing from you, Darya. Nothing given, nothing taken. Well, something given for certain. I've saved you twice now, so at least try and pretend you can trust me. I can't begrudge you your suspicion though, dear, because it's a lesson you've had to learn the hard way. But no, no yoke, at least not from me. And so hostile today! Enjoy the moment. You've won. We've won. At least for a little while, but then again, no victory is forever."

"You've always taken an interest though, Vels. Why? Even back before Mikael died, you took an interest."

"True, but I've explained this before. You have incredible potential. It is difficult to explain, so I won't."

"Try?"

"Hmmm..." He eyed her. "You're lucky I'm fond of you, dear. Very well. Think of the worlds..."

"You really aren't from here, are you?"

"Obviously not."

"Where are you from? What are the Fallen?"

"Are you going to let me answer or not?"

Darya fell silent.

"Thank you. Think of the worlds existing within a river. All peoples, all events, everything, moving from a definite beginning to a definite end. Yet the course can be changed a little, a new branch created, a new path forged, a current slowed, but only at certain points. Some individuals are those rocks tumbling in the river, the accumulated obstacles that can change the flow, even if only a little. They warp the world as they pass through, shifting the paths that would usually be so easy to see, from beginning to end. Individuals like that introduce uncertainty. Chaos embodied."

"I'm chaos embodied?" Darya scratched at her filthy, mostly burned-away hair. It itched. She didn't feel particularly chaotic. Did confused count?

"More of an above-average-sized rock. Really, don't take any of that quite so literally. I'm being dramatic and metaphorical, a poor combination at the best of times. Besides, chaos can be a very good thing, child, when the order you see around you is a collar on your neck. If you're drowning in the river—if you'll forgive me another metaphor—it can be the only way out. And when you have as much reason to hate that fledging little empire to the south as I do, it warms my cold, dead heart to see us pointed in the same direction. I've been fighting them for longer than you can imagine."

Darya waited for him to continue, losing patience. "Are you going to explain yourself any more than that?"

A pause. "No, I don't think I will." He grinned.

For some reason, today of all days, she couldn't stand him. His cryptic answers, his sly smiles, his absurd mannerisms, his entire demeanor of knowing more than anyone else and refusing to share any of it. Rivers and rocks and all his insufferable cleverness—they could all go freeze in hell. Vels had saved her, and saved her twice, that was true. But today it was too much.

"I need to talk to Duras," she said stiffly, turning away and starting toward where the Stained were gathered.

"I'll come," he said, smoothly falling in beside her and ignoring her glare. "He's an old friend, you know?"

She didn't know, but didn't bother asking how or when. Darya knew she had been lucky to get as much as she had out of him today. Vels was looking across at the battleground anyway.

"A waste," he said, sighing.

Darya ignored him, but she couldn't help but look over at the battlefield again herself. It *was* a waste. Armor and horses and spears sticking up at odd angles, with a mass of birds wheeling and landing, a feast day from hell itself. Those birds wouldn't be going hungry this winter. They would have to do this all again soon, no doubt. It would be some time until the Arkhan received word and the great warbands could make the long trek here. If they came at all. Her breath smoked out in front of her as she turned away. At least it was too cold for flies.

They approached Duras and the other leaders of the Stained at the top of one of the low hills covering the ruins beneath. Former prisoners, she reminded herself, worse off than she had been. There was a disheveled group of them, gathered around a few of their own, laid on stones. Saying goodbye. It seemed strange to her. The dead were gone. Those bodies weren't them, and any love given to them was wasted here. She hadn't bothered finding Mikael's body after his execution, because Mikael was gone. That little spark that made him who he was—a leader, her brother, everything he was and everything he could have been—had leaked out somewhere between the first and the last cut. All that was left was meat and bone.

Here they hewed to different customs, and Darya wished she could feel what they felt. She saw it on their faces and felt a hunger to understand that. It seemed human. Right. In a way that she knew their life on the windswept steppes wasn't. In a world where survival was first, second, and third consideration, there was so little room for ritual or sentiment. Did that make her less human than these? Unconsciously, she rubbed at her fingers, pinching the gaps between, where the gloves were too frayed. She felt alive. Felt pain. Hunger. Jealousy. Fear. Wasn't that the same thing?

"And with these words, we send you to that which is greater, the Rift of the worlds, which encompasses all, so that one day we might all return to the same. Goodbye, my brothers. Goodbye, my sisters."

Duras finished his benediction and nodded to the Stained from the estate. With a gesture, the bodies in the circle burst into flames. They watched in silence until—too quick, it seemed—there was nothing left. Darya listened, thinking maybe she could hear the dead, or maybe her brother. There was a Riftgate here, after all, so maybe he could speak from the other side of that wall. She thought she might have heard something, a steady whisper, but it wasn't her brother. As the fires burned down to ash, already blowing away on the wind, Darya moved closer. There were muted conversations, but the group quickly split up, most heading in their own directions, with their own instructions.

Duras turned to Darya and Vels.

"So, you survived," he said to Darya.

"Everyone seems so surprised by that."

He laughed, not put out in the least. He leaned in like he was about to share a secret. "Well, take it from one who knows. The more people who want you dead, the more impressive surviving each day is."

"The legions coming this way?" she asked, cutting to the real matter at hand. She had heard enough advice from old men for one day. For a lifetime, maybe. "I don't suppose you have any tricks up your sleeve for them?"

"No tricks. We can hold them here. Not that it will be easy. But with our knowledge of the tunnels, the ironspawn...it is more than possible.""The colonel. The Getacians?"

"We have come to a decision. Some will stay here and help us fight. Their heavier units. Most will be spread across the province though. Guerilla tactics will bleed the enemy dry and cut their supply lines. They will pour their strength over the mountains before the passes close, thinking to crush us with a decisive blow. They suspect a trap, but they are arrogant enough to think they can punch through. The legions will starve this winter."

Darya reserved judgment. It seemed a solid plan, but the accusation of arrogance could cut both ways, especially considering the devastation on the field behind her. "And our alliance?"

"Is secure. That Serik fellow came by earlier with the same question. You can tell your Arkhan we will fight with him."

"Not the alliance I meant."

Vels chuckled darkly, but his eyes were as proud as any father's.

Duras nodded thoughtfully. "Secure as well. We will work through you. We can discuss more tonight. Does that suit?"

"It does." It was all working out too well, but maybe that was what things felt like when suddenly you found yourself on solid ground after treading water all night. "And how do you two know each other?"

Duras seemed caught off guard by the question, though Vels was barely paying attention. "Vels helped us break out, along with the colonel. He...he warned us that a Riftgate was about to emerge here." He looked at the man in question. "And he told me to watch for riders from the East."

"It's true. What can I say? I'm a people person. I make connections. Speaking of..." Vels stared down the hill meaningfully, where two imperial soldiers were making their way up, people as out of place as it was possible to be. Those they passed gave them a wide, hostile berth.

"Who are they?" asked Darya.

They were lean, hard-looking sorts, both wearing an approximation of a black uniform. Well-worn leather and steel armor covered most of them, along with heavy-looking gauntlets on their left forearms. Long hilts poked above their shoulders, and Darya could see at least a half dozen other knives and weapons between the two of them. Two men, and she didn't like the look of either of them—bronze skins from the South, and cruel, darting eyes. The taller one's face looked as if he had used it to break down a wall, most of it purple and red, one eye swollen shut. As they came closer, she noticed the traces of black inscriptions on their skin, peeking out from beneath collars and sleeves. She could see the delicate runes worked onto the gauntlets, relics from another age. Oathknights. Darya felt a stab of panic and a throb in her still-healing arm. She darted a look sideways. Neither Vels nor Duras seemed surprised, so she kept her peace and studied them with nervous curiosity.

"New friends," was all Vels said. "You'll like them."

# HOPING FOR HATE

"**A**re you alright?"

From a trance, Syl looked up at Leon from where he crouched over one of the casualties on the battlefield. They had been checking for survivors all morning. There were none. What blades and fire had missed, the cold, blood loss, and looting tribesmen had taken care of. And if they had found anyone, what would they have told them?

*"Would you also like to betray every oath you've ever taken?"*

No, better dead.

"I'm fine."

It was a lie. It was like one of his dreams, only worse. A waking nightmare that there was no escaping. Today, a few Stained were his guides, or maybe gaolers, in the haze of the aftermath of yesterday. They stood at a distance and watched as Syl and Leon wandered the battlefield, making sure none of the others about took the survival of two imperial soldiers as an affront and a problem to be solved.

There should have been three of them.

One of them, the one who deserved life the most, was cold and stiff and buried. Syl had buried her this morning. Vels had offered to find someone who could have parted the earth for him, made the effort a matter of minutes. Syl had refused, and had left with her in his arms, Leon following. A few had shadowed them then too, but they had kept their distance.

The ground had been too hard, and Syl had knelt beside her, bloody and exhausted, and wondering how he had managed to fail her in death as well as in life. He had started to gather stones for a cairn when Lucky appeared, skittish and eyes downcast. Without a word, he had left a pick and a shovel. It had taken the rest of the night. The earth was frozen and unyielding, unwilling to find space for yet another. Leon had made a fire and kept watch while Syl tried to lose himself in the work.

When the first rays of light had pierced the horizon, Syl realized he had dug far deeper than he had needed to. There was no more putting off the inevitable. With Leon's help, he had lowered her gently into her resting place. At least there was a body this time. Something to bury. Perhaps that only made it harder though. They had stood over the grave for a long time, silent. Syl had found that he couldn't bring himself to pile the dirt back in. It had seemed, even more than death itself, a point of no return. An admittance that Liora was gone, and gone forever.

Once he started though, it only took a few minutes to fill it.

The stones he had piled atop her grave seemed a poor monument. A pile of rocks and a hole in the ground. What would have been enough? How could you possibly ever show someone what they meant to you once they were gone? Syl had tried with Livia and Elena, had paid everything he had for a fine headstone to be placed in the village graveyard. He had never even seen it. They weren't there, even more than Liora wasn't here.

Leon's voice brought him back.

"We should go."

Syl nodded numbly and stood. The exhaustion was in his bones now, and his face was an aching mass. He wasn't healing, not like he should be. Syl suspected he had killed most if not all of those bound to him in his frenzy to overcome Domarik. It was a mercy. As soon as word reached the capital, they would enter the Sanctum Numinary and kill any who had survived, along with Leon's own conduits. Severing a rotten limb. Syl tried not to think of how many he had failed yesterday and let himself be led away from the field. "You saved me," he said finally.

Leon looked back, confused. "What?"

"Yesterday. With Domarik. He was about to kill me, and you saved me."

"I suppose I did. You ought to be thanking me."

Syl ignored that. "Then you believed what...what Liora said? What Vels said?"

"What...oh, sure. I mean, maybe? Doesn't really matter."

"What do you mean, 'it doesn't matter'?"

"Well, you were on this side once they told you. And if he lied to you, then fuck him."

"So, just like that?"

"Just like that." Leon laughed at Syl's expression. "What? Like I said..."
He closed one eye and mimed drawing a straight line with a finger. "...
consistent." He looked around, with something that Syl would have called
nervousness on anyone else leaking into his expression. "Though, I will say,
I can't say who makes me feel more unwelcome—these fellows from out
east, or the Stained."

"We need to speak to Vels," Syl said, trying to focus on what needed to be
done. "The Twins are guaranteed to be here soon. I'm sure Domarik went
straight to them." Even speaking his name made Syl nearly sick with rage.
The broad vengeance that had driven him before was nothing compared
to this. That had been on principle and lacked specificity. He would... He
could barely conceptualize how he could bring this sort of hate into the
limitations of reality. He would start by tearing Domarik apart.

"Gods know what the Gets think about all this. Shame. I was starting to
like those kids."

"He'll have lied to them, same as he did with us," Syl spat.

The anger was a distraction, he knew, but he held onto it. It felt like
solid ground. He glared up to the top of the hill to where a small group
waited for them. Two men and a woman. Drawing near, Vels, with his
shifty, corpse-gray face, was the only one he recognized. The other man was
older, with a big frame that didn't have quite enough meat on it. One of
the former prisoners, no doubt, wearing spectacles, a mix of stolen clothing
keeping him warm now. The neck made it an easy mark, those scars from
years of wearing a collar that someone like Syl would have put there.

The girl stood out. With pale skin, wrapped in the chaotic furs and rags
of the rest of the riders, she was slight and far younger than he expected
to see at such a meeting. It looked like she had been through even more
than Syl in the past day, left arm in a sling, bruises purpling one side of her
face, and hair a burned fringe. It was her eyes that were arresting though.
Blue as ice, they weighed each of them in turn, suspicious and giving away
nothing. Here was one who had learned more than a few lessons the hard
way.

"We will be withdrawing farther into Bal Maru," Vels said once they were
close. "It would be an awful idea to stand against the full strength of the
legions in the open, so we will draw them further from their strength."

Syl approved. It's what he would have recommended. Fighting two
legions along with the Twins in an open battle would be suicide. Better

to pull them into the wilds and the deep tunnels and pick away at them. He could feel the bile rise in the back of his throat as he thought about what that entailed. Domarik had betrayed him, but it still sickened him, thinking of killing men he once might have fought beside. And that was to say nothing of the betrayal of every principle that had kept him tied to the Vigil and its mission.

"And then?" Leon asked.

Vels indicated the girl beside him. "Darya here has some friends. The Thousand Tribes move west."

Leon sucked at his teeth. "Given up on the Gates, have they?"

Darya shrugged. "A better way."

Syl stared hard at her, Lucky's words echoing back at him from this slip of a girl. He wondered how she came to speak for the grizzled savages he saw down there looting the bodies. And why, among all the other bruises and cuts, there were the unmistakable signs of a collar recently placed and even more recently removed. Questions for another time.

"We will need your help, of course," the older man added. "If you're willing. Plans to be made, traps to be laid, all of that. If you come with me, we can get to work."

The looks of distrust in that circle were palpable, but it wasn't as if anyone there had many options. Allies of necessity all. One by one, they fell into step and climbed toward the estate above them. It didn't take them long to reach the top.

Syl turned around to see Vels waiting off to the side, at a point overlooking the ruined valley and the abandoned excavation pits. With a gesture to Leon, Syl broke off and approached. He could join their planning later. He had questions first.

"Why do you need to get to the Riftgate?" Syl asked bluntly.

"Do you think your Emperor is the only one who can use those gates? That it is some sort of divine privilege that allows Him to come and go? No, the window is open for a brief time, and they are sent to take advantage of it. I simply wish to do the same. I've told you before, the world doesn't have to fall apart."

Syl's eyes narrowed. "Yes, you said, but you didn't fucking explain. And sent? Sent by whom?"

"It amazes me what is forgotten and what is remembered," he sighed. "They are the representatives of a much larger empire, older and more powerful than I think you can even conceptualize."

"They are sent by the gods," Syl interrupted, uncomfortable. "What are you saying?"

"What I'm saying is that you're not necessarily wrong, but what is a pantheon but an empire of the heavens? As far as your people's fatalistic obsession with the assumption of guilt and the cosmic justice that goes with it...it would be funny if it weren't quite so sad."

"That's a lot of talk to say not much at all. What does that make you? What Domarik said? One of the...one of the Fallen?" Even now, it felt surreal to talk of these events, these terms so casually. Wrong.

"See, they've captured your very language for the worlds. I am simply one who believes that it is beyond time for a new order, away from this infinite subjugation. A turning of the wheel toward balance, if you will. Besides, Syl, every empire needs its opposition." Vels cocked his head, examining him. "And where better to find such opposition than among those who were once its greatest champions? I think to truly hate something, you had to have loved it first."

Syl could understand that. "Then why do you care about me? Why did Lucky say you wanted me?"

"Let's say I'm someone who is interested in your potential. And you have more reasons to hate your empire than you ever knew. You only needed a push to see it."

Syl massaged his temples. "What potential? Give a straight answer for once."

"Oh, I've been far more open with you than I think you realize. Sometimes the more obvious something is, the more we fabricate alternate explanations in our minds, or distract ourselves from what is right in front of us. Do you really think your child's talent came out of nowhere?"

"But then...then what's wrong with me?"

"I thought we covered this. Nothing. It is a gift, and one that is beyond natural. Yours is just a bit unusual, and as soon as Lucky reported what he believed you were capable of..."

"Lucky? He can tell?"

"Gods before, at least try to keep up, Syl. Add that lie to your list of grievances against him. He really is a brave young man. I can't imagine what it must have been like among all you killers. And honestly, you should be thanking him. He spoke highly of you. We would have tried to kill you if he thought you couldn't be made to see the truth. Your sort of gift cannot fall into the wrong hands."

"Gods damn it! What gift?"

"Ah, and there's that temper he mentioned. Have you never wondered why you are afflicted by such pain?" Vels tapped the side of his head. "The timing of those headaches? You've done your best to ignore them, to push them aside with ritual and habit, but you can't ever get rid of it. I suspect there is some little splinter of a volseer wedged in that wreck you call a mind."

"That sort of thing is only rumored." Syl barked a bitter laugh. "And if anyone *can't* see the future, it's me. That's the one thing I can prophecy for free."

"No, of course not. Nothing so straightforward as that. And where in all the worlds do you think rumors come from? It is real, but also so rare as to be extremely poorly understood. And like all the blessings that you all try to fit into neat categories, it is expressed in infinite possible variations—prophets and seers and madmen and so on. All to say that even I don't entirely comprehend it. But I do love metaphors, so let us return to my favorite. Imagine all the worlds existing in a river." He stopped. "I really should explain these things to both of you at once, it would save me time."

Syl waited.

Vels sighed. "Anyway. River. Definite beginning, definite end."

"Definite?"

"Don't interrupt. Yes, definite. Definite, but with a course toward that end that can be changed, even if only by degrees. Little obstacles thrown up, and stones thrown in. Most of our lives, we go through following the course of that river, the choices of the day-to-day an illusion within that current. Occasionally though, and more for some than others, we have real choices. Choices that echo and ripple in the current, sometimes for a little, and sometimes changing things all the way to the end of that river when it pours back into the sea. For those touched by fate or chance or choice—like yourself, maybe—there exists the *possibility* of seeing some measure of those echoes. The ripples of what could have been or what will follow. The greater the change, the easier to see. Or so they say."

Syl didn't bother fighting this accusation. Not believing it didn't change its consequences. "Is that why they killed my daughter? Could she do what you say I can?"

"Possibly. Did you never suspect? Never notice anything odd when you were home?"

Syl looked away. "I didn't," he said finally.

*Hard to notice anything when you're never there, isn't it?*

*So it is, so it is.*

Syl pushed those truths down with the voices. Vels watched him carefully, waiting. Like he could hear them too. But Syl knew better than to give him anything more, even if he had known what to ask. Instead, he looked at the mass of humanity below them, stripping the dead and preparing to leave. He had helped to put people here, or at least in places like this. Killed them when he had to, collared them when he could, calling it a mercy. Looking down to where the famine-thin survivors of the camp toiled, he wasn't sure if *mercy* was the right word.

"So, what now?"

"Yes, that's the question, isn't it? Fortunately, your empire has grown complacent. After so many predicable cycles, they never imagined the emergence of a second Riftgate so quickly. I do take some humble credit for that. For now, there is a chance to turn the tide here. Too many peoples thrown away or kept at bay here and elsewhere, at the cold edge of empire. You might not see it, but there are allies in every direction. We start here and push south."

All of a sudden, it was too much. Another mission, another campaign, another lifetime spent fighting. Another grand cause. Syl reached for the anger, the hate that pushed him, but it was far away now, as confused as he was with revelation after revelation. The foundations of his life were gone, and it all paled in comparison to finding himself, once again, grieving and on the path of revenge. He was so, so tired.

"If I have this gift, why can't...why can't I ever save anyone? Why did Liora have to die?"

"It hardly works like that. And even if it could have, you are so far from understanding, much less using any abilities you might have like that. It's in the past now, and the river flows on."

"I don't want to hear about your fucking river," he snarled. "She's gone. Like she never was. Why should someone like me live while she dies?"

"Sometimes..." Vels paused. Those shifting green eyes took on a mournful quality, perhaps remembering something in the far past. "Sometimes I think we only get as long as we're needed."

"That means less than nothing."

"As do most simple truths. I mean that for all I say about shifting the course of the river, it still has one end. We only get as much time as we need to be who we need to be within those currents, and not a second more. Fighting against that only causes all sorts of problems. Your Liora, she was an ordinary woman. No, no, I met her," Vels continued, waving away Syl's objection. "It's true, and it's not an indictment. A flawed, perfectly imperfect person. But she touched you before she left, that's clear to see. She saved Morana too, and more than once. Stepped between her and death yesterday, and sacrificed her life so that another could live. Maybe that was enough. It was far more than many can hope for."

Syl couldn't look at him. This stranger was the last person he wanted to see his weakness, but he was hungry for more. For anything. "Then how am *I* supposed to just go on? Again..." He trailed off. "When will I know I'm who I need to be?" he asked at last.

Vels looked at him with a look sad and sly all at once. "Oh, given your starting point, I suspect that will be quite some time. I was set on my path long ago, and I'm still figuring that out for myself. In the meantime, we can focus on what those like ourselves know."

Syl was silent. There was only one answer. "War?"

"Yes, Syl. War. War and wrath and bitter justice."

"What about her touch?" Syl shifted, uncomfortable. "I'm not sure that's what she would have wanted."

Vels shrugged. "Perhaps, perhaps not. The worlds spin upon paths long since preordained. The path is before us, whether we know it or not, and the true choices on it few and far between. Their touch will matter then. Fate finds us all in the end, after all."

# INTO THE LIGHT

It wasn't their fight anymore. At least for now. Or so Domarik told Vali and Marika. Vali wondered how there could possibly be a fight left by the time they returned. He could still picture their rendezvous with the Twins' legions. The strength there was staggering. The cohorts stretched as far as he could see ahead of them, banners limp and heavy in the winter air. A cloud of steam over the thousands of soldiers, heads down, but moving with a purpose. They had already started the march toward Bal Maru, and the warning Domarik carried was redundant. Someone had reached them first.

Vali's first thought at reaching those massive formations had been relief. They had made it. They were safe. That hadn't lasted long. The outriders that found them pushed them toward the center of the column, where the command and their staff were a bustling hive of activity, even on the march. It had been then that Vali realized they weren't being shepherded toward safety. They were being corralled for judgment.

The commanders were bad enough. Domarik, that massive killer, had been meek as a lamb in front of those brutal men, faces that could have been carved from granite for all the mercy they held. His severed arm brought no pity; it was nothing but another indictment on his failure. Those commanders in turn were the embodiment of gentleness compared to the Twins. They had asked questions, at least. Had brusquely and effectively beat any information of value out of the Hunter Primary with pointed inquiries and heavy skepticism. The Twins were different. Vali had never seen any of the Chosen up close and wasn't sure he wanted to again. Certainly not anywhere other than on his side. For once, he was happy to have them ignore him. Getacians were not worthy of notice, maybe, but also not worth blaming. Domarik wasn't so lucky.

One of the Twins—Man? Woman? Impossible to tell with the disconcerting masks they wore—circled around Domarik while the other stared at him, like a hawk might watch a mouse trying to hide through inaction. They hadn't bothered to dismount and were dressed in close-fitting scaled plate that seemed more skin than armor, gleaming golds and whites everywhere. An otherworldly light leaked from the cracks in that armor, as if their mundane human forms could not bear the enormity of the divine contained within. Light, perfection, and grace embodied.

Everywhere but for their eyes. Dark as jet and as understanding as stone. They seemed to peer into Domarik's soul, and when that masked face flicked to Vali, he was shamed by the shiver that ran through him. The one behind Domarik leaned down to whisper something in his ear, before a flick of his fingers set the whole legion moving again like the sound of the earth groaning, priests and soldiers and giants all beating that ceaseless rhythm with their feet and churning the gray, snowy slop into something resembling a tilled field. A judiciar that had been summoned spoke to Domarik then, privately, and any blood that had been left drained away. It was a shell of a man that led them away from the formation.

They moved slowly at first, especially with having to stop by Breakstone to gather up a still-healing Lucan. Reaching the main imperial supply lines had sped things up considerably. The northern districts were overrun with signs of the legions' advance. Vast areas of land were flattened, as if some massive herd had slept there and moved on. Supply depots, wagon trains, and a steady stream of men and matériel choking every main road. And not all of it going north; shipment after shipment of grain and prisoners from penal colonies that hadn't fallen were being shuttled south. Seven Rivers had been busier than the provincial capital. Its population had likely doubled.

They didn't bother stopping long. Apparently, the new prefect ruled the city like a military camp, which wasn't far off from the reality of the city at this point. They crossed the mountains, shadowed by clouds of remembered violence the whole time, chased by snow flurries until they were back among the rolling farmlands of Southern Getacia. Back in Rasovus, yet more soldiers were marshalling, preparing to march north.

*Solemn* was the word. Theirs was a solemn group on that long march home. No smiles on the road, no training with Syl around the campfires, no vile jokes from Leon. Kass was bitter and withdrawn, which suited Vali.

Domarik barely spoke. Vali, Marika, and Lucan would whisper among themselves at their own fire, but they mostly kept quiet too, reluctant to break the silence. They would travel for as far as they could before the sun failed, sleep, and do it all again the next day. Ride, walk, eat, sleep, repeat. The lands and cities of the central empire, the endless miles of interlocking outer fortifications of the First Redoubt—it all passed by in a blur, until the capital had loomed before them, the shining, beautiful twin of Bal Maru. Heliopolis. It hadn't been how Vali wanted to come there. The great cannons of legend lining the ramparts, the miraculous lifts, Legio Alaris praetorians in chorusplate and flitting through the air on shining wings, twin airships circling the city, and the gleaming titans stomping around the walls... These wonders he'd dreamt of since childhood were all hollow somehow, unreal and far from where his mind was stuck.

But he was here. That was what counted. Or so Vali told himself. Domarik had been true to his word and apparently had enough authority left for that to matter: Vali was to be anointed an oathknight of the empire. Looking left and right, Vali tried to be proud of where he was. He was, truly. It still felt bittersweet. Even knowing all he had given up for this, it somehow felt undeserved. Wrong. Vali tried to focus on what was right.

The chapel was awe-inspiring, ancient and close to the heart of Heliopolis. The Sanctum Numinary itself was just beyond. Black lines threaded through the stone walls, a mesmerizing not-quite pattern that radiated outward from somewhere far behind the altar at the rear of the room. The stinging wards and inscriptions that covered him now made him feel like he was a stranger in his own skin, but they were undeniably beautiful. Mesmerizing.

His friends were here and watched from the benches. Marika had become more and more withdrawn with every day they traveled south, but she smiled back at him then, and Vali tried not to notice the lines of worry. She was proud of him. Lucan was well enough to be here, though bandages swathed his face and half his body. There was apparently only so much the healers could do, and the fire seemed to have burned a new bitterness into his normally sanguine friend. But he was alive. That was what mattered. His brother, Sorin, was here as well, beaming with pride and almost unrecognizable from the last time Vali had seen him. Tall, suntanned, and well dressed, he looked the very picture of an imperial courtier. Hell, even his father had made the journey south. He was dressed as if he expected to march straight from his bench to the battlefield, or more accurately the parade field, excitedly gesturing toward Vali from among his peers.

*Another victory for him to show off. That's it.*

Vali tried to push the cynicism from his mind. That was Syl talking. Maybe Leon. Vali had worked years for this day. Sacrificed on the altars of discipline, bravery, and loyalty. Had almost died for this. So, so many times. He smiled. He was happy. Happy.

And so, with the incense streaming from the censers, the sunlight shining through the windows, and the chants heavy in the air, Vali knelt alongside six conduits, their heads shaven and bowed. He didn't know their names, tried not to look at their nervous faces. The priest said it was better that way. Their bodies were each inscribed with an equal proportion of the same oaths he felt stinging all over, little droplets of blood staining the perfectly white robe he wore, making it stick to his skin. Standing above them all was a priest, sacred and impersonal behind a ceremonial mask, and ready to connect them, to make them one. One purpose and one weapon. The scene was mirrored on his left and right, two more groups of seven, two more would-be oathknights prepared for their own ascensions. As he finished the incantations, the priest before him grabbed Vali's own shaven head with one rough hand on the stubble and leaned forward with the other to inscribe the final link on his neck, from inscription to inscription, completing the pattern.

Vali felt it then. The sensation of healing, but tenfold. The feeling of vitality, but a hundredfold. He hardly had to think it, and it came to him. It danced through him, a second heart pumping it through him. Six more hearts, beating together with his. He could see that light reflected in their veins, could feel it in his, tracing the lines of his lifeblood, filling him with the fire and righteousness of strength made manifest. There were small gasps of surprise to his left and right as conduits and oathknights alike felt the utter newness of this sensation, of being tied together.

Vali gloried in it. Bathed in it. Felt that impossibly pure energy radiate through every pore of his body. The perfection of the moment was only compounded by the knowledge that when he rose, he would rise as an oathknight, another shield for the empire, a chosen weapon of the Emperor Himself.

All the doubts washed away. Doubt was for the weak. There would be fights ahead, and darkness, and loss, but not now or here. He would forge through all of it, same as he had to this point here. He felt a splinter of the divine, a clarity of purpose, a blinding illumination. At the priest's command, he stood and took a step forward to take his final oath. He stepped forward, with the other two oathknights, heroes from the edges of the empire.

He stepped forward, into the light.

# A WAY HOME

Darya could barely see in front of her. Between the dark, the whipping wind, and the scarf she had wrapped around her head, the world was a thin slit of shifting shapes and wavering torches. Inexplicably, almost unimaginably, she had found herself before the hundreds of riders who were dismounted now, packed tight against the cold and looking up to the small rise where she stood. Well, not to her. To Serik, who stood up there, grinning, face bared in defiance of the first winds of winter, eyes watering. He faced those torches, the clumps of men and women before him. If the clump he called his own was a bit smaller than before the battle, it didn't seem to bother him. So were all the others. And up here, around him now, were any who could have been a threat, all standing literally and figuratively, a bit beneath him. Two legions on the way, hundreds of miles from the strength of the rest of the tribes... None of it mattered to Serik. Here and now, in this little world, his victory was complete.

"Brothers! Sisters! We have come far—so far together. Further than any-one else of the Thousand Tribes has dared to come," he shouted into the wind. "You braved a long, cold road and showed the empire your strength at the end. We've lost many, it's true. My brothers, Kursagai and Taharuk, among them." The wind made the tears come easy, but the sadness in his voice couldn't quite crush his smile. "I have sent riders on the long path back to tell the warlords, to tell the Sarkhanae, to tell the Arkhan. Our way forward is here. The soft lands of the empire are all around us and stretch, ready to be taken, all the way to their cursed capital. Yet," he added, warming to his role and enjoying the rapt silence, "this will not be easy. Their empire is jealous and would wipe us and our new allies away if they could. They will try again soon."

Darya stood there, wanting more than anything to feel the hate she thought she should feel. But there was nothing. Maybe a little exhaustion.

It had been a long day after the battle, nursing her wounds. A long night speaking with their new allies. And yet another long day, which Serik threatened to stretch longer with his speech. And besides, he was right. There was not a lie among those carefully selected words. This was the way forward. There was no other. The Gates were too high, too well guarded. They would smash their strength to bits against them, year after year, season after season, as the window of open passes grew smaller and smaller. Here, where their carefully planted garrisons and governors were already in turmoil, was where the chance was. With strong new allies and a Riftgate at their back.

"They will try again soon, friends. And if they find us divided, if they find us squabbling, we are dead. We will fail." He raised a fist, shaking it at the crowd. "Our only chance is to be as one tribe. A Thousand in One."

True again. These were the words she would have used in his place. Or hoped she would have. Staring out at that sea of listeners, her heart was hammering, mind separated just a little from her body. The fire in her veins washed in like the tide. It would be her turn soon.

And there, on cue, one of Serik's lackeys stepped forward. He was a weaselly-looking man, and throwing his hood back had the opposite of the intended effect.

"Taharuk died fighting. An honorable death. Our tribe, the Temir, backs Serik." He knelt and drew his short saber, planting it in the frozen earth.

A simple statement, but it was enough. Darya knew that all it took was a few to know the play ahead of time. The rest would follow the momentum. Strength of the moment.

And there it was. One of Kursagai's knelt. "The Urgamali follow." It looked like it hurt him to kneel. But there he was, kneeling.

It was catching. The minor sycophants and opportunistic allies that Serik had gathered around him began to kneel, almost a dozen altogether, calling out his name, oaths of loyalty, or nothing at all. What mattered was that they knelt. Darya understood that. Not all allies came willingly.

Speaking of, her presence now stood out. She alone among those on the hill still stood, and stood apart from the rest. The hooded and wrapped riders in the front ranks of the crowd inched closer, tension growing palpable.

Skin burning now, she moved toward Serik. She tried to avoid making eye contact with any of those in the ranks of men and women that were closer than ever. She knew that she would see Alina, Kasym, others that had trusted her, had begun to follow her. The outcasts and castaways of a hundred broken peoples. Would they understand? Would they believe her when she told them this was the best way, the only way? It wouldn't matter. They would kneel after she did.

Every step rubbed her clothes against her raw skin, covered in gooseflesh. It felt like her body was freezing, even as the Rift burned its way through her veins. This close to it, the invisible wellspring of souls that had broken through the seals of the world begged to be used. Demanded it. More had started to manifest signs like she had. *How many of us are there?* she wondered absently. A problem for later. She knew she was distracting herself from what had to be done. Squaring her slight shoulders, Darya looked Serik in the eyes and saw the demand there. *Kneel or die.*

She knelt. Felt the front rank moving up beside her to do the same. After all, in this world, everyone knelt to someone. There was no standing apart.

Unless you were the one they knelt to.

Darya stood.

Serik had a moment for outrage to register across his handsome features, tightening his face into hateful lines. Only a moment. Fear was close behind. Figures broke apart from the crowd, brutal blows and rough hands for those before Serik. They surged around Darya with practiced coordination. As they should have; they had rehearsed this all night.

Caught between confusion and shock, the others could only watch, expressions invisible behind darkened cowls. It all happened so quickly. Darya watched as the similarly hooded men and women before her—it wouldn't be accurate to call them tribesmen; they weren't—savagely incapacitated those before them. Blows a little stronger than they had any right to be, a little quicker than they should have been. Hands like vises as they dragged their charges to the nearby trees. Everything Serik had said was true. It was good to have allies.

Alina and Kasym might not have known what she planned, but they reacted now. The motley group that had attached itself to her for want of better options formed a wall between her and those that might have considered trying to change the outcome of this night. That chance was long gone. Darya hadn't expected it to go this smoothly. She supposed she ought to feel some sort of satisfaction, some elation at seeing her plans work out, seeing those who had spat on her and her brother just weeks ago brutalized and bleeding. All she felt was resentment. This wasn't what she had wanted. Only the best choice she had left. Serik would have taken her out of the picture eventually.

They were tying them to the trees now, half of them barely conscious. She thought one woman might be dead already, a prop being pushed into place. Not Serik. One of his arms dangled uselessly, but he still struggled. The two Stained held him tight. Darya came close, examining him. It must have been excruciating. Not the arm, or any of the blows. But to have been so close. Everything he had worked for. He had been right too; they wouldn't stand a chance unless they were united. One people. The three tribes here, the Thousand Tribes themselves. She had no argument there. But she knew his type. Had watched him laugh among the rest as they cut Mikael to pieces. The sly calculations that would have seen poison in her food, or a knife across her throat within a month. She tried to imprint the impotent fury and frustration on her soul. This was what happened when you didn't strike quickly enough.

"You bitch," he slurred through bloodied teeth. "I stood up for you!"

It was impossible to fear him now. A mangled jaw stole any gravitas or venom those words might have carried. Another lesson there. People were so...fragile. Especially when they couldn't touch the Rift. Push a little here, pull a little there, they fell apart. No wonder they cursed Stained in this empire and exiled them or killed them. Why they in turn looked down on everyone else.

She cradled his head, confident in the human manacles to either side. An eerie sort of calm came over her. It felt like someone else took over at times like this.

"You would have killed me. Don't deny it," she said, forestalling any protest. "The minute I wasn't useful, or maybe the minute I was too useful, you would have taken me from the board. And it wouldn't have been your fault. It's the game we all have to play. With so many angry men like you, leading more angry men, it was the only way. Or at least, the only way we've known. I want to show them another way."

"You'll die, you crazy whore!" He was choking now, sensing the end coming and still wanting to vent his surprise, his frustration, and his hate before it was too late. As if it mattered. As if she cared. "If the crows don't get you, the Arkhan will."

"Maybe," Darya agreed. "Maybe. But that's hardly your problem anymore."

She rose and nodded to the two holding Serik. There was muttering, a few cries breaking against the thin line that stood between her and the confused crowd. It was fortunate that Serik had been so eager for his own men to deliver the good news to the Arkhan. That Taharuk and Kursagai's men suspected Serik of even more than his cunning mind had been capable of. So many little pieces of good fortune. But half of being a good leader surely had to be being lucky.

Under her watchful eye, they dragged Serik toward a thick oak tree that rose, ancient and gnarled, from the hard earth. He struggled against the two who pushed him patiently into place. *A lot of wasted effort just to die at the end,* she thought. Wasn't that life, though? One of the other men came to help now. They had brought rope for the others, but Duras had recommended something special for Serik. It turned out that even with the strength of their gifts, it took more than three to nail a man to a tree.

Duras's words rang through her, in time with the hammer blows. *"It's about sending a message. Brutality can be a mercy. Cruelty is preventative. It worked on us. It will work on them."*

She had no wish to watch though. Darya willed her stomach still. Serik was roaring now. That tone would change soon. Mikael had been strong too, but dignity left everyone in the end.

That other self turned her to face the crowd, which had fallen dead silent now. The roars behind had turned to cries. For all her talk, this hardly felt like a different path. Maybe a darker one. But Vels had been right. Damn him to hell, but he always had been. If she wanted to show them a better way, if she wanted to change anything, or even just survive, she had to speak to them in a language they understood. They would understand this. Time to change the course.

"You don't need speeches." She didn't bother raising her voice over the sobs that came from behind her. All were leaning forward now, spellbound. She loved and hated them for it. "You need a home. Ice and death and starvation are all that are left in the North. Now it is just us, and them." She pointed south, to where even now, the legions advanced to cut them away, a blight on the perfect body of their brutal unity. "The one behind me was right about one thing. If we are not united, we will never make it south, to the lands our peoples deserve. And if we cannot become one people, we do not deserve them. All we deserve is our own misery in the North." She spat. "The leadership of men like that, who will lie and cheat and steal, all to clamber over you and me. Kings of a frozen kingdom. We have a chance here, if you will take it with me."

Darya breathed hard, unsure of what to say next. She had thought so long about what words to use, but she was out of them now, and there was only the wind left. A sea of covered, silent faces before her. An amalgamation of features and emotions, hidden by clothing from a dozen regions, united by the most powerful driver of all: survival. Survival in a world gone to ice, scratching a living on the fringes of an empire too powerful and too jealous of that power to share or suffer encroachment. A greedy god with the sun locked away in his vaults. Was it any wonder they turned to savagery?

So, she would speak to them. Raising her good hand, Darya let all her anger, her fear, her self-recriminations go. She let them flow out of her and felt the molten liquid that flowed through her veins now, always present, rise joyfully to fill their place. And from her hand sprang a pillar of fire, a thousand thousand torches, blazing as brightly as the sun before becoming an incandescent, furious roar. It was so easy to move it, and it wanted more, always more. Darya let it grow, but gave it purpose. Roots snaked from the inferno that raged swirling above her to the trees of Serik and his allies. Part of the fire now. She couldn't hear their screams. She was part of it too, and she could feel it kissing her, embracing her, burning away her weaknesses. What was left of her hair burned away in a fiery halo.

Eyes glowing white with the reflected fury, Darya watched the men and women before her cringe away in fear. But there was hunger there too. They saw light, they saw heat. And in their cold, cold world, they would always follow the fire.

In a wave, torches were thrust in the air, weak shadows of the flame she held, and a roar rose from the crowd, even among those who had cheered Serik a moment ago. Her new friends would keep track of those who were silent.

*I'm coming home, Mikael.*

# EPILOGUE

"**H**urry, hurry."

Lucky stumbled in his haste to catch up with Vels. It was difficult not to be distracted in the center of the Riftgate, in a new world, veins of cobalt blue and ossanite weaving a tapestry above him in a room too big to be real. It smelled like rain and stone, and his coat was already damp to the touch. As he recovered, he put out an arm to steady himself and came—apparently—too close to touching that girl that Vels dragged about everywhere with him.

"Coming, coming," she muttered at Vels's back, sidestepping away from Lucky and sparing him a look of unadulterated disdain.

The level of contempt was impressive. It proved to have the unique quality of leaving Lucky blushing and speechless. This after a brutal childhood in the Institute, years of the worst sorts of missions imaginable on the Hunters' teams, months of the stress of passing intelligence behind their backs, the highly risky act of—for the sake of the gods before!—saving her ungrateful self.

*Gods before*—that's how he always heard Vels say it. And if there was anyone Lucky had pegged as knowing what was going on, it was Vels. He wondered what that meant, and if Vels was saying the gods *before*, what did that really say about the gods *now*, plus if...

Lucky nearly stumbled again when Vels whirled back around as he reached what was apparently a predetermined point in the massive chamber. The pulsing stone tree screamed for Lucky's attention, but he did his best to focus on Vels.

"Lucky, Morana, if you two could spare me your adolescent awkwardness and insouciance for but a few moments, I would be forever grateful.

This is important. And Tahlsan, dear boy, are you sure you want to still be Lucky?"

Lucky nodded, trying to reassert a look of bored detachment. He could feel the heat in his face. But he did want to be Lucky. That's who he was now. And honestly, it seemed like tempting fate to reject a name that had seen him through so much, especially in return for one that had brought him nothing but misery.

Vels sighed. "Very well. Well, 'Lucky', we need to find a signal in here, and we need to do so quickly. I'm..." He raised a hand, now completely unwrapped, but still mostly gray, and waffled it side to side. "... mostly sure it's time. Can't really afford to be wrong."

"Where in here?"

"Gods before, if I knew that, I wouldn't need you, would I? Open that third eye of yours, boy, and start searching. You'll know it when you see it. Morana, my dear, please be ready."

"For what?"

"Surely not to dazzle us with your winning demeanor. It cannot possibly be so difficult to guess. We are a welcoming party, and you are there to open the door."

Lucky tried not to think on what exactly that meant and focused earnestly on searching the plane of the Rift for a signal. Whenever he described what it felt like to anyone—anyone who might care (there were never many)—he tried to explain it as staring up at the night sky. Some nights, there were only a few stars peeking through the ash and clouds, some nights the moon washed away its neighbors, and yet others were a perfect velvet, stars sprinkled across it like the diamonds of every world set there for him and him alone. Picking out the right star, the right connection between souls of the Rift and where they touched the material plane, was as much about lucky guesses as it was about knowing what you were doing, and Lucky was very good at guessing.

Here, next to the Riftgate, in the very heart of Bal Maru, it was very different. As he sank into that liminal space, it was as if he emerged next to the sun itself and felt it scouring away his flesh, his mind. There would be no seeing anything here. Gasping, he pulled back, started to surface.

But no. There it was. Not another star, or even a sun next to that incredible, surging brilliance. Instead, a void, an opening blacker than any night. Not even black. A nothingness. It was like what he had seen when Morana had jumped in the tunnels, only far more distinct. It grew, stretching. Burning its way through. Lucky somehow knew that the energy expended to rip that hole was enormous. The sun would swallow it back soon enough.

"There," he breathed, pointing.

Half in and half out of the plane, his vision overlapped. His hand and the void were all that he could see.

"That's enough, my boy. Out, now."

With an effort, Lucky pulled himself completely back into the real world, to the relatively comforting unfamiliarity of the Riftgate chamber. Vels and Morana were already hurrying to one of the side entrances, apparently the one he had pointed out. Sweating and still half blind with the psychosomatic burns of that sun, Lucky once again hurried after them, rubbing at his eyes, but not wanting to miss a thing.

"Morana, please tell me..."

"Yes, yes, I have it."

Fascinated, Lucky watched as she stopped and screwed up her face into a look of the most intense concentration, eyes closed and one arm stretched out and moving slowly, like a needle on a compass. Back and forth, to and fro, and then...true north. Her arm was shaking now. Ever so slowly—so slowly, he thought he was imagining it at first—threads of black started to weave up from the point of her outstretched fingers, looking like the marks around her eye. Vels looked as if he was about to reach out—to help, to encourage, Lucky had no idea—but he pulled back, as nervous-looking as Lucky had ever seen him.

Vels settled for a whisper. "Close, so close, my dear. You mustn't let them go."

Lucky found himself leaning forward too, unsure what he was so desperate to see happen, but sensing that quite a lot might depend on it. He'd never seen Vels any way but smugly self-assured before, and it made him decidedly uncomfortable, and important-feeling somehow, to be part of this.

Intent on guessing what might be happening, Lucky almost missed the actual happening. There, before them, the void he had seen was making its way from the arcane plane to the damp bounds of reality with a silent stench of burning copper.

"Yes, yes. Almost there, a little further..."

Morana was shaking, arm now consumed by the questing little snakes of black nearly to the elbow. Sweat pattered down from her sunken face. Lucky moved toward her, confused and uncertain.

"No! Don't touch her," Vels hissed, hand seizing Lucky by the arm. His fingers were painfully tight, but his look would have been enough to freeze Lucky. "There are no second chances here." His face changed, that faraway, mad look coming over him, and he laughed. "No second chances that matter, anyhow. Now, my dear! Now!"

With a cry, Morana gave a final effort. Lucky couldn't tell what she had done, but she collapsed inward into herself. She dropped onto her knees, head bowed and then torso heaving. Vels ignored her and walked up to where the rent in the world had stayed. Had stabilized, Lucky realized.

"It will get easier," Vels muttered, perhaps to Morana behind him. But his eyes were focused only ahead.

Lucky was moving to help Morana up when he saw why. The rent in the air started to shimmer, to vibrate outward, like a rock had been dropped in that pool of night from the other side. And then, the impossible. An arm reached through the blackness into their world. Then a foot, then a body, clawing its way into being one limb at a time, the smoky threads that held on to each only letting go with reluctance. A person, whole and entire before them. Then two more, each fighting their way to the solidity of reality.

Frozen in shock, Lucky looked on as two women and a man emerged to stand before Vels. They stared at him and he at them, and Lucky and Morana were ignored by all. Lucky was used to being ignored, and knew that he had never ever been so grateful for that little convenient indignity of his life. The man was of a height with Vels, but where Vels's face was sly and prone to quick changes, the face of the man before them defied description. Lucky thought for a second he might have been furious, and felt his heart race as he wondered if it was with him, only to realize he had been mistaken. There was ecstasy there. Or was it fear, perhaps?

Lucky tore his eyes away from those liquid features and focused on the other two, who had closed the distance to Vels. The void behind them was gone, as completely as if it had never been, but Lucky thought he knew what he would see if he took the time to search the other plane.

The other two were far too arresting for that though. There was a woman with the palest skin Lucky had ever seen, to the point that he could see veins of blue streaking everywhere under that drowned marble. She pushed past Vels, loose robes fluttering around a famine-thin form as she knelt beside Morana, curiosity and life sparking in eyes of blue so dark, it looked like they were made from whatever light filled the space around them. The last woman was tall, more than a head above Vels, and in heavy black plate from neck to toe, hard surfaces so clean that they should have reflected every bit of light in the space, but instead drank it in, forming a void still where the one Morana had made had since disappeared. A squared, scarred, and brutal face looked down at Vels.

"Is it time?"

"Yes, I do think it is that time already."

A grunt from the black-armored giant. The robed woman had taken Morana's hand in her own, and Lucky watched as the blackness receded, pulled away into her and disappearing. Lucky tried to watch everything at once, and felt that for certain, he was missing something important, despite his attention.

"To be seen."

"Yes, yes. But there are three this time." Vels shrugged and leaned down to help Morana up. All were looking to him now. "Either way, it's time to try again. At the risk of bringing bad luck"—Lucky could have sworn he winked at him—"I think things are going quite well this time, if I do say so myself. Besides, cousin, what's the use of a prophecy if no one ever bothers fulfilling it?"

A sigh from the woman in white, and a measured nod from the black-armored killer. "Then let it begin."

# Thank you for reading!

Before I say anything else, I want to thank you for coming on this journey with me (and Syl, Vali, Darya, and all the rest). There are a lot of reasons I wrote this, but the first and foremost was to give people the sort of reading experience that so many authors before gave me. I hoped you enjoyed exploring this world and these characters as much as I enjoyed getting them on the page.

That said, it is also your support that makes it possible for people like me to keep doing what we do. If you enjoyed *Splinters of Heaven*, I ask that you consider rating and reviewing on Amazon and Goodreads (click for links to those review pages). The difference it makes cannot be overstated, and leaving a review is one of the most impactful ways you can help this story stand out and find its way onto your fellow readers' bookshelves.

Finding and writing this story has been one of the most rewarding experiences of my life, and I can't wait to share the rest of it with you.

Until then,
Theo Tsirigotis

By Theo Tsirigotis

**PAX TERMINUS**

**Novels**
*Splinters of Heaven*

**Novellas**
*Memory's Gate* (Coming May 2026)

Before *Splinters of Heaven*, there was *Memory's Gate*. This prequel novella reveals what exactly went wrong at Bal Maru to kick off the events of Book 1 and introduces you to the world of the *Pax Terminus* trilogy. Join my newsletter and get *Memory's Gate* delivered FREE to your inbox when it releases in May 2026.

Sign up at: www.theotsirigotis.com
Plus: Get updates on Chains of Prophets (Book 2), exclusive bonus content, and advance notice of sales.

# Prequel Novella

## Memory's Gate coming May 2026!

Set immediately before the events of *Splinters of Heaven*:

Semprys has one job: break into an ancient fortress-prison, steal a few relics from under the nose of the Vigil, and pay the debt threatening her brother's life. When everything goes wrong and she's trapped in the ruins beneath the prison, she discovers that the relics are more than she thought, the prison guards aren't her only enemies, and the price of escape might be higher than she can bear. A grimdark fantasy novella about the weight of grief, the cost of magic, and what we owe the dead.

Get your FREE copy at www.theotsirigotis.com

# Acknowledgements

Turns out, it's a lot of work to write a book. First, you have to decide to do it, which honestly is probably the hardest part. Right up until you have to get the words on the page... And then go over them again, and again, and so on.

Then, right when you think you've got it all figured out, you've got to show your ugly little baby to people! Real people with real opinions! They will inevitably have real criticisms too, which you have asked—no, demanded—of them. I'd like to take the chance here to thank them first. My brother, Demetri, is my first reader, and my "ideal reader" if I can steal a phrase from Stephen King. Demetri, your enthusiasm for the story means more than you know. My parents were right there too, and I can't thank them enough for their support and patience as I asked myself (and them) again and again if this book deserved to make its way out to you. Besides them, a host of readers have made this book a better one with their time and attention: Clay Sohn, Caleb Sessoms, Paul Broer, Noel Mrowiec, Morgan Byerley, Andrew Kress, Drew Harrison, and Nick Brennan. I couldn't be more grateful.

At that point, after you've realized that not only is there no such thing as a perfect book, but that two people can like or dislike the same thing for different reasons, it's time to get professional help. Steven Moore, Jon Oliver, and Robin Fuller all helped make this a cleaner, more professional book. Ryan Mulford designed the cover and the magnificent cover art was made by Kyle Enochs. Check out the rest of his amazing work at ArtStation or on Instagram @neonpolygon. I'd also like to thank Jason Kasper, a fellow author and Special Forces veteran, who took the time to help a new writer understand a bit of how publishing works. If you like military thrillers, check out his books!

Lastly, I'd like to thank you, the reader. I write for you and your support allows me to keep pursuing my passion and purpose. As for my end, I promise to keep giving you the very best stories I can; ones that entertain, fascinate, and hopefully speak to you in the way that sometimes only books can. On that note, I'm back to writing the next installment in the *Pax Terminus* trilogy, *Chains of Prophets*.

# About the Author

THEO TSIRIGOTIS is the author of the Pax Terminus series. Previously, he served in the 75th Ranger Regiment and as a Green Beret captain. He now lives in Austin, Texas. *Splinters of Heaven* is his debut novel.

Find out more, see upcoming work, and get a free prequel novella (coming May 2026) at www.theotsirigotis.com.

www.ingramcontent.com/pod-product-compliance
Lightning Source LLC
Chambersburg PA
CBHW030333120726
47901CB00007B/1772